Shadowstalker

Larry Patrick Shriner

criminous intent publishing

ISBN: 978-0615760476

For Elaine, with Love

Prologue

The sight of her breaks my heart.

She lies in Room 12 of the Starlight Motel, a hot-pillow joint on the Dixie Highway where people rarely stay more than an hour or two, certainly not to sleep. The room is shrouded in a dusky gloom, and only a little light comes through the single grimy window. The wall-unit air-conditioner rattles, but the room is stifling hot.

She lies - what had been her - nude, on a dingy white sheet, in repose. Her face is unmarked, angelic, in sleep it seems, eyes closed. She looks paler than she had in her pictures.

Her body is pale as well. Her hands lie at her sides, palms up, a kind of placating gesture, almost peaceful. The tattoo of the butterfly that surrounds her navel — the immutable evidence of her identity — is, in stark contrast, vibrantly colorful.

But beneath her, beneath that most intimate part of her, is a crimson stain, wet and thick on the fabric. Her thighs are mottled with streaks of red, as though a finger-painter had been at work.

I think that I might throw up, but I hold myself still, very still, and the nausea passes, and I do not throw up.

The mutilation is not subtle. Her pubic hair is matted and glistening, her sex a butchered and gaping violation.

Oddly, a childhood rhyme comes to me suddenly, softly, from somewhere in the deepest memory:

Now I lay me down to sleep
I pray the Lord my soul to keep
If I should die before I wake
I pray the Lord my soul to take

I hope that she had been able to pray.

Had she, had she in those moments when she knew — she had to have known she was living the last moments of her life — did she say some kind of prayer, something to keep the monsters at bay? Or had she been transfixed with fear, unable to look beyond the horror of the moment?

The scene in Room 12 of the Starlight Motel marks neither the beginning nor the end of this story. Rather it is a defining moment for me, an image that I will never be able to forget, the thing that changed everything.

Chapter 1

I set the kerosene lantern out on the beach. Then I waited on the porch, taking care of a big Churchill that lasted almost the entire hour. At 3 a.m. I heard the sound, at first barely distinguishable from the surf, then separating itself and growing louder. Then I could see the blinking lights in the distance as the helicopter came from the north, paralleling the beach, right at the time I had been told to be ready.

I went to the edge of the sand as the chopper descended, blades whipping the surf and throwing sand out as if the machine were the vortex of a small whirlwind. Then the skids settled onto the beach and the blades slowed. I retrieved the lantern, extinguished it and put it on my porch. Then I ran to the passenger's door, ducking my head far under the blades, stepped across the skid and got in. I bucked the seatbelt as the machine began to lift off. It was very dark outside and the interior of the helicopter was dim, illuminated only by the gauges and instrument lights. The pilot, wearing a baseball hat and headset with boom mike, nodded briefly as I closed the door and bucked myself in. Then he adjusted the throttle. The blades whipped faster, the machine began to vibrate, and then we were airborne, ascending away from the beach, away from the little lantern, up into the darkness. I settled back into my chair and watched the ground recede and felt the air get suddenly cooler.

Then the pilot abruptly swung out over the water and set a course away from land. He fiddled with the compass for a moment, tapped a couple of gauges, then stared out into the darkness.

And what a darkness it was. There was no moon, and though stars twinkled far overhead, I could see no horizon, only an indelible blackness. But the pilot kept his machine steady and clearly knew exactly where he was headed. He didn't speak to me at all. A couple of times I heard muffled sounds— a voice— from inside the headset, and then he replied, “Ten minutes.”

And precisely ten minutes later, after a ride at a height of about 500 feet over the moon swept Atlantic, I saw the twinkle of lights in the distance, and then the dim shape of a vessel.

We circled the yacht once, then the pilot set the craft down effortlessly on a landing pad on the rear deck. A man in a white uniform stood holding his hat against the wind from the rotors.

The pilot nodded at me as the rotors slowed, and I unhooked my seat belt, stepped out onto the skid and then onto the pad. I ducked my head and jogged beyond the radius of the still-turning rotors. When I got to the edge of the pad and stepped down onto a teak deck, the man walked toward me.

“Welcome aboard the Tranquility, Mr. Landers,” he said, extending his hand. “I am Captain Durance.” I detected the trace of a European accent, Eastern European perhaps. “Mr. Locke extends his regards and asks that I take you to the saloon. Please watch your step.”

I followed Captain Durance as he led me along the teak boards along the port side of the yacht until we came to an open door. Durance stood to the side and said, “Please go in, sir.”

I did, and found myself in a spacious room framed on three sides with windows. The lighting was low, from indirect sources. Classical music played softly and the moon shone toward the bow of the ship, bathing the deck in a shimmering luminescence. The room was furnished as a living area, with several couches, chairs and occasional tables. Potted plants were arranged in the corners, and the fabric and colors were cool mauves and blues. On the wall to my left, the one without windows, stood a burnished wood bar, and behind it a long counter above which were several shelves holding glasses and bottles.

The man who rose from one of the chairs to meet me looked, in a word, wealthy. In a few more words, he was quite a bit shorter than me, probably five-ten. He wore a loose white shirt and khaki trousers. He was probably around sixty. His hair was silver, worn short and well barbered. His face had a craggy look - crows feet and laugh lines, and deeply tanned skin.

He carried himself with all the confidence of a self-made man. He moved a couple of steps toward me. The hand that took mine was deeply tanned as well. The grip was firm. On his wrist a Pâté Philippe watch glittered. I had never met him but by reputation knew him well indeed.

He extended his hand. "Darwin Locke. Thank you for coming, Lieutenant Landers." Locke's voice had a timbre that bespoke breeding, the good life, and more than a little whisky. "I am truly sorry for the hour of our meeting, and the, ah, predilection on my part for privacy." He glanced at his watch as he said this, as if confirming the interesting place and time of the rendezvous.

I took his hand. "Please, call me Loot," I said. "I'm retired."

"Loot as in short for Lieutenant?" he said.

"It's what I was called when I was with the cops. It kind of stuck as a nickname, Mr. Locke."

"Please then," he said, "call me Darwin." Like we're all buddies here, a few billion dollars notwithstanding. "Darwin," I said, to get the feel of it. I knew some things about Locke, that he was worth several billion dollars, that he lived in a compound at the very north end of Crescent Key, that he had made his fortune as an investor in struggling, undercapitalized companies that needed an "angel" to help them succeed. I knew that Locke had a wife who spent a great deal of time abroad, and a couple of grown kids. He was occasionally seen on the Key tooling around in a restored Porsche Speedster or new Jaguar S-Type (in addition to the new Rolls Royce Silver Seraph), but wasn't the buddy-buddy type at the luncheonette or barber shop. He'd never been associated with any controversy that I'd heard about.

"Drink?" Locke asked, motioning toward the bar.

"Bourbon, if you have it. On the rocks."

Locke stepped behind the bar, used tongs to scoop some ice out of a silver bucket and poured a healthy dose of Maker's Mark. I took the glass, raised it to him, then took a sip. Wonderful stuff, Maker's Mark.

He poured clear liquid out of a decanter into a glass, added ice and lime and came around the bar. We took seats - he in a leather wing chair, me on a couch facing him. A low coffee table sat between us.

Locke pointed to a humidor on the coffee table. "Do you care for a cigar? They're Cuban Cohabits."

I opened the humidor, and the earthy mix of aromas enveloped me. I selected a nice plump Cahaba, lit up using an engraved gold lighter that sat on the table. Locke took a cigar as well and got his going. And now we sat around amid swirling smoke. I sipped the bourbon and waited.

It took Locke a little while, at least three puffs and four sips. Then he sighed and said, “I need you to find someone for me.”

I nodded and took a sip of Maker’s Mark.

Locke said, “Her name is Shelly. I have been seeing her. She’s been gone a week now.”

“The police are much better at finding missing people,” I said.

He shook his head. “No police. I have a wife, I have a standing in this community. This situation with Shelly was private and confidential.”

I nodded. “You say ‘missing.’ Do you have any reason to believe her disappearance was anything other than voluntary?”

“No. I mean yes.” He took a healthy slug of his drink, and ice rattled as the liquid drained. “There was no sign of, you know, foul play. I had gotten her an apartment in West Palm, on the Intracoastal. We saw each other several times a week. One day I went over, we’d made arrangements to get together, and she wasn’t there. Her car was gone. I looked around the apartment. Nothing looked out of the ordinary. I figured she had had to run an errand, so I waited. Three hours later she hadn’t come back. I called her several times that evening, but she wasn’t home. She wasn’t there the next day either. I haven’t seen her since.”

He took a folder off the table and extracted a photograph from it. He handed me the picture.

She was beautiful, in an all-American athletic way. The camera had caught her candidly as she walked along the surf. She wore a yellow bikini. Her skin was tanned, her blonde hair tousled and damp. She was giving the lens a big grin. A tattoo of a butterfly surrounded her navel.

“Here’s the problem,” Locke said. “I’m not in the habit of keeping mistresses. I have been faithful to my wife for years. But when I met Shelly, well.....” He took a long draw on his cigar. “This isn’t just an old man talking. I believed, I still believe, that we had something, that there were feelings we shared. I care about her very much. It’s breaking my heart that she’s gone.”

I looked at the picture, at her smile as she looked at Locke’s camera. She didn’t look like an old man’s mistress, she looked like a girl caught in a candid moment of happiness. If she were gone from my life I would want to get her back.

“I can’t promise much,” I said. “I’m not expert at this sort of thing, and I'm only one man. But I will make some inquiries."

Locke handed me the folder. "Here are some more pictures of Shelly. Her address is in there, and also a key."

I took the folder. "Some background would help."

For the first time Locke looked truly uncomfortable. "I know very little about her past. She mentioned that her parents were still alive, but I don't know where they live or whether she was in touch with them. Her life before we met, I just don't know much about. She didn't share much about that."

"Where did you meet?"

He didn't look any more at ease. "At...ah, through a — damn it —" he chuckled. "I met her through an escort service. Very private, very discreet operation. I would prefer, no, I would insist, that I give you no more information about the service."

"Even if it would help me find her?"

He shook his head, and a lock of silver hair fell across his forehead. "I wish I could." End of statement.

We discussed fees - not that he paid much attention. I told him I would start by going to Shelly's apartment. I didn't mention that I planned to run her name through NCIC and the local police files. She was in the life, and there might be evidence of that with the cops.

"I'll have you escorted to the back deck," Locke said. He pushed a button on a small teak box on the coffee table and in a moment Captain Durance arrived.

And then I was on the back deck, ready to be whisked back to my world.

Chapter 2

The morning after my meeting with Darwin Locke, I got to work.

Shelly Travers lived in a new condominium complex of town homes nestled on the Intracoastal. The complex was gated, and I used the code Locke had given me to gain entrance.

Each of the town homes had attached garages, so it was hard to tell if the residents were ensconced inside, off to work in their various high-paying yuppie jobs or boating on the Waterway. The whole place gave off an aura of silence and stillness.

Shelly's town home was at the far end of the complex. There were only four units in her structure; two ancient spreading oaks shaded the manicured lawns that fronted the homes, and the back patios looked out on lush vegetation and water.

I parked the Defender in a visitor's space. I cut the motor and opened the door, and was hit by oppressive heat and humidity. Not yet noon, and the Florida sun was in full force. The sky was a cloudless blue and there was no hint of an ocean breeze.

I made my way up the sidewalk to Shelly's unit. Under the canopy of shade the temperature was discernibly cooler. The shrubs that bordered her small porch and front wall were well-trimmed and tended, and some small blooming flowers had been planted in terra cotta pots on either side of her front door. There was a small wreath of silk vines on the door, and a mat that said, "Welcome." I used the key that Darwin Locke had given me and opened the door inward. A blast of cool air hit me — Shelly had left the air-conditioning running — and stepped inside.

The town home was Florida modern casual. The main room was large, leading to a dining area with a glass door that looked out to the water.

The carpet was a light cream; the furniture in the living area natural rattan and flowered fabric. There was a couch, love seat, upholstered rocker, smoked glass coffee table and a couple of end tables. The magazines on the coffee table were stacked and lined up in an orderly fashion. There were a couple of ashtrays, but no ashes or butts. A bleached wood bookcase held quite a number of hardcover books, and a few paperbacks on a lower shelf. The sunlight filtering in through the glass door gave the place a comfortable, relaxed feel.

I had plenty of time, and made my search in a slow, orderly fashion. I took a leisurely stroll through the place — two bedrooms, one clearly Shelly's, with another set of glass doors overlooking a small garden patio, the other set up as a guest bedroom. There was a spacious bath and vanity area off the master bedroom, a half-bath opening off the hall.

The dining area held a glass table on a rattan frame, and a sideboard of similar wood. The kitchen, with a large window overlooking the water, was spacious and pristine, all white, polished and gleaming.

I returned to the living area. I had no sense of the woman here; it was as if this room was more for show, or perhaps for visiting with guests.

The prints were expensively framed and modern, impersonal abstracts, one beach scene of sand, ocean and gulls, and a still life of tropical fruit. The magazines consisted of popular women's publications and celebrity gossip rags. I checked for mailing labels. There were none. All of the magazines were of recent vintage.

There were no clues under the furniture, lurking between the pages of books, behind the pictures. I moved to the dining room.

The table was set with two place-settings of Fiesta Ware and a bowl of oranges and bananas. The oranges looked okay, but the bananas had begun to over ripen and turn black. The sideboard was clean and dust-free. Inside were only more Fiesta Ware and a set of bone china dishes.

The kitchen shone spotlessly. Shelly was not a cooking kind of girl. The refrigerator yielded a six-pack of Heineken with one bottle missing, three limes, a box of baking soda, half a left-over pizza neatly put in a plastic bag. four kinds of salsa, a package of turkey that was a few days away from the spoilage date; a bottle of ketchup, a jar of spicy mustard, a half-full pack of saltines, presumably to use with the salsa. four bottles of mineral water flavored with lime. a head of lettuce that had seen better days, one slightly wrinkled tomato and two bottles of fat-free Italian dressing.

The sink and counter tops were spotless. In the cupboard were a few cans of vegetables, chili con carne, no beans, a couple of packs of rice dinners, bottles of oil and vinegar, the usual mix and match of stuff anyone keeps in a kitchen. The trash was empty, a clean garbage bag inserted in the can. The dishwasher held only a couple of cups and a few pieces of silverware.

No clues that I could find at all, but I hadn't found a lot of clues in kitchens during my years with the police.

I opened the door that led off the kitchen and poked my head into the most immaculate garage I'd ever seen. There was absolutely nothing in it but one broom and a mop. And certainly not the BMW two-seater that Darwin Locke had given her.

I shut the door, made my way to the bedroom. Bedrooms are where the clues are, I told myself. They are the most private of habitats, where one thinks that secrets are safe.

Shelly's bedroom had a strong feeling of human presence that wasn't apparent anywhere else in the town home. More natural rattan — the king sized headboard, nightstand, low chest of drawers and dressing table. On the dressing table were a few bottles of creams and lotions, some cologne - Chanel and Poison, a fairly small wall-mounted plasma TV and a CD stereo, everything tidy and neat.

In the set-apart area for tub and toilet and vanity were the usual containers of shampoo, body wash and soap. A neat stack of towels in cabinets over the toilet. Here too, everything clean and spot-free. In the medicine cabinet were a few bottles of non-prescription drugs - a mild sleeping medication, another for allergies. Bottles of aspirin and Advil, a small bottle of Ny-Quil, almost full.

I went back into the bedroom. There was a small framed photograph on the chest of drawers and I went over to it. The picture was of a smiling Shelly in a light blue summer dress, arm linked with Darwin Locke. The beach was out of focus behind them, the angle of the picture a little off center. I thought that they might have set the camera on something, a rock or ledge, and put the timer on.

I began to go through the drawers — this is the part where I always feel like a pervert. Everything neat, to the point of fastidious. One drawer held cotton bikini panties in a variety of colors. Another was filled with socks and pantyhose, another assorted T-shirts and pullovers. Bras in another — pervert that I was I checked the size and ascertained that Shelly was a 34C.

I put the bra back, feeling like a dirty intruder, and shut the drawer. So far I had learned that the woman was obsessively neat, had a 34-inch chest, was partial to cotton, rattan and tropical colors. And she made very little effort to keep personal things, keepsakes, mementos and the like.

In the closet were a few dressy lightweight outfits neatly hung on wood hangers. She had lined up a dozen pairs of shoes and sandals with an almost military perfection. On a whim I picked one up. Size nine and a half. Overhead shelves held carefully folded sweaters, jeans and slacks. There was a stack of running shorts and spandex tops, a gym bag with the logo of an upscale fitness spa.

The bed was spread with a green floral-print comforter, but there was an indentation at one side where someone had sat down. I sat there as well, opened the single drawer of the night stand.

The drawer contained a remote for the television, another for the CD unit, as well as various paraphernalia for doing nails, a hairbrush, one of those little balls you squeeze to work the muscles in your hand, a TV Guide from the week before, and a small stack of papers.

The papers were nothing really, a couple of VISA bills and some receipts, a gasoline credit card bill, a bank statement that showed only a few checks written for the usual things - clothes, groceries. No checks for rent, car or utilities; perhaps Darwin Locke took care of those. One substantial deposit on the third day of the month - an amount far more than I cleared in even my best month.

I stood in the bedroom, I thought about this house that wasn't quite a home, that bordered on the sterile, that was beyond neat and orderly. There was some of the usual detritus of day-to-day life, but the whole picture nagged at me.

I made my way to the living room and surveyed it once again, just letting my eyes wander at will. I noticed a rattan end table next to the couch, and when I looked at it closely, I could see that a drawer — not obvious at a casual glance — had been built in.

I opened the drawer. Inside was a neat stack of papers and envelopes, held tight with a rubber band. I leafed through them. Recent postmarks on various utility bills. I stuffed the bills in the front pocket of my jeans.

Standing in the living room it occurred to me that what I hadn't found was more telling than what I had. No hair dryer. No birth control pills, no other prescriptions. No suitcase. No box of keepsakes. No important papers, such as insurance or medical bills. No computer — didn't everyone have one these days?

Then something else occurred to me — something that might do more than anything else to help me establish a link with Shelly, her past, her life. Darwin Locke had seemed to know almost nothing about the woman, but I knew a way to gain more information.

I went into the kitchen, opened the pantry and found several zippered storage bags. I took a cup out of the dishwasher, lifting it carefully by the base, and deposited it in a bag. Did the same thing with a fork.

Then I went to the bedroom and lifted both cologne bottles, tilting them and touching only the base and tip of the spray cap. They went into baggies as well.

That done, I left the town home, locked the front door and pocketed the key. I looked around; holding the baggies made me feel awkward and obvious, as if I were a burglar with odd tastes in stolen goods. But I saw no living creatures.

I got back in the Land Rover, fired up the motor and let the first blast of semi-cold conditioned air bathe my face. Then I drove out of the complex, wondering if I had learned anything at all.

Chapter 3

"I need to know some things," I said.

We were sitting, Darwin Locke and I, on the aft deck of his yacht, which now was moored at the marina reserved for Crescent Key residents.

I had insisted we meet in person, as soon as possible. He wanted to go through the helicopter rigamorole, and he wasn't a man used to being ordered about, but there must have been something in my tone of voice on the phone. He said he would meet me in an hour at the marina.

"Such as?" he said. His voice was wary. "Do you have any news? Have you found her."

"Her," I said. "That's what's confusing me."

He arched his elegant eyebrows. "Mr. Landers, please don't speak in riddles."

So much for "Loot." The midmorning sun was well into its brutal ascent, but there is something about a rich man's yacht. Under the canopy the air remained cool. We sipped iced tea that Locke had produced himself. I had seen no evidence of any crew members on board.

"I found nothing in my search of the condo that helped," I said. The tea glass felt cool and damp in my hand, and I took a sip. Just right. "It appears she left on her own, things she would normally have taken with her were gone. The place was clean. The trash had been taken out."

"You insisted that we meet just so you could tell me that?" His voice showed irritation.

"There's more," I said. "I took some coffee cups, a couple of other personal things, and had a man I know at the police department take some prints off of them."

"And?"

"The prints," I said, "belong to a Sheldon Travers."

It took a few moments for this to sink in.

"Sheldon?"

"His prints were on file from the U.S. Army," I said.

He began to shake his head. "Her brother?"

"The same prints were on cologne bottle."

"Just what the hell are you saying?"

"I'm saying that the only prints I found in Shelly's condo belong to a man. Named Sheldon. Whose address listed on Army records is right down the road in West Palm Beach."

Locke shook his head. "That is impossible."

We could dance like this all day, I thought, though the prospects of sitting in the cool air under the canopy, drinking excellent iced tea, didn't seem that bad. I said, "Was Shelly — shit man, was she a man?"

"Fuck no," Locke said loudly. "She certainly was not."

The intensity of his reaction startled me, and I instinctively looked out to the dock to see if anyone was within earshot. But the place was deserted.

I held up my hands in a placating gesture. "Mr. Locke, are you familiar with the concept of transgenderedism?"

"I don't like what you are implying here, Landers. Shelly is no transvestite. And I, sir, am not a pervert."

"Not a transvestite," I said. "A transgendered. A person who changes gender. Permanently."

He was quiet for a few moments. He looked out over the water, then back at me. He said, "Of course I have heard about such a thing — this gender changing. But I would never . . ."

"After the prints came back I did some reading. It's not as uncommon as you might think. And with the advanced surgical procedures that exist today, it can be done. Quite convincingly."

He shook his head, smiled now. "Well, if that's what Shelly did, it sure as hell convinced me."

I swirled my tea glass, just melted ice now. Locke noticed and picked up the pitcher, poured me a refill. Just the right amount of ice clinked into my glass.

I looked at Locke. "Where do you want to go with this now?"

He met my gaze, held it. His eyes seemed deep, dark inscrutable pools. Then he got up, walked over to the port rail of the boat.

I watched as he stood looking out over the marina. A man of power, used to getting what he wanted. A man accustomed to the rare air of wealth and power, of private jets and convertible Bentleys, and ocean-front estates that cost millions upon millions of dollars. He was a famous man in some circles, and a power broker behind many scenes. He had everything money could bring.

But he didn't have the love of his life.

After a time Locke left the rail and made his way back to his seat under the canopy. He sat, took his tea glass and drank. Then he looked at me with deep, piercing eyes.

"Find her," he said. "Do whatever you have to do, but find her for me."

Back in the Land Rover, I thought that I had been blunt with Locke, even brutal. I had told him the truth. And I admired him for the way he had handled it.

But I hadn't told him everything. I had told him about the Army prints. But I had not mentioned that a second I.D. on the prints had come back from another source — the Emerald City Police. Four years ago Sheldon Travers had been busted on a prostitution charge, picked up in an area of the city frequented by transvestite hookers.

Chapter 4

Locke's iced tea had been tasty, but lunch beckoned, so I drove over the bridge to Crescent Key and parked in front of Lindy's Luncheonette.

I recognized a number of regulars, bellied up to Lindy's battered Formica counter, or hunched over the metal tables that took up the rest of the place.

Otis Lipscomb was eating alone at a table, and he motioned me over. He gave me a quick nod, then turned his attention back to a heaping plate of biscuits and sausage gravy.

"The good thing about that stuff," I said, slipping into a chair opposite Lipscomb. "There's enough fat in it to lubricate the arteries so the blood shoots right through."

"Slicker's deer guts on a door knob," Lipscomb said, the words slightly muddled by the mouthful of food he was chewing. "How's things in the high-rent security bidness?"

"Thank God for rich paranoids," A glass of tea materialized in front of me and I looked up into the smiling face of the hardest working gal in waitressing, Trish Simmons.

"Pastrami on rye, spicy mustard, side of fries, side of greens," she said. "Trust me." And she walked away.

"You always let her tell you what you want?" Lipscomb asked. There was a dribble of cream-colored gravy on his very black chin.

"You don't argue with Trish when she's in that kinda mood."

I looked around the Luncheonette. This was Crescent Key at its finest. Construction workers at one table, three matrons chowing down on soup and salad at another. Three gray-haired gentlemen dressed in Florida casual — pastel pants, golf shirts, soft leather shoes — took up a spot near the window. These three were residents, who could easily afford the stratospheric prices of Crescent Key real estate. Just a few of the local boys, fitting right in.

Lipscomb, a satisfied look on his face, said, “I actually gotta work today.”

“Yeah?” I said. “And why’s that?”

He chuckled, a rumbling deep in his throat. “The heir-heads are back in town.”

“Hot damn for you,” I said.

I remembered them from my days on the force. Kids — actually in their twenties and even thirties, heirs to old-money, but directionless kids nonetheless. Heirs to a soup fortune, a multi-billion-dollar software company, a group of auto dealerships, a family-controlled investment group, a media conglomerate and a perfume dynasty and a few other hefty nest eggs. We always dreaded their annual pilgrimage home from whatever college they were attending this year. They had no regard for the law, considering daddy’s money a much higher authority. And that had worked for them, so far.

“What have we got this time?”

“Bad this year. We’ve got two Vipers, a Ferrari 512, ‘67 Shelby GT500, a Lamborghini and a Porsche Twin-Turbo so far.”

“Too bad. I remember last year, they were into comfort. Bentleys and Rollses, old Jags, that kinda car.”

Otis looked wistful. “Yeah, most trouble we had then was catchin’ them screwin’ underage girls in the back seats down by the yacht basin.” He grinned. “Matrons loved that.”

Trish brought my food, which did look delicious. I looked out the front window as a Bentley convertible floated up to the curb. The top was down. The driver, a black man, got out, let the door go shut and sauntered into Lindy’s. He scanned the room, saw us, and came over to our table. Lipscomb, working a biscuit along the last remains of the gravy on his plate, used his foot to push a chair out.

“Henry, my man,” Lipscomb said. “New wheels?”

Henry Cummings was a resident, one of several black billionaires who called the Key home. “Indeed,” he said, his accent flat Midwestern. “New Azure, just come in over at the dealer in West Palm. It was beggin’ me to take it home.”

Henry Cummings had worked hard, founded a Midwestern life

insurance company owned by, and catering to, people of color. When black people couldn't get any kind of decent deal on life insurance from any other company, Henry would come through. He extended a lot of credit, took a lot of risks, and built his company. Twenty years ago, he sold his closely held corporation to a large utility company bent on diversification. They paid Henry in shares of the holding company. Last I checked, he was clearing more than seven million dollars annually — just from dividends on the insurance company alone. God knows what he brought in through investments, but it was said to be three times that much.

Henry was an easy man to respect. He held all people in equal regard, and knew the value of hard work. If there was prejudice here on the Key toward him and his black brethren, I never saw it. Henry enjoyed his life of wealth so immensely, he was a joy to be around.

"You mind if I borrow it?" I said. "I've got a hot date tonight."

Henry chuckled, a deep reverberation in his chest. "Heh, heh, Loot. You think just 'cause you got a car like that, you gonna score sure pussy? Not in my back seat." He beamed. "Besides, I've got my own plans for those hides."

We all smiled. Henry had been married to Harriet for more than forty years;. They still held hands and made dates to go to the movies. I could imagine them getting it on in the back seat of the Azure.

Henry stretched, nodded at Trish, said, "The usual," and took a deep breath. "God, you could get a contact high just inhaling the fat fumes in this place."

In truth, we all knew that Henry was more likely to nibble at a salad than wolf down cholesterol. He worked out several times a week, watched his weight and looked ten years younger than he was, which was somewhere in his mid-seventies.

We chowed down — me, the burly black detective and the wealthy resident, just three guys doing the Luncheonette lunch. Lives that paralleled at times, and were lived in physical proximity, but in so many ways were so very different. It's amazing what a few hundred million dollars will do.

After we'd paid the check, Lipscomb invited me to join him for a ride around the island — "You know, see what kinda quarter-mile times the heir-heads are posting" — but I declined. The specter of the missing woman weighed on me; the fact that she had once been in the "life" troubled me as well. The lure of such a lifestyle is like a narcotic. Even with the luxuries Darwin Locke had provided her, I knew that Shelly Travers could easily have been sucked back into some of her former habits. If she had ever completely left.

Chapter 5

Shelly Travers' parents lived in a modest sub-division north of Emerald City that dated back to the 1950s. They hadn't been hard to find; the address was the same as on Sheldon's military record, and they were listed in the telephone directory. I had spoken to Mrs. Travers, who said she would talk to me. "I doubt that my husband will, however."

The drive up Dixie Highway, permanently riddled with construction barricades and torn-up pavement, was miserable, and even with the Land Rover's air conditioning running on high, I was bathed in a sheen of dampness when I arrived.

I had hoped for Mrs. Travers. What I got was a door that opened to reveal a man with penetrating eyes, a shock of white hair and a menacing chin. I told him who I was. He simply stared at me for perhaps a full minute. Then, without a word, he stepped aside and motioned me inside.

The living room I stepped into was modest and neat, with some of the furniture seeming to date from decades ago. There were doilies and an afghan on the sofa and easy chair. The coffee table was littered with popular magazines. The only acknowledgment to the new century was a huge plasma television on one wall, surrounded by stereo speakers on stands.

A woman sat on a living-room couch, wearing a floral print dress. A serving of coffee was on a table. She seemed younger than her husband, perhaps in her early sixties. The man — I assumed it was her husband — took a seat in a stuffed recliner. He made a motion toward what was left — a very uncomfortable-looking bentwood rocker. I did my best to sit on the edge so I wouldn't fold backward, but it made my perch seem awkward and unstable.

"Listen," the man said suddenly. His voice had some miles on it.

"My wife told you that you could come here. It wasn't my place to go against her. But I'm gonna say this —"

He paused, his jaw tightened and weathered hands clinched the armrests of the chair. I saw a look of consummate sadness fall over his wife's face. He said, "That thing, that thing that used to be my son! I do not speak of such blasphemy in this house. I have no children. I had a son, but he died."

The old man's face had reddened as he spoke. His wife leaned over and touched his hand. "God damn this blasphemy." And his eyes, at odds with his anger, welled with tears.

He looked straight ahead and blinked, but he did not move a hand to his face. He said, "I will not involve myself with . . ." he didn't finish the sentence. "If my wife wants to involve herself, if she wants to care, I can't stop her. But I will have nothing more to do with this."

Then he let go of the arms of the chair, stood heavily and walked from the room.

She watched him go, and the look of sadness stayed with her. Then she turned to me, tried to manage a little smile. "What our child went through, what . . . was done, Clete has never recovered from it. He doesn't understand, I don't think he is capable of understanding. He has rejected, ah, his offspring completely."

I nodded. "He feels responsible in some way?"

She looked at me. "Of course. Isn't the father responsible for how his son turns out?"

The question seemed rhetorical; she was an intelligent woman and we both knew that the answers to such questions were complicated. But responsibility, and the bearing of it, is part of the human condition, at least in most of us. I could not condone his actions; I could, however, understand them.

"Do you remain in contact with Shelly?" I asked.

She nodded. "I don't let my husband know, though I'm sure he is aware of it. My relationship with Shelly is . . . a separate thing."

"Do you know where she is now?"

She looked up. "Why? Is she in trouble?"

I shook my head. "She was involved with . . . someone. A few days ago she left without warning. She packed up her essentials and drove off. He doesn't know where she is."

"He got involved with her, knowing about her past?"

"He didn't know until recently."

"And when he found out . . ."

"It didn't matter. He cares for her a great deal. I suspect he loves her."

"Why didn't she tell me about him?"

I shrugged. Not mine to get into.

She didn't press for more. "I just don't want there to be any more trouble," she said, as if there had been too much trouble already.

I felt myself wanting to protect her. "I doubt there's any problem at all. My client just wants some kind of closure. I've already explained to him that if I find her and she doesn't want to come back he can't force her to. In fact, I won't even tell him where she is if she doesn't give me permission. I would only report that she was okay."

"I only hope she's okay," Mrs. Travers said.

"Do you have any reason to think that she isn't?"

Her eyes drifted past me, focusing on some place beyond. "Shelly — Sheldon was always a shy child. My husband is a large man. Sheldon didn't inherit his size at all.

"Sheldon played baseball. He had no choice." She nodded her head toward the door through which her husband had exited "He was even forced to try out for football, but he didn't make it past the first cut. Then my husband enrolled him in a boxing program. He insisted Sheldon could be a champion in the bantam-weight division. Of course, Sheldon failed miserably at that too."

Mrs. Travers had been gazing at the doorway. Now she looked again at me. "We put so many pressures on our children. We expect them to be . . certain ways." The ghost of a smile drifted across her face. "We really are obsessed with our own image, so to speak."

She was silent then, and I thought about my father, and what he had desired for me, and how he had wanted to correct his own failures through my successes. I wondered how much I had let him down.

I must have drifted into thoughts of my own. I realized she was speaking again.

". . . became apparent that Sheldon wasn't going to follow in his father's footsteps. I don't think he did this out of spite or rebellion, he merely drifted in the opposite direction. He joined the chess club, never dated, never tried to grow a mustache or sideburns. He had a very slight build, but he didn't make an effort to develop any muscles."

She paused and took a breath. "You know, what happened between Clete and our child breaks my heart." She paused, picked up her coffee cup, took a sip and put it down. She looked at me, and I shook my head. She said, "There's no reason to go into all the details. Clete wrote his son off, took it for granted that he was gay. When Sheldon first came to me and told me what he thought was wrong with him, I was devastated. But I made an effort to learn about it. By this time, Sheldon was in his mid-twenties. Most of the time I didn't even know where he lived or worked. But I knew I wasn't going to change his mind.

She looked down at her hands clasped in her lap. "Clete can't understand this at all. He feels as if he failed. It truly broke his heart."

Mrs. Travers picked up her cup, put it down without taking a sip. It was just something to do while she thought. She looked at me directly, and her eyes were moist. "Just because I don't understand, Mr. Landers, doesn't mean I can't accept or forgive."

She smiled, with a bit of warmth. "You know, what had made Sheldon a somewhat unattractive man had the opposite effect when he . . . went through the change. An average sized man, he's a tall woman. What had once seemed slight is statuesque. The fine bone structure makes for a beautiful face."

She smiled again. "Of course, a few hundred thousand dollars worth of reconstructive surgery and electrolysis didn't hurt."

"And now," she said, "I have a beautiful daughter that I love dearly." And the tears ran down her face.

I sat, waiting and thinking about the lifestyle that paid for all that surgery. Mrs. Travers took a tissue out of the pocket of her dress and dried her eyes. She said, "Sorry. I hear that each day God only puts on you as much as you can handle. Me and God have had some heart-to-hearts about that."

The woman's faith and strength impressed me. I suddenly felt sorry for her husband, what he was missing, what he had chosen to give up.

"Mrs. Travers, do you have any idea where Shelly might have gone?"

She shook her head. "She did come by a few days ago, when she knew my husband would be at work."

Then she leaned in toward me. “This frightens me. You imply you don’t think she’s in any danger. But that’s not the, you know, unspoken message I get from you.

“Please,” I said. “Perhaps I’m not handling this right. I really have no information that would suggest she’s in danger. I’ll be frank, though, and I think this is something you already know. If she’s drifted back to that transsexual world she lived in for awhile, well, you know it can be a difficult place. I have no reason to think she’s in danger, Mrs. Travers. I just want to find her.”

Her shoulders seemed to relax. I suspected that she had spent more than a few nights worrying about her only child. “Yes, it can be a difficult place.” She shook her head. “I wish I could help you, but I don’t know where she is. When she came by a few days ago she told me she had moved out of her condo, and she might end up staying with some friends. I don’t know any of her friends. She doesn’t have a job, I don’t think.”

I hoped I didn’t show my disappointment. I had only learned about the woman’s past. There was little here to connect me to her present whereabouts, who her friends might be, anything like that.

I stood up. “Thank you. I appreciate your candor. I promise that if I hear something, I’ll let you know.”

She made a motion to show me out, then said. “Wait, Mr. Landers.” She got up, went down the hall and in a minute was back again, holding a shoe box.

“When Shelly came by last time, after she moved out of her place, she left this box of papers, her birth certificate, some other documents, medical records.”

She sat down heavily and put the box on the coffee table. “It seems very awkward to let you look through these things, but if Shelly is missing, and someone important in her life wants her back, I think I should let you.”

She nodded, once, decisively. “I’ll go putter in the kitchen. Take your time and call me when you’re finished.”

I sat for a moment with the shoe box in my lap. I was uncomfortable again, as I had been in Shelly’s condo. Going through the private minutia of a person’s life always made me feel unclean, and I hoped that what I found wouldn’t denigrate a person’s character. Too often it had.

There wasn't much in the box. A birth certificate for a female named Shelly Travers. Some Army papers for Sheldon Travers. A will, leaving everything to her parents. Accounting for an IRA at a local bank, some stock certificates, a few bills, nothing at all that pointed me in any direction in my search.

I shook the stack of papers absentmindedly and a business card fluttered out. I looked at the card. Dee Dee Myers, M.A., individual and family counseling, with an office in West Palm Beach.

I turned the card over. Scribbled in red ink was the name "MaryAnne," a phone number and the message, "call me anytime."

A therapist and a friend. A couple of phone numbers.

Somewhere to start.

I gave the papers back to Shelly's mother, and she walked me to the door. As we passed the television set she said, "Clete's addicted to NASCAR." She looked off into some middle distance. "Sits there every Sunday with the sound turned up nearly full blast." She brought her gaze back to me. "He always wanted a son he could watch the races with."

Chapter 6

There is another part of Crescent Key, on the mainland side of the Intracoastal. Though it is still part of the incorporated city, you must pass over the little bridge, cut up U.S. 1 for a mile or so, then cut back east to get to it. At this point there is almost a mile separating the highway from the coast, and the water's edge here is more mangrove swamp than beach. It is a strangely quiet spot amid the roar and bustle of Gold Coast life.

This enclave exists solely for the benefit of the residents of the Key. On a boulevard just off the highway there are a couple of upscale shopping centers and a grocery store. Inland a little ways, winding streets branch off a main boulevard, and along these streets are unpretentious retreats nestled in wooded acreage. It is not that these people who live here possess less wealth than the island residents. They simply have chosen to live a less obvious, more reclusive lifestyle. In truth, very few mortals can afford to live in this unassuming enclave.

Along the coast are a number of exclusive restaurants, with piers extending into the waterway.

At the northern end of "Restaurant Row" is a protected deep-water marina and a small private art institute. Just north of the art institute, on unincorporated land, a small gathering of taverns, bistros, yuppie bars and nightclubs has sprung up, along with a few art galleries, a bookstore, an art supply shop and several coffee shops with the inevitable outside patios.

The mainland side of Crescent Key is patrolled by the city's police force as well as a private security firm. We leave the bars and bistros to the Sheriff's Department.

All this is quite an advantage to the residents. Restaurants, shops, the boat moorings, and other essentials such as groceries and gas are close at hand, still within the confines of the city, and yet a little ways off our precious island.

The sun was dropping when I drove over the little bridge toward the mainland, waved to the tender, and made my way to Highway 1. I eased into the flow of traffic — there is always what we euphemistically call a "flow of traffic", that is, gridlock — on the highway. But that only lasted the mile or so it took to reach the turnoff toward the coast. Summer evenings in Florida are cooler than the days — but not by much. I kept the air conditioner on high and the windows rolled up as I turned north.

The setting sun at my back cast deep shadows in the twilight as I drove past the wooded estates to Restaurant Row. It was too early for the dinner crowd, too late for Happy Hour, and the road was virtually deserted.

In incorporated Crescent Key the restaurants are cut from the same understated elegance as the homes. They are tucked away from the road, sometimes visible only discretely among oaks and palms. There isn't much to see from the road; the real view is afforded in the luxury of impeccable cuisine served in rooms with windowed vistas to the Intracoastal and the twinkling lights of the Key.

My destination wasn't one of these serene establishments, but a place just a little ways, and a few light years, north of the city. It was a place called Desiree's Crab Shack, named after its esteemed and notorious owner, Desiree Blanca.

Desiree's Crab Shack was no shack, though through the magic of artifice it attempted to capture the flavor of nouveau sheikdom. A winding planked walkway led to a large porch of weathered wood and rope railings. The building itself was built of more weathered wood, with a rough-shingled roof. The entrance and exit doors both had life preservers attached.

I parked in the dusty and almost empty lot, made my way up the winding walkway and went inside.

The interior carried on the faux-nautical theme. To the left, off the foyer, a saltwater aquarium stood by the entrance to the bar. To the right, the hostess station stood in front of steps leading to the dining room. The paneling here was knotty pine. The seaside wall was all windows and beyond that was a wide porch with more tables. A little farther out were a few yards of sea oats and sand, and, because this part of the coast was a little north of the end of Crescent Key, the deep immeasurable expanse of the Atlantic Ocean.

The crowd that Desiree's drew was, if nothing else, eclectic. The place served some of the best seafood on the coast. The bar's drinks were copious, and if the bartender knew you, occasionally free. The music could be good, often a step up from the lounge-lizard fare to the south, and the blues jams on Sundays were legendary.

It was too early for music, and the bar wasn't crowded. I stepped inside, where it got just a little darker and a little cooler, and gave the place my best "I'm-here-to-meet-someone-and-I-don't-know-what-she-looks-like" look. A woman sitting alone at the far end of the bar caught my eye, raised her brows, nodded tentatively. I walked the length of the bar, got to her and said, "Ms. Myers?"

"Dee Dee, please," she said and took my hand. I settled in the stool next to her. The bartender, a blonde girl who didn't look a day over seventeen, coasted over and took our orders - draft beer for me, a fresh gin and tonic for Dee Dee.

She gave the impression of height - long arms, long fingers, a good bit of distance from waist to neck. She was pretty, with big blue eyes and blonde hair that fell in soft waves to her shoulders, a very feminine package. Her makeup and lipstick were impeccable.

We small-talked for a few minutes, about the heat — always the so-called ice-breaker to any Florida conversation — and the possibility that a tropical depression in the ocean might develop into the season's first hurricane. Then I said, "Thank you for agreeing to meet with me"

She nodded, and gave me a direct stare with her baby blues. "As you mentioned on the phone, you are worried about someone you believe might be a client of mine."

"Yes. Shelly Travers. I found your card in her possessions." I told her how Shelly had left abruptly, how her man was worried about her, and how he wanted her back."

"What if she doesn't want to come back?"

"Then she doesn't have to. She's an adult. My assignment is simply to ascertain her whereabouts."

"To spy on her." Myers's voice bristled.

Mine did as well. "That's not illegal."

She started to speak but I held up my hand — "or unethical, either. My client cares a great deal about her. He is worried; it wasn't like her to simply go away. That's all."

She looked at me, and some of the fire went out of her eyes. "I'm sorry. It's just that I value confidentiality, and many of my clients were — are — being abused or stalked or harassed. I only hope you are sincere."

"Can you tell me anything about Shelly that would help me find her?"

Her eyes hardened again. "You know I can't violate the therapist-client relationship."

I sighed. "So why did you agree to meet me?"

"Because I'm worried about — damn it, because I'm worried about her."

"Then we're on the same side," I said gently. "I'm really not asking for confidential information. I'm simply asking for some direction. I've spoken with her parents — her mother. Her father is a mess about what Shelly did."

"What she had to do," Dee Dee Myers said, almost to herself. Then: "God, the ways people deal with guilt . . ."

I sensed the impasse: She was worried about her client, she was an ethical therapist. But I could see the thoughtful look on her face. And she hadn't dismissed me. I hoped she could see a way through the impasse.

So I decided to give her some time.

I suggested that we have dinner. "On me."

She smiled at that. "Sure." So we took a corner table by the window in the dining area. We continued to talk about this and that - she seemed interested in my career with the police, about the mysteries of the wealth in Crescent Key, and my contacts with the residents through my security business.

After dinner — we both declined dessert and ordered coffee — she said, "I appreciate that you didn't continue to pressure me for more information. I was about to cut it off. Now I've had some time to think, and I've come up with an idea."

"To help her," I said.

"Yes. But first I have to make a phone call."

She excused herself, took a cell phone out of her purse, said, "Give me a few minutes," and walked outside. I sipped coffee, looked out at the water, thought about the brutal heat that was waging war with us.

Dee Dee Myers came back to the table and sat down. "I've spoken with someone who knows — who can help. She's not a professional therapist, but she leads a support group for transsexuals. She's agreed to meet with us. I think if you ask the right questions, you might get some help, more than I can ethically give.

"And," she added with a sudden smile. "You're going to be in for a real treat when you meet her."

Chapter 7

My sandy hair — now shot through with gray — and brown eyes don't exactly announce my Irish heritage, but it's there, as exemplified by my sometimes-too-quick temper fueled by a love of good whiskey.

My great-grandfather Eamonn O'Carmody farmed on the Emerald Isle, in county Tipperary, married a lass named Clodagh MacDonnchadaa — a mouthful there — and eventually, like so many others of his time, and in his land, saw a brighter future in the New World.

The couple, having no children as yet, made their way by tramp steamer across the Atlantic (surviving a gale that nearly swamped their little ship), made their way through Ellis Island, and eventually were drawn to the lure of riches to be made in the still-wild environs of Florida.

Great Grandpa Carmody — he had dropped the overly Irish prefix in his new home in a quaint attempt to be more "American" — eventually settled in a small town just north of the Everglades, and he worked in the fields and briefly as a blacksmith. And there he fathered two children, Padraig — Patrick — and Caitlain — Kathleen — who would become my grandmother.

Kathleen — the family encouraged the offspring to use the American derivatives of their names — was married at 16 to a man named Samuel Landers, from Sussex, and by all accounts a roughhouse, rogue, drifter, womanizer and alcoholic who knew the saddle, saloon and whorehouse equally well.

Grandpa Landers would die before he turned 50, killed in a shootout after he had been accused — wrongfully, according to family legend, rightfully, if you accept the truths of his life — of stealing another man's horse.

But before his early exit south of Belle Glade, he in 1927 he fathered Benjamin Landers — my father. Grandma did not marry again, and raised her boy by working in the sugar-cane fields and factories.

Benjamin, he of Irish and English blood, was a rogue of his own sorts. He married four times — the second wife was my mother, a sturdy lass with an Irish ancestry and the name Molly O'Farrell — and was not the type to make a career out of any job he held.

I was only five when my parents divorced, and my mother, like the other women in the family, was of the nurturing kind. She went to business college, got a job as an office manager in one of the huge farms just north of Miami, and invested her small savings wisely. She died in 1986.

My father, not of the nurturing kind at all, continued to move and marry, ending up in Nebraska working as a ranch-hand. He died in 1974 when his pickup truck turned left just as the road turned right. The truck rolled at least three times. My father was tossed through the windshield and run over by his careening vehicle, and the police found a smashed vodka bottle and eleven empty beer cans in the wreckage. Perhaps there was a streak of old-man O'Carmody in him after all.

Clodagh MacDonnchadaa and the women who followed were all red-haired, green eyed creatures. The old pictures showed them all to be exceptional beauties whose countenance of fragility belied a deep strength to endure among the less-than-reliable rogues they married.

So I come from a long line of Irish beauties. Which perhaps explains why I thought that the green-eyed, flaming-haired lass standing to be introduced to me was the most exquisite woman I'd ever seen.

Chapter 8

How I came to meet this beautiful creature:

I'd followed Dee Dee Myers to a bar on Federal Highway in West Palm, a nondescript cinder block building called The Cove. I had heard about the place during my days on the force. I wasn't looking forward to going inside.

But Dee Dee stepped inside with no hesitation at all and I followed right along. My eyes were still adjusting to the interior light of the lounge when Dee Dee stopped at a table and introduced me to the woman with the flaming hair.

MaryAnne McMichaels rose as the introductions were made. Then she motioned for us to sit and took her seat again. I sat to MaryAnne's left, Dee Dee positioned herself directly across from her.

MaryAnne McMichaels was indeed an astonishingly beautiful woman. Five ten at least, abundant in breast and hips. A wild mane of flaming hair, peaches and cream complexion with a dusting of freckles across her nose and cheeks. Bee-stung lips. My mother would have approved.

Our table was bathed in light from an overhead fixture, but the rest of the place seemed to slide into darkness. I could see perhaps a dozen more tables arranged haphazardly in a big room, and a raised area which housed a long bar. About half the tables were occupied, and a half-dozen patrons were at the bar. The people ranged from individual men and women to couples and groups. It seemed like a typical watering hole.

Except that I knew about the place. I'd been there a few times assisting on calls when the local cops were short-handed. A dozen years ago it had been a dive that drew transvestites, gays, the leather crowd. Then it had smelled of sweat and cigarettes and urine and cheap perfume.

The lights had been low enough so that the five-o'clock shadows on the girls didn't show. It had been a place where the timid didn't enter the restrooms. I had helped make a couple of cocaine busts, drug several screaming and scratching drag queens into the back of patrol cars. Just like any other dive, except for the overabundance of queen-size panty hose and pancake makeup.

The place was a hell of a lot nicer now — in fact, it was a private club that had recently been remodeled in soft colors, glass and chrome. But I wasn't sure I was that much more comfortable now than I had been before. I was the outsider here — and I always would be.

MaryAnne, on the other hand, seemed as comfortable as a cat on a windowsill. She was sipping on some kind of frothy drink. A waitress came by, an exotic thing in her twenties — though I found myself thinking about the concept of truth in advertising — and took our orders. MaryAnne got a second frothy concoction, I ordered my usual bourbon and Dee Dee Myers asked for mineral water with lime. MaryAnne looked up at the waitress and said, "Thank you, Galatea," and the waitress gave her a shy smile.

I looked at the waitress. I didn't know what was inside, and although the packaging was exceptional, I felt no impulse to unwrap it.

MaryAnne was the first to speak. "This is a safe haven for transsexuals and friends." She flashed me a dazzling smile. "It's quite an interesting place."

I nodded, thinking it best not to mention my prior acquaintance with The Cove. "An interesting place," Dee Dee Myers said, "And MaryAnne is quite an interesting woman. MaryAnne?"

Another dazzling display of teeth. "Dee Dee tells me you want to know more about transsexualism," MaryAnne said.

"I do."

The waitress glided up with our drinks and hovered at our table for a moment. She was exotic, multi-racial, Eurasian perhaps.

"Let's start with me," MaryAnne said after the girl had left. "I am what we call a t-woman. Transgendered. Used to be a man." She looked at me, eyebrows raised, as if expecting a reaction. I did my best to keep a poker face. It wasn't easy.

She continued: "I've been fortunate. My transformation is complete. I am —" she smiled — "all woman."

"MaryAnne, would you share some of the details?" Dee Dee prompted.

A dark look passed over MaryAnne's face, but was gone in a moment. "It wasn't easy. It took four years. The process is extremely complicated and often painful, both physically and psychologically." She looked at the other woman with affection. " Dee Dee has been wonderful. She's always encouraged me to be open and candid."

Dee Dee Myers just smiled.

"I started by dressing as a woman, cross-dressing if you will, but I desperately wanted to 'pass.' By that I mean passing in public as a woman. And that, my friend, ain't easy."

I shook my head. I couldn't imagine. She went on: "I started counseling; there's no way to do this right without support. I began hormone treatments. That caused a lot of physical changes and mood swings, too. It seemed like I was different every day. God, what a roller-coaster ride."

Dee Dee broke in. "MaryAnne worked hard in therapy. I never doubted that she would be an excellent candidate for sexual reassignment." She nodded again at MaryAnne.

MaryAnne said, "The hormones began to reshape my body. I developed small, but feminine breasts and my voice slipped into a higher register. My body and facial hair growth diminished but I still had to shave frequently. Yuck! Anyway, I finally had enough money saved to begin electrolysis — no way could I afford the laser procedure. That took more than a year. Mr. Landers, I wouldn't recommend it to my worst enemy. Did you know that they had to remove more than 30,000 hairs. That's 30,000 needle probes, every one of them painful."

I looked at her smooth complexion. She saw me looking and smiled.

"Then came the plastic surgery," she said. "I've had surgery to sculpt my hips. I've had liposuction to take away a little beer belly." She patted her very flat stomach. "And finally, 'cause of vanity, I went ahead with breast augmentation. Oh, and I had my Adam's apple shaved."

The last one did it to me.

"You look a little green around the gills," MaryAnne said.

I took a healthy nip of my drink. "Well," I said, "you have a damn fine throat."

We all laughed at that, and I realized that I was beginning to feel very comfortable around MaryAnne McMichaels.

"I am one of the very fortunate ones," MaryAnne said. "I can pass fairly well, don't you think." Another dazzling smile, which was quickly replaced by a darker look. "Some aren't nearly so fortunate, and still we all try and try and try."

Dee Dee Myers looked at her watch and said, "I need to go, Mr. Landers. Early appointments tomorrow. I'm going to leave you in MaryAnne's hands, if you don't mind?"

"No. Not at all."

"I'll take care of him, Dee Dee," MaryAnne said. She put a hand on top of mine. Soft skin, nice nails, manicured. A woman's hand.

As if reading my mind, MaryAnne said, "I've always thought my hands are too big." She held one up and scrutinized it. "We are obsessed with such things, the size of our hands and feet, the width of our shoulders, how well our voice modulates. Even the way we walk and gesture. It's easy to get completely self-absorbed."

Dee Dee Myers excused herself and left. Galatea came by again, and we ordered drinks. Again, she gave MaryAnne a shy smile, but this time one was directed at me as well.

After the interruption I took a good look at MaryAnne McMichaels. She struck me as a woman — I had no trouble at all with the gender reference, I realized — who had moved well beyond self-absorption. "I think your hands are very nice," I said feebly.

She laughed at that, a full, throaty, sexy laugh. "Mr. Landers, Loot, you know just the right things to say to a girl." And put her hand back on mine.

Chapter 9

MaryAnne let her hand linger there a few moments, then pulled it away. I felt her fingers brush along my skin. Flirting? And so what if she was? I was surprised I liked it. But then, she was, in her own words, "all woman."

I said, "Did Dee tell you what, ah, I'm up to?"

She laughed again. "What are you up to, Loot?" Definitely flirting. Then, "She told me you are trying to locate Shelly Travers. I trust Dee Dee, and she must have decided to trust you. It's easier for her this way. She's not breaching confidentiality and I'm not bound by it."

"So you know Shelly?"

"I do. I lead a support group, we meet at my house once a week. Some people in the group also hang out here to socialize; Shelly did not. She came to our group off and on for a year or so, but around six months ago she dropped out. I didn't know her socially, away from the group. She shared with the group that she had met a man who seemed to care for her. I think she had mixed feelings about that."

"Why?"

"He didn't know about her past. She felt deceitful."

Again I felt as if I were circling, getting at Shelly Travers, but not to her. Lots of anecdotal information, but not a clue to be found.

MaryAnne picked up on my impatience. "I know you have a sense of urgency about this. I don't know where Shelly is, and I haven't seen her in quite awhile. But I think that if she has suddenly abandoned a safe place it is likely that she has moved back into . . . this world." She looked around the shadowy bar. "I don't think she had established a great deal of confidence in her ability to make it — out there."

She scanned the room. "The trans scene isn't simple. There are so many variations, everything from the cross-dresser, usually a heterosexual male with a fetish, to the transvestite — what we call a chick with a dick — to the many stages of transsexual change, to the person who has gone all the way to having sexual reassignment surgery."

She brushed some errant strands of hair that had fallen across her face. She took a drink and looked around the bar. "Look around you, Mr. Landers. See that girl at the bar, the one in the yellow sweater?"

I looked. In the smoky light, she looked like another attractive female out for the evening.

"Her name is Amanda," MaryAnne said. "She passes pretty well here, but in the daylight it's a different story. She has very large hands and feet, and the angles of her face are quite masculine. She's had electrolysis on her face, but she still has quite a bit of body hair. That's why she is wearing long sleeves even in this heat. And —" she smiled at this — "she has no touch at all when it comes to coloring or styling her hair."

She looked over at the tables. "There," she said with the merest nod of her head. "Three people at a table near the bandstand. Louise, she's the one in the maroon t-shirt. Looks good here, looks good outside. She's tried to kill herself three times. Almost succeeded once. It's hard to miss the scars on her wrist.

"The girl next to her, the one who just let out that horse's laugh. Another girl who 'passes' fairly well. Except she has never been able to get control of her voice. Comes out sounding like a parody of a drag queen, unfortunately. And notice the three empty shot glasses in front of her. That's typical. She self-medicates that way."

The third person at the table was a man. MaryAnne said, "And that's Paul. Once Paula. He only stands about five-four. Five-foot-four women don't stand out at all, but five-foot-four men are the butt of jokes. He's tried everything to look more masculine.

"And of course," she added, "he's stuck with a cock that won't work."

I was stunned at her comment. She looked embarrassed and said, "They can construct a penis, but they haven't figured out how to make it, ah, functional sexually. Lousy deal for female-to-male transsexuals, and yet they go through with it anyway."

We finished our drinks, quiet for a few moments. I looked around the bar, but it didn't look ordinary anymore.

MaryAnne's words intruded on my thoughts. "I've always worried about Shelly. Physically, her transition was as perfect as you could wish for, but emotionally . . . she seems . . . fragile. She has been through some situations, scary stuff. I wonder. . ."

She put her hand on my arm. "Transsexuals are easy targets and they're often victimized. Then sometimes, to avoid being victims, they become the predator." She smiled sadly and shook her head. "It can be awful in our world. Dope and prostitution, of course. Lots of t-people sell sex to live on and to get money for drugs and for their therapy and surgery. Some prey on men who have no idea what they are getting into. They'll mug them and take their money without a second thought.

"These people are constantly afraid of dopers, of the cops, of johns who want to act out their repressed identity conflicts with their fists. Many transsexuals have very low self-esteem. They are isolated, alienated, broke. They are under tremendous pressure.

"A very dangerous world," she said, mostly to herself.

Then she looked directly at me, and I could see fear in her eyes. "I've never thought of Shelly as a strong one. If she's drifted back into the world she came from, I would be very worried about her. I would suggest you find her as quickly as you can."

Chapter 10

MaryAnne and I were debating how we were going to split up the drink tab when I heard a commotion near the front door — a muffled shout, a "shut the fuck up" and a door slamming shut as if shoved closed. I swiveled my head to look.

There were three of them, college kids perhaps, with those clean-cut looks and expensive casual clothing, khakis and designer pullovers, that suggested Daddy might be picking up the tab these days.

Two were of average height — not over six feet, not overly athletic in build. One was blonde, closely trimmed, with a shock of hair that fell over his forehead. The other was a brunette wearing aviator glasses.

The third was a stud: At least six-five, weighing in well over two hundred pounds. The muscles stretched his T-shirt, and his neck tapered into his shoulders in a tangle of sinews and tendons. The blonde hair was bleached, and hung over his ears and forehead. He didn't look too smart, but he compensated by looking mean as hell.

They looked drunk. They looked extremely out of place. And they clearly were spoiling for a fight.

MaryAnne said, "Oh, oh, tough kids gonna kick some transsexual ass."

I made a move to get up, but MaryAnne put a hand on my arm. "No. We can take care of ourselves. In fact —" she looked at me and her eyes were alight — "this might be kind of fun."

I raised an eyebrow — I'm one of those fortunate few who are genetically equipped to do that — and sat back.

The two average-looking guys sauntered over to the bar. Blondie said, in a very loud and affected voice, "Two Pink Cadillacs, please."

The bartender rolled her eyes and turned around. The two kids turned their backs to the bar and leaned against it, a show of confidence. I noticed the third guy, the mean one, circling along the perimeter of the dance floor near the stage.

"MaryAnne," I said. "I can do something —"

"Hush," she said. "We can take care of ourselves.

The kids made a presence in the place, but the patrons didn't seem to notice. I heard the same buzz of conversations as before. Galatea kept moving among the tables, though she cast several furtive glances back toward the bar.

"Two Caddies," the bartender said. The kids turned and got their drinks, reassumed their back-to-the-bar stances.

Blondie took a sip, bringing the glass up to his mouth in an exaggerated show of femininity. "Oh, that is sooooooo good," he mimicked, his voice a contrived contralto.

Glasses did the same. They giggled.

I noticed that the big one had sat down on the edge of the stage, legs askew in front of him, propping himself up on his arms. He looked around the room silently.

Glasses and Blondie sipped their drinks. Their eyes, what I could see in the dim light, had a glassy sheen. I doubted this had been their first stop in their drinking and carousing exploits of the evening.

The two at the bar finished their drinks at about the same time. They turned to the bar. "A second round, madam," Blondie said.

The bartender stared at them a moment, then took their empty glasses. Blondie said, "I just love your hair." The bartender said nothing, worked on their drinks.

"Does this kind of harassment happen much?" I asked. Galatea, I noticed, hovered near our table, holding her tray in front of her like a shield.

"More than you might think," MaryAnne said. "They're ignorant idiots. All they can see here is freaks."

Blondie and Glasses had gotten their drinks. They faced the room, holding the glasses in front of them. Blondie let the glass slip from his fingers. "Oops," he said in his contralto. The glass shattered and shards skittered across the wood floor. Pink frothy liquid puddled at their feet.

Glasses said, "Oh, you are sooooooo clumsy."

Blondie said, "I lost control. My little dickie-wickie wiggled."

That sent them into peals of laughter. “Dickie-wickie,” Glasses said. “Dickie-wickie.”

The bartender stood quietly behind the bar, staring at them. The patrons at the bar moved away. Those at the tables glanced toward the bar; some kept staring, others tried to continue their conversations. But clearly, the focus now was on the developing situation at the bar.

I looked at the big guy sitting on the stage. He hadn’t moved, but he had a wide smile now.

“You know,” Blondie said in a formal, contrived voice, “Not all is as it seems here.”

“Is that so,” Glasses said. They looked at one another. “Why, some of these women here —” he gestured to the room — “some of these women have . . . cocks.”

Blondie made a face of astonishment. “No. No, you say.”

“Indeed,” Glasses said seriously. “Some of these people are — I hate to be crude — chicks with dicks.”

“I can’t believe it,” Blondie said. “Some of them are so very beautiful. Let’s take a poll.”

The bartender moved back from the bar, stood with her back against the table that held the bottles and glasses. Her eyes were hard with hate.

I tensed. “MaryAnne,” I said. “For God’s sake.”

“Please.” Her fingers dug into my arm. “Stay out of it.”

The mean-looking one was standing now, weaving a little. He was quite drunk, I thought. His eyes were bright.

Blondie shouted, “Hey” — no contrived voice this time — “If you’ve got a pussy, raise your hand, if you’ve got a dick, grab it!” They both broke up laughing.

Now they had the patrons’ attention. The buzz of talk subsided. The bartender said, “Gentlemen, you’ve had your fun. I’ll even buy you a drink on the house, if you’ll please just —”

Glasses threw his drink in the bartender’s face and said, “Fuck off.”

MaryAnne said, “Landers, don’t.” She kept her hand on my arm.

The bartender stood quietly, liquid dripping down her face, onto her white blouse. Then she lifted her hand, got a rag and gently dabbed at the stains.

Blondie and Glasses were looking toward the tables. “Visual check,” Blondie said. “It’s the only way.”

"Out, goddamit," the bartender said. Her voice was a hiss.

"I said, fuck off lady, if you are a lady," Glasses said.

The big guy by the stage reached out and tipped over an amp. The cabinet fell heavily, and the reverb made a resounding sound in the room.

The bartender moved toward the phone behind the bar. "I wouldn't, bitch," Blondie said. The muscles in his jaws were working. The bartender stopped, turned around, looked calmly at Blondie and Glasses.

The big guy took a step toward the tables. "Show us what you've got," he said. His words were slurred.

A woman got up from one of the tables — Rachel, I thought MaryAnne had called her. She stood in the center of the dance floor and said, "I'd leave if I were you, before you get hurt." Her voice was as calm as the bartender's.

"Who's gonna get hurt?" the kid said. He took a step toward Rachel. She stood her ground. They were about five feet apart. I saw the kid set his legs, lean forward and ball his fists. Rachel watched him, a serene look on her face.

The big kid lunged at her. He was quick.

But Rachel was quicker. Suddenly she wasn't where she had been, and the kid was lunging at air. Then she was beside him. She took his arm in her hands, lifted it up, pivoted, applied pressure, and the kid went down like a sack of potatoes. Rachel followed him down, still holding onto the arm. He was on his stomach now, arm out to his side. Rachel knelt beside him, applying pressure to biceps and hand. The kid tried to get up, Rachel did something to his hand. The kid yelled and flopped back to the floor.

"Aikido," MaryAnne said. "Japanese martial art of non-aggression. Rachel's a black belt."

Things started to happen quickly now.

Blondie and Glasses took a couple of steps away from the bar. Blondie said, "Hey, goddamit. Bobby . . ."

A woman who had been hovering near the end of the bar picked up a bar stool, grabbed it by the legs and swung it at Glasses, hard. The seat of the stool caught him in the middle of his face with a loud thunk. The kid slammed back into the bar, blood flying from his nose and lips. He staggered to one side, slid to his knees and held his face with his hands, whimpering. His shattered glasses were on the floor.

Blondie turned around and was looking into the barrel of a very large revolver held by the bartender. The kid took a step backwards, said, "Oh, fuck man, we were just kidding around. No need for that." He glanced at his partner on the ground and tried to smile. "Really."

The bartender pulled back on the hammer. It set with a loud snick. The kid said, "Really, we were just leaving."

The bartender said, in a voice as cold as ice, "You think you can come in here and just do this?"

The bar was as silent as death now, but for the whimpering of the kid on the floor. The big guy in the Aikido pin had stopped struggling and lay there, face against the floor. Rachel knelt beside him, the serene look still on her face.

The bartender moved the gun an inch to the left and pulled the trigger. The roar of the discharge was deafening. The kid screamed and fell to the floor, onto his back. He held his ear with one hand and said, "Oh fuck, please don't . . ."

The bartender calmly came out from behind the bar and stood between the two troublemakers. She cocked the gun again and pointed it at Blondie's face. The smell of cordite was heavy in the air. The patrons watched calmly from their tables.

Blondie stared at the gun, eyes absolutely wide with terror. "Oh, God," he whimpered. He closed his eyes. Glasses had pulled himself up to a sitting position and was huddled against the bar, bloody hands still cupping his head.

The bartender pulled the trigger. The floor two inches from Blondie's head exploded in a shower of splinters and shards. Blondie rolled away, his scream a high-pitched wail. Glasses began to sob.

The bartender took a step toward Blondie. She shouted, "Can you hear me?"

Blondie nodded, eyes open again, staring at the bartender. She held the gun at her side now. She said, "Don't you ever fuck with what you don't know about. You don't know anything. You are nothing. Do you understand?"

Blondie nodded. The bartender turned toward the other kid on the floor. "Do you understand?"

Glasses, looking up at her with the eyes of a feral animal, nodded.

"Now get the fuck out of here."

Blondie pulled himself to his feet. Glasses was trying to get up but not doing a very good job of it. Blondie took his hand away from his ear and helped his friend up. Holding each other, they staggered to the door.

Rachel leaned down and whispered something to the kid she held down. He muttered something, then screamed. She whispered something else and he said, very clearly, “Yes, ma’am.”

She smiled, let go of the kid and got up. She went back to her table, sat down and took a sip of her drink. Her face was as serene as ever.

The kid got up, holding his hurt fist in his other hand. He looked straight at the door as he made his way toward it, following his friends.

The bartender, at her station now, said, “Well, I think this calls for a round on the house. Galatea, take their orders.”

“God, it’s Annie Oakley,” I said.

“She used to be a cop,” MaryAnne said. “I suspect that kid’s gonna have some real hearing problems. And the guy on the dance floor might have to deal with a couple of broken fingers. Rachel’s Aikido isn’t totally non-aggressive.”

She looked at me. “When we’re together, in our own environment, we can usually take care of ourselves.”

I heard a roar in the parking lot, the firing of a power motor. Then another growl of an engine. I got up, went out into the parking lot.

Just in time to see a black Viper skid into the highway, followed by a blue-and-white Shelby Mustang fastback.

The heir-heads. Just having their summer fun.

Chapter 11

After the bar — and the lovely smell of cordite — the night air was refreshing. I saw a Waffle House about half a block away and headed over.

I'd just gotten a cup of coffee and was looking over the menu when the door opened and Galatea, the waitress from the bar came in.

Before I knew it I had held up a hand and gotten her attention. She approached the booth slowly, stopped about four feet away, and smiled tentatively.

"Off work so early?"

She nodded vigorously. "That was enough for one night. I was supposed to get off in an hour, anyway."

"Would you care to join me?"

She hesitated a couple of beats, then slipped into the seat opposite me. When the waitress came around, Galatea ordered an omelet and coffee. I opted for a salad and a re-fill on the iced tea.

I said. "Galatea. That's a pretty name."

She smiled. "Are you familiar with the story?"

I shook my head. "Tell me."

"In Greek mythology, you've heard of Pygmalion?"

"Yes, but my memory is fuzzy."

She looked away from me, and her voice got softer. "He was a sculptor, and thought little about women or human beauty, he preferred his work, his art.

"So he sculpted a statue of a beautiful woman, which he called Galatea. As he gazed on the statue, he fell in love with it. With the image of Galatea, this image of perfection he created."

She smiled, looked at me. "So he went to Aphrodite, with his request that his statue of Galatea be transformed into a living woman. Aphrodite honored Pygmalion's request, and he was able to be with the woman he loved, that he created."

"The concept of perfection, made anew, brought to life," I said. "I think I understand why you might pick such a name."

"Well," she said, "I always feel a little silly telling it." She laughed softly. "I am hardly any kind of work of perfection, though I have been through more than my share of sculpting."

"You look very exotic," I said.

She laughed, her first full one with me. "More like a mutt."

"Hey," I said. "I didn't —"

She held up a hand and laughed again. "No, I'm just making fun of myself.. Let's see —" she held up a hand and began ticking off fingers — "one grandfather was Irish, the other Swedish. One married a black woman, the other a Japanese.

"So my mom was clearly multi-racial, but very dark. My father inherited light skin and Oriental features. Then —" she made a sweeping gesture — "they had me. Quite a pedigree, isn't it?"

It was. She had long, straight black hair, skin the color of Cafe au Lait, without blemish, and a delicate bone structure. Her raven hair framed an oval face; the subtle slant of her eyes suggested the Japanese heritage. Her nose was small and upturned. But her lips were full and lush, perhaps from the African lineage. And, at odds with everything else, her eyes were a startling cobalt blue.

It could have come out as a mismatched hodgepodge. But it didn't; she was a beautiful woman, though waif-like and fragile.

"I think you are very pretty," I said. I had the fleeting thought that, like MaryAnne, she must have had a difficult prior life in a male body that was not particularly masculine. And what had worked to her detriment as a male had gone in her favor as a female. That, and her "mutt" heritage.

The waitress brought our food, and we ate in silence for a little while. As with MaryAnne, I felt comfortable, though the distance of silence was more pronounced here. Galatea lacked the other woman's self assurance; she seemed almost timid. I had noticed her a couple of times during the bar fight, back pressed against a far wall, serving tray held in front of her.

While we ate, we made the smallest of talk, about the bar and the weather.

Then she said, “Look, you are MaryAnne’s friend. But I don’t know how much you know about . . . us.”

“MaryAnne was pretty open with me,” I said. “She told me what she had gone through.”

She gave me a smile that was tinged with sadness. “You see, those are the key words — gone through. I envy her. I’m going through what she’s already accomplished.”

I looked at her, feeling like the complete idiot. I had made an arrogant and stupid assumption — that she, like MaryAnne, had completed her sexual transformation.

And now she was telling me that she had not.

What did that change? Everything? At least a great deal.

“I wanted you to know . . .that I haven’t yet been able to have the sexual reassignment surgery. I still have . . .” she stopped and turned a crimson red.

I looked at her, at this pretty young woman who had chosen the name of a statue born in her own image. I had gotten from MaryAnne the beginnings of an understanding. Now, from Galatea, I was getting a dose of reality.

And then we were able to talk. She let her guard down and told me something about her upbringing, about her difficulties, about the tremendous guilt and confusion she had felt growing up. She told me that at one time she had accepted that she was a gay man, but that didn’t work for her. She felt something deeper, feelings of complete alienation from her biological gender. She told me of her dawning understanding of who she was, and who she could become.

As she talked the shyness fell away, and a light came into her eyes. I reflected that her beauty had a depth well beyond the physical.

And, as long as I didn’t think too technically about the physical, I found myself enjoying the company of this very pretty woman.

Then she said, “And how about you, Mr. Loot Landers?”

I hated talking about myself, but I wasn’t in a position to avoid it, given Galatea’s openness.

“Born and raised in Miami,” I said. “College there. I got a degree in criminal justice. Then I went into the Marines and spent four years in

Germany as a military policemen. Came back, applied to the cops, got accepted. About six years ago I took the job at Crescent Key, and I retired awhile back as a lieutenant." I smiled. "Hence the nickname Loot."

That wasn't enough for Galatea. "Married?" she asked.

"A long time ago. No kids. I have no idea where my ex lives."

"This is kinda like pulling teeth" she said. "Tell me about you. What you like, what you don't. Got any girlfriends? You know, the usual probing questions." She smiled broadly, which made her look very cute indeed. But not, I couldn't help thinking, all-woman cute.

"ah, gosh. I like to fish. I like to read. I like to cook sometimes, usually what I catch. I play the guitar, mostly country songs." I smiled. "How am I doing?"

She looked at me very directly. "You have a stubborn heart, Mr. Landers." The smile came and went. "You don't let people know much about you, do you."

I shook my head. "I suppose not. Habit."

"Girlfriends?"

"Not for a long time."

The smile came again. "Years? Months?"

"Okay, okay." I grinned at her to show her I wasn't peeved, even though I was a little. "Last girlfriend was, let's see, four years ago. My marriage broke up twelve years ago. I've gone out with a few women since my last girlfriend, but none was ever serious."

"Ever go out with a transsexual before?" Her grin now was enormous. She knew she'd caught me completely off guard.

"Ah, no. Not that I know of, at least."

She kept the grin going. "Just wondered."

Over dessert, she suddenly said, "What's your connection with MaryAnne. How do you know her?"

I told her about Shelly Travers, and how I had been hired to find her.

"I don't think I know her, not by name," she said. "I've probably met her if she was in one of MaryAnne's groups. But I don't think I know anything that would help you find her. Are you worried that . . . that something bad has happened to her?"

"No," I said. "Like I told MaryAnne, I have no indication that she left under any pressure. I do think she might have gotten herself involved in some of the seedier aspects of life in Emerald City."

Galatea's expression darkened then. "I've heard things . . .not about your missing person, of course, but about some things that're happening in our little community."

"You mean Emerald City?"

She nodded. "To the transsexuals here."

"Such as?"

She leaned in close. Her face was only about a foot from mine. Her eyes had an astonishing depth. "At least two girls have been murdered within the last couple of months. They were both hookers, and they were both transsexuals."

Suddenly any vague concerns I had had about Shelly's safety crystallized into harder-edged fears. "Do you know anything else?"

"Not much," she said. She leaned back in her booth. "There wasn't much in the papers, and I don't think there was any mention at all that the victims were transsexuals. In fact, I can't be one hundred percent sure they were. But that's what I hear.

"And —" she leaned in again — "There's a strong undercurrent of . . . fear. A lot of it is unspoken, and my womanly intuition might still be developing, but there's something different. I sense it at the bar, in the people I wait on. God, I sound like some harbinger of doom. I think something's wrong and when I try to articulate it, it sounds stupid.

"No," I said. "Not stupid. I was a cop for twenty years. I learned to trust my instincts. I think you should trust yours as well."

She shook her head. "The girls that were killed, I heard their names but I didn't know them. People think that we all know each other, but there are more of us than you might imagine, and within our world there are so many, ah, variations and subcultures. The people that come in the club are really a fairly moderate bunch of people who just happen to share their transsexualism. We're a long way from the chicks with dicks that work the streets in Emerald City."

She suddenly blushed crimson again. "God, I never say that. Hits too close to home."

I had absolutely no idea how to respond to that. Then I said, before I really thought about it, "I don't think of you that way."

She smiled. "Thank you for saying that, even if you don't mean it. I suggest you find your missing person as soon as possible. I just have a bad feeling about things these days, a bad feeling."

A little later, when I dropped her back off at the bar, I surprised myself by asking for her phone number. "I might need to ask you something about my case."

She gave me her number, which I scribbled down in a small notebook I always keep with me. Then, before I thought about it too long, I wrote down my phone number and e-mail for her.

She took the piece of paper and tucked it in her pocket. Then she said, "Loot — that's a nickname?"

I told her it was.

"What's your given name?"

"Samuel," I said. "Not Sam."

"Samuel. Not Sam," she said. "I like that. I'm going to call you Samuel."

Then she was gone.

Chapter 12

"You're gonna love this," I said. We were sharing bad coffee at midnight; the big detective had pulled the graveyard shift, not the most exciting time on the Key.

I told him about the encounter between the heir-heads and the transfolks.

Lipscomb raised his bushy eyebrows and grinned as I told it. The grin turned into a smile, which turned into a deep rumbling laugh. He slapped his knees, whacked the desk and sent his half-full coffee cup skittering along the Formica.

"God damn, that's rich," he said. "Gonna be interesting how they explain the bruises and cuts to daddy."

"Not to mention the deafness in one ear."

"Hell, they ain't been listening to daddy, or anyone else for that matter, since they were born. They're so damn rich . . ." He let the sentence trail off, as if he couldn't for the life him fathom at all such wealth.

"Well, our big problem is that we are around wealth, but not of wealth," I said. "Certainly puts us in our place."

The big detective nodded at that. Lipscomb and I were sitting in his cubicle in the detective division of the Crescent Key Police Department. Lipscomb had worked for me a number of years when I was a detective-lieutenant. He was an excellent investigator who had spent most of police life in New Orleans. He was also the only black officer in the Crescent Key department.

Lipscomb was perched on his desk. I sat in the interrogation chair, as Lipscomb referred to it. He was an outstanding interrogator; his blackness and largeness often seemed to have a paradoxical effect on suspects.

"Got Vipers and Ferraris haulin' ass all over the key. Probably screwing up all the pacemakers, not to mention the hearing aids."

Lipscomb took a swig of lukewarm department coffee, grimaced, said, "They outta fuckin' shoot the person who made this."

"Lipscomb," I said, "you made it."

"So shoot me."

"I'd have to borrow your gun," I said. We grinned at each other a little while, then I said, "I know you have to deal with pillaging and mayhem and so on, but I have a favor."

"Shoot," he said, rolled his eyes. "No pun intended."

I told him what I'd been hired to do, about the woman who had gone missing, about her transsexuality that might or might not have a bearing on the case. When he heard Shelly's name he had no reaction, so I doubted he was aware of the relationship between Darwin Locke and the missing girl. I told him that the only way I could think of to look for her was to go where she might have gone, back into the transsexual world from which she had emerged.

And I told him about what I'd heard, that the two prostitutes who had been murdered in Emerald City had in fact been transsexuals, and I was concerned that Shelly might have chosen a deadly time to go back to her old life. "I suppose the Emerald City cops are sitting on the details as usual. I haven't seen anything in the papers about the murders."

"You don't read the fuckin' papers."

"Your point," I said.

Lipscomb shrugged elaborately. "You know, hooker killings aren't exactly all that rare. And regarding the publicity, I'd heard about the murders, but nothing about the transsexual angle. And the Emerald City boys ain't asking for help from any outsiders. You know how they keep things sealed pretty tight over there. Wouldn't want to rock the corruption boat, so to speak. I can make a couple of calls, probably get the full reports. I doubt the dicks over there will tell me much. Hell, they think I'm a silk-stocking amateur."

The thought of Lipscomb in silk stockings was frightening. "And an honest amateur at that," I said. I had never seen Lipscomb accept so much as a free cup of coffee. He lived exceedingly modestly, drove an eight-year-old Cavalier and bought clothes at designer thrift stores. I would trust, and had trusted, him with my life.

He told me to give him twenty-four hours. Then he said, "Landers, what are you doin' looking for a missing person, and a trannie at that? I thought you were a high-priced security expert."

I shrugged. "I have no idea. I can't believe I took the case. I doubt if I can find the girl, and if I do I'll just have to go back to the client and tell him she doesn't want anything to do with him anymore. And besides, now I've gotta deal with her possibly being back where those murders took place."

Lipscomb hopped off his desk, an oddly delicate movement for such a big man. He said, "I just thought of something you're really gonna love." He let one of those deep chuckles make its way up and out. "Hold on."

He went around behind his desk, sat down and began rummaging in drawers. Understand that Lipscomb never throws away anything, any scrap of paper, any list of statistics, anything that has the ghost of a chance of coming in handy. And, though there is no discernible order to his hoarding — his office is a warren of mounds and stacks of paper and file folders — he always seems to find what he needs.

And he did, again. "Got it," he said gleefully. "Emerald City sent us the standard fax that goes out to neighboring agencies after a major crime." He whacked the paper with a pudgy paw. "Heh, heh, I thought it might be so." He handed the paper to me.

I read it: standard fax, full of police jargon, alerting other agencies that a murder had been committed, any details regarding suspects — in this case there were none — a few, in this case very few, details of the crime.

And right there at the bottom, a name. I looked at it and said, "Shit."

"Hot damn, you got to the good part," Lipscomb said. "You wanna look into those dead hookers, you get to deal with your old asshole buddy from your past, David LeGrand."

"Well, fuck me," I said, "and the horse I rode in on."

Chapter 13

David LeGrand stands as a symbol for what is wrong with Emerald City.

So, to understand David LeGrand, and the cops in Emerald City you should understand a few things about the city itself.

Emerald City is a world away from Palm Beach, and even West Palm, though it exists to serve both. It is a blue-collar town, a community of light industry and tract housing. It has slums, euphemistically called subsidized housing. It has crime, a substantial bit of it street-level — drugs, prostitution, petty graft, gambling, loansharking, extortion.

It is also home to the mid-management criminal — the gangsters who run the street-level corruption. It certainly doesn't have the organized families like those operating out of Miami, but there are people in Emerald City who do answer to the folks down south.

The cops know all this. Some of them try to fight it, some just do their best to ignore it.

And some make money off it. David LeGrand, by reputation and by the innuendo he himself perpetuated, was an example of the kind of cop that is too common in Emerald City. He'd worked patrol, and was thought to sell protection. He'd been promoted to narcotics detective and was reputed to reap a cut of the profits of pushers who expected to do business within city limits. Lateraled over to vice, he worked his cut on the pimps and independent hookers, as well as the escort agencies and massage parlors.

And he was purported to have a great deal of influence with his brethren on the force, given his propensity to let the dollars drift where he most needed them — to tighten lips, grease wheels and vaporize police reports.

If a high-stakes poker game was floating through town, David

LeGrand not only knew about it, he was raking something out of the pot. If a new dealer showed up with the latest designer drug, David LeGrand knew how it got to town and who it was being distributed to. Hookers new to town who wanted to work the agencies or the street needed to clear it with LeGrand, or one of his hired hands, first. And so on.

David LeGrand had been promoted to Homicide Lieutenant five or six years ago. He'd received numerous citations for good conduct, citizenship and bravery. He'd never been written up for any kind of major infraction at all. I wasn't sure how he was working his grift on this assignment, but I figured he'd found a way.

He was an Emerald City kind of cop through and through.

And one of the biggest reasons he was so good at his job — all aspects of his job — is that he didn't look like or act like the stereotype of the crooked cop. He didn't have to shave twice a day. His tailored suits weren't too expensive or too cheap. He drove an Acura that was just old enough not to attract attention and lived in a middle-class subdivision with the wife and three-kid family. He got his hair cut by a barber who knew what he was doing, didn't use too much Old Spice and generally treated average citizens with deference. He even occasionally made a big arrest.

I hated David LeGrand and everything he stood for. And I knew that he hated me.

The hatred stemmed from an inter-agency, area-wide task force that West Palm had put together six or seven years ago. Emerald City had been invited, of course, and of course, being good citizens, they had responded enthusiastically. (Later I figured out that they would always do what it took to get an inside line on what other agencies were doing, while never really disclosing the details of their own activities.)

LeGrand was the appointed representative from Emerald City. I had gotten the nod from Crescent Key.

It was clear from the first meeting that LeGrand considered me an amateur, sheltered by the wealth of the Key. He apparently didn't know, or had forgotten, that I had worked for years in the worst sections of Miami, both in uniform and undercover. He didn't know, or had forgotten, that I had been seriously wounded in a shootout at a crack house, and two young crack-heads had been killed by my bullets. He didn't know, or had forgotten, that I'd received numerous commendations from the force, that my resignation had garnered a front page story in the Miami Herald. He didn't know, or had forgotten, that I had once been a big shot.

The relationship between LeGrand and me had gone bad from the start of our pairing on the Task Force. While LeGrand could be charming on the streets, he had a tendency to be a condescending horse's ass among his colleagues. Most of the others simply humored him or avoided him; I had trouble doing that.

From the beginning it was clear that LeGrand insisted on collecting as much information as he could get from other agencies: what kind of priorities they set on street crime, their methods of undercover work, how they handled sources and informants. And it was just as clear, to me at least, that LeGrand wasn't nearly forthcoming about how his agency worked. Sure, he gave us information; but as I reviewed it, it was obvious the stuff he offered up wasn't anything but smokescreen. Lots of noise, no substance. After weeks, I realized I was still in the dark about how the cops in Emerald City really worked.

So I called him on it, not in front of the group, but at lunch one day, a lunch that I had set up.

I was cordial; I simply raised my concerns that many of us on the task force were volunteering quite a bit of inside information, but that, in going over my notes and handouts, I had very little substance about how the Emerald City department worked. And, I observed, we hadn't been able to get enough information to operationalize the behind-the-scenes interagency communication that might really help us work together to take a bite out of the street crime.

I attempted to express my concerns professionally. He chose to make his response personal.

He lost his temper, loudly if not particularly creatively. I remember watching the veins in his neck pulse furiously as he put me in my place. "Don't you dick around with me, you two-bit Keystone Kop." From there he continued the same theme. "You fuckers over there on Fantasy Island don't know jack about the street or real police work. What the fuck do you assholes do all day, anyway? Write traffic tickets and run off the wetbacks?"

Listening to his tirade, I was reminded of an alcoholic who gets angry at the person who confronts his drinking, all the while knowing somewhere in his dim little denying brain, that he is at fault, not his accuser.

When LeGrand came up for air, I simply said, “You really don’t want anyone to know what you all are up to over there, do you?”

LeGrand got up heavily. “Fuck you, Landers,” he said and stomped out of the restaurant.

It occurred to me that those who want to avoid prying eyes usually have something to hide. It also occurred to me that he left me with the check.

Following his tirade, LeGrand made it a point during task force meetings to either take not-so-subtle digs at me or ignore me completely. He never again made eye contact with me.

And I never found out squat about how the esteemed officers of Emerald City went about their business of fighting crime, although I had some pretty strong suspicions.

Chapter 14

You really have to go to the mountain; it generally doesn't come to you. So that's what I did. I spent my evening hitting the joints, the dives, the clubs and the streets, hoping to find a trace of the missing Shelly Travers. If she'd gone back to the old life, the old life was where I'd find her.

The evening reminded me of my days as a Miami detective — filled with oddball characters, spilled whiskey, the ever-present specter of drugs and violence, sex as a commodity and an overlay of sleaze on everything.

Shelly Travers had disappeared from the good life, and it was hard to imagine, at least while putting the spin of sober logic on it, that she would gravitate back to such a world as I had entered tonight. But, I knew too well, people did it all the time, fell victim to the strange lures that such worlds held for them. I'd seen men and women give up houses in the suburbs and Mercedes Benz automobiles, and loving spouse and children, and end up on drugs or hustling drugs or both, living with dancers and whores, needing liquor to face the day, or gambling what little money they could get their hands on the ponies or cards.

I didn't understand it; I knew it happened with alarming frequency.

But don't we all have our demons, I thought ruefully, as I fired up the Defender and prepared to leave my safe haven.

I didn't hold out any great hope of finding Shelly, especially if she didn't want to be found. I had no particular reassurance that she had gone back to her former environs, but a strong hunch suggested that she had. And over the years as a cop, I had grown to trust my hunches.

I did have a plan. At each place I let it be known that I wasn't a cop — who'd believe that, I didn't know — and left a few of my business cards. I also let it drop that there might be a "reward" for some quality information that would help me find Shelly Travers.

I dressed in the usual faded Wranglers, denim work shirt, low-top hiking boots. I had slapped on a battered Marlins baseball hat. I'd skipped shaving for the day. I wasn't trying to be of that world, I just wanted to move in that world without too much attention.

Unfortunately, when you've been a cop for more than twenty years, people tend to think you look like a cop. Especially when you try not to look like one.

I focused on Emerald City, where Shelly had lived while undergoing her transsexual journey. Emerald City has two so-called "strips," one on the north-south Dixie Highway, the main road that heads down to West Palm and beyond; the other on Everglades Drive that bisects the city in an east-west path. These streets are home to most of the strip joints, seedy bars, all-night restaurants and bottle clubs, as well as the majority of the street hookers. The transvestite and transsexual prostitutes hang out primarily at the west end of Everglades Drive.

First I drove along both Dixie and Everglades, just to get a, ah, no pun intended, feel for the place. If the streets have any saving grace, it is the abundance of lush semi-tropical vegetation. Some distant-past city fathers, in a frenzy of community zeal, slipped through a small temporary sales-tax increase to fund landscaping. Much of that effort, ironically, went into the beautification of Dixie and Everglades. Now there was the ever-present dichotomy of towering live oaks, huge flowering hedges, creeping vines, the occasional spreading banyan tree, standing in stark contrast to the gaudy neon, dusty parking lots, temporary signs and trolling women.

After making my runs along both strips — it was a little after 9:00 p.m. and the action hadn't really picked up yet — I drove back to the north end of Dixie.

My first stop was a joint called Sinful Eden, a totally nude club that featured an inexpensive buffet at noon and happy hour, and a number of big-screen televisions. Very upper crust for Emerald City, this was usually the first stop for the prettiest girls as they began their long, slow slide to the streets.

The parking lot was less than half full, a mix of pickup trucks, older model large American sedans, some Hondas and Nissans, two stretch limos — rent-by-the-hour deals — and one immaculate Mercedes 600.

Inside, the place was standard upper-class strip club — plenty of smooth, colored lighting, classic rock tunes spun by a live disk jockey, hustling waitresses in leotards, a full bar that ran along the length of one wall. Lots of mirrors, three stages, all showcasing naked girls who knew how to dance. Lots of firm, young, surgically augmented flesh everywhere. The kind of place where money is the common denominator, sex, the unit of exchange, where love and self-respect are checked at the front door.

I took a seat at the bar, put a twenty on the smooth wood and motioned to the bartender. He made his way along the length of the bar, stood in front of me, smiled and said, "What'll it be, officer?"

"That obvious, huh?"

He grinned. "Not really. You just checked out fairly high on the possibility scale, so I thought I'd take a chance. Really doesn't matter to me if you are or aren't. You definitely aren't an Emerald City cop, I know those guys. So I can't comp you, but your money's good."

"Fair enough," I said, and ordered bourbon and Coke.

I sipped the drink, got another, waited until the bartender wasn't busy and motioned him over again.

I took out the picture of Shelly Travers and asked him if he'd seen her. He flipped his bar rag over his shoulder, pushed his glasses up on his forehead and held the picture close. "I don't think so," he said. "Pretty. She in trouble?"

I shook my head. "I'm just a private cop. I'm looking for her. As far as I know she isn't in any trouble at all." I scanned the bar. "Unless being back in Emerald City is trouble enough."

He laughed at that. "Been around here before, huh? Sure, you want trouble, you can find it."

"I'd be most worried if trouble found her."

He shrugged, handed me back the photo. "Trouble happens," he said, as if it happened constantly.

I asked him if I could talk to some of the girls. "Can't stop you," he said, "but I think you'd have better luck letting me check with 'em. Can I keep the picture?"

"Sure." I handed it back. I'd had two dozen copies made at a quick-development place. I also handed him some of my new business cards. "There's some money in it for the right kind of information," I said.

He took the picture and cards and sat them by the register. "You want another drink?" he asked. I shook my head.

He took the twenty off the bar, said, "Sorry, like I said, no comps, you want change?" He grinned hugely.

"Why would I want change?" I said. I finished the last of my drink and headed out, realizing that this would be the high point of my night's adventure. In Emerald City, things mainly go downhill.

I repeated my M.O. all along Dixie, stopping in turn at the Bare Elegance, San Souci, Tit-for-Tat, Luscious Lady's, The Landing Strip, Caligula, and on and on.

After awhile, it all began to blur. I saw two alleged porn-stars strut their stuff, watched countless girls peel off tops and bottoms, watched girls who could dance like Ginger Rogers and some who couldn't keep time to a watch. I heard rock, country, rap, hip-hop, Tom Jones, Tom Petty, Tom T. Hall and Tommy Lee, David Bowie, David Allen Coe, Dave Edmonds, George Michaels and George Jones, Bruce Springsteen and Bruce Hornsby, ZZ Top and Boyz to Men. Eventually it all ran together and sounded like Muzak played at ear-splitting volume.

I talked to rude bartenders, friendly bartenders, naked girls who didn't care I was the law, naked girls who slid away quickly when they surmised I was the law, girls who politely asked for money, girls who asked for money while rubbing my crotch, girls who were pissed off before they asked for money. I bought drinks for girls, usually very expensive frothy concoctions. I drank bourbon and Coke, straight bourbon, straight Coke, mineral water and more bourbon.

By the time I finished on the south end of Dixie I had a hefty buzz on, had given away a dozen pictures and twice as many cards. I'd mentioned the word "reward" at least a hundred times. I'd also gone through two Fuentes and a Romeo y Julieta — at least these places were cigar-friendly.

Then I started working my way along Everglades, westerly. It was well after midnight now, and the energy level was soaring. Smoke-windowed limos and low-riders cruised. Girls materialized and stood on the street corners, dressed in gaudy little bits of almost nothing. Nothing subtle. Twice, as I drove by slowly, a girl pulled up her top to show me her breasts. Several times, when I didn't stop, I heard sharp curses flung in my direction.

I drove through the steamy, sultry night, the Defender a small, icy cocoon. Each joint was a cocoon of sorts, cooler though never cold enough to be comfortable. As I made my way west the places got seedier; these were the places where the girls worked when no other club would hire them. These were the places where the fringe hung out, the gaudy pimps and tired working girls, the dancers who looked to be, literally, on their last legs. If you looked close in the smoky light you might see track marks, stretch marks, bright pinpoint eyes, makeup-covered bruises. You might hear the disjointed monologues of the habitually stoned, the muttered profanities of the hopeless. Now I drank not to fit in, but to take the edge off the despair that rose inside me.

I saw police cars, cops inside their cocoons, gliding along the strip, watching, shining the occasional spotlight at a clump of girls. I never once saw a cop get out of his car. I never once saw the police stop a weaving motorist or question a hooker.

It would break my heart, I thought, if Shelly Travers had backslid into this hell.

I lasted until four in the morning. By the time I'd closed down the last joint, a dive on the east side of Everglades known for its back room blow jobs, I felt exhausted, old and soiled.

Not one person said they had seen anyone resembling Shelly Travers. I passed out all two dozen of the photographs, left every card I'd printed.

I drove back toward Crescent Key, feeling the weight of responsibility for finding one very small person in one very big, scary world. I had little hope at this point. I felt only fatigue, and an overwhelming loneliness and sorrow.

I got home without being stopped by a cop. Good thing, I wouldn't have wanted to guess what I would have blown on a sobriety test.

Chapter 15

It seems as if, more and more, I am defined by the contradictions in my life.

On one hand, I live in a bungalow that on the outside is little more than a shack, bleached and whitewashed wood and rough-planked deck overlooking woods and wetlands and beach.

But I have taken great pains, and spent quite a bit of money, on the interior. The walls are pure white, the furniture expensive antique rattan. I restored the wooden floors myself, but I had the kitchen cabinets custom built by a ship's carpenter and inlaid with etched glass from England. The tile was imported from Italy, the counter tops solid oak butcher block.

The few pieces of art that I have hung on the walls or displayed on tables I have collected from local artists. Some pieces I have gotten for almost nothing; others I have paid thousands of dollars for. But they all are of a kind — they are representative of the precarious balance of flora and fauna which surrounds us.

I bought the Land Rover with a big chunk of my severance package from the police force. Not the cushy yuppie model, this one was built for tough work, with a heavy suspension and high ground clearance, and even a winch on the front. There always seems to be a thick patina of mud and dust on the paint, but I keep the interior spotless.

I have two boats. One's an 18-foot Hawes flats boat with a hundred horses of Mercury power hanging on the back. It has state of the art GPS and fish finders, and a strong trolling motor on the front.

Then there's my skiff, 14 ugly feet of beat up camo-painted aluminum. Just a trolling motor for power, no electronics at all, and I have to position my feet just so when standing or the thing will tip over.

The skiff is the boat I most often fish in, the one in which I routinely pull in the bonefish and reds and snook.

Truly, the contradictions frame the parameters of my existence. But there is something deeper, a force that rules my life. I compulsively build walls — high, strong walls between my small, safe, controlled universe, and the big bad world outside.

I have lived here six years and by choice have never had a woman over.

Everything in this private world of mine is here, or not here, by choice. I have silence when I want it, music when it suits me. I don't have to worry about a knock on the door, or keeping the house neat (though I do in fact keep the place compulsively neat.) I can fish when I want, check my messages when I want to. I can accept only the clients I want, work on my own schedule, set an alarm or sleep as late as I want to. I can eat the fish I catch, pick the vegetables that grow in my little garden. I do admit that I have a state-of-the-art iPad with 4G capability, but I use it mostly to read the news and play iTunes.

My wardrobe consists of Wranglers and work shirts, and Nikes or hiking boots, and in winter a heavy trench coat. I'm willing to pay less than $25 for the jeans at Wal-Mart, but I own several Borsolino panamas that cost more than $600 each. And while I might buy my shirts at the discount store, I'm downright picky about how the laundry does the starch (medium, thank you, with heavy on the cuffs.)

I can sit outside at night and watch the colors fade in the Florida sky in bursts of deep purples and pinks. I can watch the summer storms approach, see the lightning flash in the darkening sky. I can stand in the rain if I want.

Or I can sit on my little protected porch, day or night, wind, rain or sun, and play my guitar, or smoke my illegal Cuban cigars, or drink my bourbon — or do nothing at all.

I have it made. And I had no reason to suspect that this recent little piece of business that I'd gotten myself involved in was going to affect the solitary, insulated life I'd constructed in any way at all.

Chapter 16

But on the morning after my fruitless jaunt through the joints, the carefully constructed wall between my public and private life began to disintegrate. And at my own hands.

I went to my bedroom, rummaged around on a top shelf in the closet until I found my portable police scanner. The batteries in it were long dead, the thing not having been turned on in several years. But the user's manual was still in the box, along with a complete listing of all the police channels in the area, including vice and tactical for all the agencies.

I knelt down, pushed aside some shirts and pants so I could get at the safe I'd installed in the back corner. I dialed the combination and swung the door open. I took out the holstered Sig that I had put away the day I retired from the cops. The gun, in its clip-on belt holster, felt heavy, but the oil I had rubbed it down with had done its job, and the finish was soft and unmarred.

It occurred to me that I had no ammunition. So I got back in the Land Rover, drove to a gun shop in West Palm and purchased a single box of 40 S&W Hydra-Shoks.

Then I used the cell phone, to call the telephone company and have call forwarding added to my office line.

In one day I had surrendered a huge part of myself, and of the life I had so zealously constructed and guarded.

I made one vow to myself, though — to never, never take any part of this, the phone, the scanner, the gun onto my back porch. There I would always have at least one place where I could retreat, where I could always count on finding a safe, serene world.

Chapter 17

The call came in a little before noon. My caller told me she'd heard I'd been hanging around the clubs, asking questions.

But first we had to do this song and dance:

"I heard you was giving out a reward."

"Could be. Depends on what you got."

"What I got's good enough for a reward. "How much?"

"I'll make it worth your while if what you have is good."

She thought about that awhile, we talked about how she'd get the reward, and then she told me this story:

It had been several months ago, she wasn't sure of the exact time. Still winter, which does come to Florida in harsher ways than many people believe.

She left the bar, huddled in a cheap imitation-fur coat that provided more warmth than style. The bartender, who was still cleaning up and would be there another hour at least, unlocked the door and let her out.

When she stepped onto the sidewalk a hard wind off the ocean hit her. "Motherfucker," she muttered and tugged the collar of the coat tightly around her neck. The coat came to the middle of her calves, but she had neglected to wear stockings — she'd ripped her good fishnet ones during a dance — and the icy wind was numbing on her bare skin. Under the coat she wore only a shimmering, clinging dress of thin rayon, and underneath it a tiny thong bikini brief. She'd looked dazzling, she thought, in the bar lights, in the dress as she had made her rounds, in the fishnets and bikini bottom, then in nothing at all, on the stage.

The wind must have kept the pervs home, floggin' their dolphins in the privacy of their heated bedrooms. The crowd at the club had been sparse, and she'd only managed four lap dances all night. At twenty bucks a dance, along with the forty dollars or so she'd hustled in "donations" for the jukebox, she'd only cleared about one twenty. Then she'd had to pay the bar twenty for the "privilege" of working there for the evening. Less than a hundred lousy fucking bucks for shucking her duds and grinding her ass on the pervs' laps and waving her tits in the pervs' faces and giving the pervs spread-legged crotch shots from the stage.

A hundred fucking dollars. At least she'd been able to hustle enough drinks to maintain a decent buzz that she bolstered with a couple of lines of coke that one of the other girls brought in and, for some unfathomable reason, gave away free.

She'd stayed an hour after closing, making small talk with the bartender and getting him to replenish her drink three or four times. The coke had worn off, but she had a pretty good the whiskey buzz going when she finally left.

She'd lost track of time in there. She'd thought she'd be able to catch one of the cabs that cruised this strip of bars — another twenty bucks down the drain for the ride to her place — but it looked like it was even too late for the cabs. Damn. She made her way to the t-bar across the street and hunched down in the protected entrance. They were still open for their after-hours crowd, and she figured a cab would be by any minute to unload the usual bunch of late night queers. But after a few minutes of waiting there in the cold, she hadn't seen anybody come or go, and still no cabs had showed up. She gave up on it and leaned into the wind and began to walk down the street. A cab would eventually come by this way, she thought.

She wore the same high heels, black pumps, that she'd worn on stage. Now, with the whiskey working in her, they seemed unstable, awkward. She clomped along, hearing only the sharp sounds of the heels on the sidewalk. She was the only soul on the street. The wind did not let up.

A couple of cars drove by. One driver honked his horn but didn't stop. Another slowed, came up beside her, the driver just a shadow behind smoked glass. She shivered, turned away from the street, huddled more furtively in her coat, and trudged resolutely ahead. The car stayed with her a few yards, then sped up and disappeared around a corner.

"Cold, fucking cold," she muttered. Her hands were numb, exposed to the bitter wind as she held her coat to her body. The wind whipped her hair, an expensive bottle-blonde job. The twenty pounds of "baby fat", as she called the weight gain over the last year, didn't help insulate her at all.

She walked another block, and no cab came by. The wind picked up even more and gusted, and whipped the coat up and away from her legs. Icy air sliced up between her legs, and she went into a shiver that almost became a spasm. She felt the freezing air all the way up to her belly and breasts.

No cab. Bitter wind. Lousy coat. No gloves. "Motherfucker," she muttered again.

Another car came by, slowed, took up a pace that just kept up with her as she walked. New and expensive, some kind of foreign car she thought, but she didn't know cars very well.

The window slid down, and the driver said, "Too cold to walk. Would you like a lift?"

He was damn right about that. She looked at him. She saw men all the time, the pervs in the bar all blurred together. She'd been in the face of hundreds of men, dozens a night. Men didn't make much of an impression on her.

This one was in his forties — fifties? — she wasn't good at ages, either. He was wearing some kind of cloth cap. He looked rich, had this really nice car. He didn't look like a perv, but she knew, from much experience, that looks could be very deceiving. Just as many rich pervs as poor ones, if not more.

Just then a brutal gust of wind whipped into her, blew the coat up again, slapped her skin. She looked up and down the street. No cabs. She looked at the man and then made a decision. She said, "Sure."

She went to the passenger's door, heard the automatic door lock go up with a snick. Opened the door, got in and immediately felt the rush of warm air from the heater. The interior was wonderfully warm.

The driver said, "No cabs, huh?" He had a nice voice, soft, easy-going.

She brushed the tangled hair out of her face, held up a few strands in front of her and scrutinized them, flipped them back over her shoulders. "No fuckin' cabs, too fuckin' cold." She smirked. "Excuse my French."

He grinned at her. "No fuckin' problem."

She grinned back. God, the heat felt good.

She checked him out again. Average looking guy, wearing the hat and slacks and a leather jacket, unzipped and a button-down shirt, and soft leather gloves, looked expensive. Definitely a guy with money, perv or not.

She told him where she lived, a five-mile distance. He told her he wouldn't mind running her over there, he wasn't doing anything anyway, just out cruising. He emphasized "cruising," and raised his eyebrows. She had seen the raised-eyebrow look a million times. She knew what they all wanted. What she wanted was a ride home.

"You work there?" He asked, jerking his head back toward the strip of bars.

"Nope," she said and shook her hair. The men in the bar liked it when she did that, in their faces, and she had begun to do it almost unconsciously when she was around men. She thought she was very sexy, even with the extra twenty pounds. Men liked lots of curves and tight dresses and boobs that bounced. Thank God some of her weight gain had been in her tits. "Just there visitin' a friend, kind of slumming." Let him think she had a little class, a higher level of gal than just a dud-shucker.

"Good," he said. "I'm glad to hear you don't work there." She looked over at him. Odd answer, most men got hot for strippers in a pervy kind of way.

He looked at her hard then, and she felt the weight of his stare. It almost took her breath away, the depths of his eyes.

Then the stare closed down, and he was just a guy again, checking her out. He told her his name, something she'd never remember, like Bob or Bill or Ed. She told him hers — the one she had been using the last few days. He said, "Nice name," patted her on the knee — she'd let her coat fall open to reveal the tight dress and bare legs.

She took a moment to study the man's face. Not bad looking, nothing she'd remember. Of course, men in a general way had become forgettable, just faces and hands in the bar, night after night. But this one was okay looking, nothing special, kinda old. At least he was white, she got really tired of the Spics and Mexes who came into the bar, drunk and hollering. Colored, she had no opinion of. Very few coloreds came into the bar and those that did usually left a short time later. She'd never given a private dance to a colored.

The man reached over and opened the glove box, took out a silver flask. “Cold night, a good drink’ll warm you up,” he said. He offered her the flask, held it out in his gloved hands.

The wind had wiped out most of her buzz and she gratefully took the flask, uncapped it and took a long swig. Not ladylike, she thought, but some men found it sexy. She swallowed the burning liquid and felt the warm glow begin to grow in her belly. She sighed, comfortable now, beginning to feel the high return.

She held the flask toward the man, but he said, “No thanks. Driving, you know.” So she took another gulp, capped the flask and rested it on her lap. She thought the hammered metal looked sexy against the thin material.

They drove through the deserted streets. A couple of cars passed them, a cab, a police cruiser. She noticed that he avoided Dixie, some of the other main roads. She didn’t say anything. He knew his way around.

“Do you live alone?” he asked, looking straight ahead. She thought she knew what he was leading up to. That didn’t bother her. She knew what men wanted. She liked it when they wanted her, even when she decided not to let them have her.

She nodded. Her kid was staying at her mom’s for a few days. She needed a break from the squalling. “All by my little lonesome,” she said in her best little-girl voice. She liked the guy okay so far. She figured, the car and the clothes, he had money to spend on her.

She thought about the eighty dollars in her purse. Eighty fuckin’ dollars and not a penny more at home, and no food or booze in the place. “Yep,” she said again. “All by my little lonesome.” She wondered if she had picked up all the rug-rat’s toys.

“Well . . .” the man said, and let his voice trail off. She had gone through this a thousand times, just let the guy do it his way, feel his way along. Be patient, they all got around to it one way or another.

But she enjoyed helping them along. She stretched, shrugged out of her coat, let the man see her boobs stretch against the fabric of her dress, crossed her legs so she could flash some thigh. “Gettin’ warm in here,” she said. She uncapped the flask, took another swig. “Boy, that makes me feel mellow.” She capped the flask and nestled it back into her lap, pushing it between her legs a little, kept her hand on it. “Mellow,” she repeated.

A couple of blocks later he said, "But you are a, ah, working girl?"

She loved this, watching guys fall all over themselves, beating around the proverbial bush. A lot of times she was tempted to say, "Cut the shit and tell me what you really want," but the times she'd tried it the guys had looked embarrassed or mad. She'd learned to let them do it their way.

"Well, sure, we all gotta work, honey," she said, putting a lot of sexual innuendo in her voice. She liked sexual innuendo, she'd read an article in a woman's magazine on it, had to look up the word but once she got the hang of it she found she could use it to great advantage on men.

She opened her little clutch purse — leatherette, it looked like leather but it didn't smell like leather — and got her lipstick. She also checked to make sure she had rubbers, gotta be prepared, wasn't that the Scout's motto? They were there, five or six, she kept a range of styles, lubricated, neon, ribbed, one French tickler with antlers on it, just for amusement.

She didn't think of herself as a hooker, though, if you wanted to split things really fine, she might have hooked a time or two. She thought of it as spending some quality time with a guy, mutual attraction and all that, and one thing leads to another. And the guy would leave her a token of his appreciation for her time.

Even though she wasn't a hooker, she didn't want to get busted by an over-zealous cop. A police-officer friend whom she had spent some quality time with had told her to always ask the question, "Are you a policeman, law enforcement officer or government agent?" — those exact words, some court somewhere had approved them — and the cop had to be honest and answer truthfully. So she knew she'd never be arrested.

She went over the wording in her mind as they drove along the deserted streets of Emerald City.

She said, "Well, I'm not working now, but I always like to spend some, ah, quality time with a generous man." She smiled and looked at him, pushing out her chest just a bit for effect.

He glanced over at her, smiled, and said, "Yeah, I like the idea of spending some time. I think of myself as a very generous person." He reached over and brushed his gloved hand against her leg for just a moment. She knew that he had played this game before. She began to worry less about the meager amount of money in her purse.

“There’s an all-night convenience store right around here,” she said. “I know the clerk, and he’ll sell us some wine or beer, something to make things a little, well, you know . . .” she kept the smile going.

“Romantic,” he said.

She nodded happily. Things were going to work out just fine.

Chapter 18

They pulled up to the all-night market and she looked at him expectantly. He got two twenties out of his wallet and she smiled, made sure her fingers lingered on his hand as she took the bills.

She came back with two bottles of Gallo chardonnay and two six-packs of Heineken. He didn't ask for the change, and she didn't volunteer.

At her place she unlocked the deadbolt, asked him to wait outside the door while she did a quick run-through. There were only a few toys scattered on the floor and she quickly scooped those up and tossed them in the house-ape's room. She checked the bedroom, picked up a couple of pairs of underwear and a bra, tossed them in the closet. She straightened the quilt on the bed, went back to the door and let Bill or Fred or whatever his name was in.

She watched as he looked around, a little awkward now, as if assuring himself that they were alone. Then he sat down on the couch, hands on his knees, back ramrod straight.

She sat beside him a moment, put a hand on his neck and said, "Honey, you just relax. I'm glad you're here. I'll open the wine and bring it in. Why don't you get out of that jacket and make yourself more comfortable? I sure am.

She went into her bedroom and quickly got out of her dress, unhooked her bra and shrugged it off. Leaving her panties on she got into a thin silk. flowered kimono. Just the right mood for her new friend.

Then she came back with two bottles and two glasses. She noticed that he still wore his coat, hat and gloves. They sat in silence and drank the wine. She sat beside him, not quite thigh to thigh, but close. She smelled his cologne, nothing overpowering.

That glass of wine and a second one seemed to help him relax; he started looking over at her and smiling, gazing at the front of her kimono where it gapped open, revealing more than a little cleavage. Then he leaned back on the couch and draped an arm behind her, and she leaned in on him and rested her head on his shoulder. The cologne smelled good; it smelled expensive. She couldn't quite place the brand, but she knew she liked it. She liked Old Spice too, that smelled like her grandfather, and English Leather. She hated all that new crap.

She went into the kitchen to get the second bottle of wine. But when she came back he wasn't sitting down. He was walking around the room, looking at her things. He had stopped at a block-and-board bookcase and was moving some knicknacks around. He picked up a picture of her parents, one of the few things that meant anything to her. "Family?" he asked. He looked odd standing in the heated room in his coat and gloves.

She nodded. He put the picture down, continued scannning the shelves, touching things, shifting them around. She felt a chill. Then he gave her that look again, the dark eyes, bottomless, bearing into her, just for a second.

She sat down. He circled the room, moved to the front door. She thought that he might have checked the deadbolt, made sure it was locked. Then he came back and sat down beside her. He took the wine bottle and poured the wine and they drank a glass, and then another.

Did she feel just a flicker of fear now? She forced her thoughts back to the present moment. He was treating her nice. He wasn't making her feel like a whore. She actually was kind of attracted to the guy, and she decided to not mention any tokens of appreciation he might leave behind. She didn't think he'd let her down.

They leaned back and he kissed her, and she kissed him back, and let it get kind of hot. She knew that hookers usually didn't kiss, so she let him have a lot of tongue so he wouldn't get the wrong idea about her. She tried to get her arms around his neck but it was awkward with the jacket.

"I do have to ask you one thing she says. He looks at her, his face only inches away.

"Are you a policeman, law enforcement officer or government agent?"

He waited a moment, then he laughed, a good hearty laugh. "No ma'am, I'm not a cop. I'm just a guy out to have a good time."

She felt better now. That was always awkward, saying that and not feeling like a hooker.

She kissed him again, with a lot of tongue. When she was finished she said, "God, my back is hurtin' something awful. You wanna let me lay down and you can rub it for me?" She gave him one of her best smiles.

So they went back to her bedroom and lay on the bed and one thing led to another and she pulled her kimono open to show him her breasts. She knew that guys just about lost it when they looked at her tits.

He stood by the bed, slowly took off his jacket and hat. He made no move to take his shirt or pants off. Shy little fucker, she thought. Then she saw that he still hadn't taken his gloves off, and she really didn't get that at all. That didn't make sense. But she'd stopped trying to make sense of men.

She pulled her arms out of the kimono and worked it down to her waist. It was still held by the sash. She rolled on her stomach and took the bottle of baby lotion she had placed on the nightstand. She reached behind her and squirted lotion on her back. "Rub my back, honey," she said in the sexiest voice she could muster.

He sat down on the edge of the bed and began to stroke her back. She felt the brush of soft leather against her skin. Strange sensation. Leather and lotion.

Then, without warning, he rolled her over, a bit roughly. . He looked down at her, and he didn't look shy or awkward now. He looked in control. He ran his hands along her tits, let them linger on her nipples, took them in his hands and squeezed them and moved them around. She kept watching the leather on her skin.

He undid his belt, began to work his pants down to his knees.

"Blow me," he said, his voice hard.

She started slow, like she knew men liked, but he grabbed her hair and pulled it, arching and shoving his cock into the back of her throat. She almost gagged, but kept at it. Some guys liked it rough, she thought. That was okay, as long as it didn't get too rough.

She did him that way for a minute or two, him shoving it into her hard, pulling her head up and down, coming almost out of her mouth, ramming back in.

Then, suddenly, he pulled out of her mouth. She started to come up toward him, but he sat up and twisted and then he was beside her, pushing down with both hands on her back. He got her onto her stomach. “Don’t move,” he said, his voice a harsh whisper.

This was beginning to feel different. She wasn’t in control now, and she hated losing control.

Now she feels a stab of fear. Now he’s astride her, leaning his weight against her body, facing her feet. She feels the kimono being tugged up, just to the bottom of her ass. She hears the sound of the baby lotion bottle being squeezed, feels the sudden coldness of the liquid on the crack of her ass. He is breathing hard now, rocking back and forth on her back, pinning her. His hands grip her legs at the knees and she feels them being pulled apart.

She tries to move, realizes that his legs have pinned her arms to her sides. Another chill of fear — he is humming softly, tunelessly.

She is afraid — and wet with anticipation. She feels his fingers at her crack, spreading her, feeling up and down her, rubbing her. A finger massages her anus, rims it, dips into it, one time, two, deeper, then deeply into her. She gasps with pain and almost orgasms.

The humming is louder now, he rocks back and forth, she thinks he is masturbating. He shoves another finger into her ass, stretching her painfully.

Then the fingers are gone, now they are below her ass, probing, sliding, around toward her cunt, starting to . . .

Suddenly, silence. Stillness. A sharp intake of breath. The probing fingers are gone. His weight begins to lift off her.

She wonders what she has done wrong, what she has done to offend him.

He is standing now, at the side of the bed, she twists to look over her shoulder, God, she’s scared now and he’s staring at her, those dark fathomless eyes.

And now his eyes begin to burn with a deep fire. His face is a mask of anger. His mouth opens as if to speak but no words come.

She slowly, slowly turns over until she is on her back. She barely breathes, is afraid to talk, cannot help but look into those eyes that burn now with rage.

He begins to clench his fists, clench them, unclench them. She thinks he will strike her. Getting hit has always terrified her, caused her to have nightmares.

Now his hands go slack, and he slumps and the tension is broken. He looks away now, looks down at himself, embarrassed. He pulls up his pants, eyes averted from her, muttering to himself. She hears, "God damn it, God damn, damn. . .I thought, I thought . . ."

Belt fastened, he cuts his eyes to her once, quickly. He grabs his jacket and hat, put them on. Then he is moving out of the room, gone. She hears the door open, then quickly close.

She makes herself move, get out of the bed. She puts her arms back into the kimono, wraps it tightly around her. She goes to the living room, looks around. Empty. The door is closed. She glances into the kitchen. Empty. To be sure, she goes to her kid's bedroom, looks around, sticks her head into the hall bathroom. Empty.

She goes back into the living room, moves to the door, throws the deadbolt closed. She leans against the door, begins to breathe deeply, lets her nerves untangle. She goes to the kitchen, opens the second bottle of wine, takes it back to the bedroom and swigs down half of it within a minute. Then she crawls under her sheets, turns out the light, clinches her eyes shut and, eventually, sleeps.

It is not until after she wakes up the next morning that she realizes the son of a bitch didn't leave her a dime.

When she'd finished telling me her story, she asked me if it had helped me. I had no clue whether it had, but I thanked her for calling.

Then she said, "So, what about the reward? I came forward to you."

"How 'bout we get together?" I said. "I have a few more questions to ask."

Chapter 19

"As I said, when I got up the next morning I realized that the son of a bitch hadn't left me a dime," she said.

Her name was Maggie and we were sitting in the Tanga Lounge where, in spite of what she had told the man, she was employed as a dancer.

I shook my head, letting her know how terrible I felt about his inconsideration.

We were sitting in the gloom of a back table in the lounge. It was mid-afternoon, though you couldn't tell anything about the outside world from inside the bar. No windows, loud jukebox, semi-naked girls, waitresses in thong bikini bottoms and halter tops, a few men alone at tables, alone in chairs lining the stage.

Maggie was one of the semi-naked girls. She wore a blue sequined bottom and a filmy negligee that hid nothing.

"So about the reward," she said. "Do I get it?"

"Maybe," I said. "Let me ask you a few questions."

"Okay, but I went out of my way to tell you this. I think it ought to be worth something."

"This man," I said. "Can you describe him?"

"I told you, he was just kinda average looking. I'm not good with faces." She looked around the bar. "I see too many of 'em."

"Did you notice his hair color?"

"Kinda grayish, I think."

"What about his complexion, was it dark or light?"

She scrunched up her face, thinking. "In between, like I said, he wasn't a spic and he wasn't colored."

I took a deep breath. "Was he tall, short?"

"Well, I'm five eight, and he was taller than me."

"Quite a bit taller?"

"Well," she said. "Just taller is all. I'm not good with heights."

"Was he heavy set?" I asked. "Thin?"

"He wasn't skinny. He was in pretty good shape for an older guy, like I said. She was starting to sound impatient, like she wished we'd get to the important stuff, such as the reward money.

"You had mentioned his eyes, when he got angry. Do you remember anything about them?"

She leaned over and put a hand on my arm. "God, honey, they was something. Like the fires of hell."

"Would you say they were brown?" I said helpfully.

"I guess," she said.

We went around like that for awhile. I ascertained that he was probably Caucasian, probably middle-aged, probably taller than five eight, that he was not obese and not wasting away. He had no obvious scars, warts or moles. He didn't wear glasses, but she had no opinion as to contact lenses. He was clean-shaven and wore his sort-of grayish hair in a conservative cut. And his penis was somewhat large. (I could see myself using that line of questioning on a suspect.)

He could have been any one of a thousand men.

I looked at my informant. Not bad looking in the dim light of the bar. Course skin, big bone structure, prominent features, most likely breast augmentation. Not a small woman.

"Did I do good," she said expectantly.

"You did great," I said. I took two fifty-dollar bills out of my wallet and slid them across the table.

I left her staring at the cash as if she thought the concept of a reward involved a lot more money. I was glad Locke was such a generous man, because I'd just thrown away a hundred bucks of his money.

Chapter 20

"I don't feel real good about the way things are . . .out there," I said.

We were sitting, MaryAnne and I, at an outside table at an ice cream stand. The stand was on a short boardwalk on the mainland side of Crescent Key. In addition to the ice cream stand there was a newsstand, several upscale casual boutiques and an overpriced Italian restaurant with fake-grapevine decor. I'd called the meeting twenty minutes earlier.

"Okay," she said. "What is it?" She was wearing a light yellow summer dress with tiny straps. She had on leather sandals. Around her neck was a simple gold chain, on one wrist a similar bracelet. The sunlight flattered her smooth, sun-bronzed complexion and highlighted the dusting of freckles across the bridge of her nose. Looking at her, you'd have trouble believing she'd ever been anything but a female. Unfortunately, looking at her, I had trouble forgetting she had once been a man.

We were both wrestling with enormous sugar cones overfilled with scoops of ice cream — hers coffee-flavored, mine rocky road.

I said, "Two people have been killed in Emerald City within the last month. Both were prostitutes. And what seems to tie them together, both were pre-op transsexuals."

She stopped eating and stared at me. "God, you'd have thought I would have heard something about this." She shook her head. "Who were they, what —"

I held up a hand. "Whoa, I don't know all that much. I spent some time hitting the joints in West Palm and Emerald City, looking for some sign of Shelly. I didn't have any luck there, but I found out about the murders. This morning I went down to the Emerald City police station and went through the police reports. I wanted to talk to the detective working the cases, but he was out." I grinned. "The detectives in Emerald City are notoriously unavailable. After I got the dates of the killings, I went to the newspapers. I found about what you'd expect — just a mention in the regional briefs."

As MaryAnne listened I could see the tension in the set of her jaw, the way her hands clinched. "And?"

I took a lick of ice cream that had melted and run down the cone. "The first victim was killed about three months ago. Her body was found in hot-pillow joint on Dixie in Emerald City."

"Hot pillow?"

"Sorry. Cop slang. A motel used by hookers. Sometimes they rent it all night but mostly they rent it by the trick."

"Was it . . . how did it happen?"

"All I know is she was strangled. The cops there have been pretty tight-lipped. They treated it as just another hooker murder, just that the victim happened to be a transsexual. Figured it might have been a john who went berserk when he found out the truth about her, but no suspects."

MaryAnne nodded. "A lot of the pre-ops who hook try to 'pass' on the streets, but they're usually hustling the quick blowjob and nothing else. Sometimes they are quite good at deceiving the johns. More often than not, the johns want to be deceived."

Her use of the profane term for oral sex startled me, but I plowed ahead. "You know what kind of place Emerald City is. Armpit of the county. What's another hooker murder to anyone there?"

She sighed heavily. "Especially if it involves a transsexual."

"Apparently. The second murder took place a little more than five weeks ago."

"Emerald City too?"

I nodded. "About three blocks from the first one. It's that area of cheap apartments and motels on the south side."

"Suitcase City." That was the name for an area of what had once been so-called "luxury" apartments that had slid way down, where hookers worked one of the main drags and apartments rented month to month or even by the week.

"Yeah. The victim fit the same general profile as the first murder. Street hooker. Pre-op, well along on the hormones."

MaryAnne thought for a moment, then said: "I sure wish I knew their names. Some of the people who live over there are friends of mine."

"I've told you just about all I know. Like I said, the details weren't publicized. I did get some additional information through a cop I know on the Crescent Key force." I paused. "The first murder was a strangulation, as I said. But the second one, there was some mutilation."

"What?" She said, "You mean sexual?"

I nodded. "The guy, and they're assuming it was a guy who did it, went after the sex organs. The mutilation was focused there."

She shook her head, looked off into the distance. "It's as if . . . he was angry at the penis."

"You've heard of something like this before?"

"Unfortunately, but never carried to this extreme. Nice heterosexual male discovers he's just gotten a blowjob by a quote man. He lashes out at the source of the deception."

I said, "That might speak to some kind of sick motive, but there's not really much to connect these two murders, other than the fact that the victims were both fairly attractive pre-op transsexual hookers. Murder isn't all that uncommon in Emerald City."

MaryAnne said, "I read somewhere it takes at least three killings for the cops to start treating them as serial murders."

"That's right," I said. "Nothing points to this being a serial killer at this point. Except my instincts."

"Loot, you said the cops didn't release any information about the murdered women being transsexuals?"

I nodded.

She said, "It seems like it would be important, especially after the second killing, for Emerald City to at least alert the other local police departments. Why are they keeping that information to themselves?"

I chuckled. "Because we're dealing with Emerald City. The whole town is crookeder than a snake in heat. The police force especially. They'd hate to have any outsiders poking around. Someone might uncover something dirty. That could really screw up some Emerald City cops' income brackets."

"So if there's another murder, and it happens in Emerald City, we probably won't hear squat about it."

"Well, not quite squat. Like I said, I have contacts in the Crescent

Key department, so I'll hear something. But the Emerald City guys really hate Crescent Key, so I can't count on many details."

She had finished her ice cream cone. She leaned toward me and put her hand on mine.

She had done it before, in the bar. Was it merely a gesture of kindness, or something else?

Her hand patted mine, felt just a little sticky from the melted ice cream. She smiled. "Your job is to find Shelly, and I think you will, Loot, if she's out there. Those dead girls —" she shrugged her shoulders — "hookers get killed all the time, right?" It was a throwaway line, but she said it with profound sadness.

"My leads haven't gotten me anywhere so far." I told her in some detail about my visit with the dancer who had taken the man over to her place. "The guy was a sicko, I guess, but I don't see any connection to my case."

"Why did he pick her up do you think?" MaryAnne said.

"Who knows," I said. "Why pick up a prostitute and freak out just when you are getting to the best part?"

She shot me a pained look. "No reason, unless — unless what he was after was a cock."

Chapter 21

It didn't take me long to break my only rule.

MaryAnne had given me a lot to think about. I drove along the road that bordered the waterway, stopped at a couple of bars but didn't hang around. I ran into a couple of acquaintances, but nobody I wanted to share a drink with.

After that I'd shuttled over to the Dixie Highway and stopped at a steakhouse with a Western motif and a decent steak for the money. Sixteen ounces, medium rare, with a baker on the side and a tossed salad made me feel better, metaphorically washed away some of the residual grime from Emerald City.

After my meal I drove back along the A1A, the coast highway, through Palm Beach and south through condo heaven. It suddenly occurred to me that I might be avoiding going home, for the first time in years. I thought about that.

And came up with an answer. I'd ravaged my sanctuary. Now it was wired, hooked up and tuned in.

Hey, I told myself, it was a temporary condition. I'd find the elusive Shelly Travers, she would or wouldn't go back to Darwin Locke, and there would be at least some increase in the relative level of "lived happily everafter-ness." Then I could hock the shit I'd brought home, toss the cell, disconnect call forwarding, and go back to being a high-priced security consultant to the rich and reclusive.

So I got home, glared at all the contraptions on my kitchen table, vowed to at least get a computer desk the next day so I could get the mess organized, steadfastly refused to log on to the internet, and made myself a stiff drink.

And turned on the damned police scanner.

I shouldn't have done it, shouldn't have let my ear become accustomed to the long-forgotten chatter of the police airwaves. I shouldn't have gotten out my owner's manual and list of frequencies, and programmed every God-forsaken Emerald City frequency, including vice, tac, rescue — even the medical examiner's numbers — into it.

I shouldn't have sat there like an idiot, eyes glazed over with memories, ear attuned to the strange, disaffected, almost lifeless police chatter.

I shouldn't have taken it out on the back deck with me. Broke the cardinal rule. Invaded the last bastion of solitude left in my world.

But I did, and fuck me for it.

I must have become mesmerized; I lost track of time. I noticed that scudding clouds drifted in front of the waxing moon. I saw some night birds gambol in the sand. I heard the animal sounds — crickets and critters — from the swamp around me.

And I listened to that damned scanner.

And a little after three in the morning, the tenor of the chatter changed. Suddenly there was just a bit more affect, increased numbers of transmissions. I watched the readout: the channels with increased activity were Emerald City. I heard backups dispatched to a motel on Dixie, a few minutes later heard the code for a dead body. Then nothing of note for a few minutes.

A medical examiner was dispatched, along with the body baggers. Fire rescue was pulled off, reassigned. Several detectives were making their way to the crime scene, then I heard a lieutenant heading that way.

Dead body. Sleazy motel. Right in the middle of one of the strips I'd gone slumming in the night before.

I stood up and looked out toward the surf and said, "Shit," as loud as I could. Nobody heard. The birds and critters didn't even flinch.

And then I went back inside to do what I knew I would do, from the first time I'd heard the increased activity on the scanner — pull on shirt and shoes, drag myself out to the Defender and start toward the crime scene, Room 12 of a hot-pillow joint called the Starlight Motel.

Chapter 22

I stood and stared at her, stood just inside the door I'd quietly entered, unnoticed by the crime-scene personnel at work in the room.

She was lying - what had been her - nude, on a dingy white sheet, in repose. Her face was angelic, in sleep it seemed, eyes closed. She looked much paler than she had in her pictures. The tattoo of the butterfly that surrounded her navel — the immutable evidence of her identity — was vibrantly colorful against the pale skin. Her hands lay at her sides, palms up, in a kind of placating gesture, almost peaceful.

But beneath her, beneath that most intimate part of her, was a crimson stain, wet and thick on the fabric.

I thought that I might throw up, but held myself still, very still, and the nausea passed.

The mutilation was not subtle. Her pubic hair was matted with blood, her sex a butchered and gaping violation. Rivulets of blood had run between her legs and pooled, and her inner thighs were mottled with red, as though a finger-painter had been at work.

I did not throw up. I think back on that and, for some reason, feel a measure of pride.

Had she, had she in those moments when she knew — she had to have known — she was living the last moments of her life, did she say some kind of prayer, something to keep the monsters at bay? Or had she been transfixed with fear, unable to look beyond the horror of the moment?

I stood and looked at the body of Shelly Travers. I hoped with all my might that she had been able to pray.

Chapter 23

I was still staring at the body of Shelly Travers when David LeGrand walked up and said, "What the fuck are you doing here?"

I looked at him. He was staring straight at me, first time in years. "Looking at the body of a girl I was hired to find," I said.

"Well, you found her. Now leave."

"In the interest of good police work and inter-agency cooperation," I said, "aren't you interested in what I might have to offer?"

He continued to stare at me, his jaws working. He had to make a decision: do some actual decent police work or shut me out of the investigation.

He said, "Come with me," turned and strode toward the front door, elbowing a suit and a uniform out of the way as he went. I followed, said to the other cops, "Excuse me for both of us." They grinned.

Outside, he said, "Give me what you've got."

I did. I told him who she was, where her parents lived, how I had happened on the scene. It didn't take long.

"So who hired you, sport," he said.

I shook my head. "You know I can't tell you that. Besides, it has nothing to do with —" I jerked my head toward the room — "with this."

That angered him. He flexed his jaw muscles a couple of times, said, "Listen, shithead, I'm the investigating officer here. I tell you what's important, you don't tell me."

"Attorney-client privilege," I said. "I was hired through an attorney so the privilege applies."

He took a step toward me. "Don't you fuck with me." His voice got louder. "You pansies try to hide behind that attorney shit all the time. I'll subpoena your ass, and then if you don't tell me I'll have you up for contempt."

I didn't point out that he had no authority to find me in contempt; only judges can do that. I only said, "LeGrand, I'm not trying to make trouble. I've given you important information that just might help your case. I've cut your time line down for I.D. and next of kin. So don't go threatening me with the little bit of information I can't tell you."

He stared at me, gave me a small dismissive wave, as if I were not important at all. He said, "Hot out here. I'm going back in. You're finished here, now beat it." He turned and went back inside. I tagged right behind him.

Inside he surveyed the room, his back to me. A photographer was working his way around the bed, taking flash shots of the body from various angles. The strobe rifled off the walls, catching the dimly lit room in a moment of frozen clarity. Another tech was dusting for prints on the dresser, while a third was placing clothes in plastic evidence bags.

Flash. The body of Shelly Travers is suddenly front lit by excruciating light, caught in a timeless moment. Pop. The mutilated body seems to jump from the shadows, bathed in an instant of intense brightness.

LeGrand, his movements strobe-like, moved toward the bed. He must have sensed me behind him. He turned around and set his jaw.

He caught me looking over his shoulder, horror-stricken, as the strobes popped and flashed. He said, in a voice calculated to be sneering and offensive, "So you think your queer friend's murder here is tied in with the others? Was she a bitch pervert who decided to lose the cock and buy herself a cunt?" He leaned in close to me and leered. "Or maybe she still had one and the killer cut it off and took it with him. You know, a trophy." He grinned. "Imagine that trophy case."

It must have been his use of the words, bitch, cunt and cock in the same breath. I rocked back on my heels, then stepped forward with one foot. I got a lot of leverage and put an outstanding roundhouse left into the middle of his face.

His head snapped back. A geyser of bright red blood exploded out of his nose, arcing in the air and splattering his shirt and tie. He made a small, feral noise, stepped back, put his hand over his face. Blood seeped through his fingers. His eyes bulged, black with pure hatred.

Then he lunged at me — directly into a right uppercut to the belly.

He bent forward, went, “Woof,” and slid to his knees. He stayed there, one hand on his face, the other cradling his guts. Through clinched teeth he made a noise that sounded like a cat choking. Then he took his hand away from his bloody face, leaned forward and threw up.

In seconds three cops were on me; one pulled my hands behind my back and cuffed me, another stood in front of me, hands on my shoulders, the third took a position a little to one side, swiveling his head between me and the heaving David LeGrand.

Two other cops — the whole Emerald City crime-scene contingent was occupied with the fracas now — got down beside LeGrand, helped him to his feet and led him to a couch. He moaned a couple of times, but still managed to turn his head to stare at me, mouth open and bloody teeth bared. As he got to the couch he made an effort to shrug off the cops, but they firmly pushed him down. He sat.

In another few seconds I was in the back seat of an Emerald City police cruiser. I stayed there, rubbing my aching fist and replaying the satisfying images of LeGrand catching the punches, until the brass showed up.

The brass in this case was a Capt. Scanlon, whom I vaguely remembered. He was a hound-dog of a man, with deeply etched wrinkles on his face and folds of loose skin on his jaw and neck. He had the doleful eyes of a man who’d seen everything and didn’t want to see too much more until retirement. I remembered him as a peacemaker, and a guy who tried to avoid crises, which might be a point in my favor.

He opened the cruiser, looked in at me, said, “Landers,” and motioned me out of the car. He crooked his finger, gesturing me to follow, and walked over to the shadows of a nearby hedge. He lit a cigarette, offered me one, which I declined.

He said, “Did you enjoy hitting LeGrand?”

“Yes, sir,” I said. I rubbed my fist again just to let him know I’d put some muscle into it.

He broke into a lopsided grin; I almost expected his tongue to loll out one side of his mouth. “The boy does ask for it. What’d he do to rile you up?”

I told him about LeGrand’s unfortunate choice of words in describing someone I’d grown to care something about.

“I know that we all make our jokes around crime scenes just to keep from going crazy," I said. "But in this case he was baiting me."

"Didn't take much, did it?" He gave me another loopy grin.

"Sir, I had been trying to cooperate with him. At first he didn't want to talk to me at all, even though I could identify the victim. Even after he decided to interview me, he was still angry that I had shown up at all."

Scanlon took a long pull of the cigarette, looked down and pushed some dirt around with his shoe. "Anybody hear him try to hustle you out?"

"Only everybody in the room, including the medical examiner's people. Your cops might not say that, but there's others that can corroborate my account."

He scuffed the dirt some more, then looked at me. "No matter which way you cut it, we got you for assaulting a police officer. That's a felony, and most judges these days are inclined to apply a little jail time for that."

I looked at him, saying nothing. I'd already raised my best defense, which wasn't particularly solid. Scanlon was in control.

"Well," he said. "I got several choices. I know you from when you was over in Crescent Key, and I never had any trouble dealing with you. You got a reputation for honesty, which —" here he looked out across the lights of the police cars — "I wish I could say was more common these days."

I understood Scanlon's larger dilemma; he worked for a corrupt force, and I doubted he was a particularly corrupt cop. But he was also a realist with just a little time left to retirement, not the best combination for a whistle-blower. I started to think he'd go for the peacemaker solution.

He said, "Doesn't do any of us good for the story to get out that our cops were having a free-for-all, even if this one was a little one-sided."

He turned and took a couple of steps toward the motel. Then he stopped and faced me. "This isn't entirely my call. Wait here."

Scanlon walked back to the room. I waited, fired up a cigar and smoked, letting the smoke curl up and mingle with the fetid air. No breeze, too far inland to get anything cooling off the ocean tonight.

After about ten minutes he came back. "It's not over. I'm not going to make any decisions tonight. We might arrest you, some of that depends on how hard LeGrand wants to push it. I told him to go home, take care of his face, see me tomorrow. We'll take it from there."

He gave me that loopy grin. "Now, I'd suggest you beat it in case the media shows up, or LeGrand decides cooling off ain't cool and comes out here after you. Now git."

I walked back to the Defender, the visions of Shelly Travers's naked and mutilated body cast in brutal relief by the unforgiving white flashes of the camera strobes.

Chapter 24

I stood on the back deck of Darwin Locke's yacht and said, "I don't know any other way to do this, sir." I paused, took a deep breath. "Shelly's dead. I'm sorry. I'm sorry I didn't find her before. . . ."

He faced me, shoulders squared, the set of his jaw firm, his eyes depthless. I'd heard that he was a war hero, had led a group of Marines to safety, men under his command, by taking up a rear position with an automatic rifle and standing in a rice paddy, firing away. He'd been hit four times, but was still standing when the enemy melted back into the jungle, and his troops had come back for him.

He'd killed at least twenty Viet Cong, it was said. He never talked about it.

Now he stood there, pulling on that reserve. His eyes glistened, and a few tears ran down his cheeks. He made no move to wipe them away. He made no sound. He said nothing.

Then he turned from me and walked to the ship's railing, looked out past some smaller craft moored at the marina, out over the water and the Key. He stood there for a very long time. After awhile I took a few steps back under the canopy, just to get away from the sun's brutal strength. There was a table and chairs, and a pitcher of iced tea and glasses. I stood where I was, I could not let myself sit or drink until my host invited me.

And my host was occupied with only himself and his grief right now.

I waited, and eventually he turned and looked at me like he'd forgotten I was there.

He held a hand out, swept it in a small arc to the table. "Please, sit down, Mr. Landers. Forgive me. I'm not thinking too well at the moment." His eyes were dry now.

We sat, and he poured tea for us. He even took a bowl of lemons and held it to me, and I took a slice, and a sprig of mint as well.

He sipped at his tea, locked his gaze on me, and said, "Tell me how it happened — everything." There was a hard edge on the last word.

I told him. I left nothing out. I spoke of the motel room and how she'd been when I found her. I spoke of the mutilation without going into excruciating detail. And, finally, I told him of David LeGrand, his attitude, his comments, and my reaction to those comments.

He nodded as I spoke, clinched his teeth when I got to the part about the mutilation, let a small, choked sound come from his throat. But he sat and listened to all of it before he spoke.

"I have to tell you, Landers —" he gave me a ghastly smile — "I'm not sorry for what you did to that, LeGrand, you said his name was?"

I nodded. "I'm not sorry I did either. I do wonder if I'll be arrested, though."

He gave that a dismissive wave. "I know an attorney . . ." He let the words drift away. Then he hardened his eyes and said, "Do you think she was a random victim?"

I shrugged, and told him about the earlier murders. "I don't know," I said. "The first two victims were also transsexuals. Pre-op, though. Shelly was found in the vicinity where the other two murders occurred. All three killings took place in motels known to be frequented by — ah, by prostitutes."

He kept his eyes on me. "Go on."

"In each instance, genital mutilation occurred. But if the killer — and this is assuming the killings are related at all — if the killer was somehow lashing out — at the male genitals, you know — a psychological thing, Shelly's case, then, wouldn't fit in with the others."

"Unless," he said with sudden utter clarity, "he had known her — before."

It could have been so, I thought. I calculated that her arrests for prostitution had to have occurred before she had her sexual reassignment surgery.

"Mr. Landers, I'm terribly sorry about the deaths of those other girls," Locke said. His voice was very calm, too calm I thought. The shock had to be hitting him. "But it's Shelly I care about." I saw his hand tighten around the tea glass, forgotten.

He breathed deeply, and his shoulders suddenly slumped. He said, “I loved her. And it wasn’t what you might think, the sugar daddy, or the father figure. We loved one another, we told each other that. She wasn’t demanding. I had to make her buy that nice little car. I chose her condo, gave her the charge cards, she wouldn’t even run up bills on those. She was frugal, for God’s sakes, she clipped coupons and insisted on using her two-for-one card for dining.”

He looked down at the glass he was holding, saw it as if for the first time, lifted it and took a drink. “My wife — there is nothing there, hasn’t been anything for years. She has had affairs, though it has never been brought out in the open. I used to think she needed me. But I’ve come to realize that all she really needs is my money.

“Ten years ago, I would have had the affair and stayed with my wife,” he said. “Now — I’m making plans to divorce. Shelly’s death won’t change that.”

I nodded. There was nothing at all for me to say to any of this. This was Darwin Locke talking, making his statement.

He said, “I appreciate what you’ve done for me, and I want to assure you that you’ll have full use of the attorney I mentioned in the event of any problems with the police.”

I told him I appreciated that. I made a move to slide the chair back, to leave Darwin Locke with his grief and his decisions. But he wasn’t finished with me. He said, “You can’t leave it like this, can you?”

“No sir, I can’t. I believe there are other lives still in danger, including some friends of mine.”

“I would have expected nothing less of you,” he said. “I’d very much like to continue to retain your services, Mr. Landers.” His eyes bore into mine, and I saw a silent fury simmering there now.

“I’m hiring you to do exactly what you would have done anyway,” he said. “Go find him. Find the monster who killed my Shelly.” His hand locked onto my arm, his fingernails digging into me through my shirtsleeves, like the talons of a hawk. “Find him and fucking bury him. For all of our sakes.”

Chapter 25

It was deep night when I made the phone call.

She answered on the third ring. A soft voice. “Hello”

“Galatea, this is Sam Landers. Ah . . . remember me?” I paused, not finding the words for a moment. Then I went on. “I'm sorry. I don't even really know you. I'm sorry I woke you up. But you did give me your number?”

“It's okay,” she said. I could tell she was trying to wake up, focus. “Are you all right?”

I chuckled, but there was no mirth in it. “Not really. I've been sitting here on my porch. I don't really have anyone to call. I just remembered you saying I could call you. So,” I paused. “Here I am.”

“I'm glad you called,” she said, sounding more awake now. “Did you want to talk?”

I thought about that. Why did I call this person I barely knew? Why was I sitting out on my porch in the deep night with a bottle of whiskey beside me, some of it already gone?

“I don't know,” I said. “I've, ah, now I feel kinda stupid. I'm a little drunk. I'm sorry about that. It's a little embarrassing.”

The line was quiet for a few moments. Sitting on the porch I could feel the seabreeze and the coolness of the nighttime. I could hear night critters and insects making their sounds out in the woods by the house.

Then she said, “I'd offer for you to come over, but . . .”

“Probably not a good idea to be driving,” I said. Suddenly, I began to feel as if this long thin connection was the only thing that was keeping me sane, and I knew what I had to talk about. I took the chance.

I took a hit off the bottle, liquid courage. I felt the wind. I felt the connection through the line. Ah, to hell with it.

"I get this way sometimes, here by myself. I told you I live alone." I paused for a moment, then went on. "I don't really have friends I can call, not about this . . . this thing I need to talk about sometimes."

I stopped, suddenly feeling foolish. "I must sound crazy." I felt light-headed from the booze, and lonely as hell. I hated it when I got this way, and here I was talking to this person I'd just met. A phone number to call. But I had come too far to stop now. I wasn't going to sit here another night on my porch alone with the thoughts that seemed to come close killing me when they came over me, when I couldn't shake them and I couldn't bury them.

Like tonight.

"I need to talk to someone, I said. "I need to talk to someone about how I killed my daughter."

Chapter 26

I heard a sharp intake of breath, then the silence of the line.

"Not the way you think," I said. I paused a moment, then went on. "It happened a long time ago. And now I'm drinking and I don't have anyone to talk to, and I'm here by myself and I came across your phone number . . ." My voice trailed off.

The line was quiet for just a moment, then she said, "I want to hear about it, Samuel. Tell me."

So I did.

I told her that twenty years ago I had been a detective for Miami's Metro-Dade Police Department. But on the day in question, I wasn't acting as a detective. I was in uniform, like every other available cop on the force.

"A hurricane had hit, Hurricane Eliza, and it was a pretty bad one. There was quite a bit of wind damage and flooding, and a lot of power had been knocked out.

"My daughter Linda was on the streets that day, too. She was a cop. She'd been on patrol for two years and she was the light of my life. It had always been her desire to follow in the old man's footsteps.

"I had checked out a cruiser and was driving on the outskirts of Little Havana when I got the call to respond to a looting in progress. The store where the looting was going down wasn't that far away. I could be there in four or five minutes."

I paused to take a drink. There was no hint at all of light in the eastern sky. I went on.

"I heard Linda's call number go out too, and a sense of pride went through me. I was actually responding to a call along with my own daughter. Two cops side by side.

“So I took off, but I'd gone maybe three blocks when I saw this guy I'd been looking for. He was one of my informants. I had really been trying to track him down. He had some information I needed to make a serious bust.”

“So you stopped,” Galatea said.

“Yes, I stopped, I said. “I wanted to know where my snitch had been. I figured I'd talk to him just a minute or two and then go ahead and answer the call. There were plenty of other units responding.”

I paused, and brought the bottle to my lips and drank, and suddenly hated myself for being so weak while I talked to this good and honest woman. I put the bottle down and took a long breath, and continued.

“I really only talked to him a couple of minutes. He told me where he was staying. He gave me a new cell phone number, which might have been good or not, I had no way of knowing. But I couldn't hold him there. I figured I had a better chance of finding him than I did before.”

“Couldn't you have arrested him, or just put him in the back of the car or something,” Galatea said. Then she caught herself. “I'm sorry, Samuel, this isn't my story. Go on.”

I had been about to get angry, but her voice calmed me. “To answer your question, no, not without probable cause at least. I had to let him go.

“When I got back in the car I could hear more units being called to the scene of the looting. I didn't hear Linda's number, so I thought she must have arrived. I really put the car in gear now, I figured the scene might be getting out of hand. Looting can do that pretty quickly sometimes.”

I stopped talking then, feeling a little out of breath. But I didn't want more whiskey. I took a couple of gulps of air, and I heard Galatea say, “Go on, Samuel.”

I told her that by the time I had gotten to within about three blocks of the scene the radio went crazy. “ 'Shots fired, shots fired, officer down,' I heard. And that's when it really hit me. Linda was there.

“I pulled up to a scene of chaos. There were five or six cruisers and an unmarked. The strip center had a foot of water in the parking lot. Most of the windows were broken out, and I could see people running out of the interiors of the stores and slogging through the waters. Some of the cops were going after the looters, but some of them were huddled by a figure on the ground, lying in the water. I could see the figure's pants legs, they were uniform issue. I knew then that a cop was down."

I paused. We both knew what was coming, but Galatea let me get to it in my own way. This time I turned away from the bottle and wiped my hand across my forehead. The night breeze had a chilling effect.

"You can figure out what happened," I said. "It was my daughter. She'd been shot in the throat. She was wearing a bullet-proof vest but it hadn't helped her. She was still alive when I got there.

"A cop was doing CPR. I could hear sirens in the distance. I just held her hand, Galatea, I just held her hand and she looked at me for a moment and then she was gone." I realized I was crying now, but I didn't try to stop.

"Samuel," Galatea asked after a little bit. "Why does any of that make you feel responsible?"

"I stopped. I was late. I could have been beside her. I could have protected her." I kept crying. "She was my baby girl, my only child."

Galatea let just cry then, for a little while, and then that was over, and I began to get hold of myself. And I felt, like I always felt when I had let myself go this far, used up and drained. I never, ever, felt better.

Galatea seemed to realize this. She only said, "How can I help?"

I thanked her for listening. I told her that I did this every so often, and when I was finished I just went on about my business, but the emptiness never went away.

"I know I can't ever say anything that will help take that loss away," she said. "As you might expect, I have been through quite a lot in my young life and I do know a lot about loss. I'm glad you called."

We left it at that. I thought that I could sleep then, and I knew that I had to get up and begin to work on the case of Darwin Locke's missing mistress. I hung up feeling a bit awkward, but with the thought that we would talk again.

Then I went back in from my lonely old porch, and in the stillness of the deep night went to bed.

Chapter 27

I woke to the sound of Charlie Daniels playing "The Devil Went Down to Georgia" at about a thousand decibels. The sound was coming from somewhere at the back of my brain. Someone had put at least four microphones on the bass drum. A thousand demons were dancing the two-step and Gabriel was blasting a trumpet into my eardrum for good measure. The smoke-and-light show was impressive.

It's amazing what a night of drinking whiskey will do to the morning after.

At 9 a.m. — after four aspirins, a very long shower, a careful shave, and a breakfast of corn flakes with fresh cream and blueberries and a hefty cup of coffee — I was on my back deck, a second cup of coffee in hand and sunglasses on to guard against the rising sun. Charlie Daniels had taken a break and the dancing demons were still. Gabriel still punched a few notes now and again.

The case that had started out so simply — just find the girl, see if she is okay — had mushroomed, pulled me out of my cocoon, rattled any semblance of protection I'd built up, and threatened to shove me right into the path of a serial killer.

I did not need this. But now it was mine, and I could not turn away from it.

I thought about that, and fortified myself with a huge gulp of cooling coffee. I winced. Just too cool is way too cool. I tossed the remains of the cup out onto the sand and turned back toward the house to pour another.

I heard a snuffling sound beyond the brush line near the house. Snuffling, a kind of low snort. Some kind of animal that had wandered onto the island? That didn't seem likely, though there were a few deer in the wooded areas on the mainland side. But here the largest critters I'd come across were raccoons and 'possums.

The brush moved and I heard the snuffling sound again. I stood still on the deck and watched and waited. Was I about to be attacked by the only remaining wild boar on the Gold Coast? Was a disgruntled client lying in wait to do me harm?

Then the brush and weeds parted and a huge brown shape launched itself at me.

And I found myself face-to-face with a huge chocolate-colored nose, and a very active pink tongue that was having its way with my face. Two large paws had been planted on my chest.

Man versus dog, and a very friendly dog at that.

I stepped back, and the dog's front paws fell back to earth. He stood there, looking up at me, tongue lolling, tail coming close to falling off from wagging.

A dog.

I said, "Woof."

His tail wagged harder, if that was possible, and he said, "Woof" right back, though his version was much more dog-like.

I said, "Sit."

He wagged his tail some more.

I said, "Lie down."

He took a few steps toward me, and sat.

I said, "Lie down," again, and he picked up one paw and held it out.

I knelt down and shook it.

A dog.

The dog, which from my limited canine experience appeared to be a Labrador retriever, dark brown in color, wore a collar, but no tags or I.D.

I noticed that his rib cage was rising and falling, and he seemed to be panting. I got up and said, "Stay," and walked toward the house.

He followed right behind me. I opened the door. He went in before I had a chance to. He walked into the middle of my kitchen and sat down. He said, "Woof," and held up his paw.

"Damn," I said. "Woof."

I rummaged in a cabinet and found a fairly large plastic bowl. I filled the bowl with water and sat it down in front of the dog. He immediately got back on all fours, dropped his snout into it and lapped.

And lapped. And lapped some more, until the bowl was dry.

I have him another bowl and he drank half of that. Then he got up, walked backwards a few steps and sat down. He held up a paw.

I went over and knelt down and shook the damn paw. The tongue came out and the tail went into high gear, sweeping back and forth across the floor, like the world's fastest whisk broom

I knelt there and held on to the dog's paw, shook it up and down

Just what I needed.

I had been befriended.

By a dog.

Woof.

Chapter 28

The dog was either poorly trained, or stubborn. I suspected it was a little of both. It seemed that he knew the standard commands, he simply ignored them.

One thing was sure — he surely did like me. I couldn't budge without him jumping up and tagging along. If I went outside, out he went. When I came back in, in he came.

When I went for a mid-morning run along the beach, he jogged beside me. Then he ambled into my bedroom to watch me change.

He wouldn't do a thing I told him, but he made no effort at all to run away. In fact, he made very little effort to get more than about five feet away from me.

During the late morning I decided to take a short rest. I got into bed — and up bounded the dog. He sniffed the bed cover, sniffed me in a couple of awkward places, made three circles counterclockwise, and plopped down right beside me. He sighed deeply, lay his head on my thigh and was instantly asleep.

I found out that he snored. Loudly. It wasn't rhythmic, either, but a series of belches, mutters, snorts, sighs and gurgles.

Just before I drifted off, I reached a hand down and patted his head. He sighed deeply and blew some snot out his nose. He was in dog heaven.

"You are just too cool," I said.

Too cool.

When I woke up an hour later he was sitting on the bed, looking at me. When he saw that I was awake, the tail started its sideswipe motion and out came the tongue. I barely dodged a long string of drool.

I did not need a dog.

This dog, I was sure, had a master somewhere who was probably frantic over his disappearance.

And, I thought, I already had a case that had torn my protective walls into rubble. I didn't need another intrusion, another responsibility.

I really, really liked this dog.

So I came up with a plan. I wouldn't run the dog off (as if I could). I would give him nourishment and shelter, but I wouldn't let myself get too emotionally attached.

And I would place an ad in the paper under the "found" column, perhaps even put a card up at a couple of nearby
animal clinics.

I would do that, the dog's happy owner would show up, the pooch would be ecstatic and I'd be able to start rebuilding my walls.

I thought this was such an excellent idea that I bought myself a couple of drinks from the house bottle. Then Cool and I — he was assisting through his extremely close proximity as I sat at the computer — checked my e mail. There were messages from MaryAnne and Galatea.

MaryAnne's said:

Please call and let me know how it is going. I am terrified to open the newspaper every day for fear of finding a story about another death. I hope and pray you can help — God, that sounds like pressure, and I am sorry for that. I have no idea if I have helped you at all, but I will do anything within my power to help you catch this monster.
Smiles :):):) and hugs ((((())))) MaryAnne

And from Galatea:

Hello, Samuel Landers and how are you? I am really happy that you asked me out for dinner the other night. I really enjoyed your company. I think you are a handsome guy:) blush! Anyway, on a more serious note, I want you to know that I am really glad you called me and talked to me. I am so sad about your daughter! It is always good to feel you have someone else to talk to, and though I haven't known you very long, I want you to know you can talk to me anytime you wan or need to. On a very somber matter, it is so scary to think that someone is out there, intending to do harm (!!) to us (you know who I mean.) I realize that in spite of my amazing (:)) transformational journey there is a lot of the big bad world I haven't been exposed to. Be that as it may, if you want to have a cup of coffee, or a drink or even a bit to eat again I would love to do that. Or we could always just talk Please let me know how it is going.

Hoo boy, talk about them walls comin' tumblin' down.

Chapter 29

Too Cool and I were sitting on the back porch after dinner when suddenly he leapt up, spun twice, ran to the edge of the deck, peered around the corner of the house and commenced to barking.

His bark could wake the dead. It was a deep bellow that tapered off into a yowl that disintegrated into a mournful mutter that drifted off to a guttural sigh.

I got up and went to the edge of the porch. I looked out toward my front drive and watched as a white Ford Crown Vic with basic wheel covers and three antennae on the roof cruise my way.

The door opened and out came Capt. Scanlon. Cool tensed and let out a soft growl. I said, “Stay,” and Cool ran straight toward the cop. He skidded to a stop about three feet away and went rock-solid still, muttering.

Scanlon slowly edged his hand toward the back of his pants. Cool growled some more. I bounded out to the scene of the confrontation and said, “If you shoot my dog I’ll kill you and skin you alive.”

Cool looked up at me lovingly and relaxed. I said, “Sit,” and he lay down in the sand.

Scanlon looked down at the dog. “Fine looking animal,” he said. “Well trained, too.”

“What do you want here,” I said, my voice hard. I didn’t like company; I especially didn’t like an Emerald City cop as company, even an allegedly decent one.

He must have sensed my edginess. He backed up a step and put his palms outward in a placating gesture. “I just wanted to tell you that we won’t be taking any further action on that little altercation you an’ LeGrand had out on Dixie.”

"Fine," I said. I hadn't really expected any other result, but I was relieved nonetheless. "While you're here, why don't you tell me what you've come up with so far."

Scanlon stared at me, as if he couldn't believe I would ask such a thing. I looked at his hound-dog features and couldn't help but think that, as dogs went, Cool was much handsomer. I kept my opinion to myself.

Scanlon said, "Everything is under control."

"Ah," I said. "You've made an arrest?"

The baggy eyes narrowed as best they could. "God damn it, you know how things are in something like this."

"So you haven't made an arrest. Any leads?"

Scanlon must have realized that he was responding to my line of questions. He said, "Fuck you," and turned to get back in the car."

"Scanlon," I said sharply.

He turned very slowly, looked at me over the top of the open car door.

In a voice as even and cold as I could make it, I said, "I want you to understand a few things. Number one, I never would have put my fist through your man's face if he hadn't made insulting and demeaning remarks. Number two, I was there because I was involved in an investigation I care about. I have a personal stake that goes way beyond money in finding who killed — and tortured, God damn it — Shelly Travers.

"Number three —" I could feel the heat rise in my voice — "you can warn me off, and you can keep me away from your crime scenes, but you can't make me walk away from the case. Somebody's got to care, Scanlon. That girl was loved by a number of people. She didn't deserve to die, and she sure as hell didn't deserve to die at the hands of some sexual butcher."

Scanlon took it, watched me and stood as still as can be. I realized I was almost hyperventilating and forced myself to gain a measure of calm.

In a softer voice I said, "Listen, Scanlon, I never heard bad things about you. But you and I both know what kind of department you work for, and we both know what kind of shit a lot of your cops are into. I don't even really want to know what you all have to hide. I don't really care. Emerald City has been corrupt for years. I just want to find out who killed Shelly Travers.

"So now I've been warned off this thing twice, once by your boy LeGrand and now by you. And I have just one response to that: fuck you."

Scanlon just looked at me, with the same tired expression he'd had while I'd gone at him. Then, without a word, he eased himself into his car, closed the door and started the engine.

He backed slowly out of my driveway, put his car in gear and was gone.

Cool looked up at me. I looked down at Cool. I said, "Him's a bad mans."

Oh, my God, I thought, now I'm talking baby talk to the damn dog.

Chapter 30

The drive down Florida's so-called Gold Coast is a quick course in all that is wrong with our state.

We were headed, Galatea and I, to Miami. My telephone calls to a couple of FBI agent friends from my years on the Miami force had borne fruit. One contact had led to another, a fellow I knew who had spent some duty time in Quantico called in a favor, and within a day I was talking with an agent by the name of Eldon Wainwright.

But Eldon Wainwright was more than just another FBI agent. He was famous — the man who for a number of years was the Bureau's chief profiler out of Washington, who had in fact been instrumental in developing the science of profiling as it exists today, and who now served as a kind of special consultant, flying here and there across the U.S. and abroad to train profilers and lend his expertise to particularly difficult cases.

How we had come to be headed to Miami: Wainwright told me that he had been meaning to go to Miami for a couple of months to talk to some agents in the field office there. "What you've told me about your little situation kinda piques my interest. I've got to the point where I can do just about whatever I want to, so how 'bout I jump a jet and meet you down there tomorrow."

How Galatea had come to be coming along: I called her. I didn't think about it much, I just picked up the phone. I was tired and weary and perhaps feeling a bit vulnerable; in any event I thought that I wouldn't want to make the drive alone, and Galatea came to mind. I thought that I might be embarrassed about my deep-night phone call, but then I thought about her e-mail, and I even believed that I might want to talk to her again. I had felt a little less blue lately.

In any event, when I called her, She had been enthusiastic about going, had told me that she would only have to make a call to the bar and she'd be able to take off.

So here we were, driving south, into that vast nightmare that is the Gold Coast. South of Palm Beach are several hamlets for the wealthy. Here the land and the beaches have, for the most part, been well cared for. Sea turtles lay their eggs on the beach, the estates are carefully tended, lush and green. There are even a few public beaches with white sand and sea oats.

But a little further down, it starts to get ugly. The estates and compounds give way to condos. Towering high-rises sprout. And sprout, and sprout, like ugly, hairy warts on creamy skin.

The blight really began back in the 1970s and '80s, when everyone north of the Mason-Dixon Line wanted to move to Florida. Our powers-that-were at the time said to hell with zoning, and to hell with the environment. Let's drain the swamps, dredge the rivers and lakes, add a few artificial waterways, build roads that cut right through the delicate aquifer of the Everglades, add some industry and a few million hydrocarbon-producing cars, and call it paradise.

Which is why you can drive miles along A1A, within yards of the Atlantic Ocean, and rarely catch a glimpse of sand or water. There is so much concrete that it radiates with shimmering heat waves, and there is no respite from the sun's torture.

You will, however, see thousands of northern license plates, especially during our winter tourist and snowbird season. Beware then, for to drive is to live dangerously.

So Galatea and I drove, searching vainly for a glimpse of sand or ocean, watching the condos and hotels whiz by on either side of the road, keeping our windows up and the air conditioner on high.

I felt comfortable in her company. I said, "I really want to thank you for listening to me the other night. I don't talk about that subject very often, but it's always on my mind."

"It's good that you called. I wouldn't have wanted you to just sit there by yourself."

"Just for the record," I said, "It's not a subject I want to talk about today."

"That's okay too," she said, and patted me on the knee.

South of Fort Lauderdale we hit the love bug swarms. We didn't have love bugs a few years ago. Now, during certain times of the year they are thick as, well, love bugs. These little creatures flit about in pairs, permanently coupled in a copulating dance.

Until they die a sudden death on your grille or windshield.

Coming and going at the same time, I said to Galatea. She groaned. I told her that puns were high humor. She disagreed.

So for awhile, I threw puns at her, and she groaned.

Such as:

"And that's why they call it the amber graves of Wayne."

Groan.

"That's the beer that made Mel Famous walk me."

Oh, groan.

"You can lead a whore to culture, but you can't make her think."

God, groan, groan.

At least it got our minds off the high rises that spread like skin cancers.

Just north of Miami, it got worse — not my puns, the congestion and construction. Traffic slowed to a crawl, but I was determined to stay on the shore road, hoping against hope to catch a glimpse of that scenic Florida now seen only on postcards.

I longed to cut inland. If I drove far enough, I would be in the heart of the Everglades. If I went far enough, I'd get past the best efforts of man and find myself deep in the swamp, where the stars shown by the billions because there was no electric light, where the bugs buzzed and darted, and the swamp was alive with the sounds of nature's creatures. Where you could hear the jump of a bass, and the croak of a bullfrog, and the bellow of a bull gator.

I kept driving along the coast. Dead hookers can certainly reorder one's priorities.

We trudged into Miami, drove — slowly, very slowly — into downtown and finally found what we were looking for, a seedy diner just south of the business district.

We parked and hurried to get out of the afternoon heat, went up a few steps and entered the air-conditioned coolness. The place was almost empty. I looked around, and a man in a back booth raised his arm.

We went that way, past a waitress with way too much hair and hands full of coffee pots.

When we got near the booth the man slid out and stood up. He said, “Mr. Landers?”

I nodded. He stuck out a hand and said, “Eldon Wainwright, nice to meet you.”

I introduced Galatea, who smiled shyly — she was so good at that, and we all sat down.

This was no faux diner we were in. I doubted it had been remodeled since the 1950s: Yellow-and-blue tufted vinyl upholstery, flecked Formica table tops, an honest-to-God jukebox station at each booth. Even a call button for the waitress. The place mats were maps of the Sunshine State, with tourist traps highlighted. I immediately spotted Monkey Jungle, Sunken Gardens and Reptile World.

Special Agent Eldon Wainwright fit right in with the decor. He in no way resembled an FBI agent, unless your idea of an FBI agent dated back to J. Edgar’s reign. He was thin and reedy — I’d noticed that when he stood up — and was dressed in a gray suit that had been out of style long enough that it was starting to come back into style. The shirt was crisp and white, with a traditional spread collar. The tie, done in a full Windsor knot, was dark blue with coats of arms running in angled rows. He had affixed a gold tie clasp, the kind that has a little alligator clip and snaps down from one side.

There was even a gray fedora, sitting brim up on top of the little juke box. And a cigarette was sitting in an ashtray, slowly burning down to a long, gray ash.

He said, “Great place, huh? Reminds me of the days when. . . never mind. He gestured to the menus that had been left on the table. “Anything’s good, as long as you like grease.”

I said, “Far out,” flipped through the menu and settled on a Western omelet, hash browns and whole wheat toast. Galatea, grimacing all the while I ordered, had the fruit plate — “Does that have grease?” she asked the waitress seriously. Wainwright stayed with coffee.

I had pegged the agent as a man my age when I first saw him. Now, watching him as he poured another cup of coffee out of the carafe on the table, I thought I had been wrong by at least a decade. His hair was a washed-out brown, cut FBI regulation. His face was thin, almost gaunt, with deep lines running down from the sides of his nose to either side of his mouth. There were a lot of worry lines at the corners of his eyes, and the eyes themselves were a washed-out blue. His lips formed a thin, almost bloodless gash against a sallow complexion.

He was either quite a bit older, or quite a bit less healthy, than me. While I thought that, he tapped another cigarette out of his pack, fired it up with a battered Zippo with the Marine Corps insignia on it, inhaled deeply, blew the smoke through his nose, and coughed.

We made a little small talk about the Miami heat, the humidity, how wonderful things must be up where the rich folks dwelt, how Washington had to be so very nice this time of year, the meaningless chatter of people trying to get a feel for one another. During the meal we talked a little less and made quick work of the food. Wainwright finished off three more cups of coffee and two more cigarettes while we ate.

Then we all pushed our plates away, Wainwright lit up yet another cigarette, Galatea and I had some iced tea brought around, and the agent said, "So — from what you told me on the phone, it sounds as though you might have an interesting situation in your area." He said interesting situation in a totally noncommittal way.

While Galatea watched, we fell into cop talk. I briefed him about the three murders, noting both the similarities and the differences. I took him through the time line. I told him about the call I'd gotten from the topless dancer, and relayed her description of her trick gone bad.

"And, in checking our files, I find out that, what's the name of that place, Emerald City? The cops there haven't asked for our services."

"Not surprised," I said. Then I filled him in a little on Emerald City's finest.

He nodded; he'd been this route before. "Couple of quick observations," he said. "First, the local cops are under no obligation to call us, even if they have Jack the Ripper running around — as long as he doesn't kidnap for ransom or drag someone across the state line." He might have laughed then, but it came out as a dry rasp. "Second, from what you've told me, there is a chance you have a serial killer at work. There is also a very good chance that you don't. These killings could be entirely coincidental."

I nodded, and reiterated the delicacy of my rather unofficial position. "I'd like to speak to you off the record for now, at least. It's not going to do any good to get the Emerald City cops even more pissed off at me than they already are. And, if I start crying wolf and it turns out to be just coincidence, my credibility is shot. And I still haven't gotten any farther at solving the death of the woman I was hired to find."

He nodded; he'd been this route before as well. "I have no problem working with you on an informal basis for now. I'd rather you not let my superiors know. And if this turns into something we can stick the 'serial' tag on, I go official and on the record immediately. Okay?"

I told him I understood.

"Okay," he said. "Remember, since I only have limited information, and we are talking, ah, hypothetically, would you mind if I did a bit of speculating?"

I nodded my head emphatically, ready to listen to a man whose experiences and expertise were legendary in cop circles. He had, I remembered, worked on some of the most famous serial-killer cases: Ted Bundy's sorority murders in Tallahassee; Son of Sam, The Hillside Strangler, John Wayne Gacy. His two books on the subject were required reading for any student of profiling.

"I just want to say, sir, that it's an honor —"

He waved a hand to cut me off, grinned hugely and said, "Oh, shut up." The grin transformed him from the tired FBI agent to a man of depth and complexity. I thought that I was about to see the hunter of killers I had heard so much about.

He got down to work.

"You've read my books?" I sensed no ego in the question, rather an assessment of how much basic material he'd have to go over.

I told him I had. I suddenly realized that we had completely excluded Galatea from the conversation, and said as much, but she patted my arm and said, "I'm just an amateur along for the ride." She gave no hint as to her investment in the case, but I got the feeling that Wainwright knew.

Wainwright gave her a beatific smile. Then he turned his attention back to me.

And I got an earful.

Chapter 31

"You're familiar with the generic serial killer profile," Wainwright said. "You know, white male, twenties or thirties, quiet, likely a loner. Maybe he still lives with his parents. He appears average, normal to his acquaintances and neighbors. In the cases of sexually motivated murders, the killer may in fact be married and carry on a quote unquote normal marital routine."

Wainwright paused to ignite the Zippo and fire up another cigarette. After a hefty inhale, he went on: "That's good as far as it goes, but the description also fits a huge number of entirely innocent people."

He smiled. "But I've been doing a bit of thinking about your guy — I use the term 'guy' here without regard to gender. Okay, first of all he focuses on a very unique minority — transsexuals. How much do you know about transsexuals, Mr. Landers?"

Galatea snickered.

Wainwright took a long look at her, smiled and said, "Okay, we can continue." He took another long pull on his dwindling smoke.

"I think the guy is evolving. And I think the psychosexual pathology at work here is somewhat different than any I've run into before."

"You mean different from other sex killers?" I asked

"Yes, right," Wainwright said distractedly. He rubbed his eyes and blinked. He had that inward-focused look now; the discussion had really become a monologue.

"Different in the sense of his focus on transsexuals," he said, "both pre-op and post-op." He looked at Galatea. "Is that the correct terminology."

"Right on," she said and smiled.

"Yes, well. What does a transsexual, especially one who is pre-op, offer that ordinary men and women don't." He looked directly at Galatea now.

She might have been caught off guard, but you wouldn't know it. She looked down at the table, and her forehead scrunched into tight wrinkles. She said, "The best of both worlds?"

He nodded rapidly. "Exactly."

Galatea continued, "I've known men —" she cut a glance to me, then said, "Not intimately. But there are men who will deny any possibility that they might be gay or bisexual, even to themselves. But at some level the urge exists to be with someone of the same sex. At least sexually."

"Right," Wainwright said with some feeling. He leaned toward her. "Go on."

"To these men, being with a transsexual is equivalent to being with a woman. And that's basically true. Many pre-op transsexuals live as woman, act like women. They feel they are women. They simply haven't had all the necessary physical modifications made to bring their body in line with their sexual and gender identity."

"So," Wainwright said, "what's the added attraction the transsexual brings to the table, or the bed in this case?"

"A cock," Galatea said a little too loudly. But she didn't notice. She went on, with some animation. "Of course it makes sense — the man needs to convince himself he is with a woman, but he craves the experience of sex with a man, or at least with a man's sex organs."

"Yes, yes," Wainwright said. "You are right on the money."

Galatea flashed him a momentary smile, then looked serious again. "So he hasn't actually been with a man, but he has experienced being with one," she said. "For a lot of these closet cases, that's the end of it."

"But not always," Wainwright said. "Here's where it gets a little tricky. Think about the concept of shame."

"Shame," I said. "I do something I feel badly about, I feel was wrong. I feel guilty."

"Guilty, yes," Wainwright said. "But shame takes us beyond guilt. When we feel guilt, it is about an action, something we have done. When we feel shame, it's about who we are. It is a much deeper and complex emotion."

"Guy screws girl in order to really screw guy, and afterwards his defenses get rattled and he becomes extremely ashamed. He is diminished, he is not worthy." This was Galatea talking now, and I had a new respect for her insight and intelligence.

And it appeared that Wainwright did as well. He nodded vigorously again and said, "Take it a step further. The majority of people deal with the shame within acceptable societal limits. They might work it out themselves, they might decide not to undertake the shame-inducing behavior, they might seek counseling. But they do something appropriate."

"But not our killer," I said.

"Nope," Wainwright said. He jabbed a finger in our general direction. "Have you ever had a dirty little secret?"

Galatea laughed, and this was no giggle. She spewed spit on the table. Then she caught herself, inhaled and grunted sharply. "Wow," she said. "I'm really sorry." Her eyes bulged and she looked deeply embarrassed. "Ah, transsexuals have tons of little secrets."

We gave her a little time to get her breath. Before I realized it, I was patting her back. Then Wainwright said, "How did it make you feel when someone found out one of your secrets?"

She looked at him, serious now. "Depends on the person. Transsexuals share a lot of deeply intimate stuff. But with an outsider — I guess I would feel — I get it — shamed."

"So very correct, Ms. Galatea," Wainwright said. He smiled. "We've noted that Mr. Landers isn't commenting on his dirty little secrets, but we'll let that go for now."

"Oh, thanks," I said.

"No problem," Wainwright said. "So you hate to have another person know something you might be ashamed of, that shames you further."

"So —" Galatea's voice was going up again — "If the killer can't stand the thought of another person knowing his secret . ."

"He gets rid of the only person who knows about that secret," Wainwright said. "Then, he can avoid a measure of shame, in fact, he dehumanizes the source of his shame. Our killer kills to assure that his shame will remain a secret, and will diminish by remaining a secret.

"And that may well be at the root of our killer's psychosexual motives when he murders the person with whom he has shared his little secret."

For a moment there was nothing at all to say. Could it be this simple?

"Of course," Wainwright said, "it's not that simple. First, I must caution you that only the first two killings have similar victims, and two killings don't qualify as serial. The third victim, she may simply have been a coincidence. And if she wasn't, it raises some confusing questions about the killer's pathology, which makes him harder to predict."

"Perhaps he went into number three assuming she was pre-op," I said. "Could he have killed her out of anger, that she misled him, or maybe he felt misled simply because she wasn't what he expected."

"Still," Galatea said, "he could have just packed up and left when he found out. She wouldn't have shared his so-called shame. That's what happened to that dancer who called you. The guy, right when he found out she had a —" she caught herself abruptly — "you know, then he leaves. She isn't hurt."

Wainwright held up his hands. "Okay, at a certain point the speculation reaches diminishing returns. We don't have enough information yet to understand how the third victim fits in, assuming it's the same killer."

"So now what?" I asked.

Wainwright looked expansive. "We haven't exhausted our research capabilities. I must say this little situation interests me. I'm going to run it by a psychologist friend at the Academy. And I'm going to run a check through VICAP, that's the Violent Criminal Apprehension Program. It's a database on violent crime information we collect from local forces across the U.S. Could be that something similar happened in another part of the country."

Then his expression changed to that of deep concern. "And, unfortunately, we might have to collect more data. We might have to wait for him to kill again."

Chapter 32

A guy was waiting in my driveway, leaning against the trunk of a burgundy Eldorado with dark smoked windows. I hate that. I hate anyone coming to my little slice of paradise uninvited. And hardly anyone ever gets invited.

The guy was out of Mafioso Central Casting. He had the requisite swarthy Italian good looks — olive complexion, sharply chiseled features, black hair slicked back and worn a little long in the back. Wraparound shades. More than a few rings on his fingers.

I stopped behind the Caddy — that really pissed me off, blocked off in my own driveway — and got out.

The guy eased up off the trunk lid, a liquid motion, and faced me. He had no discernible expression, and he was tall, almost my height, but weighed at least thirty pounds less. He wore a blue suit with wide chalk stripes and significant lapels. There was even a small white flower in his buttonhole. It was at least ninety-five degrees, but he hadn't popped a drop of sweat. I would have bet my pension that a gun lurked in a shoulder holster under the beautifully tailored, loose-hanging, coat.

I walked up to within two feet of him and said, "You're uninvited, and you're blocking my driveway. I don't appreciate that."

The muscles in his jaws tensed, and he pressed his thin lips together for a moment. Then, to my surprise, he said, "I'm sorry. It wasn't my intention to intrude. I bring a message." His voice, like his expression, was flat and without inflection. Didn't go at all with the Mediterranean looks.

I nodded; it felt odd, as if his politeness had given him some power. I said — and found my self being polite when I said it — "What business do you have with me?"

He said, "There is a gentleman who would like the pleasure of your company." God, a politeness contest. "His name is Frederico Corcacan. Do you know of him?"

Ha. Who wouldn't know Frederico Corcacan, ranking made guy on the upper Gold Coast, a minor figure by Miami standards, but powerful here. Made guy even though he was of Mexican descent rather than Italian.

There was another reason Corcacan was memorable. He stood no more than three and a half feet tall — a dwarf — and besides that, affected tuxedos fitted to his twisted body, frilly starched shirts, string ties and patent-leather shoes. He cut a dapper figure for a guy who was abnormally short and strikingly distorted.

"Oh, boy," I said. "Mr. Corcacan wants to see little old me —" I could feel the politeness slipping away. "I must have won the sympathetic cop of the month award. He needs a new numbers runner?"

He didn't break an expression. He simply nodded and said, "Shall I drive you, or do you wish to follow?"

A choice. You usually didn't get that with Corcacan. His temper had a one-pound hammer pull, and he supported the giant chip on his shoulder by being relentlessly ruthless. It was said that certain hits, if they were interesting and challenging enough, he opted to do himself. Men had died looking down — way down — at the deep black business end of his .45 Colt.

I said, "I'll drive myself."

He slid into the big car — he seemed to glide in everything he did — got it started up and waited. I got in the Defender, backed it out of the driveway and gave him room to pull out.

I followed him at a stately pace off of the Key, onto the mainland, and into the depths of Emerald City.

Corcacan lived in a castle — a real one — nestled inside a neighborhood, a ghetto, actually, littered with run-down apartment buildings, out-of-control graffiti, junk cars and drug dealers. His place would have stood out anywhere, but here it was Oz. A ten-foot wall surrounded the two-acre estate. Shards of glass had been sunk into the concrete at the top, and above that was some vicious-looking concertina wire. The front gate was heavy wrought iron, and a guardhouse with bullet-proof glass stood just outside it. A guard usually stood outside, holding an Uzi or M-16, in flagrant disregard for the law.

Above the wall could be seen the top story of the castle. medieval ramparts, Moorish minarets, Celtic engravings, Crusader turrets, all of it was thrown together.

The Cadillac stopped just outside the gate and the driver spoke with the guard a moment. The guard looked back at me, then turned back to my escort and nodded, and as though by magic, the gates rolled open.

I followed the Cadillac into the compound. The first story was another nightmare of Crusader, Gothic and Renaissance angles, curves, nooks and crannies — architecture afflicted with multiple personality disorder. There was even a moat with a drawbridge over it surrounding the castle. I wondered if somebody lurked above it, ready to pour boiling oil on whomever dared enter without permission.

The short gravel drive from the gate ended in a turnaround outside the drawbridge. The bridge was down, I saw, indications that there was no siege scheduled today.

We both parked, got out and I followed along, over the wood planking of the bridge, along a flagstone path bordered by English Ivy to a front door roughly the size of Idaho. The guy I was following — he'd not told me his name — opened the door without knocking and stepped inside.

And here I came, out of the sunshine and into a pervasive gloom. The room I'd stepped into was, as near as I could make out, a large hall two-stories high. A balcony ran along three sides, and at the top of the walls were small barred windows. The wallpaper above the wainscoting was red- and silver-flocked. Italianate statuary was positioned near the walls. Above the wainscoting hung paintings in heavy, ornate frames. I recognized a Rubens, a Botticelli, another Rubens, a Bosch — even a Klee that looked as if it had lost its way and showed up completely by accident.

The furniture consisted of several heavy refectory tables, a couple of ancient leather wing chairs and a rough-hewn desk set out from one wall. Behind the desk were bookshelves heavy with leather-bound volumes and what might have been original Medieval folios and quartos. A pedestal, I could see even in the gloom, held an open volume of an illustrated Inferno.

My God, I didn't know whether to laugh, cry, whimper or just ask to be let alone for an afternoon so I could touch things.

As if reading my thoughts, my escort said, "Something, isn't it? And there are rooms here that make this pale by comparison." He smiled, his first expression of emotion. "I spend most of my time here. I am Mr. Corcacan's curator."

"Curator?" He had to notice my eyebrows shooting up in surprise.

He smiled again, with genuine warmth. "Mr. Corcacan is a world-renowned collector, whose tastes are exceedingly eclectic."

He must have sensed my continued surprise. "I know," he said. "Some say I look like a hood. But I am not. I am actually, believe it or not, Dutch, though I was educated in England and the United States. No accent, I know. For some reason the accent seemed, ah, affected. So I worked at losing it."

I nodded. He said, "I have a degree from the London School of Economics and a Ph.D. from Stanford in art history." He looked around the room. "I realize it's a bit overwhelming, but I love it here. Much of what you see is priceless."

"I've got one question," I said.

"Yes?"

"Is that a gun under your coat?"

"Of course," he said without elaboration.

Another man entered the room, from an arched entry into the rest of the house. He too was dressed in the official Mafia uniform, though shorter and beefier than the curator. But when he spoke it was all Sicily by way of New Jersey. "Hey buttwipe, this way." He jerked a head that looked to weigh as much as a bowling ball and was approximately the same shape as one toward the interior of the house.

"Buttwipe?" I looked at the curator. "Is he for real?"

The curator looked at me with alarm, as if he couldn't understand why I wasn't frightened by the guy. He said, "Ah, I believe Mr. Corcacan is asking for you."

"Well, in that case," I said. I walked by Bowling ball Head, stepped to one side and said, "After you."

The ugly hood gave me a killer stare, as cold and deep as polished onyx, and underneath my bravado, I truly did feel some apprehension. Being in the company of killers and gangsters — even gangster-curators — will do that.

Bowling ball Head led me through more gloom — an ornate living room filled with extremely uncomfortable looking Queen Anne furniture and heavy tapestries on just about every square foot of wall, then along a long hall adorned with oil portraits of quite a number of elderly men, presumably long dead, all of whom looked Italian.

About half way along the hall, I felt it — the hurry-up push from behind, the push for no reason other than to establish dominance. I tensed, but didn't turn around. Nor did I speed up. He said nothing.

Then we went up a winding staircase, and I slid my hand along a banister smoothed by hundreds of years and thousands of hands. I had heard that Corcacan had purchased all the pieces of the house, all the wood and fixtures, and had it shipped and assembled here. The banister might have been as old as Shakespeare, hell, it might have been touched by Shakespeare.

At the top of the stairs was a small landing, brightly lit by a floor-to-ceiling window of leaded glass. On the far side of the landing was another wooden door, this one of less-substantial proportions than the monstrous front door.

Bowling ball Head pushed through the door without hesitating -- the hinges actually gave off a few gothic squeaks. I looked up by reflex, preparing to duck if a bat swooped down on me, but all I saw inside the door was an English study that I would have sold my grandmother into slavery for.

I stepped inside, and hoped that my jaw would stop falling before it hit the floor.

The light in here was brighter, coming from three stained glass windows on the far wall. The glass looked as if it had come out of a Renaissance cathedral. It probably had.

Along the walls to my right and left were enormous oak bookcases. Here were more leather-bound volumes, thousands of them, most looking old, worn, and heavily read. Here and there were bookstands, on which were perched individual volumes, opened to pages of beautiful woodcuts, ornate calligraphy and delicate drawings. I saw the influences of the Celts, Goths, Huns, the Anglo Saxons and the Italians, and the Dutch and Spanish.

There was no art hanging here, no sculpture, no carvings or pottery. This was a room in which to worship books, and a proper church it was.

In front of the middle stained-glass window was a Victorian writing desk. On the desk were only an old leather-edged blotter and fountain pen in a marble holder. Behind the desk was a huge leather chair, not an antique most likely, but comfortable looking and in keeping with the motif of the study. And behind that was a small Queen Anne credenza that held a pewter pitcher and six matching drinking vessels.

And standing on the chair stood Frederico Corcacan. At full height his head still didn't reach the top of the chair. His tuxedo was immaculately shaped and pressed. His little body was as warped as I had remembered.

He made a sweeping bow and said, "Mr. Landers, please sit down.."

And so I sat, in a leather wing chair that almost swallowed me. And, as I'm sure he had planned all along, looked up at Frederico Corcacan.

Chapter 33

Corcacan said, "It seems our paths are crossing."

I said, "And how's that?"

Bowlingball Head had taken a position to one side of the dwarf's desk. Corcacan, now that he had made his point about who was in charge, slid down into his chair. Still, and I suspected this was orchestrated in the adjustment of the desk chair's height and the low chair I sat in, I still had to look up at him.

"I understand you were looking for a girl who ended up dead," Corcacan said.

He hadn't asked a question. I waited. He said, "There's some concern that the killing might be tied to a couple of other murders here in Emerald City." Still, no question. "You've found the girl you were looking for. Why are you still nosing around?"

Now a question. I said, "Because I want to find out who killed her."

"And you can't depend on the Emerald City police to do that?"

"Ha, ha," I said. "Seriously, you live here. Would you rely on the Emerald City cops for anything at all?"

He shook his head. "It is not my intention to play games." He spoke with a trace of accent, but beyond that his speech sounded as if the words came out of the back of his throat. "I have no problem with you trying to find the killer. In fact, I think that would be a good thing."

I raised my eyebrows. "Are we at odds, then?"

"I don't think so." He reached for the pen — it was quite a stretch, but he made it — and held it tightly in one little paw. "The other two deaths, do you think they are connected, with each other and with the death of, what was her name, Shelly Travers?"

I nodded. "Don't know. Some similarities, some differences. The two earlier killings were alike in a number of details, but I don't have that much information. The Emerald City cops, you see, they aren't —"

He jabbed the pen at me. "I heard about your little fracas with David LeGrand." He laughed, which came out as a choked cackle. "Didn't help your standing there much, did you?"

"Didn't have much standing to begin with," I said.

Another cackle, then Corcacan's features composed, and he began to tap the pen on the blotter. "Those girls, the first two. They were employed by my organization, in an indirect way."

"You mean your operation has its hand in the prostitution network in Emerald City, so you control the pimps and the escort agencies, who in turn control the prostitutes, and you provide protection and the right to operate in return for, ah, monetary considerations, do I have it correct?"

Bowlingball Head said, "You got a smart mouth, buttwipe." He took a step toward me. Corcacan lifted his hand and shook his head, and Bowling ball Head stopped abruptly.

Corcacan said, "That is unimportant. What is important is that there is fear now, fear that some kind of psycho's running loose out there, on the streets."

"And it's hurting your business," I said.

"God damn it," the dwarf said suddenly, and with some heat. "It's not your business to concern yourself with my business. I want you to understand that I'm concerned with your business."

"Yes, sir, boss," I said as flatly as possible. "I'm glad I understand that now, sir." I heard Bowling ball Head mutter something under his breath. It might have been "fuckhead."

Corcacan ignored my comment. "The point is, the two of us got a mutual goal here, and that's to find the psycho who's killing these girls."

"If there's only one psycho."

"I got a feeling," Corcacan said. "Point is, I want to hire you."

"I've already got a client."

"So?"

"My client's more powerful than you are."

Bowlingball Head made a noise in his throat.

Corcacan said, "Who gives a shit? I just wanna know that we aren't working at cross-purposes."

"Mr. Corcacan, with all due respect, I don't give a rat's ass what your purposes are. I know you run the rackets in this part of the state, and it's pretty clear you have the local cops in your pocket. So why don't you just apply your leverage there? You'll probably get a lot better results that way than you will by depending on little old me."

He shook his head sadly, as if I were an ignorant child. "I want the killer found. It might not be in my best interests to have the cops find him."

"Are you setting me up to find a guy you already know the identity of?" I said, beginning to rise off the chair.

"No, no." He spread his hands. "I mean, sometimes it's better not to have to work within all those bureaucracies, you know?"

"You mean, all those folks who'd have to bother with the niceties of the law, protection of individual rights, due process, that kind of thing?"

Another sad shake of the head. "Even if I put the full force of my authority behind persuading the police to find the killer, have you ever considered that they might just be too incompetent to do that?"

"Incompetent, or unwilling?" Then, suddenly inspired: "They have something to hide."

He ignored the remark; I noticed that he was good at that.

"So, will you continue to look for the murderer?" the dwarf asked.

I hated looking up at the little bastard, but the looming presence of Bowlingball Head kept me in my seat. I said, "What the fuck do you really want, Frederico?"

He tensed and his eyes bore into me. Maybe it was my use of the profanity, maybe it was my use of his first name. Bowlingball Head hissed at me, "stupid motherfucker" and made a slight shift in my direction.

Enough was enough. Maybe it was Corcacan's presumption that we understood each other. Maybe it was his presumption that, though I might pop off, I would ultimately do his bidding. Maybe it was his presumption that his power was all-powerful, that I was only significant as a means to an end. Maybe it was those sad shakes of the head, his determination that I just didn't understand.

Or it may have been the irritating insults Corcacan's hood continued to growl at me under his breath or how he pushed me along on the way up here to establish his dominance. Or maybe it was none of those things, maybe it was all of them, that accounted for what I did next.

I rose off the chair, as if making to leave. I leaned down, brushed at my pants. Then I leaned forward and took hold of a pewter waste basket that stood near my chair.

Holding the pewter basket with both hands on its top edge, I came up fast and hard, aiming a hard swing at Bowlingball Head's head. He had an instant to register surprise and turn toward the movement before the heavy pewter basket slammed into his face with a heavy thunk.

He screamed. Waste paper flew like confetti from the basket. Blood erupted from the thug's nose, and he staggered back a step.

I'd held onto the basket during the rebound. I swung it again, getting more arc into it this time, and caught him hard on the ear. He screamed again, the ear seemed to explode in a pink mist and he fell like a shot. He curled up in a ball, clutched his bashed-in face with his hands, and whimpered like a kicked dog.

I stood over the crumpled man, still holding the dented pewter can, breathing hard.

And behind me, I heard the sound of hands clapping, louder and louder, and then the cackling laugh.

I turned, and looked at Corcacan. He'd jumped up on his feet, still in the chair. He was stomping his feet onto the leather. He began to slap his hands on his thighs. He was cackling so hard his face had turned a bright red.

I just stared at the little dervish.

After at least a minute he finally began to get himself under control. He took several deep breaths, leaned forward and rested his hands on his knees. His cheeks were wet with tears.

"Oh, my, Mr. Landers," he said in a voice hoarse from laughing. "I like you. I really do. We are going to do so well together, you and I." He paused and took a couple of gulps of air. "Though I'm not sure Carlo there —" he pointed at the still-whimpering thug huddled on the floor — "I'm not sure how he's gonna feel if he has to deal with you in the future. Yep, he could be real upset by that." And he commenced to cackling again.

I carefully placed the bloody trash can on the floor, said, "Fuck you," and knew it came out exceedingly lame, and walked out of the room.

He was still laughing as the doors shut behind me.

Chapter 34

The encounter with Corcacan left me feeling depressed and directionless. I hung around the house for awhile, hung out with Cool for awhile (and tried, unsuccessfully, to stay emotionally aloof from him) and finally made a plan to do what all real men do when the going gets rough — go fishing.

I went to bed early, fell asleep quickly and awoke before my alarm went off at 4 a.m. I made coffee, fed Cool a savory breakfast of Field Trial Chunks, and went out onto the back deck for a few minutes.

I've always loved the promise of the day that the time before dawn brings. If you sit quietly and watch and listen, even sometimes in the rush of the city, you can sense it: listen to those first chirps of the birds as they begin their day of swooping and soaring and foraging. Feel the crisp air just beginning to be warmed by the heat of the new sun. Watch the dark skies and see them slowly lose their blackness, and begin their subtle progression to bright blue.

Feel it, see it, hear it. And then it's easy, if only for a little while, to share the hope and promise that this is a new day, and anything is possible. At dawn — when that very edge of the burning sun peeks above the horizon, casting tongues of reds and oranges and violets into the sky — I pulled my battered aluminum skiff from its snug place beside my house and pulled it toward the water's edge.

Which caused enormous excitement in Cool. He ran around the skiff in concentric circles, narrowing the gap each time. He skidded in the sand, barked, jumped, darted and skidded some more.

When I got the boat into the edge of the water I got in and checked the connections on the battery, made sure my rods and reels were secure and the tackle box was fully stocked. Then I looked at Cool, watching my preparations at the edge of the shore, tail splashing in the water, said, "Stay," and used an oar to push the boat out into the surf.

At one moment, Cool was standing — head cocked with curiosity — watching me drift away from the beach.

The next moment, he was dashing into the surf after me. He made it to the boat and threw his front paws over the low gunwale, pushing and paddling furiously with his back legs.

I leaned over and removed the dog's paws and placed them back into the six inches of water we floated in. I said, "Go on back," and pointed to the shore and, to my amazement, the pooch tromped through the water back to the sand.

My amazement was only momentary. He stood there for a moment, then threw himself enthusiastically into the water and did a run-and-swim comedy routine toward the boat. This time his momentum carried the upper half of his body all the way into the bow of the skiff, leaving his back legs to churn furiously in the water like little outboards, pushing us away from the shore.

I gave up. I grabbed the poor wet dog's legs and pulled, and he pushed, and finally he launched himself out of the water into the front of the boat, panting and dripping. He looked around happily, shook off the water in a rain of spray and sand that soaked me, barked once and sat down. Game over, game point to Cool.

Shaking my head, grinning in spite of myself, I tried standing in the stern. Cool, to his utmost credit, sat calmly, perfectly still. Standing wasn't difficult; I'd done it hundreds of times in the skiff. I took hold of the long vertical shaft and handle of the trolling motor, gave it some juice, and got us pointed in the direction of the south edge of the key, where bonefish and reds lurked in the flats just off the mangroves and brush at the shoreline.

My intended prey were the bones — skittish, cautious fish who will dart away at the slightest provocation, and who are the best pound-for-pound fighters I've ever tangled with.

The way to snag a bonefish is to use your eyes. Drift as quietly as possible, use polarized sunglasses, stand and let your eyes adjust to the very shallow water of the flats. When you see a bone, gently, very gently, toss your bait — generally a live shrimp on an neighed line — out in front of him and let it drift. Nineteen times out of twenty the bone will beat a path in the other direction. The twentieth time — you're in for a treat. He'll run and pull and zig and zag, and you'll think your rod is going to snap, or your line will break. And if you're good, and if you have the right equipment and the reel's drag is set just right, and you're willing to play him patiently for as long as it takes, you'll boat a beautiful bonefish — which is good only for throwing back. Bonefish are barely edible. It's all in the sport — real men armed with thousands of dollars worth of state-of-the-art fishing gear against one small, wiley fish. Usually the fish wins.

My other goal was to snag a redfish. Not as much sport as the bones, but a good fight, and a fine feast.

An hour into my foray, I'd seen several bones, all of which swam away before I even had a chance to present the bait. A little later I dropped a shrimp about four feet in front of a bone and he came up to it, took it in his mouth, jerked it a couple of times, and stole it before I could set the hook.

Three hours later, the sun bright and hot in the mid-morning sky, I'd gone through two bottles of Evian, Cool had gone through two more. I was letting a shrimp drift in the flats when I got a sudden tug, the rod bent double and the line zinged out of the real. A straight pull, which could mean a redfish. Of course, it could also mean a catfish.

It was a red. It gave me a decent fight, tired after a couple of minutes and when I got it into the boat I knew I'd done my shopping for dinner. I sat in the rear of the boat, used a filet knife to cut the head off the red and gut it, rinsed it in salt water and wrapped it in damp newspaper.

Then Cool and I headed back, him panting, me fantasizing about a cold beer. At home I got the skiff into its nook, took the battery to the edge of the deck and connected it to the charger. The red ended up in the refrigerator, a beer ended up in my hand, and several basted dog biscuits ended up in Cool's belly.

For the first time in days I'd gone several hours without thinking about the case, about Shelly Travers or David LeGrand or the dead hookers or even Galatea.

And, as I stood in my little living room I remembered, the thought coming unbidden, the stack of mail I'd taken with me when I visited Shelly Travers' apartment.

I'd stashed it in a desk drawer, forgotten until now. I retrieved it and took it to the kitchen table, spread it out among the debris of computer components, cables, wires and disks.

There were perhaps a dozen pieces, not counting a few junk-mail flyers and ads. An electric bill, cable bill, statement from an investment broker, flyer from a CD mail-order house.

And a cellular telephone bill, postmarked just over a week ago.

I tore open that envelope and extracted the bill. It ran to about nine pages, and there, on three pages, was what I was hoping for — an itemized accounting of calls, both incoming and outgoing, with telephone numbers listed.

I went to a kitchen drawer and got a pen and legal pad, and returned to the desk. I did a line-by-line analysis of the bill.

And found out some interesting facts: Three numbers appeared repeatedly — one more than a twenty five times. I suspected that would be Locke. I reached in my billfold and got the card Locke had written his number on. This number was listed as his cell phone. I crossed those off the list.

The second number appeared ten times. I called it and got Dee Dee Myers' answering machine. So Dee Dee knew Shelly better than she had let on; thankfully she had at least steered me in a direction that bore some results. I could only wonder what Myers knew, but wouldn't or couldn't tell, that would help me.

Another number appeared seven times. It didn't look familiar, so I used my cell phone to call it. A woman answered it by saying only the last four digits of the number. She had a very seductive voice and I said, as sweetly as I could, "Oh, is this the — ah, whom did I reach?"

She disconnected without another word.

I went back and checked the dates of the calls to Locke, and the calls to the mystery number. The calls to Locke had been frequent during the first part of the billing period, which ended just a couple of weeks ago. But they began to diminish, and the number hadn't been called at all the last two weeks of the bill. The other number exhibited the opposite trend. A couple of calls during the first two weeks, then more and more toward the end of the period.

Well. A number that Shelly called repeatedly, with increasing frequency. Each time had been in the evening. That number was shown as having called back a number of times as well, generally in close proximity to the outgoing calls. A pattern. Evenings, calls back and forth.

What kind of business worked that way?

I had an idea.

Chapter 35

I checked my e-mail; it was getting to be a new habit, and I looked forward to the frequent correspondence from MaryAnne and Galatea.

Just one this time, from Galatea. It was flagged urgent, showing up in red. I opened it and read:

Hello big tough guy and how are you doing?:) Sorry I haven't written in many hours, but hey, hey the working' girl (betcha didn't know this ethnic mutt listened to Merle and Willie, didja?) Anyway, the reason I'm writing is actually kind of serious. I was talking to someone at the bar last night -- I was actually tending bar for a few hours if you can believe that:) Anyway this girl is in there and she is toast, I am not kidding you. And she wants to talk. She's high on booze and I'm sure something else, and she's kind of excited but scared too. So we talk for awhile and I feed her a few drinks — great interrogation technique, huh? — and she tells me some really interesting things. Too complicated to try to explain in writing, so can we get together, like soon? Like, call me, you have the home and bar numbers. I'm off today so what do you say?:):-:);-)
g-girl the t-girl

Hoo, boy, the friends I make.

And though I liked hearing from Galatea, liked the fact that she wanted to help, liked the fact that she was witty and easy on the eyes — I just couldn't help thinking about who — and what — she was. And that was enough to define the, ah, parameters of the relationship.

I picked up the cell phone and dialed her number, and she answered and sounded glad as could be to hear my voice, and we agreed to meet.

So here we were, this time at an upscale restaurant on the shore side of Crescent Key, sitting catty-cornered at a corner table. Candle on the table, cloth napkins delicately folded, silverware shining in the flickering candlelight, stars twinkling in the night sky outside the big windows of the restaurant. Aware of the ambiance, I hoped Galatea wouldn't construe this friendly meeting as a date.

"This case may suck," I said, "but it sure has made for some elegant social events."

Galatea smiled. I had to admit that she looked absolutely stunning in the soft light, as feminine as could be. Truth in packaging, I reminded myself.

"So," she said after she'd finished off an enormous bite of flounder, "this girl comes into the bar, and she's pretty wasted. And she's in a talking mood."

"And since you are the shy one," I said, smiling, "you let her talk."

"Hey," Galatea said and kicked me under the table. "Anyway, she is toasted. She's drinking straight scotch on the rocks, and she isn't stopping with one or two."

She paused to dive into her baked potato. The girl could eat, and she weighed next to nothing.

"I should add here," She said, "that she is the classic chick with a dick, God, every time I say that get totally embarrassed, you know, because . . . well, anyway."

I waited for the crimson flush to fade away while Galatea fiddled with her fork and took a sip of water. Then she said, "She wasn't bad looking in the bar light, but I gotta be honest, she hadn't done nearly all the things she could do to really pass well. She was coarse. She had a masculine throat and I don't think she had had electrolysis, it was more like she might have shaved extremely close. A lot of the, you know, 'chicks' do that and put on a whole lot of pancake makeup.

"Anyway, she's the kind of person who may not take the transformation any farther. I figure her for a hooker, she had the boob job and definitely got some whoppers, stood out to here —" she held her hands out in front of her and cupped them in the universal tits-out-to-here gesture. "There's a demand for these kinds of hookers, as you know, ah, I don't mean from experience." She chuckled.

"And the important part of this, see, from what I can tell, is that she fits the profile of the girls who were killed.

"The first two -- not Shelly Travers, " I said.

“Except remember that at one time Shelly Travers was in the life, just like her.”

Galatea was right. I just didn’t like to think of the dead woman that way. I watched a ship far offshore, just a brighter twinkling of lights that formed a shape on the horizon. I thought of Darwin Locke, perhaps out there somewhere, grieving alone in the solitude and luxury that great wealth provides.

I felt Galatea nudge my arm. “Anybody home, big buy?” I turned to her smile.

“Sorry,” I said. “The whole case has gotten to me. I go into these melancholy funks. I’m back.” I returned her smile.

“Back to business?” she said with a little hesitation.

“Have to,” I said. “Later we can talk about fun stuff. So go on about your new-found drinking buddy.”

“Not my buddy,” Galatea said seriously. “Anyway, she drinks, drinks, drinks, and talks, talks, talks. If I ever talk that much try some duct tape.”

“I’ll do that. I take it her talk wasn’t just idle chatter.”

“Nope,” she said. Hesitated. Then, “I don’t know why I’m hesitant to get to the important stuff. Maybe it’s because I -- well, we, you know, the transsexual community, we’re really private. Even this kind of person, we think of her as one of us, at least kinda, and we respect her, you know. But she wasn’t exactly talking to me in confidence, so . . . “

“So you might save somebody’s life by telling me.”

“Yes.” She nodded solemnly. “Okay. Well, she does the usual thing about ‘I’m a working girl.’ Then she talks about what assholes all the guys are.”

“Perception of whores everywhere,” I said.

Galatea nodded, looked out at the darkness, then returned her gaze to me. “So for awhile it’s bitch, bitch, bitch, you know she’s a tough broad, talks about her gorgeous tits and the seven inches she got down there, okay I am seriously not going to get embarrassed here. And I’m like, yeah, yeah, have another drink and let me do some work.

“Then she gets maudlin. That’s no surprise, she’s drunk as a skunk and her life sucks. I can understand that. But she says things are looking up since she hooked up with this new escort service. She says it’s real secretive setup, only the men who are members can call in. There’s even some kind of screening process so the girls know they're safe when dates are set up. She's real happy about that.

"All of a sudden, her mood heads south. She gets this really scared look on her face, this could just be the alcohol talking, but it seemed genuine. She says, 'The whole thing's really a little hinky. First, these men, they want some really weird things. She uses her finger to underline really. I figure that's like role-playing, bondage, maybe some water sports -- God, I guess I sound like I'm a pro or something."

She focused those wide eyes on me and said, "Samuel, I've never, never done anything like that. I've never sold myself to anybody. I like sex just as much as anybody, and I don't have a problem with being, you know, open-minded. But you've gotta believe that I never did the bad stuff."

Her eyes were wet. I put a hand out and covered hers, and it felt warm beneath mine.

She looked at me, and looked at my hand over hers, and she said, "Thank you, Samuel."

I took my hand away. She smiled again. Said thank you again. Took a deep breath and another drink of water. "Okay, so she makes her point about the kinky stuff and then her voice drops to a whisper. I have to strain to even hear her. I'm leaning in, she's leaning in, her breath smells like a distillery, not to mention cigarettes, and she says, 'Someone's killing us off.'

"So I pull my head back and think. She's talking about those girls who were killed. I ask her what does she mean? She says, 'You hear about those killings? Those dead girls all worked for this same service. That's no shit.'"

I felt the adrenalin push my pulse up a few notches. Galatea had stumbled on the connection that I had suspected but couldn't find. I said, "And you got the name of the service?"

She shook her head. "She wouldn't tell me. Told me she was sworn to secrecy. By this time she looked really nervous. Then she said something else, remember she is nine sheets to the wind by now, she says, 'remember that gal got killed a few weeks ago?' That would be the second girl who got murdered, Victoria Chance, right?"

I nodded, and neglected to mention Galatea's truly stunning use of the run-on sentence.

"Victoria Chance, who according to my drunken friend was another 'chick with a dick,' worked out of this same escort agency. Weird, huh?"

"At this point, nothing's weird," I said. "Anything else?"

"Just one thing," Galatea said. "She looks at her watch -- I can't believe she can actually read it by now -- and she gets up real quick, says, 'Gimme the check, I gotta go. I gotta meet a cop.'"

"And?"

"And that's it! She paid her tab, which was substantial, left a pathetic little tip and wobbled out like she'd never worn four-inch heels before."

"This is good, Galatea," I said. "This is very good. I have a telephone number I think may just belong to that escort service. At least it's somewhere to start."

"So you can call them up and find out the name?"

I shook my head. "I tried. Whoever answers the phone is cagey. Just the last four digits of the number. I would have to have some kind of password to get any farther. But I do have a guy trying to run down the owner of that number."

"Or," Galatea said very carefully, "I could call them and inquire as to whether they were hiring."

"No!" I said. I wagged a finger at her. "No! I'll take it from here. I am absolutely not going to put you in danger."

She argued. I was adamant. She argued some more. I got more intractable.

And we left the restaurant better friends than ever. Emphasis on "friend" for me. I was a bit uncertain about what road Galatea thought we were headed down, but I knew I wasn't willing to go there.

Chapter 36

The day had worn me out. I'd gotten up before dawn to go fishing, spent some time with Shelly's mail, walked the beach to ponder the significance of the cell phone information. During the afternoon I'd surfed the transgender newsgroups, just trying to get a feel for the people who posted. There were several such groups; some were sex-oriented, filled with posts from people who wanted to meet a t-girl, or inquiries about transgender-friendly bars, or pictures of naked transsexuals and transvestites.

Then the meeting with Galatea, which, while bearing significant fruit, kept my mind scurrying around all the corners of the case. Shelly Travers, and the perp who might be out there killing t-girls, was a weighty specter.

When I got home it was almost midnight. Cool bounded out to meet me, as usual, but something was wrong. He appeared agitated, running toward me, then pulling back. His eyes were bright. This was not a mood I'd seen before.

I reached into the glove box and took out the Sig — I'd been carrying it in the Defender when I made my night jaunts, and keeping it in a drawer in my dresser each night.

I got out of the Defender and stuck the Sig in the waistband of my jeans, then closed the door and locked it. I knelt down, and Cool moved to me, pushed his head right into my midsection and snuggled up as hard as he could. I could see his chest heaving and hear his pants.

"Hey," I said. "It's okay. I'm here, buddy." The dog kept burrowing and for a time I just patted his head and scratched his ears. Even this late the air was hot and muggy, and I realized that only the softest of breezes was coming in off the Gulf. Too long here and I would become dinner for some of the millions of mosquitoes who buzzed the coast at night.

Then I got up headed to the front door but Cool cut down the side of the house, barking. I followed, not liking the darkness I had to travel in.

I got to the corner of the back deck. Cool stood, peering around the corner. I stepped by him, wary now, and onto the deck.

And saw the reason for Cool's strange behavior.

A snowy egret, at least five feet from head to foot, and clearly very dead, hung from one of the wooden poles that supported the roof over the deck. A large nail stuck through the center of his head. A puddle of blood had formed beneath him.

I pulled the Sig out from under my belt. I racked a round into the chamber and flicked the safety off. I scanned the deck, the beach beyond, and the brush on the far side of the house. Nothing. I stood very still, heard nothing except the soft sounds of Cool's whimpers.

I took several deep breaths and approached the egret. He was very cold to the touch, and had started to stiffen. The blood was thick and dark.

Something caught my attention. I turned to the back door. On the white paint someone had traced words with the egret's blood. Don't meddle, in ragged six-inch letters. In a couple of places rivulets of blood had run down on the paint.

Holding the Sig in my right hand, I got my keys out of my left pocket and got the door unlocked. My heart was pounding. I reached in and turned on the inside light, and stepped inside and held the gun out in a combat stance. Nothing out of place, nothing moving.

Cool stuck his head inside and stood still, half his body still on the deck. He watched me intently.

I went quickly around the house, starting in the bedroom and working my way back to the kitchen. There had been no entry that I could see. Nothing had been disturbed. No windows had been jimmied. Apparently whoever had come had been content to do his mischief outside.

Don't meddle!

I tucked the Sig back under my belt, after making sure the safety was securely on. I got a hammer, flashlight and small army shovel I kept in the broom closet. By now Cool had ventured inside the house, but he stood stock-still in the middle of the living room, sniffing.

I dug a grave a few yards from the house, in the moonlight under the branches of a spreading oak. When I knelt I felt the hard metal of the pistol dig into my leg. It was a little painful and greatly comforting. While I dug I thought about the poor bird. Egrets are so graceful as they swoop low over the water, so ungainly as they gambol on spindly legs pecking at small critters in the surf. They hurt no one; they were a reason why parts of Florida can be as close to paradise as you can come on this earth.

I held the hammer and went back to the deck. I hated what I had to do next.

I saw immediately that with the hammer alone I couldn't get the leverage to pull the nail out without mashing the bird's head. I went back inside and got a large screwdriver. I held the handle of the screwdriver next to the head, then carefully slipped the fork of the hammer over the nail. That done, I made sure the hammer head was against the screwdriver, then applied pressure. The screwdriver was wide enough that the hammer didn't push against the bird, and after a few moments the nail gave way and came out. I caught the bird before it fell, and scooped it up in both hands. It weighed next to nothing.

Back under the tree I placed the bird in the grave, filled the dirt back in and tamped it. Then I stood and said a short, silent prayer for all of nature and the land for which we served only as God's caretakers.

During this, Cool had come out on the deck. He sniffed the blood, then scuffled at the door for a minute. Then he came to the edge of the deck nearest the bird's grave and lay down. But his head still was up, and he was vigilant.

Up 'til then, I could only think of the tasks at hand: secure the house, make sure Cool and I were safe, bury the bird. The facts of the case, when I did try to bring them to mind, ran together and collided like so many out-of-control bumper cars. I gave up trying to make sense of anything and just concentrated on the moment.

But the bloody words kept coming back to me: Don't meddle! Don't meddle!

The message was clear, and it was equally clear that my little bastion of safety could be intruded on even more easily than I had thought.

Don't meddle! If someone wanted to warn me off the Shelly Travers case they'd picked the wrong way to do it. Now I was really pissed off.

Chapter 37

I slept fitfully; the two stiff bourbons I gulped before bed only seemed to further agitate me. They certainly weren't good medicine.

I slept with my pistol, cocked and ready, on my nightstand. Cool, for the first time, lumbered onto the foot of the bed before he faded and started his version of snoring.

Before 8 a.m. I was awakened by the shrill ring of the cell phone. Cool's head snapped up — he didn't appear to have moved all night — and looked at me expectantly.

I crawled out of bed, feeling aged and stiff, and made it to the phone. I stabbed at a couple of keys until it stopped ringing and said, "Hello," in a phlegmy voice.

"Well, well, you private licenses don't like to get the early jump on the crooks, do you?"

I had to think for a moment to place the voice. "Wainwright?"

"It is," the chipper voice said. "Can you talk or should I call back when you're conscious?"

"Give me half an hour, I'll call you back." I took down the Washington number. Then I made a pot of coffee, drank two cups sitting at the kitchen table. I tossed a few biscuits Cool's way, and he did the usual, snag, put down, sniff, lick, and eat routine.

I went to the bathroom, ran water over my face, brushed the oxidation from the night before off my teeth, poured another cup of coffee and called Wainwright.

He answered the line himself. When I mentioned it, he said, "Hey, I'm a big shot now, a senior consultant or some shit. What it means is I get a small office and no secretary." He chuckled as if that didn't bother him at all.

“I called to say,” he said, “that I’ve had some time to turn my attention to your little predicament down there.”

“And?” I said, suddenly hopeful.

“And I haven’t turned up anything new on the three killings down there.” Hope plummeted. “But —” he paused and I could hear the intake of breath, a small cough — “I ran a search on VICAP and turned up a couple of interesting items of information.”

“You’re killin’ me here, Wainwright. I haven’t been able to do much except step in shit on this case. Get to the point.”

“Testy guy,” Wainwright said happily. “We don’t get reports from every agency, but the numbers’ve gone up since we’ve offered the locals computers and tie-ins from quite a number of agencies, especially the larger ones. In return for the computers they have to input information on all their violent crimes from years ago to the present.”

I remembered from previous talk that Wainwright would tell it his way, in his time. I wrapped my hands around hope’s wings and waited.

“Got some hits,” he said after another draw on the cigarette. “Four, to be exact. Murders of transsexual prostitutes. Pre-op. Mutilations, though I’m not yet clear on the exact nature of those.”

I let my hands go and hope soared. “Where? When?”

I heard paper rattling. “Ah, New Orleans, back in July 2000. And —” more shuffling — “Atlanta, January 2002. Then, here’s an odd one, Honolulu, February of 2003 and, hmm, Pensacola, that’s up in the Florida Panhandle, January of this year.”

A pattern, just like in the textbooks, I thought. Similar murders, decreasing periods between killings.

“I’ve put calls into the various agencies. Pensacola and New Orleans are an hour earlier. Hawaii, they haven’t even thought about waking up yet. But I have some detectives’ names, and I think I might get some calls back today.” He chuckled. “They might have heard a little about me.” Then, “Are you breathing hard because you’re glad I called, or is that Florida air just too humid this time of year.” He inhaled again and tried to chuckle, which turned into a cough that sounded like a car about to throw a rod.

“Are you having the agencies send you their complete reports,” I asked.

“By fax I hope, end of day at latest. Or I’ll threaten to take their computers back. I'll call you tomorrow. Or I'll call you tonight, on the home phone number you've probably forgotten you gave me."

I made sure he had the cell phone number before we hung up. Then I looked at the dates I'd written down. July 2000. January 2002. February 2003. January 2004.

An interval of 18 months.

Then 13 months.

Eleven months.

Now eight months.

The pattern of decreasing intervals was clear. Except that I'd only included Shelly. If you factored in the two other killings, only about a month apart, you had an extreme acceleration of the killing timeframe.

And there could be others. Wainwright himself said that not all agencies reported, and those that had couldn't be relied on to get all their crimes into the computer.

Five similar killings, perhaps seven. The timeframes bode well for isolating this as the work of one killer. The bad news: The guy had become a killing machine, his obsessions were mounting, and the needs were just about out of control.

Sure sounded like good news, bad news to me. Throw in a crooked cop, strange telephone calls, scared hookers and a dead bird and it made quite a stew.

Chapter 38

The only good at all to come out of this, I told myself, was that I got to use some of my toys.

In this case, the toys — sophisticated gear that I sometimes employed in my security business — consisted of my late model iPad with the cellular capabilities, a GPS transmitter with a magnet that attached easily underneath a vehicle and a monthly subscription service for the GPS system. I could attach the transmitter and track a car in real time from anywhere I had cell service.

The toys didn't stop there. I'd also gotten a sophisticated digital camera with a long lens that would upload into my computer, a night-vision scope, a small laser light that pulsed and could only be seen with the scope and a long-range shotgun microphone coupled with a small digital recording device.

With all of this I'd be able to track my target from the privacy of my own home and from my car using the iPad. If I wanted, I could keep a visual tail from quite a distance using the pulsing laser light, and with the camera get some striking photo evidence without him ever being aware of my presence.

The target I'd chosen was David LeGrand. It wasn't that I thought he was running around hacking up transsexuals. It was more that I really didn't have any better lead. LeGrand worked for Emerald City. He was the lead investigator in the killings. He was less than forthcoming with information about them. Emerald City was known to be a corrupt town. Put all of that together and you get — what? I didn't know, but I figured if I followed LeGrand he might lead me around the underbelly of the city, perchance set me onto a clue or path of action.

The transmitter for the tracking system — no larger than a can of sardines — would be affixed to the underside of his car. The laser I would put inside his taillight. Unless he did a thorough inspection of his undercarriage he wouldn't find the transmitter. And I doubted he'd ever go inside his taillight assembly to look for anything.

With all this equipment I could choose to follow along behind him as he drove, or simply fire up the iPad, boot the software and track him from just about anywhere as a little pulsing dot on the map on my iPad's screen.

Sure made tailing a suspect a lot simpler than the old days. Lots more expensive, too.

I didn't think putting the device on LeGrand's police car would be a problem. One of the perks of working for the Emerald City force was that everyone, officers and detectives alike, got an issue car they could take home.

So I simply waited until the wee hours of the morning, drove by LeGrand's house, said a silent thank-you that the police car was parked in his drive way, rather than his garage, and stopped a few blocks away. I walked to LeGrand's, noted the absence of light in the windows, detoured up his driveway, dropped onto my back, slipped a hand underneath the vehicle and felt the magnets pull themselves onto the frame.

That took about ten seconds. I sat up, looked around. No activity, no dogs barking, no lights. I took out a screwdriver, unscrewed the right taillight assembly, tucked the little laser inside and made it fast with duct tape.

I was just starting to tighten the last screw when the floodlight at the corner of the garage came on, bathing the driveway, the car and me in bright light. I sucked up my breath and held it, and slid slowly to my haunches. Still, my head and shoulders were visible above the trunk of the car.

LeGrand came out of the side door carrying a bag of trash. He stumbled a little coming down the steps that led to the driveway, looked both ways and started walking toward the garage. He wore long-sleeve pajamas and bedroom slippers with tiger heads on the front. Then he turned, looked toward the street — I had to be right in his line of vision — and began coming my way.

I had no choice. I slid to my right, toward the rear wheel well, and hunkered down as far as I could. My shirt, wet with perspiration, clung to my back and chest. I let my breath out slowly.

LeGrand, whistling some nameless tune, walked right by the car. He stared straight ahead, holding the trash bag at arms' length in front of him. As he got closer to the street I slipped back farther into the shadows made by the car. I heard a rattling sound, then the noise of the sack being dropped. Then LeGrand, still whistling, shuffled back along the driveway. The whistling receded, then I heard the sound of the side door opening and closing. A moment later, the floodlight switched off.

I waited a minute, seeing nothing except flickering light patterns in a deep darkness. Then my eyes began to adjust and I slipped back around to the taillight. I finished screwing in the last screw, took a quick look at the house, and took a deep breath.

Then I duckwalked a few feet across the lawn away from the house. When I was almost to the sidewalk I stood up, stepped onto the concrete and began to stroll away as casually as I could, just another burgher out for a late walk around the neighborhood.

Back home I turned on the iPad, punched up the software and logged onto the Internet. In less than a minute I had a map of LeGrand's neighborhood on my screen, with a that pulsing dot hovering right on his block.

Now I could follow along in the Defender and use the iPad to get an instantaneous fix as LeGrand moved about. Or I could log on at any time and backtrack his movements for as far back as I cared to.

The thing was unbelievably accurate — literally down to specific address points.

I was fairly sure that LeGrand wasn't on a specific shift; rather, he probably put in some daytime hours and got called out when a crime took place that required a detective or supervisor. That meant that I'd have to be flexible if I wanted to tag along real-time.

I checked my watch — after 3 a.m. I decided I'd try to catch a few hours myself, though my usual insomnia was rearing its ugly head. God, I thought, to actually be able to get in bed, turn out the light, and let sleep come easily.

So I got into a pair of boxer shorts — and went straight to my kitchen cabinet where I kept the bourbon, poured up a jelly glass of straight hootch, took my guitar to the back deck and spent a couple of hours serenading myself with cry-in-your-beer (or in this case, whiskey) songs so I'd be sure to be in a really surly mood when the morning came.

Chapter 39

The next morning I got up around 10 a.m. After gulping enough coffee to light the old spark plugs, I spent an hour discussing the pros and cons of the designated hitter rule with Cool. I talked, he listened. For the most part, he was an excellent listener, content to lie at my feet and cast his eyes upward. A couple of times he lost the train of thought when squirrels happened by the deck. Off he went, on the mistaken notion he could actually catch one.

When I booted up my iPad, I found that LeGrand's car was still in his driveway, and hadn't moved since I'd bugged it. So he was probably scheduled for the evening shift.

I spent the rest of the day tinkering with my equipment, honing my net-surfing skills, and hanging out with Cool.

About 5 p.m. LeGrand started moving. For a couple of hours I simply stayed at home and tracked his movements. The equipment was amazing; it was as if I was right alongside him in a way, knowing almost exactly where he was.

First LeGrand went to the police station. He stayed there more than an hour. Then he drove up Dixie to an area where I knew were a string of restaurants that comped cops. So far, business as usual.

My police scanner told me that nothing extraordinary was happening on the Emerald City frequencies. So I fooled around with Cool, sat on the deck and had a drink, snacked on some crackers and watched over LeGrand's virtual shoulder.

Over the next couple of hours he cruised some middle-class residential neighborhoods. He made three stops, each about twenty or thirty minutes. This was likely routine. Detectives spent a lot of time interviewing people regarding cases they were working on — victims, suspects, witnesses, and so on.

Then, from about 10 p.m. on, the tenor of LeGrand's evening changed. He drove back from the outlying neighborhoods, made a couple of quick stops at what might have been shopping plazas, then got on Dixie.

And began to bar hop.

It was almost as if he were tracking the stops I'd made when I'd joint-hopped. He worked his way south, stopping every several blocks, staying fifteen or twenty minutes at each place.

I thought this might bear some closer observation. So I filled Cool's water dish, fed him a late snack of beef-basted dog biscuits and avoided his forlorn look as I backed out of the driveway.

After I got over the bridge to the mainland I stopped in the parking lot of a convenience store. Under the glare of a sodium vapor light, I fired up the iPad, logged into the software and I was up and running. In a minute I was back on LeGrand's tail. He was moving now, still making his way south on Dixie, almost to the intersection of Everglades.

I doubted that LeGrand knew what kind of vehicle I drove. And anyway he wouldn't be expecting to be followed. The Land Rover is somewhat conspicuous, but traffic on Dixie and Everglades is always heavy, and the laser strobe and my night binoculars gave me the advantage of keeping some distance. It was a loose tail that could tighten up quickly.

I could tell by the vehicle tracker that he was near the intersection of Dixie and Magnolia, about ten blocks north of Everglades. He was moving south at a leisurely pace. I quickly cut north a few blocks until I got to Everglades, then headed toward Dixie.

I need not have hurried. LeGrand's vehicle stopped a couple of blocks later; I assumed he had pulled into another joint.

So I pointed the Defender toward the spot marked on the tracker's screen. Sure enough, in the appropriate block of Dixie was the Bare Facts, a still somewhat upscale nude club. LeGrand's unmarked car was parked in the back lot. It wasn't clearly visible from the street, but LeGrand had made no special effort to conceal it.

I drove up Dixie a couple of blocks until I found a Krispy Kreme. I parked on the side, locked the Defender and darted in for a cup of coffee to go and a half dozen of their namesake donuts.

Fortified by a number of the essential food groups, I took up the loose tail again. I was driving past Bare Facts when LeGrand's car whipped into the street and almost sideswiped me. Surprised, I slammed on the brakes and resisted the urge to lay on the horn. LeGrand wheeled his car into the outside lane and began to head south at a stately pace. I waited until several more cars had passed, then eased into traffic behind him.

I reached behind the seat and got the night-vision scope. Holding one hand steady on the wheel, I chanced a quick peak through the binoculars. I used two fingers to focus, glanced back at the road to make sure I wasn't about to rear-end someone, then took another look.

The laser was outstanding. Through the scope the world was a surreal sight, bright phosphorescent shapes moving through a moonscape. But the images were crystal clear, and the laser strobe seemed to explode from LeGrand's taillight in a series of brilliant flashes.

Like shooting fish in a barrel.

And down Dixie we went. Then onto Everglades and west along that strip. A couple of times, had I been conducting a traditional tight tail, I would have risked exposing myself. Now I simply picked up the scope, peeked quickly, and latched onto the flashing strobe. Even two blocks ahead it was a brilliant winking eye, yet without the scope it was invisible.

Along Everglades, LeGrand followed the same MO. He'd stop at just about every strip joint, cabaret, bar and adult book store and movie rental place along the strip. I wasn't ready to risk going in; if he saw me he'd do something, and I was sure it wouldn't be pretty. So I just drove around, used my equipment to check his movements, and recorded his journey.

He took three hours to make his way along the complete length of the Everglades strip. I had no idea what he was doing, or who he was talking to, but it seemed extremely odd for a detective to spend his shift in the way LeGrand was.

Finally, close to 2 a.m., LeGrand left a bar on the far west end of the Everglades strip, and headed back in the general direction of the police station. I headed back to Crescent Key. Sure enough, my screen told me that he made a non-stop trip to the cop shop, was there about fifteen minutes and then headed in the direction of his home.

According to the screen, we both arrived at our respective homes at the same time. I suspected that he went on to bed.

I know that I did.

Chapter 40

The next evening LeGrand and I did the same dance.

His itinerary: a few visits to outlying residential areas, then the slow journey along both strips. I kept a loose tail on him, only this time I ventured into several of the clubs after he'd left.

The interiors of the clubs were depressingly predictable: dark and smoky, garishly lit stages with women in various stages of undress, other dancers sitting at tables with men, drinking and smoking cigarettes. Waitresses in French-cut leotards, stockings and garters and lots of cleavage. Rock music just this side of ear-splitting, booze flowing, men looking dazed, waving dollar bills at the stage, dark corners where girls danced privately — and did more than dance — for men sitting against the wall.

At each place I got a seat at the bar, chatted with the dancers who came up, watched them drift away when they realized I wasn't going to open the wallet wide for them. I suspected that I looked enough like a cop that I discouraged a number of come-ons. At each place I had one drink, tipped neither too much nor too little, and made sure I gave a couple of dancers money for the jukebox. That way, I wouldn't raise too many suspicions; in fact, I doubted I would be remembered if I came back again.

LeGrand's itinerary was identical to the previous night: South along Dixie, west along Everglades. Then, after the last club, he stopped at a Waffle House. I drove by and eyed him through the plate-glass window. He was eating alone, and I fantasized about piping hot pancakes, warm, thick syrup, hash browns, steaming mugs of coffee. I scanned the interior of the Defender. Lots of surveillance gear, two empty McDonald's bags and three Styrofoam cups stained brown with dead coffee. And not a convenience store in sight.

Forty-five minutes after he'd entered the Waffle House he came out. I figured he'd head back to the station, so I let the tail get very loose. I was tagging along at least four blocks behind when suddenly the flashing locator cursor on the screen stopped moving. He'd stopped, but he wasn't far enough along Dixie to be at the intersection he'd normally take to the cop shop. I put my foot into it and in two minutes was driving along the block the stationary cursor led me to.

I found his car behind a bar in the middle of the block — Forbidden Dreams, it was called. I pulled the Defender into the far edge of the lot. I hunkered down and watched the front door.

And a few minutes later my evening got a lot more interesting.

Chapter 41

“Have you ever observed,” Lipscomb said, “how racial and urban stereotypes are so right on. I mean, like fulfilling the prophecy of the urban myth.”

I stared at the big detective. “You take a night course in social anthropology over at the J.C.?”

He laughed that big rumble. “There you go. See, you’ve responding by typing me. Large, black man, career police officer no less. Has to be a product of his darky upbringing. You can take the detective out of the ghetto, but you can’t take the ghet-to out a da nigger. Or something that.”

“Touché,” I said. “By the way, weren’t you brought up in some white-bread section of Ormand Beach?”

“Beside the point, mo-fo.” He leaned back in his chair and patted his ample belly. “Note, my man, that you called the meeting but I chose the place.”

He spread his arms expansively. “The Boar’s Butt BBQ — motto: None Too Clean — in the beautiful ethnic quarter of Emerald City. Do you feel a little out of place?”

“Wanna talk social anthropology?” I said, “Or do you want to hear about my scintillating evening with David LeGrand?”

Lipscomb nodded, chewing fiercely on a rib bone. “Lay it on me.”

I outlined the case so far, what he knew and what I’d come across since we’d last talked. I went into a great deal of detail about my meeting with Frederico Corcacan, the discussions I’d had with Galatea and what she’d recounted from her bar encounter. I told him — off the record — about what Wainwright had uncovered, and how Emerald City had neglected to call in the Feds. I spoke of my concerns about David LeGrand, and detailed how he spent his evening shifts.

“Last night I’m following LeGrand, a fairly close tail,” I said. “He does the usual routine, goes from one bar to another, stays for a little while, heads on down the strip.”

“Hard workin’ cop, he is.”

“After doing that for most of his shift, he goes in this one bar and a few minutes later comes out with a girl in tow. I figure he’s actually making an arrest, you know, look good on paper. But he puts the girl in the front seat and drives off. So I tag along and he drives all the way out of Emerald City, across Dixie, and into the outskirts of the inland side of Crescent Key. Not within corporate limits, but close. There are some upscale homes there, near the waterway.”

I had the detective’s full attention now. He nodded me on.

“LeGrand drops the girl off at this really spiffy house. It’s not big, but it’s obviously expensive, and it’s nestled in a hummock of trees and very dense foliage. Privacy from the neighbors. The girl uses a key and lets herself inside without knocking. LeGrand drives off.

“Now, with my tracking system, I have LeGrand nailed, so I figure it’s best to watch the house. Of course, I have to pee, so I hurry off to a nearby convenience store, bleed the lizard and pick up a six pack of beer. I head back and it looks the same, but I don’t know if anybody’s shown up while I was gone. I also don’t know who was already at the place.”

“Wow,’ Lipscomb said. “All this intrigue in our little piece of heaven. The suspense is killin’ me. What happened?”

“Well, I drank several of the beers and I have to pee again. But you already figured that. About an hour later a car pulls up in the driveway and kind of drives back under the shade of a big tree. Car wouldn’t be noticeable if you weren’t looking for it, and even then it would be hard to identify.

“Man gets out, does the suspicious I’m-not-really-supposed-to-be-here-so-I’ll-act-natural thing. Looks around a few times and saunters to the apartment.”

“Saunters?”

“Well, you get my point. He uses a key, goes in without knocking. He’s there about forty five minutes, then he comes out, looking really natural now. Gets in his car and leaves. About thirty minutes after that, LeGrand comes back in his plain vanilla wrapper, the girl comes out and they drive away. He takes her back to the club. End of story.”

At that point Lipscomb held up his beefy hands. “It doesn’t surprise me that LeGrand’s in on some kind of procuring operation. But do you honestly think LeGrand is involved with the murders?”

“No, at least not directly. Here’s what I do think. LeGrand and the boys over at Emerald City PD might like to solve the killings, but they want to do it on their own. They don’t want outsiders looking in. That’d get too close to all the nefarious stuff they got going on.”

Lipscomb grinned. “Nefarious?”

“Hey, it’s a way of life over there. In any event, I came away from my chat with Frederico Corcacan with the feeling that the killings were hurting his business. He’d like the cops to solve them, and in fact has most likely put some pressure on them to do so. Though from what he tells me, he has no confidence in them.”

“And since Corcacan controls a big chunk of the crime and cop operations,” Lipscomb said, “that puts the cops in an awkward position.”

I nodded. “Cops are kind of damned if they do, damned if they don’t.”

“Corcacan, too. If the killings don’t stop, his business suffers. If somebody looks too hard at the cops, his business suffers.”

“And since the Emerald City cops are largely incompetent, they might have a great deal of trouble solving the killings without some outside professionals.”

“All in all, Ollie, a big fuckin’ mess,” Lipscomb said. “And as interesting as all of this is, you already had it figured out. So why are we really having this meeting?”

“Well, I need your valuable insights, big guy.”

“Shit, man, you mean my official access to information.”

“Well, there is that,” I said. “I haven’t told you all of the connections between Shelly Travers and at least one of the dead hookers, maybe both. According to Travers’ cell phone records, she made a lot of calls to an unlisted number in Emerald City, mostly during the last few weeks of her life. She got a number of calls from the same number. It’s answered by a woman who simply repeats the last four digits of the phone number. I tried a couple of tricks but I can’t find out what sort of business this is.”

“But you have an idea.”

“I do. According to a source, one of the murder victims mentioned that she was working for a very discreet escort agency. I suspect that the number Shelly was calling is that agency. I know that Shelly was in the life at one time."

"Really." Lipscomb's eyebrows shot up. "This do get interesting."

"Did I mention that the club LeGrand got the girl from is a hangout for, among other lowlifes, more than a few transsexual hookers."

"Okay. Wonder if Corcacan knows about this?"

"I would think so," I said. "He made the point to me that the killings of those t-girls was bad for his business. So it stands to reason that Corcacan is running t-girls as part of his operation."

"Although, LeGrand could be freelancing. It's interesting that there might be some kind of very discreet call-girl operation going on, perhaps outside of Corcacan's influence."

"It would have to be somebody more powerful than Corcacan to get away with that."

"Well, hell," Lipscomb said. "Think about it. There are more than a few folks right on our little key that are more powerful than Frederico Corcacan. Money talks, brother."

In an odd way, it made sense. I would be making a mistake if I assumed that Corcacan was the top control dog. There were billions of dollars available here, and more than a few folks with too much time on their hands. LeGrand would freelance if he thought he could be protected from Corcacan's wrath. If Corcacan couldn't apply direct influence on a freelance operation it made sense that he might come to someone like me, an outsider. He wanted the murders stopped. Did he also want a freelance operation pulled down in the process? Oh, so much to think about.

"You know," Lipscomb said. "You still haven't said what you really want from me."

I took a piece of paper out of my breast pocket and handed it to the detective. "Could you run a check on this plate for me. I could come in to the station and do it, but I don't want to draw too much attention to myself right now."

Lipscomb looked at the number. "That's easy. What else?"

"How about finding out who that phone number I called belongs to. I've kinda used up my source at the phone company for now."

Lipscomb sighed. "Gimme the number."

I wrote it on the same piece of paper.

Lipscomb looked at me, shook his head. "Oh, and how about I run a check on the address on the possible hooker heaven, see what kind of owner pops up. And wait — while we're at it, should I run a check on the property where the club's located?"

"If it wouldn't be too much trouble," I said with as little guile as possible.

"You know," Lipscomb said, serious now. "You were my boss for a few years. You are one of the best cops I know. But you used to let it all get to you. Lose sleep, hell, one case you were losin' your hair. And that was in Emerald City. I can't imagine what you went through in Miami. How else can I help?"

His genuine warmth surprised me and touched me deeply. He was perhaps the only person I could call a friend. And I'd never even had him out to my home.

Chapter 42

On the phone he'd seemed like a nice enough guy. He'd made the effort to find his dog.

I wanted to kill him.

But I held my fire and instead opened my front door and nodded to him as he got out his car — a new Lexus, I noted — and walked onto the front porch.

I looked at Cool lying on the cool wood of the deck. He seemed content, happy. His chest rose and fell gently with his breathing.

I had done the right thing. Master and best friend would be reunited. I hated myself for placing that damned ad in the newspaper.

The wait for the man to come over had been agony. I'd sat quietly in the chair for awhile. Cool had sighed a couple if times, got up once and circled three times counterclockwise - the way he always circled - before he moved to a spot next to my chair. He'd sighed again, put his head on his forepaws and went back to sleep.

I had held on to the arms of the chair and stared off into distance of the ocean, waiting. I knew who was coming over; Cool didn't.

Now, three interminable hours after he'd contacted me, my caller stood a little uncertainly, it seemed to me, underneath the overhang. He told me his name was James Newell and that he was a banker who lived and worked in West Palm Beach.

"Got the dog for my kid," he said. "But I've really been the one who takes care of him, the dog I mean. Kid's way too interested in video games." Newell gave his head a quick shake and came into the house.

"Coo...ah, the dog's out back," I said, heading through the house to the deck. Newell followed. For a guy just about to get reunited with his beloved dog, he didn't seem all that enthusiastic.

I opened the screen door and held it for Newell. He stepped onto the deck, and looked down at Cool. Cool looked back, got up, stretched, walked over to the far edge of the deck, circled three times - counterclockwise - and lay back down.

I looked at Newell. Newell looked at the dog. Then he looked at me.

“You have a nice place here,” he said. “Out in the woods.” He took a couple of steps so he could better see the mangroves and palmettos that lead to the south shore. “I brought the dog to one of those little parks on the mainland side, first time I’d taken him near the water.” He smiled. “Dog romped in the surf for awhile, then he took off. I chased him but he’s not really that well trained. Guess you’ve noticed that.” He shrugged his shoulders. “Last I saw of him he was going full speed down the beach.”

Cool looked up at Newell, took in a deep breath and held it. Not relaxed like he was before, but keeping up a good front. Newell still hadn’t taken a step toward the dog.

I stood as still as I could, did my own version of controlled breathing. Tried to keep my eyes on Newell and not Cool. A wind picked up off the ocean and rustled the trees near the house, dropped the temperature a few degrees.

Cool got up, stretched again, walked across the deck and lay down again, this time with his nose on my boot.

Newell kept his place, glanced at the dog, then at the overgrown wilderness that was my yard. Then he looked at me.

“I appreciate all the trouble you’ve gone to for Wellington.” Wellington, I thought. Good God. “And he seems to have grown attached to you.” He looked out at my property again. “You have a great place here for a dog. Water, woods......” Just then a squirrel darted across the far edge of the deck and like a shot Cool was off the boards and into the brush. Newell laughed. “And critters that need managing.”

“He does seem to like it here.”

“My son, he isn’t interested. I have no time, and all we have is a small yard.”

Cool ambled back onto the porch, tongue lolling. He flopped down against my leg, panting.

Newell knelt down, patted the dog on the head. “How do you feel about keeping him?”

I said that I would.

Newell stood up. "I think he would do well here. He really does seem to have become attached to you."

"And I to him," I said.

"Yes, I can see that, Mr. Landers. I have papers on him that I'll be happy to drop in the mail."

"That would be great," I said. "Let me get my check book. . ."

He cut me off with a wave of his hand. "No. You've already had expenses. You took him to the vet, you ran the ads. Besides, this isn't an issue of money. I really do want to see him happy. He is a pretty neat dog."

Got that right, I thought.

We exchanged cards. Newell bent down. For a moment it seemed that his eyes got damp. He stroked the dog and said, "You're a sweetheart. You be good. You have a nice man to take care of you."

Newell got up, quickly wiped the back of his hand over his eyes. "Thank you, Mr. Landers. I think this will work out really well for Wellington."

Not to mention Landers.

After I had walked Newell to his car and watched him drive away I went back to the deck. Cool had gotten into my chair and was fast asleep.

I said, "Wellington?" He didn't budge. I said, "Cool?" He cut his eyes up to me, sighed as deeply as a dog could sigh, got up, lumbered out of the chair, came around in front of me, sat, and raised a paw.

I grinned and shook it. "Okay, my friend, Too Cool it is. Forever."

Chapter 43

Her voice was quiet but urgent, over the phone line.

"She's back, Samuel."

Galatea. Calling from the bar.

"Who's back?" I asked.

The call had awakened me from an unscheduled nap, and I felt disoriented and thick. I glanced at my watch. A little after 7 p.m. LeGrand, whom I was planning to follow that night for lack of anything else to do, would already be well into his nightly routine.

"The woman, the hooker. You know, the girl I told you about."

It took me a moment to put it together. "The one who got drunk and spilled her guts?"

"Yes. When I saw her come in, I hit up Samantha to give me bartender duty. I'm feeding her drinks. She's relatively sober now but I don't expect that to last."

"Okay," I said. "Keep her going, let her talk. Try to engage her and don't let her get away. Buy her drinks, do whatever you have to do. I'm coming over. When I do, pretend like you don't know me. I might come to the bar. I might get a table. I'd like to watch her a little before I decide how I want to handle this."

I took the world's quickest shower, jumped into Wranglers, work shirt, and sneakers, slipped the Sig under my waistband and headed to the door. I hurled some biscuits in Cool's direction as I went through the door and yelled "Stay cool, Cool."

The trip from my place to Galatea's bar normally takes about half an hour. I made it in twenty minutes, partly through luck, partly because of some serious downward pressure from my right foot.

The parking lot was three-quarters full. Inside the crowd was happy-hour in nature — quite a few people still dressed in work duds, knocking down two-for-ones and congregating around the food table. The noise level was rising with the size of the tabs.

I stood just inside the door and scanned the room. My eyes met Galatea's, and she gave me the merest hint of a nod. Then she sat a glass down in front of a woman sitting alone at the bar.

I looked her over. In the dim light — hell, have you ever been in a bar that wasn't dim? — she looked pretty good. Lots of blonde hair piled up on her head, a real Texas-style, big-hair do. Her skin appeared tan. She wore a lime-green dress that hugged her body. The side I could see was split high with a lot of leg showing. She wore white pumps with heels that could have been six inches high.

There was an empty seat to her right, then two seats taken by patrons who were chatting with each other. Beyond them, the bar made an L-turn and there was an empty seat on that side. I went over and took it. I was far enough away that I could observe without being obvious. I was close enough to see her in detail, and perhaps catch some snatches of conversation.

Galatea turned out to be quite an actress. She came over to me like it was the first time she'd ever laid eyes on me. "Hey big boy, first time here?" She gave me a huge smile. Flirting with me.

I said I'd been around a time or two, told her I'd never seen her here. She gave me another grin and said, "Hope it won't be the last time."

I ordered bourbon on the rocks. Galatea made a show of selecting a top-shelf bottle and pouring it with a flourish. She sat it down beside me and said, "Hey cowboy, why don't you move down to this empty seat and join me and my friend here. We're just making girl talk."

I stared at her. "Well, sure," I answered.

She whisked up my drink before I had a chance to grab it, walked down the length of the bar and sat it at the empty stool next to the solitary woman. I came around and took my seat.

The woman didn't fair nearly as well on closer inspection. The tan turned into a leathery patina. Her features were coarse, the forehead broad and the jaw strong. There might have been a hint of an Adam's apple, but I'd been around so many transgendered people in the last few days, I didn't trust my judgment. Everybody looked suspect to me these days.

Galatea gave me another “howdy partner” grin and said, “I’ve made two new friends tonight, and I don’t know either of your names.” She raised her eyebrows at me.

Taken aback, I said, “Ah, Tom.”

“Tom. That’s a fine name, Tom.” Nicely sarcastic.

She turned to the woman. “And what about you, honey?”

The woman had been swiveling her head between Galatea and me. “Trina,” she answered. Her high pitched voice sounded forced and unnatural.

“Well, Trina, meet Tom. Tom — Trina.” Another big grin. “Isn’t this nice?”

I wanted to brain her.

The glass in front of Trina was filled with ice and an amber liquid. Trina hefted it to her mouth, and downed it in three gulps. She put the empty glass back down on the bar, hitting glass to wood a little too hard. “Hit me again,” she said to Galatea.

Galatea took a bottle of well-brand scotch and poured Trina a stiff one. She sat it on the bar and Trina eyed it like a hawk contemplating a sparrow.

For a little while Galatea chatted about this and that: bright conversation about the weather and how much she loved the Journey song playing on the sound system. She asked me about myself, phrasing her questions so I’d see what was coming and have time to frame an answer. For the night’s purpose, I was Tom and I worked in some facet of the insurance business. I was divorced, had a bitch of an ex-wife and a kid out in Des Moines who didn’t bother to write very often. I was bored, I was a nice guy, and hey, we all like to explore new interests, we’d seen some of those interesting women on Jerry Springer. I respected other people, no matter what they chose to do with their lives. And it didn’t hurt to be looking for a little action.

Trina did a lot of nodding when I told my spur-of-the-moment life story. She threw in a few you rocks, ain’t that the way it ises, and I can understand wanting a little action.

Then Galatea deftly shifted the conversation onto the reason for our charade.

“You know,” she said, “I’ve just been going on and on about all these little trivial things. But just before you got here, Tom, Trina had started to tell me how things weren't going so good right now for, you know, girls like us."

"Got that right, honey," Trina said. A sad look passed across her face. The timbre of her voice was dancing around now, settling on a contrived contralto. "Bad time to be a t-girl." She turned to me and grinned. "Bet you didn't know I was one a' those, did you?" Behind her, Galatea rolled her eyes.

"No kidding?" I said. "That's pretty interesting."

She took another drink, more of a sip this time. Another dark look colored her face. She swirled the liquid in the drink and ice cubes clinked.

Galatea said, "C'mon, talk to him. Tell him about it."

Trina cut a glance to me. Galatea said, "Hey, it's okay. I can tell already, Tom's good people."

Trina finished off her drink and looked longingly at the empty tumbler, then at Galatea, who smiled, took her glass and without a word filled it up again. Single-malt stuff this time.

Galatea sat the drink down and Trina smiled, the dark look commuted and the dark thoughts forgotten. She raised the glass, "To good people."

I figured Trina was past the point of inhibition; I hoped I could get some information before she became completely incoherent. I said, "What do you mean, bad things are happening?"

Trina nodded to Galatea. "Shit man — I mean girl — you tell him what I told you."

Galatea leaned in toward me and dropped her voice to a conspiratorial whisper. "Tom, have you heard about the girls who've been killed recently?"

"What? No, I haven't heard anything." I tried to sound shocked. "Who were they?"

"Prostitutes," Trina said thickly.

Galatea rolled her eyes again. "Trina says that two local t-girls, working girls, you know, have been murdered within the last couple of months in Emerald City."

"Three," Trina said. "Just that the third one, dint hava dick anymore."

Galatea picked up Trina's now-empty glass. "I'll buy you this one, hon'."

"Heavy stuff," I said. "You know any of the girls, Trina?"

"Fuckin' A." She stared toward the mirror behind the bar. She was wasted, and I doubted we'd get much more out of her.

"Trina worked for the same escort agency as one of the dead girls," Galatea said calmly.

Trina nodded sharply. I saw that tears had wet her cheeks. I felt like a vulture.

"Do they think the same guy killed all these girls?" I asked.

Galatea said, " Trina knows a couple of cops, she told me. She says one mentioned it, kind of in passing. When she asked him for more information, he clammed up."

"What's the cop's name," I asked, and regretted it as soon as I'd said it. There'd be no reason for "Tom" to want to know that.

But Trina missed it entirely. "LeGrand. David Fuckin' such-a-big-shit LeGrand. Like the chief in-fucking-vestigator in the killin's."

"I'm sure he's doing all he can to find the killer."

"Sure," Trina said. "Just so's it don't fuck up his action."

Galatea glanced down the length of the bar and noticed that at least four patrons were gesturing to her. "Oh, oh," she said. "Neglecting the paying customers." She went that way to take orders.

Trina cut a couple of glances at me. I could only wonder at how much booze she'd put away. She wasn't particularly coherent, but she was at least conscious. Sort of.

"I'll buy you another drink, Trina." I leaned toward her. "And maybe you'll tell me how I can get in touch with that escort agency so you and I, you know, could get together."

She snickered and gave me the once-over. "No way you can get me through that agency. It's like private, you gotta have a code and be referred and all." She cast a knowing look at me. "And you gotta be, you know, like really rich."

"Damn," I said. "That's too bad. I was hoping we might get together sometime. I'll bet you could show me a thing or two."

She let out a laugh that sounded like cloth ripping. "A thing or two is right. Tell ya what, I'll give you my home number. That way we can get together without the middleman." And she reached over and grabbed my crotch.

I swallowed hard and moved her hand as gently as I could away from me. She didn't seem to notice. She was doing her best to keep her blurry gaze fixed on me. "A thing or two," she said again.

I turned to watch as Galatea returned. When I turned back to Trina she had put her head down on the bar and was softly snoring.

Chapter 44

Galatea roused Trina long enough to elicit her phone number and address. Twenty minutes later we were helping the semi-comatose hooker out of the bar and into a cab.

The driver protested, but Galatea convinced him with her huge smile, two twenty dollar bills and an address that was less than two miles away. The last we saw of Trina was her head lolling against the window, mouth open, eyes closed.

"God," Galatea said. "I feel like a heel feeding her those drinks."

"And I feel like a pervert," I said. I told her about my seductive overtures and the crotch-grabbing interlude.

"Well, Samuel, what you grab is what you get." She immediately turned crimson, which she always seemed to do whenever anything the least bit risqué slipped out.

We went back inside the bar. Galatea found the other bartender and begged off for the rest of the night.

"Let's go eat somewhere nice, Samuel." Not a question. And off she went, out the front door, with me tagging along.

We drove to Palm Beach and wound up on the open-air patio of an popular Italian restaurant.

"I'm confused and frankly overwhelmed by this case. I feel like I'm in way over my head," I said as I watched her tear happily into a large, steamed artichoke.

She patted my hand. "Why don't you just talk to me about it? Maybe we can sort some of this out together."

"Okay. Well, point number one, we have three deaths. Two victims who were pre-op transsexual prostitutes and one post-op who had once been in the life, had gotten out of it, and more than likely was back in again."

Galatea nodded, held up two fingers. "Number two. Don't forget the girl who called you, she wasn't a transsexual but had the size and physical characteristics to suggest the possibility. Her john lost interest as soon as he discovered she was, ah, all woman."

"Number three," I said. "We have the fact that the Emerald City PD doesn't want any outside help in the investigation. Which leads me to believe they have something to hide, which might be something to do with the murders, but more likely it's just that the boys over there don't want their den of corruption exposed."

"Good so far," Galatea said, gamely jabbing for the heart of the decimated artichoke. "What's next?"

"Number four — did I tell you about my visit with the dwarf?"

She snorted. "Dwarf?" Her eyes twinkled. "No. You did not."

I told her about my meeting with Corcacan. I downplayed the part about crowning his goon with the pewter wastebasket.

"I think I might have seen that guy, Corcacan, around," she said. "Always wears a tux — right?"

"That's the guy," I said. "A real piece of work. Shortest made guy I ever met."

"And you think he might even be on our side in this?" She shook her head. "With friends like that . . ." she said. "Which brings us to number five. Our new friend Trina. She's definitely pre-op and has been in the business for awhile. That means she's a potential target for the killer, Samuel."

"And she works for an escort agency that is extremely low profile and very exclusive. She takes one look at me and essentially tells me I'm not rich enough to qualify as a customer, at least through the agency."

"But," and Galatea smiled at this at this, "she did give you her home number. You have an open invitation for some off the books action."

"Oh. Boy. Anyway, and I guess this is number six, at least one of the girls who was murdered had worked for that same agency."

"Anything else?"

"When you call the phone number I found in Shelly Travers's phonebook, a sexy-sounding chick answers, says 'six, five four seven' and that's all."

"Didn't Trina say something about needing a password?" Galatea said.

"Yep," I said. "Which we don't have. But I've been following LeGrand. He picked up a girl at a bar and drove her in his police cruiser to a very secluded house on the Intracoastal and dropped her off. I staked it out and got pictures of some men with expensive cars coming and going."

"The pad the agency uses to hook up the johns and the hookers," she said.

"Probably," I said. "What do you think of this idea — what if the agency is actually owned and run by the customers, like a private sex club? And the place is their members-only club house."

"I think it makes a lot of sense," she said. "They could really control who knows about it that way." I noticed that since the demise of the artichoke heart, she was working her way through the basket of rolls. I motioned to the waiter. "So, number seven, an assumption, but a good one — LeGrand is hooked up in this somehow."

"I wonder if LeGrand is running the girls himself, or if he just helped set it up and handles, err, security. Either way, I'm sure he wouldn't want a pesky little murder investigation to blow the lid on his lucrative prostitution racket."

"And," Galatea said, "think about where we live, Samuel. If a group of local citizens went together and purchased property on the water, if they're bankrolling a secret escort service or call-girl ring for their private use, it stands to reason that the membership would be comprised of some of our extremely wealthy and influential Palm Beach citizens."

"Or Crescent Key."

"Of course," she said. "Even richer, more powerful and reclusive."

Our salads came, and we worked at them in silence for a little while. Then I said, "This could be very big, if it involves any of our billionaire residents."

She nodded, and used her napkin to dab a dribble of salad dressing off her chin. "Rich johns, kinky call girls, crooked cops, a serial killer. Sounds like a Harold Robbins novel."

"Only worse," I said. "Real people are getting killed."

The main courses were delivered in time to distract us from those sobering thoughts. Over our meal, we slipped into a comfortable exchange of small talk. Galatea talked a little about her job, told me about some “ah ha’s” as she called them, that she had experienced in her support group.

And then, before I realized I was speaking my questions out loud, I said, “Galatea, where do you go next with . . .” my voice trailed off.

“That’s a valid question,” she said. “I think you need to know these things, Samuel.”

And as she said it, I realized that I did.

“A little history first,” she said. “I started the process about three years ago.” She gave me a little smile and said, “I’ll save the ‘before’ story, you know, what led me to my decision, for another time. Anyway, three years ago I made the decision to live my life as my true gender, to live as a woman. I didn’t care if I ended up the most half-assed-looking woman in the world, I was going to be true to myself.”

I smiled. You don’t look half-assed at all.

She pushed her plate away from her. “I know MaryAnne was pretty upfront with you about her story. She and I are both fortunate. We weren’t built like linebackers to start with. We didn’t look like Bigfoot. Thank God.

“But even with a slight build and not too much body hair, the process of transformation has been an ordeal.

“Did you know that at one time I was quite a successful businessman? When I started the transition, I dressed as a woman only at home, trying to get used to the feel of it. I still worked and lived as a man outside the house.”

Her use of the word “man” in reference to herself was startling, but I just nodded.

“I imagine the people I worked with thought I might be gay. I never had girlfriends. I kept to myself. I suppose I had feminine mannerisms.”

She laughed softly. “What am I saying -- of course I did. I was a woman, and I was determined to eventually live like one.

“And I did, more and more. I went into therapy with Dee Dee, and she helped me emotionally and psychologically. At first I worked on dressing as a woman, using makeup, learning how to walk. Then I started taking small trips, like to the grocery store or the mall, as a woman. God, I felt like a freak. I was sure everyone was staring at — laughing at — this weirdo walking around in public.”

I thought, God, what a nightmare. Then: What incredible

perseverance.

She was talking. ". . .gradually built up a little confidence. Most of the time I made sure when I went out I headed somewhere out of town."

She gave me one of those sad smiles. "I am making this a long story. I'm sorry. But I want you to know."

I nodded and swallowed. I wanted to know, but it was hard to hear.

"I started hormone treatments as soon as I could," she said. "That's about the same time I quit my job. I simply dropped out of one world and into another. I got a job at the bar — I must have looked a sight back then — and started hanging out with other transsexuals.

"I had some money saved, so I went ahead with the electrolysis treatment and some of the sculpting surgery. I didn't elect breast augmentation. I figured I'd just let the hormones do their thing. I did have some body sculpting on my hips and throat. But mainly I just got better and better at being myself. Not just acting like a woman, or dressing like a woman, but truly being a woman."

She paused and sighed deeply, and took a long drink of water. "And that brings us up to where I am today."

Another smile. "And to your question. What next?"

She smiled at me again, and this time there was no sadness there. "What next is getting closer to being a reality. Sexual-reassignment. Do you want to hear about that?"

I wasn't at all sure that's what I wanted, but I nodded anyway.

"At one time it was extremely difficult to find a doctor in the United States to do it. People spent many thousands of dollars and ended up under God-knows-what-kind-of-doctor's knife." She shuddered. "Now more and more docs have the vision to understand why this type of surgery is viable and why it's needed. It's still very expensive, and most doctors won't do it until you've lived as the appropriate gender for a few years and undergone extensive therapy.

"And I've done that, maybe not quite long enough, but Dee Dee and my doctors say I'm getting close to being ready. I have most of the money for the operation saved up." She smiled at me, sadness there again. "God, Samuel, it has taken so long. So very long. I love what I'm becoming, but I hate the way I am now. It's almost as if I have two bodies. I look in the mirror. That's me I'm looking at. I think like a woman, I feel like a woman. Look like a woman. Hell, I have always been a woman. But part of my body is still male – and it's just not me. It doesn't belong." She put her head in her hands. "I hate it."

Then she looked up and said, "Does this help you understand how incredibly difficult people like Trina have it?"

People like Shelly Travers, too, I thought. I nodded. I had no idea how to put in words what I felt.

Instead, I did something that astonished me completely. I raised up out of my chair and leaned over the table. I brushed my lips over Galatea's forehead. Then I kissed her, gently, on her lips.

She must have been as astonished as I. When I sat back down, she simply stared at me for a moment. Then tears welled in her eyes and flowed down her cheeks. And still she looked at me.

She made no attempt to wipe the tears. She just reached her hand across the table and covered mine. She said, "Samuel, I've never had a kiss mean so much. I love you for who you are, and I respect you immensely." She squeezed my hand tightly. "I'm very fortunate to have you for a friend."

No more fortunate than me, I thought. No more fortunate than me.

Chapter 45

"I need a plan," I said.

We had left the restaurant and were walking to the Defender, which was several blocks away. Along our stroll we shopped the windows of a newsstand and a place that specialized in extremely expensive casual clothes in various sherbet hues. Several times, while peering in the windows, I felt Galatea's hand or hip brush against me. It might have been by accident. I hoped it was, for the nearness caused me some tension.

In the car she said, "A plan. Any ideas?"

I eased into the insignificant traffic and said, "Would you like to ride down the beach road? We can cut over a few miles down. It might be pleasant."

She reached over and smiled and patted my arm. "I'd like that."

So we drove south on A1A through the little downtown area of Palm Beach. What passes for downtown is really just a few blocks dotted with private banks and brokerage firms in unassuming stucco buildings. Then you come to the world-famous Worth Avenue, one of the two or three most exclusive shopping areas in the world. I cut down Worth for three blocks, and I counted five Rolls Royces, four Bentleys, including one new convertible, three Ferraris, one Lamborghini and at least two dozen Jaguars.

"We are among them," Galatea said, "but we are not of them."

The Defender suddenly seemed like a lumbering oaf. I made a couple of turns, got back on County and headed south again. Soon we were driving along a narrow road that bordered heavily wooded estates with high fences and locked gates.

A few miles later, after a few hard twists and turns, we left the big gates and huge hedges and could see the ocean. Then came the low condos of South Palm Beach. Eventually those gave way to more palatial estates. Welcome to East Florida living. To paraphrase Everett Dirksen, a few billion here, a few billion there, and the first thing you know, you're talking real money.

After we passed one of the roads leading off the beach to Lantana — home of the National Inquirer and the post 9-11 anthrax scare — I turned off the air conditioner and rolled down my window. Galatea followed my lead, and we were inundated by the rush of wind and the relative coolness of the ocean air. The scent of the water and beach was intoxicating.

I slowed down to about 25 miles an hour, a little under the posted limit, and the wind subsided a bit. We could talk without shouting.

"A plan," she prompted again.

I glanced at my watch. "I'm waiting for some information from a detective I know. I'm trying to get the phone records of the first two girls who were killed. I'm also trying to get copies of the complete police reports. I wrote down a couple of license plate numbers from cars that visited the Intracoastal party pad — I want to get those checked out, too. And I'm having somebody look at some pictures I took out there. It's not much of a plan, but it's all I have to go on right now."

"Not much?" she said. "It sounds like a lot. And you haven't really had any help at all."

"Not true." I smiled. "I've had you and MaryAnne, and my detective friend and the FBI profiler. I've got a damn good team helping me." And Cool. Couldn't forget Too Cool, my crime fighting canine.

She smiled back. "And don't forget Trina."

"Right," I said. "There is Trina. I doubt we've heard the last of her."

"When are you going to see your cop friend?"

"The FBI profiler is flying in the morning. After I pick him up, I want to set up a meeting with him, the detective and me. The FBI man is here on his own hook. My detective friend is also helping me off the record. And of course I have no official standing, so we really don't have much leverage."

"But by tomorrow you'll have some phone records and tag information. Maybe you'll even learn something from the pictures you took. That's a lot."

I shrugged. "Maybe, but none of it seems to be getting me any closer to the person who killed those two girls and Shelly Travers."

Galatea said, "So what about LeGrand? You've been tailing him every night?"

I nodded and glanced at my watch. "He's only halfway through his shift." I gestured to the gear in the back seat. "I can track his car electronically. I'll catch up with him and tag along some more after I take you home."

"Take me home, hell," she said. "Tonight, I'm coming along."

Chapter 46

So she did. We caught up with LeGrand halfway down Dixie. His unmarked cruiser was parked in the back lot of a nudie bar aptly named the Barely There.

Galatea motioned me over to the side of the road fifty feet from the bar's main entrance. "Wait here," she commanded and was out the door and headed into the bar before I could stop her.

Five minutes later she was back. "Fire up the A/C, boy, it's hot in there. Naked, too."

"God, Galatea, what the hell did you think you were doing —"

She cut me off with an upturned palm. "Hey, hotshot. Think about it. You can't go in there because LeGrand knows you. I can go inside all these places because he doesn't know me. And I'll bet there're folks in every one of these places I'll know."

I started to protest, but I had the sudden revelation that arguing with the woman when she was strident would be fruitless.

"Fuck," I muttered. What I meant was, I don't want you to get hurt.

"I'm not going to argue with you over this, Samuel. I can help you. I know what you're thinking, but this is fine. I'm not going to do anything to raise his suspicions. I'm not gonna get myself in trouble. What I am going to do is see who he talks to in a few of these places. I'm gonna see if I know any of these people. Maybe we can go back and talk to them later. I'm especially gonna see if he connects with either bar managers or hookers. I can get close to him in these places without him ever knowing it."

"Won't you stand out in there?" I said a little lamely.

"You mean, because I'm wearing clothes?" She laughed. "You've been in those places. They're filled with hookers and off-duty dancers all the time. I'm just another chick." She said it as if she was very proud of being just another chick.

The interior of the Defender was a jumble of wires and equipment. I had my laptop propped precariously on the console with a cord running to the cigarette lighter. Another line out the side of the laptop connected the cell phone, which was lying next to Galatea's thigh. The screen of the laptop lit the interior with a greenish glow. In my lap was the night scope and the long-lens camera.

I looked at Galatea in the green luminescence. I wasn't sure what having her go in the clubs would accomplish, but I had already become familiar with LeGrand's nightly routine, and I wasn't particularly interested in reprising the monotonous scenario yet again. Nor did I see how just going inside and looking around could put her in any danger.

So we parked a block down from a strip of bars on LeGrand's venue, and Galatea followed him inside each one as he made his rounds. She assured me she was careful not to be obvious so he wouldn't sense the tail.

At two places LeGrand ordered drinks he didn't pay for, nodded to a few people, and made what appeared to be small talk with the bartender and a couple of dancers. He stayed no more than fifteen minutes in either bar.

In the third club, Galatea noticed that an oily-looking man came out of a back room and signaled LeGrand. The cop followed the man down a hallway and they entered a room, maybe an office, together. Ten minutes later LeGrand came out alone and headed back to the bar. He was smoothing his coat, and Galatea wondered if he had put something in the inside pocket. As he approached his chair, she got a good look at him, and he seemed unsteady and dazed. He walked a little past his seat and had to backtrack. His movements seemed too controlled, she thought, like he was trying to look normal.

"Betcha he got treated to a few lines of nose candy back there," Galatea said as we traveled down Dixie. I hated to have to agree with her.

I decided to cut loose from the close tail for awhile. I didn't want LeGrand to make Galatea. So we went to a 7-Eleven, fueled up on coffee and some Little Debbie cakes and let LeGrand find his own way onto Everglades.

"God," I said as we picked up his trail again, following along a few blocks behind. "Doesn't he have to answer to anybody at the station? He obviously isn't spending much time on any real police work. His arrest record has to stink. Hell, I haven't even seen him write a ticket."

"Maybe he's doing some — heh heh — sniffing around in the drug business."

The LeGrand-blip on my screen stopped moving. I figured he was stopping at a low-class joint a little ways ahead called the Pussycat Club. I pulled over as usual and Galatea took off.

The tail was tedious, and I was tired from the long day. Neither LeGrand nor Galatea came out for awhile, so I retrieved the scanner from the back seat and switched it on.

To a very quiet hell breaking loose.

I almost missed it at first, but then I began to make out the gist of several transmissions.

Deja Vu. Patrol units had called for assistance at a duplex on the north side of Emerald City. The original call apparently had been a report of a disturbance, but for some reason there had been a delay in dispatching units. Now I heard a couple of extremely agitated voices.

And then — silence. Strange to go from more than the usual amount of chatter to dead air.

I shook the scanner — nothing was loose. I checked the batteries — plenty of juice. I checked the squelch and volume. No problem there. Either I had misread the urgency of the chatter, or the cops intentionally had silenced their transmissions. Radio and television stations monitor the emergency and police frequencies regularly. Some even scan the medical examiner's and detectives' bandwidths. I was beginning to believe the cops didn't want anybody to know about this one.

I set the scanner back in the seat, and looked up just as LeGrand hurried out the door of the bar. He got in his car and squealed the tires heading out of the parking lot. In a moment Galatea came out.

She got in the car looking a little bewildered.

"Something's going down," I said, nodding toward the scanner. "What happened inside?"

"His pager went off. It must have been some kind of emergency code because he looked like he'd swallowed a hot poker. He beat it to the door and the pager started going off again just as he left."

"Mmm. I don't like this. The call came from a location north of here. Could be nothing, but . . . let's go."

She was still buckling up as I hit the gas and skidded out onto Everglades. I kept the screen on and followed LeGrand's quickly changing position.

A few blocks later another police car, running without lights or siren, hurtled by me going well over the speed limit. In a big hurry, but still not wanting to draw attention. The cruiser almost clipped my front bumper cutting back in front of me. I pulled my foot off the accelerator and cut a glance toward Galatea. She sat ramrod straight, peering straight ahead through the Defender's huge windshield. Her face was drawn tight.

I slowed down when we were a block away from the disturbance. The neighborhood was a mix of frame houses and small four-and-eight-plexes. The yards, what I could see of them in the darkness, were overgrown and ragged with weeds. The cars in the driveways and scattered in the apartment-house lots were a assortment of old American models — beat-up Cadillacs and Oldsmobiles — and ratty-looking foreign jobs, Datsuns and Toyotas and Hondas. I glimpsed a couple of motorcycles peeking out from under canvas covers. Ragged tarps and plastic garbage bags half-covered missing car windows, and duct tape seemed to be the number one customizing statement.

I took a slow turn around the block. When I turned onto Eastfield, where the disturbance call had come from, the scene was bizarre. At least seven patrol cars were grouped in the middle of the block, parked haphazardly and blocking any traffic that might try to get by. But only one of the cruisers had its lights popping. And just as I registered this piece of information, those lights went out. With no street lights to improve visibility, I could make out only shadowy human forms moving about among the cars and in front of one side of a duplex. Like a stage crew hurriedly making a set change between acts.

Neighbors had spilled out into the yards and street to watch the action, but a couple of cops had blocked them from getting close enough to see anything. I eased in behind a massive '70s model Pontiac with multicolor fenders and cut the Defender's ignition and lights. We sat there a moment, listening to the cooling ticks of the engine. As my eyes adjusted to the darkness I could better make out the scene.

What I saw continued to strike me as odd. Beyond the marked cruisers were two unmarked cars and an unlit Emerald City ambulance. I saw a man who seemed to be directing things standing beside an unmarked, talking to a small knot of other men in suits and casual clothes.

I reached behind me and picked up the night scope; I'd almost forgotten about it. I turned on the ignition and rolled down the windows; the air outside was only slightly less stifling than what had built up in the interior. I zeroed in on the little group and focused. There, captured by the scope's ghastly green-white light, was LeGrand. His expression was severe. He was talking and gesturing a little wildly, and after a minute a uniform and a suit nodded vigorously and headed off toward the duplex. The others drifted off toward the cars. LeGrand stood there a minute, staring at the duplex. He shook his head, then kicked the side of the unmarked car hard, definitely hard enough to dent it if he caught it right. Then he spat and started walking toward the duplex.

Galatea said, "What the fuck is going on?" Then, in a small voice, "ah, sorry."

"This is strange," I said. "I've been on a lot of crime scenes and this just isn't typical. Lots of cars, uniformed officers and detectives, but no lights. And LeGrand is pissed."

Then I heard motors begin to fire up, and within minutes six of the seven marked cruisers drove off slowly, one after another. That left LeGrand's car and another unmarked, and the ambulance.

I scanned the area with the scope and saw two men carrying cases that looked like big fishing tackle boxes. The paramedics. They loaded their equipment in the ambulance and got in the cab. Then the ambulance's motor fired up and the unit eased off down the street, very quietly.

Then a detective came out to one of the unmarked cars and got in. He too drove off.

That left a grand total of one car — LeGrand's.

Then I put the scope on the front door of the apartment. Two patrol officers stood on the porch. Odd. They'd been left behind.

As I thought about this, the two cops moved out to the street. They confronted the few neighbors still outside, made a few gestures, and the people began heading back to their homes.

Two men passed by the Defender, taking swigs out of cans hidden in paper bags. “Fuckin’ Miriam’s drunk again,” one said. His companion said, “So why the fuck they need so many cops?”

“Cops,” the first guy said. “They hear about a little somethin’ happening around here and they haul ass. Fuckin’ gotta roust all of us.”

That got them both to laughing. I heard one say, “That fuckin’ Miriam. Would you wanna fuck that?” And his friend said, “You’d more likely get fucked yourself. Don’t you know that ugly ol’ whore’s got her a cock, man? Shee-it!”

And in the Defender I said, “Shee-it!”

And Galatea said, “Did I hear what I think I heard?”

I nodded. “The Emerald City boys, and LeGrand in particular, are clearly sitting on this one hard.” I looked at Galatea in the shadows. “There’s a maniac on the loose and they don’t want anyone to know about it.”

I saw tears on Galatea’s cheeks. “A maniac,” she said in a very quiet voice. “A maniac hunting down women — just like me.”

Chapter 47

Galatea said, "How could Emerald City keep a crime like this, a murder, a secret?"

We were following about half a mile behind LeGrand. I hardly needed to watch the screen; I knew where he was headed.

We'd hung around the crime scene a few minutes longer, but I thought the Defender would start to be more obvious once the action died down. I did a circle of the neighborhood once, and when I swung back by the scene, an unmarked black van was just pulling up. I knew what that meant. No reason to stick around now.

"I've been thinking about that," I said. "It's not as hard as it might seem. I noticed that after a few transmissions, the cops went totally off the air. I'm sure they switched to cell phones pretty quickly. And did you notice who was at the scene? Emerald City cops. An Emerald City ambulance."

"But don't they have to call in the people who, you know, take the body away and find out how she died?"

"Even in that Emerald City can keep a secret. They're an oddity around here," I said. "Did you see that black van that drove up right as we went by the last time? That belongs to Emerald City. They don't use the country medical examiner's office. They have their own staff and an elected coroner. God only knows who does the autopsies. I doubt if it's state of the art."

"So if Emerald City wants to keep things quiet, it's not that difficult for them," Galatea said. "They don't have to rely on resources outside their jurisdiction?"

"Right. And I'm sure they haven't set it up that way by accident."

We drove a few blocks in silence, bathed in the chill of the air conditioner. Then I said, "I've been running through every possibility of who could be killing these women. Of course David LeGrand himself has come to mind more than once. He's a hard son of a bitch. He's dirty, and he's obviously tied up in this hooker mess somehow. But after tonight I guess I'll have to rule him out as the killer."

Galatea looked at me. "Why?"

"We've had him under surveillance most of the night. If he killed, ah, Miriam, he'd have had to have done it quite a bit earlier. But earlier in the day I know he was at home."

"You didn't check on him while we were eating dinner."

"I know, but his pattern just doesn't fit. He followed the same pattern today. Stay home, go out, hit the bars. And — either the surprise we saw on his face when he got the call tonight was genuine or he is one hell of a gifted actor."

She nodded. "He truly seemed shocked when he looked at his pager."

"And the way he looked at the scene. It was as if he was thinking, oh God, not again. He was clearly angry and frustrated. The killings are increasing, and they're cutting into whatever good thing he's got going on."

Another nod from Galatea. "You aren't driving like you're paying attention to the computer. You know where you're going, don't you?"

I told her about LeGrand's probable destination. "It was important that he secure the scene. Now it's important that he get over to his little hideaway. Maybe to deliver news. Maybe to find out who is there, and who isn't. Hell, I don't know. I've just about given up on doing anything in this case except following along."

She reached over and patted my thigh. "Seems I saw a show on TV once where the famous detective said the same thing, that good detective work is just tagging along and seeing what develops."

I glanced in the back seat, then at the iPad, scanner and camera. "Hell of an expensive way to tag along, ain't it."

Ten minutes later we drove by the house on the Intracoastal. LeGrand's car was barely visible behind the structure. I couldn't tell if other cars were parked back there or not. I glanced at my watch. It was nearly 4:00 a.m. and the place was deader than Des Moines. A couple of dim lights shown through curtained windows. I saw no movement. I nosed the Defender in behind the trees that had provided cover before. We sat in the dark and waited. Again, I could see no other house lights nearby. But with the windows down we could hear the soft distant sound of water slapping against a sea wall, and here the sea breeze cooled the air.

We waited ten minutes, sitting silently. Then I saw sudden movement behind the house. LeGrand's car began to nose slowly around the back corner. Its headlights were out. The car edged along the drive bordered by the big hedge. Then, still running without lights, it pulled onto the road. As it gathered speed it drove within ten feet of where we were hiding.

I watched the car pass. LeGrand was not alone now; I caught a glimpse of a man sitting in the passenger's seat. As the car passed it was caught in the sudden light of the one street lamp near the house. And in that one instance I could see the man clearly. Old. White hair, tousled. An open-necked shirt. Scrawny neck. Pasty complexion. Tortoise-shell glasses fronting a frightened expression.

Son of a bitch. Could it be? The mayor of Emerald City? The man who'd held office seemingly since before Noah built the Ark? I shook my head. Think about it, I told myself. Emerald City. David LeGrand. It sure as hell could be the mayor.

Chapter 48

"The mayor of Emerald City?" said Wainwright.

"The mayor? Charley Bragg?" said Otis Lipscomb.

"I couldn't get a picture, but I'm ninety-nine percent sure," I said. "I got a short but very clear look at the man, and I was closest to his side of the car. LeGrand obviously had high-tailed it over there to pick him up right after the discovery of the body. He was trying to protect him."

Our unofficial task force had convened at a Pancake House in West Palm. It was 10 a.m. Wainwright's flight had gotten in an hour earlier, and he'd taken a cab to the restaurant. Lipscomb and I had driven there separately. After introductions, and the stirring of cream and sugar into coffee, we'd gotten down to business.

"Where did they go?" Wainright said.

"A shopping center parking lot a few miles north of Emerald City. Dropped the man off at beside a Lincoln Town Car. Guy got out of the cop car and scurried over to his car like a crab outta water."

"And of course . . ." Lipscomb said.

"Five nine two, D four three," I said. "Otis, would you ever doubt me?"

Lipscomb jotted down the number on a piece of paper contained in a worn leather portfolio he was never without. "Lucky for you I've fought crime to a standstill over on the island, so I happen to have a little time on my hands right now to do some diggin' around on your little problem."

Wainwright looked at the big detective with apparent respect, even admiration. Not standard operating procedure for federal types to respect any locals, but Lipscomb had that effect on people. His sheer size, the dark ebony cast of his skin, the overriding gentleness of his manner did not completely disguise a deeper presence. Lipscomb was the man you wanted on your side in a dark alley. If you were on the other side I'd suggest you run like the wind.

I drank cups of coffee while the other two made small talk, got to know one another. I listened, but I was more aware of the creeping anxiety and fatigue that were beginning to mark my mood. My sleep patterns had gone to hell, I hadn't been able to do the things I normally did to maintain my own sanity. The edge of fear for those poor girls working the streets and my anger at the violations of my homestead were both working on me as well. And I was alternating between hefty doses of caffeine and alcohol. No way to live.

Lipscomb seemed as calm as ever, but he didn't have the emotional involvement I did. And Wainwright came across like the graduate school professor lending kindly expertise. For him, I sensed, the case was an intellectual exercise to be puzzled out.

Still, I knew I was extraordinarily fortunate to have these two men helping me. It made my job seem a little less lonesome, my outlook a little less bleak.

We spent a few minutes briefing one another on the case. Lipscomb had been able, through a couple of phone company sources, to gain access to the cell phone records of both of the murdered hookers. He said he could pick them up sometime in the afternoon. His other source hadn't gotten back to him on the phone number of the escort agency.

Wainwright picked up his cell phone and stared at it as if it was a magical thing. "Used to be," he said, "that only rich business executives and doctors carried cell phones. Now they're like pagers, every hooker and drug dealer in town has one."

"I had less luck with Emerald City P.D.," Lipscomb said. "I know a detective over there, but as soon as I even mentioned the murders, he clammed up so hard his ass was watertight. I had to back off before he got suspicious and started asking questions. Good thing, I don't think he knows you and I are friends."

I nodded. I hadn't expected much out of Emerald City anyway. "I'm becoming more and more convinced," I said, "that this escort agency operation is tied into the murders. Even though I'm pretty sure LeGrand isn't our killer, he's into this thing pretty deep. He's dirty and I want to know just how dirty."

Lipscomb and Wainwright both nodded. Lipscomb had done his part. We'd have access to the phone records today, and he'd run a check on the Town Car license plate. I turned to Wainwright. I said, "I'm frustrated. It's like I've been spending all my time in restaurants or nudie bars or driving around all the while some fuckin' psychopath is out there sharpening his razor. What do you think? Do we have a serial killer out there who's gone completely over the edge? There were only, what, five or six days between the murder of Shelly Travers and last night's murder."

Wainwright, ever the professor, said, "If they are connected. We know very little about last night's death, except by inference — all we've got is that its location was in an area frequented by prostitutes and an oblique suggestion by one of the neighbors that the victim might have been a transsexual."

Wainwright looked off into the distance. He opened his notebook and studied it, shook his head. "The one thing that doesn't fit is Shelly Travers murder. We've got three other deaths. Two victims were pre-op transsexuals for sure, according to your source. The third is probably one. The Travers woman wasn't pre-op. If you exclude her murder when you look at the killings, our guy's pattern makes a lot more sense."

"So," I had a sinking feeling when I said it, "if I'm trying to find Shelly's killer — which is what I was hired to do — maybe I'm looking for the wrong guy. Maybe I'm going about this all wrong."

"Unless," Wainwright said in his professorial voice, "He killed Ms. Travers for a different reason. Not because he's just had sex with her so he has to hide the shame of his secret fetish, but . . ." He stared off in the distance some more.

I felt as if my mind was a redlined engine, screaming, about to explode, and still not going fast enough. Could Shelly's past, not her present, be the key? I said, "We know that Shelly hooked, probably during the time she was pre-op. Then she went through the rest of the process and by all accounts got her life together. We also know that Dar — my client — met Shelly through an agency. We also know that Shelly had recently gone back to working, probably hooking, through an agency. We have that agency's number, and by this afternoon, we'll be able to look at phone records and start making some connections. If they exist."

“So, Wainwright said with sudden clarity. “As I was saying, what if it’s the same killer, different motive.” He nodded to himself. “Let’s make a working assumption that we are dealing with one killer. That makes the most sense to me in light of what I know now. If we’re wrong . . .” He spread his hands and shrugged. “I can fit the other three murders into a reasonable pattern of escalation of intensity, decrease in interval. So — what about Shelly?”

He took a sip of coffee, grimaced, picked up the carafe and filled his cup. “Just like you trail people, I do the same thing, only psychologically. I wish I knew more about the latest murder, but from what you’ve told me in general, it’s pretty clear that the killer is becoming more and more disorganized. That’s not unexpected. In any event, he’s become quite a concern to the Emerald City police, or else they wouldn’t be trying so hard to keep a lid on things.

“As I’ve said, I believe he kills to hide his shame, to dehumanize and diminish the victim, to right the wrong of his fetish, so to speak. Loot, the girl who called you, she indicated that her john lost interest in her right about the time he discovered she was a woman – no male genitals. Right?”

I nodded. Wainwright drummed his pen on the table. “With that girl, he would have been able just to leave. She didn’t know him, there was no connection, and he wouldn’t make that much of it in his mind afterwards. He just lost interest. He figured it had happened to her before, so she was a non-problem in his mind. And, in truth, she probably wouldn’t have given it a second thought if you hadn’t come along asking questions.

“Which brings us back to Shelly Travers.” He swiveled his gaze from me to Lipscomb, and back to me. “If her murder is connected to the others, and in my gut I think it is, the killer must have known Shelly before — when she was pre-op. But at that point in his development, he wasn’t murdering his victims. Now his shame is so great he has to kill anyone who knows his secret.”

“And,” I said, “Shelly Travers knew the truth about him. It may have meant nothing to her, but he couldn’t stand the thought of someone holding that knowledge about him.”

Wainwright nodded slowly. “She was working again, out of the same agency. Our killer found out and set up a rendezvous. Then he killed her. Very methodical."

"Oh, God damn," I said. "This is incredible. A serial killer on dual tracks, one disorganized, the other highly calculated and organized."

Lipscomb said, "Holy shit." Wainwright nodded again, slowly. "I've never seen anything like it. And it scares me to death."

We looked at the profiler. He looked back at us, each in turn. Then he said, "There's something I have to do. It ain't pretty. And I'll need your help."

Chapter 49

That night I was doing what I do best — watching, waiting.

I'd given Lipscomb copies of Shelly Travers' phone records. He was to meet his source and get whatever he could. Then he would spend some time cross-referencing the records. Wainwright had held off on giving us any of the information he'd been able to obtain; he said he wanted to make some more phone calls. We were all to get together after midnight, along with Galatea, at the bar where she worked. If I thought something significant was going on, I was to stay with my surveillance.

LeGrand was wandering around Emerald City according to my computer. Currently, he was neither on the Dixie Highway or Everglades, so he might even be doing some real police work. He hadn't gone back to the scene of the most recent crime.

The house I was watching was still and dark. As near as I could tell, no cars were parked out back. The sun had set an hour ago, but the heat was still oppressive. Not much of a breeze tonight. No sweet scent of honeysuckle or jasmine. Heavy humidity.

I decided to leave the Defender in an apartment complex parking lot several blocks away and hike the distance to the house hauling my gear in an oversize backpack. I was afraid my vehicle had been too visible lately in all the places David LeGrand frequented. I was prepared to spend some time in one place tonight, and the clump of trees provided outstanding cover for a solitary individual.

Nothing happened for two hours, except that I had to pee twice. LeGrand had finally moved onto Dixie and was working his way down. Did the man ever get tired of being around so much naked flesh? Did he even notice anymore?

At 10:30 p.m., a car finally showed up. It turned into the driveway and parked behind the house. A late-model Taurus. I caught a glimpse of a lot of blonde hair as the driver passed through the illumination of the vapor street lamp.

In a minute, a light came on downstairs. In another thirty seconds a light went on upstairs.

Ten minutes later, a smoke-gray Mercedes came down the road from the other direction. When the car moved through the light I saw that the windows were darkly tinted so I didn't get a peek at the driver. The Mercedes pulled into the driveway and drove behind the house.

Nothing else happened for the next forty-five minutes. I thought about sneaking behind the house to get a closer look at the cars, but decided against it. If I was caught, it would blow my cover for the rest of the investigation.

I did get the night-scope fixed to the camera. I checked the computer. LeGrand was now drifting down Everglades.

It was now approaching 11:30 p.m. I had a decision to make: wait and see what developed at the house, or leave for my appointment with the others.

I elected to stay.

Just after midnight another light came on downstairs. I saw a curtain part, and I reflexively pulled back into the shadows, although I knew I was invisible from the house.

Five minutes later I heard a motor start. Headlights came on in the back of the house and a moment later the Mercedes nosed around the corner. It got to the edge of the road and stopped. Then it eased out and began to accelerate. The driver's side was closest to me, and when the car passed by me, I saw that the side window was rolled down.

I could see the driver clearly. And the driver I could see was clearly a man I knew.

Henry Cummings.

Chapter 50

Henry Cummings. Someone I knew. And respected. Multimillionaire citizen of Crescent Key, community leader, self-made man. Proud father, loving husband. Some judge of character I was.

I stood in the darkness, stunned at this revelation. An upstairs light flicked off inside the house and yanked my attention back to the present. The upstairs was completely dark. I watched as the downstairs light went off as well. Shutting up for the night? A minute later another car rolled down the driveway. The Taurus. As before, lots of blonde hair visible behind the window.

Still unable to recover from my sighting of Henry Cummings, I watched the Town Car disappear around a curve. Then realized that I was too far from the Defender to reach it in time to follow.

I looked at my watch. There might still be time to catch up with the others at the bar. I packed my things in the backpack and trudged back to the Defender. I felt as though I could only move in slow motion. Henry Cummings. God, the webs that we weave.

We reconvened back at the restaurant. Wainwright, Lipscomb, Galatea, all with more than one glass in front of them. They stared at me when I sat down.

"See a ghost?" Lipscomb asked.

"Worse," I said. "I saw Henry Cummings."

"You mean you ran into Henry . . ." Lipscomb stopped. He looked hard at me and his forehead creased. "You saw Henry Cummings at the house?"

I nodded. Lipscomb yelled, "Someone bring this man a drink, and make it a double." To no one in particular, he said, "Henry Cummings. Motherfucker, motherfucker."

"Someone mind enlightening me?" Wainwright said.

"Really," echoed Galatea.

I told them who Henry Cummings was, and why I was so shocked at seeing him.

"At least he had the sense not to drive the Bentley," Lipscomb said.

"And the other car?" Wainwright said.

"I fucked up. I stood there like my feet were stuck in cement and watched it drive off. All I can tell you was that it was dark red or burgundy, and the woman driving it had a serious quantity of blonde hair. And don't ask me if I got the license number."

For a moment, no one spoke. The waitress, a woman I'd never met before, brought a drink for me. I had no idea what it was, but it was large, and filled with a little ice and a lot of amber liquid, and that was enough for me right then. I drank half of it down in one long swig.

Then Lipscomb said, "I was able to cross reference the two hookers' phone information with Shelly Travers' records."

I wiped my mouth with the back of my hand. "And?"

"Calls were placed from all three cell phones to the same number, the one you called with the sexy voice that answers with just the last 4 digits."

Wainwright chipped in. "All three of the murdered girls were apparently working through the same agency. And . . ." he turned to Lipscomb. "That number we think belongs to the escort agency is a cellular number so it could be answered anywhere. At the house, anywhere. It's registered to a Pristine Entertainment, a business line. The address for Pristine Entertainment is a P.O. Box in, ta-da, Emerald City.

"One thing's for sure," Galatea said. "These people certainly don't want us commoners to know about them."

"Here's what I think," Wainwright said. "And this takes into account the new information about your friend Henry Cummings. A group of men has set up their own exclusive service, kind of a members-only thing. I suspect many of them are wealthy or well-known or both, so privacy is essential. We have Cummings and the mayor on record here, and that's with only a few surveillances. Given that at least two of the people working for this agency were pre-op transsexuals, the service probably specializes in kinky sex. Someone, most likely the cop LeGrand, is in charge of procuring the right girls for the job. To submit a request, the member must produce a password. They meet at the house you've been watching, Loot. Which — did I mention? — is owned by, you guessed it, Pristine Property Group."

We all did things with our drink glasses while we digested this information. Then I said, "So there's a possibility the murderer is a member of this little club."

"Or," Wainwright said, "at least somebody intimately aware of its operation. Narrows it down some."

"Right," Lipscomb countered, "to a select, secret membership that we have no way of identifying."

"Mind if I share some profile information?" Wainwright said.

"Sure," Lipscomb and I said together.

Wainwright consulted his notes again, but I was getting the idea that this was for effect. He said, "It's amazing how accurate some of this is, so it's safe to trust it, at least to a point." Another nod at the notes. "We are probably looking for a white male, single. Or, if he's married, he gives the appearance of being happily married. Family man, may have kids. I would normally say he was in his twenties or thirties, but I'm gonna revise that, given the types of men frequenting this house. Could be in his forties, even older.

"We get into the psychographics now. Probably has latent homosexual or bisexual identity issues. Likely participated in male-to-male sex at one time, most likely as a youth. I suspect he felt a lot of guilt about that, but on some level, maybe subconscious, he enjoyed the experience. He probably fantasizes now about these kinds of experiences, probably while masturbating."

A lovely image, I thought. I knocked down some more of my drink.

Wainwright wasn't finished. "Now we get into some tertiary stuff. Might help, might not. But this guy probably was raised by his mother with an absent or distant father. He has always had bonding issues with both sexes. His marriage, and I suspect he is married, looks wonderful from the outside. But I doubt he has much marital sex. Either he isn't interested, or he can't, ah, get it up." He looked at Galatea. "Excuse me."

"Would you guys just chill? Drop the double standard thing. Especially with me. We all know my story. Just stop, ah, all the pussyfooting around." Now she looked embarrassed, but she managed a healthy grin. "As it were."

Wainwright studied her a moment then looked at the me and Lipscomb. "If you want my professional opinion, I'd say we're after a sick fuck who's just about to kill again."

I felt bile rise in my throat, and thought, yak, yak, yak, and I slammed my fist on the table. "Yak, yak, yak. The question is, what do we do?" I glared at my companions.

Wainwright levied a steady gaze at me and nodded. "You're right. Time's over for yakking. We need to do something."

"Fast," Lipscomb said.

"What we gonna do, we gonna shake the tree," Wainwright said. "We gonna shake the tree and see what falls out."

"I'm taking suggestions," I said.

"How 'bout leaking the whole thing to the media," Lipscomb said.

We all thought about that for a minute. Then Wainwright said, "Upside and downside to that. Upside is that is that the tree starts to shake really fast. The downside is that we lose a lot of control. If the media make a big deal, we'll be overrun by reporters. And then the Feds, and I use the term with utmost respect, will be on us like stink on shit."

"The media might pick up on it anyway if there're many more murders," I said.

"Which means we don't have a lot of time," Wainwright said.

"FDLE?" Lipscomb asked.

Wainwright cocked his head. "State agency?"

"Yep," I said. "Florida Department of Law Enforcement. I think that would be like bringing in the Feds. If we got them interested, and that's a big if, we'd get their bureaucracy. We'd probably accomplish the same thing we would if we alerted the media."

"We could roust a few characters," Lipscomb said.

"True," I said, "but we have to be careful. If we make a wrong move our killer may strike his tent and lay low. Or move to another part of the country and continue killing."

"Which brings me to something else I wanted to share with you," Wainwright said. "I used VICAP — our violent criminal apprehension database to see of there have been other murders with similar MOs."

He used a moment's hesitation for dramatic effect. The waitress came by and wordlessly brought fresh drinks. Then he said, “There actually have been others. Not exact, but pretty close.”

He opened a notebook and scanned some papers. “Nothing real recent. The first murder here was in, what, 2004? There’ve been no reports in other parts of the country since then. But if we go back another decade, we find some interesting things.”

He flicked a finger at his notes. “Detroit, 2000. Transsexual with a history of prostitution is found dead in a seedy apartment. Her throat had been cut. There was some genital mutilation. She was a pre-op.”

Another tap at the notes. “Here’s one a little closer to home. Miami, 1997. This one was strangled, same type of victim, some mutilation. Miami, not that far away, is it?

“And here we have New Orleans, 1995. Hooker dead in the French Quarter, actually in a fairly nice hotel. Pre-op. No mutilation. No leads, no suspects. All of these cases are still open.”

“If it’s the same guy,” I said, “the level of violence was clearly escalating. At first he simply strangles them and leaves. Later he’s cutting their throats and hacking up their genitals.”

I noticed that Galatea had a sick look on her face.

“So much data,” I said. “So little time.”

“And nobody ever suggested that these crimes could be part of a series of murders by a single person?” Lipscomb said.

Wainwright shook his head. “Isolated incidents. Never in the same jurisdiction. Also, our database wasn’t nearly as efficient back then.”

“You think these murders are connected to ours?”

“Yes. We have a pattern of killings now, and I suspect it may go back even before 1995.”

“I like the idea of rousting someone,” Lipscomb said.

“The idea of leaning on some of the players isn’t a bad idea,” Wainwright said. He downed the rest of his drink. We all used the pause to do the same. I wondered if our plan wouldn’t be colored by more than a little alcohol-influenced judgment.

“So let’s look at our list of likely suspects for leaning on,” Wainwright said.

“David LeGrand,” Lipscomb offered.

“I dunno,” I said. “He’s a key player in that he probably knows the most about this little agency operation. He could also shut it down real fast if he thought someone was checking around.

"And I think, and I know this sounds wicked," I said, "we need to keep that operation viable if we are going to nab the guy."

"Trick is," Galatea interjected, "to catch the guy just before he kills again. Ugh."

"Yep," Lipscomb said. "Timing could suck."

"Next candidate. Corcacan."

A moment for thinking. Then Lipscomb said, "He called you because he's getting hosed in this deal somehow. He's lost control of LeGrand. I doubt he's got a hand in this gig. I suspect he's pissed off it's going on at all, and I'm kinda surprised he hasn't reeled LeGrand in already. LeGrand must have something on him."

"Doesn't want the publicity," Wainwright said. "If LeGrand attracts too much attention it ain't gonna bode well for Corcacan's other, ah, business interests."

"What about Cummings?" Lipscomb said.

"I like that idea," I said. "I don't know how much he knows, but we might learn something about the set up. Also, we have some leverage with Cummings."

"Threaten to tell the little woman?" Lipscomb said.

"Well," I grinned. "Only as a last resort."

"Who else?" Wainwright said.

I thought. And the more I thought, the more I thought that we had very few trees to shake, let alone suspects to roust.

"I think we should increase the surveillance on both LeGrand and the house," I said.

"I agree," Wainwright said. "And to do that we need more people."

"I can get a couple of people," Lipscomb said. "If we can pay them, there's a couple of good Crescent Key cops who could break away. You know Forbes and Deitrickson?

They were good people. I nodded. "Check it out with them. I think we need to tighten the tail on LeGrand. I'll do that myself. But we can put some people on the house with some photo equipment. I'd like a detailed record of who comes and goes from that place."

Lipscomb raised a hand to signal the waitress. Serial killers make for serious drinking

"I have a thought," Galatea said suddenly. There was something strange about the way she said it. I looked at her, said, "Yeah?"

She gave each of us carefully measured looks. "All this surveillance stuff is a really good idea, and talking to Henry Cummings, that's a good idea too. But . . ." She let her voice trail off and looked at us.

"And . . ." I said.

"And we set up a Judas Goat," she said.

"A what?" Lipscomb said.

"Judas Goat," Wainwright said, nodding. "Put somebody out on the point. A set-up. Bait. Make the bad guy come after the bait."

The concept didn't sound so bad. Conceptually. I kept looking at Galatea.

Lipscomb said it for me. "So who we gonna use as bait?"

Galatea smiled. "Why, me, of course."

Chapter 51

The drive back to my place seemed long and lonely. We'd settled nothing at the bar.

I'd said, "No fucking way will I use you as bait."

Wainwright had said, "The concept has merit."

I'd said to Wainwright: "Fuck you."

Galatea had said to me: "Who are you to tell me what to do?"

Lipscomb had said to the table in general: "I'm keepin' the fuck out of this one."

I'd said to Galatea: "It's my investigation, and you'll do it my way."

Galatea had said to Wainwright: "Who put him in charge?"

Wainwright had said to Galatea: "He did."

I had said to the table in general: "This is fucking absurd."

Galatea had said to me: "Hacking up girls with knives isn't absurd?"

And it had gone on that way for ten minutes. No one was making friends, and I finally put a stop to it. "I'll think about what to do next." I'd pointed a finger at Galatea when she had opened her mouth. "You shut up."

Which really went over well.

By the time I turned into my gravel driveway I was feeling a little better. I'd rolled down the Defender's windows and the ocean smelled fresh and pure.

I pulled up close to the house, cut the motor and got out. I locked the door and made my way in the darkness to the front door.

On the front porch I fumbled with my keys, trying to find the right key. "Yo, Cool, I'm home," I said. "Biscuit time."

I didn't hear any commotion from Cool. Probably out on the beach. I got the door unlocked and went through the house to the back door. I opened it and looked out on the back deck. Cool wasn't there. I yelled, "Cool, I know you don't listen to a word I say but I'd appreciate hearing from you." Feeling stupid, discussing my feelings with a dog.

I went out on the deck. Cool's food dish was there. It was full.

For no logical reason that I could think of, I took the pistol out of my belt, where I'd stuffed it when I got out of the Defender. I racked a round into the chamber. The sound was shattering in the silence.

The moon shone bright in the lower sky. I heard the usual night noises. Nothing unusual.

Which was unusual.

I knew that I had left Cool outside when I'd left. That had been many hours ago. Had he gotten mad and gone off, like he did with his former master?

But when I was around I'd literally had to pry him off me. He wouldn't run off. I suddenly wished I'd put an I.D. tag on him. Suppose he'd wandered off and gotten lost?

I didn't think so.

The night felt suddenly hot and sticky. My skin was damp under my shirt. My hand was sweating on the butt of the Sig.

I moved along the length of the deck, warily, hackles up. The night sounds began to amplify, sign of the adrenaline flow.

I got to the corner of the house. I looked out into the moonlit woods that led to the water. I listened.

And heard something. Very low. Like a low, soft moan? The wind in the trees?

I didn't think so. I left the deck and moved into the brush, not knowing at all where the sound had come from. I cursed myself for not getting my flashlight.

About twenty feet into the woods I heard it again. Yes, a moan, very low and soft. Coming from —?

I stood as still as I could and listened hard, tried to simply let the sounds come to me. Suddenly the night was alive with noise — a billion insects, the scurrying of ground creatures, the distant screech of an owl.

I took the easiest route through the brush, stepped over small clumps of vines and stunted saplings. I moved between the palmettos, silhouetted in the moonlight.

Almost to the shore, in an area where the tree roots ran on top of the ground, I had to step gingerly. I was under deep cover here, and the moon provided little illumination. I glanced back, and could barely make out the lighted windows of my house through the thick vegetation.

I tripped on something — an exposed root? — almost lost my balance, blundered ahead a couple of steps and grabbed a low branch to steady myself.

Too soft for a root.

I bent down. In a furry heap, looking way too small and still, lay Cool. I put a hand out and touched him. No response.

I got down on both knees. I heard someone saying, "No, no," and realized it was me. I ran my hand up his body, along his chest. His fur was wet and matted. My hand reached his head. I bent down very close to his face. "Cool," I said. "Please, Cool."

Nothing. And then, after what seemed an eternity, his eye, the one I could see, opened ever so slowly. As he focused on me he let out a great sigh and his mouth went slack. I said, "God, no." But then his chest began to rise and fall. He took in great gulps of air, and his tongue came out. He got his front legs going and before I could make him lie still, he'd drug himself a foot toward me and laid his head on the hand I'd placed on the ground to steady myself.

I put my head on Cool's, and put my hand on his chest and felt the steady beating of his heart. I told him that I was sorry. I told him that I loved him.

Then I scooped him up in my arms and made my way to the Defender. I had no purpose but to get help.

Save one other thing, one other purpose.

"The motherfucker who did this," I said, "will pay for it."

Chapter 52

The lunatic who lived inside my brain decided to start with Henry Cummings.

I came to that decision this way:

After I'd taken Cool to a twenty-four-hour emergency animal clinic in West Palm Beach, I'd driven back to my house in a daze, thinking about what the vet had told me. He'd been shot near the shoulder. A miracle the bullet hadn't hit anything vital. Probably missed heart and lungs by centimeters. Most likely a medium-bore bullet. The exit wound wasn't much bigger than the entrance. Very fortunate. A mushrooming slug would have killed him for sure. He'd lost a lot of blood.

He'd live.

At home I'd stripped off my bloody clothes — my image in the mirror was that of an ax-murderer, or a ghoul out of a grade-B horror movie. I'd thrown the clothes in the washing machine and gotten into the shower, and spent half an hour under water as hot as I could stand.

I drank a cup of coffee. I avoided alcohol; I didn't want anything to blunt the rage I was feeling.

I got maybe three hours of tortured sleep before the sun came up.

My plan now was a product of my rage. How dare anyone shoot my dog? Fuck surveillance. Fuck getting together with Wainwright and Lipscomb and yak, yak, yaking 'till the cows came home. Fuck LeGrand — though some small part of my brain had the sense to stay away from him for now.

I was a mad motherfucker and I was gonna shake some trees.

Starting with Henry Cummings.

I had never kicked ass on someone worth $8 billion before. The prospect didn't feel good or bad. My rage put me way beyond that. I was working now for the ghost of Shelly Travers, and the battered body of Too Cool. I didn't give a rat's ass whether Henry Cummings was worth $8 million or eight dollars.

I found Henry Cummings by staking out the luncheonette. At 7:00 a.m., I parked a block away, the other side of the street. I watched Lipscomb go in an hour later.

At 9:15 a.m. Henry Cummings drove by. He didn't stop at the luncheonette, but kept going, south, toward the mainland bridge. I made a U- and followed, resisting the urge to simply run up on him and ram the rear of the $325,000 Bentley.

I didn't care if he spotted me. But it didn't matter; Cummings drove as if he didn't have a care in the world.

He didn't — not yet.

We traveled over the bridge. Neither of us had to stop at the toll booth; we both had the little scan decals on our windows that allowed us to go through without even slowing down.

I kept a couple of cars between the Bentley and me as we drove onto the mainland. Traffic was light, and the sun was already blazing hot in a hazy sky.

I thought Cummings would likely go to Dixie and turn. Whether he went straight or turned made little difference; either way was wall-to-wall humanity, parking lots and buildings.

I had no plan, other than to follow and confront. I just wanted a place secluded enough that I wouldn't get interrupted or shot.

I got a break. He turned north on Dixie, but then doubled back on the road that led into the inland side of Crescent Key and wound through the wooded estates. Now I was directly behind him, but he didn't drive as if he noticed anything unusual. Just another day tooling around in the Bentley, top down, blasting air conditioning all over the Florida shoreline.

As the road curved through woodlands about a mile from the shore, I saw my chance. The Bentley and the Defender were the only cars on the road. I sped up, pulled alongside Cummings and began gesturing wildly and blowing the horn. Henry jerked his head sideways, pulled the Bentley to the right and looked at me wide-eyed. When he recognized me he grinned broadly. I pointed to the side of the road. Cummings obediently pulled over. I whipped the Defender onto the shoulder in front of him, hopped out and pointed to a secluded driveway. "Pull in there, Henry," I shouted.

He said, "Loot, what the —" but he shut up when I screamed, "Now!"

I got back in the Defender and gunned the motor fiercely. Henry got the Bentley going and eased it into the driveway, which wound through the woods for some distance. A slim-to-none chance of being disturbed back in there.

I followed within inches of his rear bumper. I could see his face in the rear-view mirror; he wasn't grinning now.

A hundred yards along the drive I backed off, hit the horn and pointed to the grassy shoulder. Cummings eased off the pavement, stopped the car and got out. He left the door open and stepped to the edge of the road. I stopped parallel with him, rammed the Defender into Park, jumped out and came around to meet him.

I walked directly up to him, put the palm of my hand on his chest and shoved him backwards. "I'm a fucking madman, Henry." I shoved him again. "I'm a fucking lunatic." I shoved him another time and he staggered backwards. "I am really fucking pissed off," I said evenly. "I am out of control. You understand me, Henry? Out of fucking control." I shoved him again and he backed up a couple of steps until he hit the fender of the Azure. "Somebody," I said, "shot my dog.

"So, Henry, you are gonna cooperate with me, or I'm gonna start kicking things. I might kick in the door of your Bentley. I might kick in your teeth. I might knock you down and prop your leg up on a rock and stomp your knee until it snaps backwards. Would that be kicking or stomping, Henry? Or is that putting too fine a point on it?"

Henry blinked at me like a cornered animal. His lime sherbet outfit made him look like a clown. A very rich clown. He gulped air and said, "What the hell are you doing, Landers." Another huge gulp of air. "Are you crazy?" He was backed up against the Bentley, just behind the open driver's door.

I couldn't shove him any farther, and I didn't want to hit him. I moved back a couple steps and stared at him.

I willed myself a calmness I wasn't sure I had. I looked at Cummings steadily. He'd gathered himself somewhat and he wasn't leaning on the car anymore. He stood, swaying a little, hands balled into fists, nose flaring as he breathed.

Thunder rumbled overhead. The usual mid-morning thunderstorm was on its way, earlier today than usual. I had the odd thought that it would serve Cummings right if the Bentley's precious interior got soaked.

"I want some answers, Henry," I said, keeping my voice level. "Last night you drove a gray Mercedes to a house on the mainland. You stayed there more than an hour. After you left a blonde driving a Ford Taurus drove away. No one lives there. It's a place to go to fuck isn't it, Henry?"

He glared at me, a feral stare, but gradually the bravado faded and was replaced by — what? — fear. Worth so many millions and filled with fear.

But he wasn't ready to cave in. He shook his head. "I don't know what you're talking about. You're crazy."

"I'm crazy all right. Last night someone shot my dog. He almost died. Shooting him was a warning to me to drop an investigation I'm on. It wasn't the first warning." I wanted to shove him again, put him back against the car, but I held off. "I love that dog, Henry. Do you understand love, or do you just go to whorehouses to get laid?"

"The fuck," Cummings said. Angry now.

"I want to know everything about this little operation you folks have going on."

He shook his head. "That is none of your business. I —"

I hit him in the stomach, hard. He doubled over, said, "Oof," and dropped to his knees. He knelt there in the sand, bent over and holding his guts. Then he slowly raised his head until his eyes met mine.

I said, "It seems kind of old-fashioned to beat the information out of you but I'm willing to do it if that's what it takes."

Cummings took a couple of deep breaths. He shook his head, slowly. He wasn't used to losing. But he wasn't going to come at me, either.

And suddenly, looking at the man, kneeling there in the heat and the sand, defeated by a few shoves and one hard punch, my anger fizzled. Knocking Cummings around any more would accomplish nothing, except possibly to get me arrested.

I reached down and put out a hand. Cummings flinched. I shook my head and said, "No more, Henry. Get up. We gotta talk."

Cummings hesitated, then took my hand. He made an effort to get up, and with some pull from me, made it unsteadily to his feet. He leaned back against the Bentley, spent.

"Henry, there's real trouble," I said. "I'm not gonna hit you again. But you're involved in something that's way over your head. We're talking about murder here."

His head, which had been hanging down, snapped up. His eyes got that feral look again, but then they darkened as he composed himself. "I've been no party to murder," he said.

"I don't think so either, but people have been killed — at least three so far, probably more. The murders may go back at least a decade. That house I saw you go to last night, I think that ties in with the killings. I need the truth, Henry. I need to know what's going on there. I need to know everything."

"I don't know anything, Loot."

"God damn it, Henry! I want to do this civilized. I apologize for hitting you. But I'll hit you again if you don't tell me what I want to know. Now."

Thunder rolled again in the distance, out over the water. I looked beyond Cummings and saw a blackening sky and a sudden duskiness as the clouds obscured the sun. I usually love a morning thunderstorm coming in off the ocean to drop the temperature and cleanse the air. Now it felt foreboding and ominous. Probably because I had a sick puppy. Probably because I was doing such a swell job of finding the psycho who was hacking up innocent transsexuals. Probably because I was spending my morning beating up a man whom I'd always considered a friend.

Lightning flashed in jagged streaks out of the deep darkness of the clouds. The temperature had plummeted at least fifteen degrees in the last five minutes and I felt the first fat drops of rain.

Cummings wiped his brow with the back of his hand, but he seemed unconcerned that the interior of the Bentley was about to get soaked.

So we stood there a few moments while the rain fell in those fat splattering drops, increasing now and beginning to wet my face and shirt.

I said, "Henry, why don't you put the top up on your car. We'll get in and talk. I really don't want to hit you again."

Henry turned to look at the car, then at the sky. He got in and switched the key on. But he wasn't looking to run. He didn't start the motor, just activated the electric top and let it rise slowly, then drop just as elegantly until it sealed against the top of the windshield.

I went around and got in the passenger's side. Cummings started the car and let the air conditioner blow over us. I saw the windows slide up electronically, but I didn't hear a thing. That's what three hundred grand will buy you. That and eight miles to a gallon of premium gas.

"Who was killed?" Henry said. He looked straight ahead.

"Several women that I know of so far. Each one was a call-girl, most likely working out of the agency that's hooked up with that house. All of the victims were transsexuals. They were all killed in Emerald City, all within the last several months."

"Jesus God," Cummings said under his breath. He turned to me. "I only went there a few times."

I felt my anger returning. "Henry, I don't care if you went there weekly to fuck sheep. As long as you aren't the killer I don't care. I just want to know about the place. Who, how, why, you know the drill."

Finally he said. "It's a long story."

Chapter 53

Here's how Henry Cummings told it, sitting in the Bentley as sheets of rain pelted the car:

The Club — innocuous name, that's what the members called it — had come into existence years ago. Who started it, and when and how it first got going is lost in obscurity.

The Club functioned within a cloak of expensive secrecy. Men were admitted only upon referral by a member. You might not even know who referred you.

The Club cost money — a great deal of money – which, upon acceptance, the new member deposited in a foreign bank account. There was never any acknowledgment of the payment, never any receipts. The dues were hefty, and if you paid them you heard nothing. If you didn't, your access to The Club ceased abruptly.

Members' only contact, if it worked the same way for the others as it did for Cummings, was via the one telephone number. Members were issued an I.D. number, password and a security entrance code to the house on the Intracoastal. If they forgot the password or security code they simply weren't members anymore. There was no appeal. Hell, there was no one to talk to about it. The woman who answered the phone — it was always the same one, the one with the sultry voice — was their only human contact.

The house. The House, as members called it. Apparently a slice of the initiation fee and dues went for upkeep and taxes. Cummings had inquired once and found out the property was owned by some nondescript private company, he couldn't remember the name right now. The place was always immaculate, and every week a yard service came by to do a complete mow and trim. The air conditioner was always set to

68 degrees in the summer, 74 in the winter. The furnishings were expensive Florida casual. The bar was always fully stocked with expensive liquor. The refrigerator had soft drinks, imported bottled water and snacks.

A rule: No food in The House. A snack might be okay, but it wasn't a place to bring in KFC or a catered meal.

Members were under strict orders not to answer the door. The partner they'd chosen for their interlude was always there before they arrived.

The House received no mail. Cummings had never seen a maid but the linens and towels were always fresh, soap and toiletries were always set out in the bathroom.

The House had four bedrooms, all with a different motif. One was simply a continuation of the Florida casual theme. The second was English oak, with hunting prints on the wall. The third was actually a large sauna-steam room, covered with tile from floor to ceiling, with several shower nozzles on one wall and a small vanity and dressing area off to one side. The fourth was a dungeon, fully equipped with the usual whips, chains, feather dusters, rope, electric vibrators, leather masks, panties, collars and vests. There were shackles bolted into one wall and a pallet equipped with shackles and velvet ropes as well.

Cummings had never seen another man there. He had never seen another woman other than the one he was with. There was always a discreet note that told him what time he had to be out; there was always plenty of time.

All Henry had was the number for the foreign bank to which he could wire his dues and fees. He offered to give it to me, but I didn't see how it would help. I took it anyway, and tucked it in my pocket. Nothing illegal about depositing money offshore. In fact, to split legal hairs, there probably was nothing illegal about The Club. For years, escort agencies had been skirting the prostitution laws. It worked this way: The agency set you up with a "companion." Nothing illegal in the state of Florida about paying a person for spending time with you. Of course, if you two hit it off really well, and one thing led to another, hey, that's between the two of you. And if you were feeling generous and wanted to leave the girl a tip because you'd enjoyed her company, that's okay as well. The point is, you never paid for sex. And therefore nobody had done anything illegal at all.

So the wealthy members of The Club didn't worry about having their names entered into Central Booking at the courthouse. They didn't worry about having to call a stranger for a little tryst. They didn't have to pick up a girl — or a guy — at a bar or on the street. They could order the "dish" — no pun intended — and have it served up just to their liking. Straight, gay, kink, no kink, twosomes, threesomes, moresomes, whatever they wanted. Their trysting partners didn't know who they were. In fact, Henry doubted that the woman who answered the phone knew identities, since members used I.D. codes and passwords.

Cummings said that he loved his wife. He had thought he could separate the love for his wife from the occasional fling. He said that in any marriage boredom sets in. He should have concentrated on breaking through the boredom with his wife, not by looking for meaningless indiscretions. He said he felt guilty after each tryst, that the guilt only dissipated over time.

He dropped his eyes as the rain pelted the soft top of the Bentley, thup, thup, thup. He said he thought it was best if he never went back to the House again.

Henry Cummings told me all of this as the storm rolled over us and headed inland. He also told me he regretted the day he'd joined The Club. His eyes filled with tears when he told me this.

I believed him.

Chapter 54

I had roughed up Henry Cummings. Now I was roughing myself up.

For missing the obvious.

A phone call to Darwin Locke's cell phone got a quick answer. Locke was on his boat — since Shelly died, he said he seemed to seek the comfort and privacy of the water. He asked me to come to the boat.

"I don't think that's a good idea," I said.

He must have heard something in my voice. "Bad news?"

"I'll tell you when I see you." I realized I was being unnecessarily brusque, but Locke's feelings — anyone else's feelings — weren't too high on my list at the moment.

"All right, where then?" Locke said.

I told him about a place in Ft. Lauderdale, a seafood joint on the beach. He said he had to complete some transatlantic business that would keep him tied up on the phone until late in the afternoon. We agreed to meet at 7:00 p.m.

I went home. The place, so long my bastion of solitude, now felt lonely without Cool's company. So I drove over to the animal hospital and sat with him for an hour. He was on the mend, the doctor said, but very weak. There wasn't much to do but let the wound heal and keep him full of fluids and some soft food. I had taken him a dog biscuit, but he only sniffed and licked it.

"Not much into chomping, huh, boy?" I said. Every time I spoke to him his tail took to swishing along the floor and his eyebrows twitched up and down. He managed to drag a wet tongue across my face a couple of times when I bent down to nuzzle him.

I left the vet feeling much better. I could possibly take Cool home tomorrow if he kept his soft food down, or by the next day at the latest.

I got back home just before rush hour traffic started to build up on Dixie. I showered, shaved, changed into fresh jeans and work shirt and logged on to check e-mail.

MaryAnne had written once, just to tell me that she had heard nothing new, but that if I wanted to get together to talk, she was always ready.

Galatea had written me four times. Hmm. Just since we'd seen each other last night. The first one was a nice "enjoyed the evening" note. This morning's first note was a "can I help you with whatever you're doing today?" message. The next message was "I'm not working today and I sure would like to hear from you." The fourth message said, "WHERE ARE YOU? DON'T YOU EVER CHECK YOUR E-MAIL?"

Whoa. I fired off a quick note that I had been out of pocket for most of the day. I told her I had a dinner meeting. I couldn't tell her it was with Locke, and after I re-read the note I thought I had sounded evasive. So I typed a postscript saying I'd really like to see her, but that I had to meet with Lipscomb and Wainwright to set up the surveillance. Then I thought that the last sounded like I was avoiding her by not inviting her along, so I added that I would call her late and perhaps we could get together for a drink.

I sent the message. Then I logged on to the cellular tracking system to check on LeGrand. He'd stayed home all morning. Early in the afternoon he'd gone to the police station and was still there. Finally catching up on his paperwork, I thought.

The morning thunderstorm had been long and intense, but no showers had developed during the afternoon, and by the time I got the Defender headed south toward Ft. Lauderdale, the place was an inferno. Steam rose off parking lot asphalt. The road gave off shimmering heat waves. The air conditioner struggled against the mercury and the humidity.

But to my left, when I could glimpse it between the houses and the condos and the thick vegetation, was the deep blue sparkle of the Atlantic. Three-foot whitecaps rolled onto the beach, turning the white sand a darker tan, then retreated back into itself.

I made the drive in a little less than forty-five minutes. When I pulled into the very dusty parking lot of the restaurant I saw a new Jaguar S series nestled among a collection of heaps and has-beens. Locke had beaten me here.

I found him sitting at a table on the back deck that overlooked the beach and ocean. Clouds were building up in the eastern sky, but it was too soon to tell if we'd get any rain out of them. I didn't expect the temperature to dip much below eighty during the night.

Locke stood up when I came over. He wore a cream-colored linen shirt, stone-washed jeans and topsiders. No socks, no belt. His silver hair was tousled by the sea breeze. He looked tan, fit, and very weary. We shook hands and sat down.

He got right to it. "I was disconcerted by your mood on the telephone. What is going on?"

I tried hard to meet and hold a gaze that many men had faltered under. I took a breath and said, "I need to know about The Club."

To his credit he took it calmly. He simply stared at me a few moments. Then he said, "How does that have any bearing on what I've hired you to do?"

I told him. About the dead girls. About the common phone number on their cellular statements. About Shelly's recent involvement with the escort service. He winced at that. About the house. About LeGrand. I did not mention Henry Cummings, nor did I go into detail about what I'd learned about the machinations of The Club and how it operated. I wanted his version.

Locke stared directly at me while I talked. Then he nodded. "You have been doing your homework. What I hired you to do. So you think this club somehow holds the key to a serial killer?"

"I do."

"And you think I can tell you something you don't already know about this club?"

"Mr. Locke, with all due respect, don't bullshit me," I said. "If you want me to find Shelly's killer, you aren't going to help by editing the information you give me. Because technically I'm working for your attorney, we have a confidential arrangement." I paused and looked hard at him. "Mr. Locke, it's not just Shelly. Other girls are getting killed, and it isn't stopping. The intervals between the murders are decreasing rapidly. He's gonna kill again. Soon. The Emerald City cops are looking the other way. They don't want any help, and they aren't too good at actually catching criminals even when they try. Will you level with me?"

Locke did a little staring of his own, and he worked those remarkable eyebrows a bit. Then he said, “Yes, I met Shelly through the agency that uses that house. I am a member.”

I nodded. He said, “I was not a founding member, but I know some of them. Who they are is not, I think, important. Wait —” he held up a hand as I started to speak. — “hear me out. The couple of men I know who started the thing are very old now. I don’t know them well, and I doubt they would tell me anything if I asked them.”

“So you’re saying that there is no way at all to find out who the members are?” I asked.

A sailing yacht idled just offshore. Three people on the bow looked at the mere mortals on the shore and waved happily. The sky was starting to darken, and some rough-looking clouds had begun to form in the ocean. Could be a night for storms.

Locke shook his head and said, “The policeman, LeGrand?”

“LeGrand, that’s his name.”

“I know that a policeman is heavily involved in the operation of The Club. He may run it completely for all I know. If LeGrand’s the kind of man you describe, I wouldn’t put it past him to blackmail the members. That way he could extort money from them and take a cut of The Club’s business as well.”

“It would,” I said, “give him ample motive for keeping the murders from being linked to The Club.”

“Yes,” Locke said. “I take it that, ah, taking down LeGrand would be difficult.”

“It would be if he has the goods on some wealthy and powerful people.”

Locke smiled with no trace of humor. “My colleagues and I, people like us, we’ve always believed that our money would protect us. If all else failed we could use it for leverage, for power, to get what we wanted, to own what, or who, we wanted. Doesn’t seem to be the case here, does it?”

I returned a smile that was as bleak as his. “No. There’s always been one thing that seems to wield even more power than money.”

“You know,” Locke said. “I heard a rumor awhile back, after I’d been a member of The Club for some time. The rumor was that we’d each been videotaped at one time or another while we were using the

House. That being the case, we'd be in a rather untenable position, don't you think? We thought the people who ran the place essentially worked for us. If the rumor turned out to be true, we wouldn't control The Club after all — it would control us.

"So what did I do about it? The same thing I suspect others did who heard the rumor. Nothing. If we had been taped — and we had no idea who would be doing the taping — what could we do, except continue as before? Nobody was rocking anybody's boat. Nobody was getting extorted. So that's what we did. Nothing at all."

I didn't want to tell him everything I thought. I looked out over the water. The yacht had sailed on. Lights twinkled far out at sea, on the horizon — party ships going beyond the three-mile limit so the gambling tables could open.

When I looked back at Locke he was staring off into a middle distance of nothingness, a look on his face of infinite sadness.

After awhile he reeled himself back. "I have money. And so people defer to me, treat me like I am so much more important than they are. There goes Darwin Locke, he's a mighty and powerful man. They get tongue-tied when they get around me. I hire them and fire them. And do you know what? None of that means anything at all. Nothing. Hell, Landers, what are we? Nothing. We're both just blips, mere specks in the cosmos. We'll be forgotten just as soon as we're gone."

He looked out to sea now, his face a specter of grief. "I'm worth over a billion dollars, according to my accountants and lawyers. I don't even know what a billion dollars means. I do know that I don't have the one thing I want. I can't buy her back. I would if I could. But her precious life is gone. And mine isn't worth a damn."

We let all of that lie there awhile. Then I said, "I think David LeGrand runs the whole show."

Locke nodded. "If the men who started The Club enlisted LeGrand to run the operation, they essentially sold their souls to the devil. They were naive. By allowing an outsider access to our secrets, they surrendered their power."

"I don't think I have much choice but to challenge LeGrand," I said. "I just want to do it from a position of strength. And right now, I don't have much strength."

"He seems like the kind of man who responds to threats," Locke said. “What could you threaten him with?”

“I don’t know,” I said with as much enthusiasm as I could muster. “But I’ll think of something. I usually do.”

Chapter 55

"I told my client I'd think of something, so I've gotta think of something," I said.

"Well," Galatea said, "there's my suggestion."

We were at a burger-joint drive-in in West Palm, the kind of place with real honest-to-gosh carhops wearing roller skates. We had the windows rolled down, and the sea breeze made it bearable. So did the massive all-the-way burgers, fries and thick milkshakes — strawberry for Galatea, chocolate for me.

Between us my iPad screen displayed the familiar David LeGrand blip. He was parked on a block of Everglades where three strip joints were located adjacent to each other.

Avoiding Galatea's comment, I took a huge bite of the burger and felt dressing dribble down my chin. "You know," I mumbled, "I'd do better handling this burger if I could unhinge my jaws like a snake."

"Better at a few other things, too," Galatea said, her voice similarly muffled.

I decided absolutely not to go there. Instead, I said, "I think I can pick up Cool tomorrow."

"Poor Cool," Galatea said. My first chance to tell her about his assault was only a little while ago, after I'd called her — she'd been testy that I'd been remiss in getting back to her. But she tamed down quickly when I suggested food — and brought her here to Jake's (Best in the Free World) Burgers.

I had trouble thinking about Cool without feeling an explosive mix of pain and anger. And when I felt like that, I just wanted to hurt back.

Who I wanted to hurt right now was David LeGrand, if only because he was an accessible target. I couldn't get my hands on a serial killer, so LeGrand would have to do.

"Have you given any thought to my idea, Samuel?"

The large bite of chewed burger I'd been coaxing down my throat almost backed up. I looked at her, fetching tonight in an oversize man's shirt unbuttoned at the top and tied at the waist, and tight, very tight blue jeans. Her dark hair framed her face, and her skin was pale in the soft light.

"No," I said.

"No, you haven't —"

"No, as in no, I won't let you do that."

"Let me?" she bristled. "Since when do you let me or not let me do things?"

"ah, poor choice of words," I said. I watched a waitress skate by balancing an impossible load of trays. She had great skater's legs and blonde hair that whipped in the breeze.

Galatea stared at me. Glared, actually. I chewed on my burger and kept my mouth shut. Eventually, she resumed eating, the subject apparently closed. I like a woman who doesn't have to have the last word. Unfortunately, Galatea was not one of those women.

"Samuel," she said quietly, "this subject is not closed."

The blip on the screen blinked and began to change position. LeGrand was finally on the move, and I had an excuse to table the discussion. We paid — actually Galatea insisted on paying — and after the carhop had skated off with our tray I eased the Defender out onto the street. I turned north, cut through a couple of back ways I knew and within ten minutes hit Dixie Highway a few miles south of Emerald City.

In another ten minutes we had crossed the southern limits of Emerald City and were close to the intersection of Everglades and Dixie. By this time LeGrand had turned west on Everglades and was moving slowly along the strip.

As we got closer to him, I began to experience the feeling that permeated the case — a kind of deja vu, a sickening sensation that I was a rat trapped on a wheel, running, running, yet getting nowhere. I told Galatea this, and she just smiled and reached over and patted my leg.

I sped up and passed LeGrand, who was setting a leisurely pace along Everglades.

A block later LeGrand passed me, still doing the speed limit in the inside lane. I let him get half a block ahead and fell in behind him. I doubted he was looking out for a tail. At this point I really didn't care if he spotted me.

He pulled into the next nudie joint — pardon me, adult cabaret.

"I'm not going through another night of this shit," I said. My jaws were tight and I realized I had been clinching them relentlessly.

"Let me go in," Galatea said. "I'll —"

"No. I'm going in this time. I'm gonna be in his face before the end of the night, so I don't really care if he sees me. I want to watch him in his element, see for myself what he's up to."

I left the keys in the Defender and got out and made my way to the bar. From cool air to infernal heat to more cool air, but this time smoky and clinging.

I felt as though I had stepped into some kind of surreal battleground.

Smoke hung in air lit by shards and streaks of tinted light. Hard rock roared at almost intolerably high decibels; the bass banged away at my chest. On a stage brightly lit by white spots, a girl lay on her back, propped up by her elbows, legs in the air, writhing to the beat of the music. A man was leaning over the stage, his head buried between her thighs. If he pushed much harder, I figured, he might die of suffocation. No one else in the place seemed to notice. Other men at the stage watched without much interest. Others drank at small tables, many of them accompanied by naked girls who draped arms and legs over their prey. One guy was leaning over, holding a girl's very large breast in both hands, mouth locked on her nipple like a baby suckling. She gazed beyond him with a look of utter boredom, and inspected her nails.

I went to the bar and ordered a drink. Within two minutes I'd been approached by four girls in various states of undress, all offering wonderful private entertainment for a mere twenty bucks a dance. When I shook my head they disappeared like smoke in the night. One of them muttered, "Narc," as she drifted away.

I didn't see LeGrand, but that didn't mean much. He could be somewhere in the back or off in a shadowy corner getting serviced. Galatea could see his car from the Defender, and she would come get me if he left by a back door.

I was on my second drink – it had been an effort to get the very bored-looking bartender's attention —when LeGrand walked up to the bar. He got the bartender's attention a lot more quickly than I had and didn't have to name his drink. The bartender immediately served up a tall glass with the right amount of ice and a healthy dose of liquor.

He drained half of the drink in one long series of swallows. He returned the glass to the counter then swiveled around and scanned the room. Another girl, plump with a baby face and long black hair, was dancing now, if you could call it that. She stood, legs spread, wearing only a huge grin, as a patron poked a finger deep into her crotch. He looked as if he was about to die of pleasure; she looked as if the whole thing was immensely funny. I noticed a twenty dollar bill in the man's free hand.

I felt a hand land heavily on my shoulder. I turned and LeGrand was looking at me with a very tense expression. "What the fuck are you doing here?"

"Drinking and watching the action. And what the fuck are you doing here, Officer LeGrand?"

He worked his jaws a few times. "It'd be healthier if you left," he said.

"I couldn't help but notice," I said, nodding my head toward the stage, "that Emerald City does a real fine job of enforcing the obscenity laws."

"Fuck you," LeGrand said. He hadn't taken his hand off my shoulder.

I grabbed the offending hand, squeezed it hard and pulled it off. "I really hate to be touched like that," I said. Then I let go, giving his arm a little downward push as I did.

His eyes bulged. He glanced down at his hand and reflexively slid the other hand under his jacket. I stiffened. But LeGrand's hand stopped, although he continued to stare at me. "You don't have a fuckin' clue, do you, Landers? You and that dick-chick you're hanging out with."

I resisted a strong urge to deck him then and there. Instead, I stood, which gave me the height advantage. "I'm just curious, LeGrand. Why does a career cop with less than five years to retirement get himself assigned to cruising two-bit sex slums like this dump?" I threw a few dollars on the bar. "Must be the perks. Free booze and all the pussy you can eat." I waved an arm toward the plump dancer who now had one foot propped on the shoulder of one of the men seated at the stage, giving him the view of a lifetime. “Enjoy,” I said. I pushed past him and headed toward the door.

I didn’t look back.

LeGrand’s profane reference to Galatea had stunned me. I had been so careful; I thought my surveillance had gone undetected. Now I wasn’t so sure of that, and the knowledge disturbed me.

“God, what a pit,” I said, getting back in the car. “LeGrand and I had a little chat. I don’t think he’s onto our tail specifically, but I think he knows we’ve been hanging around. He mentioned you.”

She gave me an astonished look. “How could he know . . .”

I shook my head. “I’ve gotta move on him pretty quick. Like tonight. He’s on edge, and he’s drinking like a fish.”

Galatea nodded.

“Let’s get away from here for a little while,” I suggested. We drove a couple of blocks west on Everglades until we found a Dunkin’ Donuts. The blip indicated that LeGrand was still at the bar. So we took a few minutes to sit at the counter while a fresh batch of hot donuts came out of the oven. Ten minutes later we were back in the Defender.

LeGrand had changed locations while we were in the donut shop. “Whoops,” I said, “let’s catch up.”

I drove as quickly as I could without breaking the law. Five blocks later we came to a section of Everglades devoid of bars and restaurants. One solitary 7-Eleven sign beckoned from the far end of the block. LeGrand’s present location, according to the computer. I slowed down to almost a crawl. I eased the Defender along the street. When we were about a hundred feet from the store I heard tires squeal and suddenly a black Grand Am careened out of the parking lot, tires fighting for control. The rear end slithered on the pavement and swiveled toward my bumper. I whipped the steering wheel and jumped the curb to get out of the way.

I stopped a foot from a street sign and turned to watch the fugitive vehicle’s taillights disappear around the corner.

“I got a bad feeling about this,” I said. I bumped the Defender over the curb and stopped at the entrance to the convenience store’s parking lot.

Only one car was parked in front — LeGrand’s. I could discern no movement at all inside.

I pulled up next to his car. I reached over and opened the glove box. I took out the Sig, checked the clip and chambered a round.

"Stay here," I told Galatea.

"No, I'm coming too." Her hand was on the door handle.

I turned to her. "No." Harshly.

She glared at me, started to open her mouth. I raised my hand and shook my head.

She must have seen something in my eyes. She took her hand off the door. "Be careful."

I got out. I kept the pistol down, next to my leg, and walked slowly up to the front door. Still no activity inside that I could see.

The exterior lighting was harshly bright, and I felt extraordinarily conspicuous. I put a hand on the door and pulled it open and stepped inside.

The interior was lit by a garish fluorescent glare, and much cooler. And very still. I heard the buzzing of a couple of neon beer signs, the hum of a compressor. And I noticed the faint scent of something that didn't belong. I sniffed. Cordite.

I raised the Sig slowly, and took a two-handed stance, gun in front. I moved slowly, slowly, looking right and left, listening for human sounds. I made it to the checkout counter and leaned over. Behind the counter was the body of a man. He was – had been – young, in his twenties, with stringy blonde hair. He wore a red 7-Eleven shirt. He lay on his back, arms thrown out to the side. There was a small puckered hole in the middle of his forehead. His eyes stared sightlessly at something beyond the ceiling. A pool of red blood haloed his head and matted the blonde hair.

I stepped back abruptly, turned, and swept the room with my gun. I heard the sharp hissing of my own breath. I looked out to the parking lot. Galatea was sitting very still in the Defender. I shook my head at her and turned again.

I moved past the counter to the rear of the store. On a stainless steel counter several coffee pots steamed on their hot plates. A few chunks of melting ice glittered on the shiny surface. A soda cup was overturned, and the metal in front of the counter glistened with rivulets of dripping cola.

I moved down the aisle, made my way to the refrigerator cases where the beer was stocked. The smell of cordite was strong here.

LeGrand was sprawled on his back, arms outstretched, as if he were mimicking the kid behind the counter. His eyes were closed; perhaps he had clinched them shut as he was shot.

The hole in LeGrand wasn't particularly large. The slug had caught him high on the chest, at heart level. A scorch mark on his pale blue western shirt circled the rim of the bullet hole, and a patch of blood the size of a silver dollar ringed the wound. The force of the slug had apparently knocked him back, into a pastry rack, and an assortment of cookie and cupcake packages were scattered around the body. On one shelf was a pinkish mess the size of a fist, and a fair amount of blood. Large bore hollow points will do that.

About six inches from LeGrand's right hand, partially hidden by a box of Little Debbie cakes, was a small revolver, typical cop backup weapon. I knelt down and put my nose to the barrel. No cordite odor there. LeGrand had cleared leather, but he hadn't had time to pull the trigger.

I placed a hand on his neck. His skin was warm, but there was no pulse at all. I hadn't thought there would be.

I made my way back to the checkout counter. I heard a compressor kick on, and a moment later felt the slight stirrings of cold air. The place was very cold.

Like a morgue.

I took another look at the kid behind the counter. He was as dead as ever, and a couple of flies had found his eyes. I glanced at the register. The drawer was open, but there were still a fair number of bills inside. I wondered, had this been a robbery gone wrong, had the robber been surprised during the heist, maybe killed LeGrand first when he drew his gun, then popped the kid to alleviate the pesky problem of witnesses? Or had he shot the kid first, then popped LeGrand?

Or did it really matter who got it first, or how. One way or another, the robber had panicked and ran before he'd emptied out the cash drawer.

I looked out toward the parking lot. Just LeGrand's police car, and the Defender.

I went outside, pushing the door open with my elbow. After the unnatural coolness of the store, the heat and humidity was suffocating. I felt sweat break out on my forehead, and my armpits felt suddenly sticky.

I went to the Defender and got in. I met a very wide-eyed stare.

"I am really pissed off," I said.

She arched her eyebrows. "Why?"

"Because LeGrand had the audacity to get himself killed before I had a chance to do it myself. Ain't that a bitch?"

Chapter 56

It had taken hours with the cops, and a lot of it wasn't pretty.

Especially when Scanlon showed up.

The 911 call I'd placed from my cell phone had summoned a covey of cop cars – first, marked cruisers with lights and sirens, then, several unmarked detectives' units. I stood outside, smoking a cigar, until the first car got there, then passively let the officers handcuff me and place me, not too gently, in the back of a cruiser.

Galatea was nowhere to be seen. I'd instructed her to disappear and wind up someplace else fast, to find a restaurant or bar, go inside, call a cab, and then look calm and collected.

So it had been just lonely old me, and two stiffs, when the cops arrived.

And for the next three hours, directed by Scanlon, the cops had come at me: out in the parking lot, in the cruiser, and then down at the station.

But what could they do to one so pure of heart? I was just an ordinary citizen, desiring late-night sustenance, who had, in an amazing coincidence, ended up at the very 7-Eleven where LeGrand had bought the farm.

They'd had a field day with the surveillance gear in the Defender, including the mud-caked transmitter I'd had the foresight to remove from beneath LeGrand's car. But having such equipment isn't illegal, and there was really nothing they could hold me on.

In the end, just as the sun was breaking on the horizon, they let me go, after the usual warning to "stick around town."

I called Galatea. I told her where I was. "You're in the slammer?" she cried. She obviously had watched way too many detective movies.

I assured her I wasn't in the slammer, that in fact I was about to hop in the Defender, which the cops had so graciously let me drive to the station, and head home. Or somewhere. "I'm a little wired."

"I've had three calls from Detective Lipscomb," she said. "He heard about it. He called Agent Wainwright, so he's been calling, too. They thought it would be best to stay away from the police station for now."

"Call 'em both," I said. "We gotta get together. Let's meet . . ."

"Another restaurant?" She almost chuckled. I said, "Actually, yes. I need to eat something. Police stations aren't known for their cuisine. Besides, I've gotten no sleep. I need coffee."

We agreed to meet at a restaurant on the inland side of Crescent Key. They served an upscale breakfast, and I was tired of Emerald City and low-class joints.

I was the first one there. I got a table and the waitress brought a carafe of coffee and a plate of sweet rolls. I was on my second cup of coffee, and staring at an empty plate, when Galatea came in. She hurried over to the table, looked me in the eye, and said, "Some night, huh?"

I nodded. She sat down, got a cup of coffee going. She said, "Detective Lipscomb can't make it. He has to report for duty."

Just then Wainwright came in. He wore a suit — you can take the FBI agent out of Washington, but . . . .

He took a seat. He said nothing, just poured a cup of coffee. He looked like he'd slept in the suit, and not slept much at all. He said, "Hell of a night."

Galatea and I nodded.

Wainwright said, "What have we got?"

I said, "We got shit is what we got. We got a dead cop who might have been the key to the whole thing. We got a real exclusive whorehouse we can't get anything on. We got God knows how many dead girls, we got a maniac with a blade. And we don't have one fucking idea of how to catch him. That's what we've got." I sounded as if I felt sorry for myself. That wasn't too far from the truth.

"Well," Wainwright said when I'd finished, "that about sums it up." He looked at the empty plate. "Listen, next time, don't wait for me."

I said, "I'd made up my mind to confront LeGrand. I was out of patience. Then somebody shot the son of a bitch. So now we get to eat yet again and hash the shit we ain't got over and over. I've had it."

"I agree," Wainwright said. "Bad news is, I have to get back to Washington tomorrow." He looked a little forlorn. "I hate to admit it, but right now I'm out of ideas. I guess I could lean on Emerald City to let us in."

"Might try," I said. "But Emerald City will be circling the wagons now that LeGrand's been killed."

"Who do you think killed him?" Galatea piped up.

Wainwright looked at me. I said, "It could have been a case of wrong place, wrong time. Someone comes in to rob the place and LeGrand tries to be a cowboy. A drunk cowboy. And he gets a slug in the chest."

"Yep, might have been that way," Wainwright said. He looked skeptical. He took a sip of coffee and replaced the cup on the table. "Somebody put you on notice to find out what was going on with the murders. You were told that things were getting out of control. And that LeGrand was a big part of pushing things out of control. And who told you all of this?"

"One shrimpy little dwarf by the name of Corcacan," I said. "Could be he decided to take care of things on his own. LeGrand might have pissed him off just a little too much."

"Do you think LeGrand's death will have any effect on the killer's strategy?" Galatea said.

Both Wainwright and I shook our heads. "The killer is decompensating, losing control. He is operating on pure obsession and very little else at this point," Wainwright said.

We sat silently for a few moments, sipping coffee and waiting for a waitress to come by and take our orders. The place was starting to fill up with the weekday business breakfast crowd. I felt like a side of beef that had been dropped in the sawdust.

"Remember my idea?"

I remembered. "No," I said.

Wainwright said, "Landers, it's not a bad idea. We've got to flush the killer. I suspect that LeGrand's death will greatly hinder the operation of The Club. If our man was setting up his liaisons through that, he's going to be looking for alternatives. Not only that, when word of LeGrand's murder gets out, the girls working the street are going to be on guard. I suspect LeGrand was a big part of the protection for the girls.

"So if our killer can't use The Club, and if the street trade dries up, he's going to have to search out his prey using other means." He refilled his cup from the carafe, added sugar and stirred. "Every bone in my body tells me he's escalating. He's going to kill again. And it's going to be soon. Emerald City isn't going to be able to keep the lid on this for much longer, especially if the media starts sniffing a story."

"We'd talked about leaking a story to the press," Galatea said.

I shook my head. "Not yet, not until we've exhausted the alternatives. I want to catch him, not run him underground."

"Which brings us back to my idea," Galatea prompted. "The Judas Goat. I've even thought about how we could do it." She looked at me expectantly.

I felt control slipping away from me. I'd tried to control the investigation, tried to make the right decisions, and what had it gotten? Nothing, except a few more dead people. Yet the thought of placing Galatea at risk was agonizing.

As if reading my thoughts, she said, "You've done everything you can. We're all in danger now. Your dog's been shot. LeGrand's been killed. If LeGrand knew about your investigation, it's possible the killer does, too. I for one don't want to sit around and wait for him." She suddenly leaned very close to me and grabbed my arm. The pressure was painful. "Damn it, Samuel, we are running out of choices. Do you understand that?"

That was the problem. I did understand it. I didn't want any more murders. But there was one person in particular I didn't want killed. And she was sitting very close to me now, holding my hand. I'd just about given up trying to fight against the feelings I had for her. I felt absolutely miserable.

She took my silence as affirmation. "We can do it, and if we do it right we'll catch that psycho. And then —" She looked at me and left the rest unsaid.

Wainwright said, "Admit it when you're beat, Landers." He smiled at us both.

I said, "Fuck you," with no force at all.

Chapter 57

I longed for a shower and a few hours in my bed. I had a couple of stops to make first, and I had no complaints at all about making them.

First I stopped at a pet store, where I bought a large dog bed, a blanket, matching water and food dishes with a decorative bone pattern, a large sack of beef-basted dog biscuits, some rawhide chews and three sacks of flavored doggie treats.

I lugged all of it to the Defender, wedged it amid the electronics gear and drove to the animal hospital.

When Cool saw me he almost fainted. His eyes rolled up in his head, and for a moment I was afraid he'd pass out. But then he let out a healthy woof and ran as fast as he could in his weakened condition until he got to me. He got a paw in the air and his tail slapped against the tile floor.

The attendant smiled. "I think he's glad to see you."

I walked Cool out to the Defender and he got in the passenger's side, with quite a bit of help from me. I got the motor going and aimed three a/c vents at him. His tongue came out and he looked at me with what could only have been love.

"I love you too, Cool."

When we got home I ran around to Cool's side and helped him out. When his front legs hit the ground they nearly buckled. I held on and got him steadied. Then I watched as he slowly walked up to the front porch and sat down. I opened the door and he went in, got to the kitchen, lay down on the tiles and got tongue and tail to working again.

I lugged my purchases in. I put the dog bed and blanket at the foot of my bed. I opened the sack of biscuits and gave a couple to Cool, along with a rawhide bone. He didn't go for them, but he pushed his nose close to them and sighed. I set out the food and water dishes, filled them and placed a few doggie treats on top of the food, like a garnish.

I looked back at Cool. He had fallen asleep, and though I thought the new bed would be much more comfortable I didn't have the heart to wake him.

I stripped off my wilted clothes and tossed them in the hamper. I showered, shaved and flopped down on the bed.

And that was the last thing I remembered doing until I woke up completely disoriented, with the strong sensation that I wasn't alone in the bed.

I wasn't. Somehow Cool had managed to hoist himself up into the bed. He was sleeping peacefully next to me, sighing gently as he breathed.

I patted him gently, then got out of bed. I dressed and called Galatea.

She answered a bit breathlessly and said, "I was hoping it would be you."

"Do you have to go to work?"

"No. I'm going to take a few days off. I told my boss I had personal problems to take care of."

I waited a minute, then said, "Galatea, ah . ."

She waited.

I said, "He's going to kill again. I don't want you to be his next victim. I, ah, . . ." The words trailed off.

She said softly, "It's okay to care about me."

I said, "I'm willing to work out a plan, but only if I could be convinced that you won't be in danger."

"Samuel," she said, her voice still soft. "I'm not a hero. I don't want anything to happen to me either."

I shook off a sudden vision of the dead Shelly Travers. I thought about Darwin Locke, and the grief that had descended on him after he lost the one he loved. I thought about dead girls in squalid motel rooms. I thought about frightened hookers plying their trade in spite of the dangers they sensed. I thought of the woman on the other end of the line.

"Okay," I said, feeling utterly defeated. "I'd like to hear your plan."

There was a long silence on the line, and then she said, "I'd like it very much if you'd come over here. I don't think I could stand sitting in another restaurant. You've never been here." She laughed. "In fact, no man has ever been here. Will you come, Samuel?"

I told her I'd be there in half an hour, but only if I could bring my dog.

Chapter 58

We sat, Galatea, Cool and I, in her extremely comfortable and cozy living room. Cool got to be guest of honor, perched on the couch with an afghan tucked around him. Galatea sat on one side of him, stroking his head lightly. I sat on the other side, patting his rump gently through the blanket. Galatea had opened a bottle of white wine, and we both had had a couple of glasses. Cool occasionally took a couple of chews on his rawhide bone, but mostly he just snuggled happily and closed his eyes while he got patted and rubbed. The sun was just going down, and Galatea had lit a couple of candles which she had placed on the coffee table next to the wine bottle. A track light turned low burned over a built-in bookshelf. The whole thing smacked of home and hearth.

But we had deadly business to discuss.

"There're only so many ways a hooker has to advertise," Galatea said. "And only so many ways our killer could find the kind of hooker he wants.

"There's the escort service. Although you say it might shut down now that LeGrand is out of the picture." She smiled. "Like really out of the picture. And the word will get around to the other services about the killer. This kind of news travels fast.

"Next, there's the street. But the rumors will be flying, and there will be a lot of fear. Only the hard cases will be out for awhile, the ones who need the money for booze and drugs.

"Of course, there's always the bars. But the fear factor will be at work there as well. I just don't see our man working the clubs. Too many things out of his control.

"There's on-line advertising – women who develop their own

websites with the appropriate keywords and contact information, or ads for escort agencies that girls hook up with, and provide a call-in service." She paused. "I could hook up with agency, but that might take a little too long, or make a webpage, but that also would have a lag time before it got on Google.

"So finally —" here she looked at me knowingly "— there's this." She reached down on her side of the couch and came up with a tabloid newspaper. "Viola. The Sunset Exxxpress, the West Coast's premier adult newspaper." She waved it at me.

"In here," she said, "in the back, are dozens of ads for escorts and nude, heh-heh, companions and such. I know it's not real high-tech, but the johns use it all the time. You know, pay the girl for an hour's worth of her time, scintillating conversation, see what develops. I checked the ads. There are two for transsexual companions. I called both numbers. Both times I got answering machines. One just said to leave a number, so I did. Never got a call back. The other machine said Yolanda was on vacation for the rest of the month. I wonder what prompted her holiday?" We decided on a two-pronged approach – upload a website and put the ad in the paper.

She went on to explain that the ad would run in the upcoming edition of the Exxxpress, which would hit the racks on Friday, three days hence. We would set up my phone as the callback number. I would listen in on all of the calls by putting it on the crystal-clear speakerphone function. We'd have a room reserved if Galatea agreed to meet a john, and I would be in the adjoining room.

We'd hide microphones in Galatea's room as well as a couple of strategically placed cameras. From the next room I would monitor everything that happened.

If it got to that. I didn't want it to get that far. What I wanted to do was to lure our john to the hotel. I'd watch him as he arrived, get his tag number and car description, and a picture. Unless Galatea received a signal from me via cell phone, she would stay quiet and not answer the door. Then I'd trail the man from the location and find out where he went. From there . . . I wasn't sure. Wasn't sure how I would connect him with the murders. Wouldn't be sure if he was the murderer. Maybe it wasn't such a great plan after all.

But it was a plan. And it would lead us to men with such

proclivities as we sought, and the chance of our killer being one of them emerging was a lot more than zero.

"It'll be enough to lure the guys to the location," I said. "I don't want to let anyone in and put you in danger."

She shook her head. "I don't think we'll have to let anyone in, but it'll be good to have the option. There might be someone we want to confront once he's in a compromising situation."

I agreed, reluctantly. "But you will open that door only — only — if I give you the okay."

She nodded, and scratched Cool behind the ear.

Chapter 59

There was one person I wanted to see before I put any plans in motion.

I found Scanlon seated behind his battered government-issue metal desk, a defeated look on his face. A Marlboro smoldered in an ashtray. It wasn't 10:00 a.m. yet, but at least a dozen butts occupied the ashtray. In front of Scanlon was a ceramic mug, filthy with coffee residue, full of steaming black brew. It looked like hot mud, and about as appetizing.

He looked up as I entered and said, "Most folks knock."

"Don't mind if I do," I said and sat down in the visitor's chair. "How are you this fine morning, Captain?"

"Fuck you," Scanlon said. "What do you want?"

"What I want to know is, what the fuck is going on in the investigation of the murders of those hookers. And I'd like to know if you have any idea who killed LeGrand."

"Is that all?" Scanlon said sarcastically. "Why didn't you say so. I'll tell you what's going on in the investigations. None of your fucking business is what's going on."

I sighed and shook my head elaborately. "Such cooperation from my law-enforcement colleagues." I leaned over the desk, got a little close for Scanlon's comfort. He edged back a few inches.

"Stop dicking around with me, Scanlon. You don't want to talk, then listen."

Scanlon said nothing. The hot mud steamed. The cigarette smoldered. I said, "You've got an out-of-control crisis on your hands. You've got a serial killer on the loose. You even suspected LeGrand might have been the killer, but you don't have the evidence to tie him to it, so you've got to keep investigating. But you don't have dick in the way of evidence, just a few dead throw-away girls. You don't want outsiders poking around, because — especially with LeGrand's death — if they look under a few rocks they are going to find lots of slime. You've got a town up to its eyeballs in corruption. Scanlon, you're fucked if you sink, fucked if you swim. They'll get you as accessory, at the least, when it all hits the fan. You can't find the killer, you can't ask for help. So what are you going to do, wait until a couple more girls are killed? The reporters'll get hold of it and the Feds and the boys from Tallahassee will be all over your asses. You're fucked, Scanlon. So now's the time to acknowledge that I might actually be your ally in this. If you'd stop spending your time being so goddamned defensive and protective, you might just realize I'm trying to help you."

Scanlon stared at me for a long time, and it seemed that the resilience drained out of him. What was left was a defeated, pathetic, overwhelmed man. He said, "What can I tell you?"

I told him a little about my plan. He tried to press me for details, but I remained intentionally vague. The last thing I needed was for Emerald City to make a play at operating this sting.

"What I need is a couple of your men, good officers who can be put on notice that I may need them for tracking and some stake-out work."

He nodded slowly. "Only way I'll do that, you'll have to keep me up to the minute as to what you are doing."

"I don't think so," I said. "It's been nice chatting. See you around."

I'd risen about two inches off the chair when Scanlon said, "Okay, sit down. I can't get you the personnel. You're still persona non grata around here. But I might be able to beef up patrols in some areas. I might be able, just between you and me, to let you in on a little information. But that's about it. I hate to say it, Landers, but in a way you're on your own out there." He sighed deeply. "This whole department is folding up around me."

"Damn, Scanlon. I never thought I'd realize the cooperation, however unofficial, of the esteemed Emerald City police. I'm honored."

Scanlon jabbed the smoldering butt into the ash tray. "You know, just fuck you. I'm trying to be helpful."

"Sorry," I said. "I'm a little on edge. You know somebody shot my dog?"

"Damn. Is he okay?" Scanlon was probably the kind of man who had more respect for animals than he did for humans.

I nodded. "Almost killed him."

"Do you know who did it?"

"No. I think there's a good chance it was LeGrand, a way to try warn me off the case. I'd be really surprised if shooting my dog was coincidental to this investigation."

"Hell, I wouldn't put it past LeGrand to do something like that. He was out of control. Jesus, he'd been dead four hours before they got him downtown and he still blew a point two on the breath-o-meter. Just kidding."

Chapter 60

"I'm going to get a little cooperation from Scanlon, strictly off the record," I said. "I asked for some cops. He said he'd put a couple on notice but I'm not sure how fast I can get them."

"So," Galatea said, "when it comes right down to it, it's most likely you and me out there."

I nodded. "Wainwright's back in Washington. Lipscomb had pulled all the time he can for right now. The cops I was using off duty have to work, too. I know one person I might hire to help out on the surveillance, but I'm not even sure about that."

"Okay," she said matter of factly. "I can handle that. Remember, I was the one who suggested this plan."

I smiled at her. "Yes, you did."

We were back at her place, plotting. I had almost invited her out to mine. Almost.

Earlier that morning I had gone online and visited several adult sites until I'd found the photo I wanted — a picture of a woman with an oriental look, just resembling Galatea close enough to constitute some truth in advertising. I'd loaded the photo on a flash drive; the newspaper could make the ad from that. We'd come up with some creative copy: The girl who has it all, and Fully functional seven inches, and 38-24-36, and The ultimate companion for the gentleman who's ready for the ultimate experience.

"We need a name," I said.

She put a finger to her cheek, thinking. "How 'bout Desiree?"

"Hmm. Maybe too exotic."

She worked her cheek with the finger. "Ah, Brandy?"

"Too dippy."

She laughed. "Okay, sport, you come up with something."

I snapped my fingers. "Shavonda."

She rolled her eyes. "Too ethnic."

I thought some more. "Morgan."

She shook her head. "Kinda too butch."

"God," I said. "Where's a name when you need one."

So we both thought for a minute. Then Galatea said, "Wanda?"

I raised an eyebrow. "It's just dumb enough to work. Wanda it is."

Galatea said, "I'm glad that when I picked a name it wasn't Wanda."

So we invented Wanda, a twenty-seven-year-old transsexual, of mixed ethnic heritage, some oriental. About five foot seven, big boobs (at least in the ad), all woman — except for that pesky seven-inch cock that worked quite well, thank you.

"If I were going for a transsexual," Galatea said, "she'd fit my expectations."

"If I were going for a transsexual," I said, then stopped abruptly. She grinned, then we both laughed, and left the rest unsaid.

A little later, fortified by some of Galatea's exceptional coffee, we drove around the Emerald City strip in search of just the right digs for a transsexual hooker. The first three places we tried bombed — no rooms with connecting doors.

The fourth, a place called the Zanzibar, fit the bill nicely. It was at the extreme west end of the Everglades strip, where the road began to wind its way into the far edges of the north 'Glades. The Zanzibar looked like a motel called the Zanzibar ought to look — another forgettable joint on the highway to hell. At night it would look almost pleasant, with its pink and purple neon sign and lighted pool area. But now, in the harsh light of the Florida sun, it was only shabby.

The Zanzibar might have been a small step up from a hot-pillow joint, but the clerk wasn't interested in providing four-star service. While he checked us in he mostly kept his eye on the television set behind the counter.

He didn't ask any questions when I produced several hundred dollars in cash.

We had two rooms on the second floor — 234 and 235. Each had a king bed, chest of drawers nailed to the wall, low dresser similarly affixed, and one armchair. The window looked out over the front walk and railing. Thick privacy curtains cut out almost all light. The place seemed fairly clean, and the bathroom had little bottles of shampoo, conditioner and soap. The towels, while not luxurious, were better than the postage-stamp-sized ones that usually came with a place like this.

"There's a good chance we'll be here a lot for a few days," I said. "Can you stand it?"

Galatea stood in the center of her room and sniffed. "It hasn't been invaded by rogue mildew. That gives it at least one star." She looked around at the room's shabby furnishings. "Faux Formica and a swag lamp, what more could you ask for?"

Chapter 61

I had packed my surveillance gear in two large suitcases, which I lugged up the stairs and into the room.

While Galatea unpacked some clothes and toiletries she had brought — we hoped we wouldn't be spending nights here, but had decided to come prepared — I made an inch-by-inch inspection of the room. The cameras I planned to use were tiny; the lenses were no bigger than an eraser tip. But they had to be placed strategically so that I could monitor the bedroom, vanity and bathroom at any given time. The hidden microphones would be easier to place. I could put one in a lamp or fixture in each area, and I'd have no trouble picking up even the softest of mutterings.

The air conditioning unit wasn't the worst, but it was working overtime during the late afternoon heat to keep the room comfortable. I stripped down to my t-shirt and felt better, but I still felt damp and clammy as I moved about the room.

I placed a camera with a fish-eye lens in one high corner and drilled a hole through to the other room. I could bury the lens in the wall, with only the very slightest of protrusions. A little touch-up paint and it would be invisible.

I found that a second wide angle, placed just above the mirror in the vanity area, would cover vanity and bathroom both, as long as the bathroom door was left open. I was able to snake the wire behind the mirror, then along the baseboard where it met the carpet, and finally under the connecting door and up to the monitor.

The audio wiring was easier. I set up one very powerful omnidirectional microphone behind the television set and ran the wire straight through the wall. A few well-placed articles of clothing or food and it would be invisible to any casual observer.

In each hole I installed small connectors, so when I was set up I could plug a wire into the connector, then into my gear. When I wasn't using the equipment, I could take a small piece of white gum and plug the holes. There were enough scrapes, bruises and dents in the walls that a maid wouldn't notice.

The gear I would need to monitor the activity in the other room was all contained in one large suitcase. Plug in some wires, plug into the electrical outlet, pop on some headphones, and sit back and watch the show.

Only where Galatea was involved, there would be no show. I was adamant about that. We were going to lure johns here, not answer the door unless we — meaning me — thought it would help us gain some information, then log and identify the men.

Beyond that, I hadn't the slightest idea what I would do. But I was sure set up to do it.

Chapter 62

Now the waiting game. Wait two days for the newspaper to hit the stands at all the adult joints. Watch The Club's house and note the complete absence of activity since the David LeGrand's murder. Check with Wainwright, who had nothing new to report. Contact Vivian Rivera, a private detective I knew who could help with surveillance if I needed her.

And wait. Kill time around the house. Listen to the scanner with trepidation. Scan the police bulletins in the paper. Return some calls on jobs I'd been putting off for way too long. Have dinner with Galatea. Have lunch with Galatea. Sometimes, have breakfast with Galatea.

Sleep alone. Or with Cool.

Do a little fishing with Cool. Do a little walking on the beach with Cool so he could build his strength back. Try unsuccessfully to get Cool to sleep in his expensive doggie bed. Try unsuccessfully to get Cool to obey my commands. Surf the transsexual websites and newsgroups online, and learn nothing useful.

Wait. And pray this was the day the killer would strike again.

Wait, through the daily grind of the Florida summer: the relentless heat and humidity, the daily afternoon thunderstorms, the cooling evening sea breezes and the night of stars over the ocean.

Wait, and play the guitar on my back porch, a seemingly endless assortment of melancholy tunes. And then worry I'd missed something on the scanner.

Wait, and smoke illegal cigars and drink legal whiskey.

Wait, and refuse to let anyone — read Galatea — come over and wait with me.

Late on the day the paper was due out, I got a call from a breathless

Galatea. "It's here. I've got it. The ad looks great." She stopped. Then, softly she said, "God, that's really sick, isn't it?"

I told her it was okay, that we were so deep in it now I doubted if we had much perspective left at all. "The better the ad, the better the chance our man will notice it," I said. "That's what we want, isn't it?"

I agreed to come to her place – me, Cool, and my cell phone. I threw the bag I'd packed days earlier in the back of the Defender, which was now devoid of tracking gear.

I made it to her place in a half hour. By the time I arrived I was tense and impatient, looking at the phone as if I could will it to ring.

We sat on the couch, with Cool between us.

And waited. The phone didn't ring at all despite my frequent checking and rechecking to make sure it was operating the way it should.

At 11:00 p.m., she said, "Ain't gonna happen, is it?"

I told her not to give up. "These people get going late. Could happen at any hour."

She shook her head and went to the kitchen to refill the coffee carafe. We spent another hour drinking coffee and harassing the dog. The phone was making about as much noise as a dead possum.

At midnight Galatea went to the bathroom and then made even more coffee. While she was gone Cool got to his feet on the couch, scratched himself, circled a couple of times and stretched out right across Galatea's place.

He, he, he, I thought. Just try to move this slumbering pooch.

Galatea came back bearing the coffee carafe. When she saw Cool she put the carafe down, placed her hands on her hips and said, "I don't think so, big boy."

Cool raised his head — an effort, there — and looked at her.

Galatea said, "Too Cool, down."

To my astonishment, Cool got up and slithered off the couch. He came over to Galatea's feet and stuck his nose in her crotch.

"Hey!" She giggled and said, "Bad dog."

Immediately, Cool pulled his head back and looked up at Galatea. She said, in a very firm voice, "Too Cool, sit."

He sat.

"I can't believe this," I said. "The damn dog won't do a thing I say. How do you do that?"

She patted Cool's head and smiled at me. "You gotta have a woman's touch. You treat 'em right, men'll obey just about any command, at least from a woman. Maybe using his whole name helps."

I sighed and raised my hands in an "oh-well" gesture. "What can I say? He obviously responds better to women." I gave her my tough-guy stare. "But I'm still the master of this here mutt."

"Whatever you say, Samuel," Galatea said, pouring coffee.

Half an hour later I went to the bathroom and peed for a very long time. As soon as I got out Galatea went in. I tried not to think of the mechanics of her peeing.

While she was gone Cool got up from where he had been lying and hoisted himself back on the couch, careful this time not to take Galatea's space.

At 2:00 a.m. the phone rang. We had both began to doze and the harsh trill caused all of us, Cool included, to snap our heads up.

It rang three more times before Galatea said, "I suppose I ought to answer it."

I nodded, pulled on the headphones and turned on the tape recorder. I heard a voice say, ". . . can you describe it in detail?"

Galatea looked at me, horrified. I took off the earphones, left the tape running and went into the kitchen. I didn't want to listen to what she said anymore than she wanted me to hear it.

I killed five long minutes flipping through a People magazine I'd found on the kitchen table. When Galatea came in, she looked stunned, and a little frightened. She walked past me to the refrigerator, took out a gallon of milk and poured a glass. Then she put the milk back, closed the fridge door and walked out of the kitchen.

I found her nestled on the couch next to a sleeping, snoring Cool. She was resting her head on his back and patting him absently. Cool was in sleep heaven.

I sat down by her and put my hand on her neck. "You okay?"

She turned to me, tears welling in her eyes. The only sound was the soft whooshing of the cool air blowing through the vents and Cool's soft snoring. I kept my hand on her neck.

Then she turned to me and pulled me to her, and burrowed her face against my neck. "Saying those things, playing along with that . . that, creep. God, Samuel, the things that man asked me —"

I stroked her hair. “I know, baby. We won’t have to do this for long.”

That’s what I hoped. Hope and expectations can be very different things.

No other calls came in during the early morning hours, nor did the thing ring while we slept in the next morning.

And we did sleep in. Together, in her big bed, her in a long flannel nightgown, me in sweats and a t-shirt. Cool between us.

I expected we’d be spending a good deal of time at the motel room, that the chances of sleeping over there were high. So the private pleasures of spending time with Galatea in her home were intensified, as we woke up, as we worked together in her kitchen to prepare breakfast, as we visited over coffee, as we studiously avoided, if for only a little while, the gravity of what we were attempting. As we looked at the phone, both willing it to ring, and dreading the thought of it ringing.

Chapter 63

The next couple of days didn't serve our killer up on a platter, but we did experience the fodder for some stories we couldn't ever tell our grandkids.

Such as:

The several men who wanted descriptions, in minute detail, of the sexual member in question, including length, width, hardness and duration of erection, skin color, foreskin status, prominence of veins, head size. A couple of times we got the distinct impression that just hearing the description was enough for the guy at the other end of the line, judging from the heavy breathing that increased, then subsided. Those were the ones who didn't make appointments.

And the several callers who wanted to describe to "Wanda" — in detail — exactly what she would be expected to do for them after they arrived. We heard relatively unimaginative fantasies that involved, among others, handcuffs, a nurse's uniform, a feather duster, velvet ropes, and whips. It was sometimes unclear who was supposed to dress in what, or do what to whom. Most of these callers stopped short of trying to make an appointment.

Two women called, and "Wanda" blew them off — no pun intended.

Then there were the serious callers, and for each of them an appointment was set up. Our plan was this: I would station myself discreetly outside the motel, walkie-talkie in hand. I would eyeball the john, get a picture and his license number. Then I'd radio Galatea and tell her what to do. Which, as far as I was concerned, would be, don't answer the door. It would be enough to nail down the identification, run computer checks.

If the john got too persistent, knocking too long or otherwise making a nuisance of himself, Galatea was to go in the adjoining room, lock the door and radio me. Then I'd casually go up, as if I were just a guest, and let myself in. I figured my arrival would be enough to drive the guy away.

Six men visited and knocked. Six times the door remained locked. Each time, I got a picture and license plate number. I hoped nobody would show up in a cab.

And six times I wondered if this half-assed plan was getting us any closer to catching our killer. Each of the men could be the one. Each of them probably wasn't.

Chapter 64

On the fourth day I descended into a black funk. Maybe I had the Monday blues. Maybe I had cabin fever. Maybe I was thinking that a killer was loose and I hadn't caught him.

"Maybe for some inconceivable reason," I said, "the Emerald City PD will catch him."

"Maybe they will," Galatea said soothingly.

"Or," I said, "maybe he ran off to Phoenix or Des Moines to cut people up."

"Could be," Galatea said soothingly.

"Or could be," I said, "that he simply isn't ready to kill again and all of this is for nothing."

"Maybe so," Galatea said soothingly. Then she said, "Doesn't change anything for now, does it." It wasn't a question.

We were both propped up against pillows on her room's queen-size bed. She put her hand on my neck and began to massage some incredibly bound-up muscles. I said, "No, it doesn't change anything. We're going to stay with this for awhile, if for no other reason than it's the only thing I can think of to do."

The phone rang and my muscles snapped back to attention. Galatea said, "Damn," and picked up the phone. She said, "Hey, baby." Then she made a face and handed the phone to me. "It's Detective Lipscomb."

I took the phone and said, "Hey baby."

Lipscomb said, "Sounds different coming from you."

"Bite the big one," I said. "I speak metaphorically. What's up."

"I ran checks on the tags you gave me, then ran the names through NCIC. And the news is: no news. Not one of these guys has been in trouble. They seem like just your average middle-aged joes, or in this case, johns."

"Lovely," I said. "And there lies the root of our problem. According to Wainwright and everything I've read about it, that's the profile of the killer, just your average Joe."

"You might as well come by and pick up the info," Lipscomb said. "Or, if you get on line and give me your cell phone number I can fax it over. You do have a fax program on your laptop, don't you."

I had no idea if I did or not. I said, "ah, I'll run over later and get it."

"Don't have a clue about the fax software, do you?" Lipscomb chuckled.

I gave him a friendly, "Fuck you," and hung up.

I went into to the adjoining room where all the surveillance gear was scattered, unused and pretty much useless, and fired up an illegal corona. I lay back on the bed, closed my eyes and smoked, letting the smoke linger in my mouth and curl up into the room. The tobacco haze was comforting, as was the gentle drawing on the cigar. My kind of meditation.

I must have dozed off. The shrill ringing of the phone startled me awake. I looked at the ashtray; at least I'd had the foresight to put the stogie there instead of letting it light up the room.

I quickly flicked on the recorder, but I just wasn't up to listening to the pervert on the other end of the line. I could hear Galatea as she went through the usual routine. Suddenly, she snapped back angrily, "Fuck you, buddy." And slammed the receiver down.

I walked into her room. She sat on the bed, staring at the phone, clenching and unclenching her fists. She looked at me and said, "I'm sorry. I shouldn't have hung up on him. My nerves are shot. He wasn't saying anything the others haven't said. Just sitting here doing what we're doing isn't going to get us anywhere."

"I have an idea," I said. "How 'bout I take you out this evening for a nice seafood dinner — tablecloth, candles, view of the ocean, the whole thing."

"A date?" she said.

I looked at her a long time. "Yes. A date."

"I want to dress up, then. I actually do have nice clothes. But we'll have to go by my house so I can change."

I said we could do that. "But right now, I need to run over to

Lipscomb's office and get the printouts he has for me. You want to come? Or I guess I could drop you off at your place first."

She thought about that. "That'd be way out of your way if you're going over to Crescent Key. How about I stay here while you run your errand. I wouldn't mind getting it as cold as possible in here and taking a nap. Maybe I'll even take a long, hot shower while you're gone."

So we agreed that I would go see Lipscomb, then come back and pick her up. "I doubt I'll be gone more than an hour, hour and a half," I said. "Is that time enough."

She smiled. "Wouldn't hurt if you maybe stopped a place or two. A couple of hours of solitude sounds wonderful." She opened her eyes wide. "Hey, I don't mean I don't enjoy —"

"S'okay," I said. "Take it from a guy who loves his solitude, I understand completely. But, if you don't mind, I'm gonna leave Cool here. He'll protect you. And it might be best if you didn't answer the phone while I was gone."

"Yeah, okay," she said. "Kiss on the cheek?"

I did that, and it seemed completely natural. I could handle kisses on the cheek. No problem at all.

Chapter 65

I had miscalculated. The drive from the motel to the Crescent Key Police Department took me almost an hour. In an effort to ensure that not a single block of the Dixie Highway was without construction, the county had obviously dispatched additional crews. Now they had the whole highway clogged from end to end.

I crept along, glancing at my watch every few minutes. Finally I took a hard left in front of an oncoming dump truck, darted and turned through about fifty side streets, and came out near the bridge to the island — all in about the same time I'd have gotten there had I stayed on Dixie.

To find that Lipscomb had already left for the day. The detective on the duty desk said he didn't know where he'd gone, whether out on the job or home.

On Lipscomb's desk was a manila envelope with my name on it. Inside were several sheets of dot-matrix printouts, along with a handwritten note. The note said:

Yo Loot. Here is the stuff I was able to pull up. I checked our local data bases and NCIC. Nothing. Sorry. I also poked around the Emerald City PD, Big mess over there. The chief left town suddenly on ha-ha vacation. Scanlon is ostensibly in charge. They're treating LeGrand's death as him being in the wrong place, at the wrong time. (Cash drawer open, no money taken. Hmmmm?????) Be enlightening to get the Dwarf's take on it, wouldn't it? I'm off tomorrow. Can you use my help? Call me. P.S. I don't think you're gonna get any help at all from Emerald City. Feds still aren't involved. I think your plan is the best so far.

Nice to know somebody thought so.

I braced myself for the drive back. I'd already been gone almost an hour and a half, and I wasn't going to make any better time on the return, even though I'd decided I might as well take on the stop-and-start traffic on the Dixie.

I got the Defender going and reached for the cell phone to call Galatea's room.

The cell phone was not there. I looked under the seat, around the interior. It wasn't there. I thought back. I didn't remember having it with me when I left the motel.

I smacked the steering wheel in frustration as I backed out of the parking space. I would stop at a convenience store on the mainland and call the room. I didn't even know the number. I'd have to go through information. The whole thing seemed to demand more energy than I could muster.

At the pay phone it took the operator more than a minute to find the right number. She couldn't get the name right, at first looking for a motel named the "Sand Bar," then screwing up the spelling. But she finally found it, and she was probably more relieved than I was just to get rid of me. I jotted the number down, dropped in more money and dialed. After fifteen rings a very bored desk clerk muttered, "Zanzibar."

I asked that he ring the room. He did. The phone rang. There was no answer. Then I remembered — of course, there would be no answer. We'd agreed for her not to answer the phone when I was gone. But I let the phone ring a dozen times. Each ring sent a kind of shooting dread through me. I called the clerk back. He assured me he had rung the right room. I asked him to ring again, stay on the line and if there was no answer, to ring our other room.

He did as I told him. Again, no answer. No answer at the other room. "Gotta go, buddy," he said. "Gotta customer waiting."

I hung up and jumped in the Defender, feeling as if I was lugging around a huge stone in my stomach.

The drive back to the Zanzibar was excruciating. I stopped at another pay phone, thinking Galatea might have been taking that long, hot shower she'd mentioned. Same clerk. Same drill. Same empty ringing.

The sun went down while I drove. I went as fast as I dared, hoping that now, of all times, I wouldn't be stopped by Emerald City's finest.

And finally, after what seemed an eternity of lugging the rock in my gut all over west Florida, I careened around a corner on two wheels and stopped just short of the Zanzibar Motel's flashing neon vacancy sign.

Chapter 66

The parking lot of the Zanzibar was only about half full when I veered in, and I could hear a radio playing in an upper room with an open door. Several couples lounged by the pool, drinking beer and laughing.

I parked in a space right below our rooms. The room with the monitoring equipment was dark; the privacy curtain had been drawn in the other room and only a tiny sliver of light showed where the curtains met.

I took the Sig out of the glove box. Every cop nerve ending I had was zinging — twenty years in the trenches will give you a sixth sense you never shake. I was perspiring heavily and it wasn't all from the heat. I tucked the gun into my waistband until just an inch of it showed. I kept my hand over it and made my way up the stairs. At the top I turned left; our rooms were midway down the open walkway, at least seventy five feet away.

I stood very quietly for a moment, let myself feel for movement, for vibes.

Nothing.

I walked briskly down the walkway, past the first of our rooms and stopped at the second door, my room. I listened again. Nothing. I put my ear to the door. I heard nothing. I looked down toward the pool. The people there were intent on their merry little party.

I stepped over to the door in front of Galatea's room, put my ear to the wood. I heard something, perhaps only the television or radio. But also something softer. A voice? I started to knock but held back.

I listened again, but the door muffled and distorted any sounds coming from inside. I moved back over to my room, gently slipped the key into the door and unlocked it. I held the knob and very slowly eased it inward. The room was pitch dark, except for a few winking green and red lights on the equipment. The connecting door was closed.

I told myself I was just being paranoid, that she was only taking a nap, as she'd planned, and that I had better pull myself together, that it was only the television. I didn't want to freak her out by barging in waving my gun.

I closed the door to my room, heard only the soft click of the lock. I walked silently over to the equipment, pulled the chair back and sat down.

I had almost reached the switch to turn on the video monitors when something brushed against my leg. I almost screamed, and it took every bit of my self-control to keep from bolting out of the chair.

When I'd gotten my heart pushed back down my throat I reached down and gave Cool a few pats. I said, "Shhhh," very softly, as if he would understand. Other than a soft swishing of his tail on the carpet, he kept quiet.

I flipped on the monitor and looked at the screen.

And saw a vision straight from hell.

A man, his back to me, stood over the bed. Beyond him I could see two legs, spread apart. He blocked the view of the rest of her.

The legs weren't moving.

Then one of them did. Just a little. It moved inward a few inches, and the toes on the foot curled up.

I looked at the man again. Dressed in jeans, a light colored shirt. A floppy hat.

He held a straight razor in his right hand, down at his side, casually.

I realized I had the sound off. I turned it up just a little, so it wouldn't filter into the other room.

". . .'s going to come, you little whore. Don't bullshit a bullshitter."

The voice sounded muffled and tinny. I eased the volume up just a little. I heard Galatea answer, in a very scared and trembling voice, "Sir, just do what you want to do and then leave, okay? Please?"

"Oh, you're a little one, aren't you?" He took a step toward the bed. "But you sure do come as advertised. Look at that."

I saw Galatea's hands inch out, one on each side of the bed. They grabbed handfuls of bedspread and held on.

The man's pants dropped to his knees. He wasn't wearing any

underwear.

I thought. The connecting door on my side was closed. That didn't mean the other one was. So if I opened my door, and the other one was open, I'd telegraph my entrance. If her door was closed it could be locked or unlocked.

One thing at a time. I stood up and took the Sig out of my waistband. I flicked off the safety and realized I'd forgotten to chamber a round. There was no other way. I took a deep breath and racked the slide. The sound of the mechanism was like a clap of thunder in the room. I slowly let out my breath and looked at the monitor. The grim tableau hadn't shifted.

I went to the connecting door, put my hand on the cold metal of the knob and turned it as slowly as I could. I felt the bolt give way with a solid snick and I froze. I glanced back at the monitor. Nobody had moved very much. I heard the man through the tinny speaker. "You understand, I'm not gay. You are a woman, isn't that right?" He paused. Then, louder, "Right?"

Galatea said, "Yes sir," very softly. I thought she might be crying.

"No! Your a liar!. You're a freak and a whore. Admit it. Say it. You seduced me, then you tricked me.

Galatea told him that she had.

The man said, "And you begged me for it, didn't you?"

"Yes sir." Her voice was barely audible.

"So I had to do it. With you, with a woman, but with — that —" Now the voice was rising on a quality of hysteria. "So what should I do now? I'm not gay, but you'll lie, say things about me that just aren't true."

I eased the door open, slowly, slowly. No light showed. The other door was closed. I realized I had been holding my breath and slowly let it out. I tested the knob of the other connecting door. Locked.

I had no options now, and I had no time. I stepped back, thankful I was wearing boots. I banged my right boot as hard as I could against the door, next to the knob. The door rattled and shook. Something tore in the wooden jamb, but the door held. I reared back and gave it another boot. Another woeful shaking, and more tearing. This is taking too long, I thought as I stepped back for a third try. This time I put a shoulder into it, using my legs like pistons, and this time the door tore off its hinges and crashed into the room behind it.

The force of the lunge threw me off-balance, and I staggered into the room trying to get my feet planted.

Chapter 67

And came face to face with Darwin Locke.

He had pulled Galatea up and held her in front of him like a shield. She was naked, her hands attempting to cover herself. Her eyes were wild with fear. She'd been slashed above her left breast, and blood dripped from the cut.

Locke's eyes were those of a cornered beast. His pants had fallen to his ankles. He had one arm around Galatea's midsection, under her breasts. The other held a glittering straight razor to her throat.

He shuffled backwards, awkwardly in his dropped pants, and pulled Galatea along until his back was against the vanity. The razor never wavered; the shining steel pressed against the smooth flesh of Galatea's throat. A thin rivulet of blood ran down below the blade.

He'll kill her if I make a move, I thought.

He'll kill her if I don't.

"Darwin," I said as steadily as possible. "Let my friend go. I'm sure we can work something out."

His eyes never left mine. His mouth was working, mouthing soundless words. He had his body pushed up hard against Galatea's and he might have moaned.

"I don't think so," Locke said in a voice as calm as the times we'd talked on his boat. "I don't see how it could end that way."

"Galatea, honey," I said. "Are you okay?"

She started to nod, but stopped abruptly as the blade pressed against her. In a whisper she said, "Yes, Samuel."

"I'd appreciate it if you'd put that gun down, Mr. Landers," Locke said. "On the bed."

I tossed the Sig onto the bed, where it lay looking ugly, useless and out of reach.

Locke's expression began to change, to lose the fear. He said, "Congratulations. You've completed the job I hired you to do. You found the killer."

"You hired me to catch him, not just to find him. So we really aren't quite finished."

His eyes lit up, this time in a kind of rage. But when he spoke his voice was that of a pitiful child. "You were supposed to catch the killer before now." He looked at the razor with wonder. "You were supposed to fix it so this wouldn't happen again."

I took a deep breath. My hands were shaking. I tore my eyes away from the bright steel of the blade and fastened them on Locke's. "Darwin, Galatea is my friend. My heart would break if something happened to her."

"She's a trickster, you know," Locke said. "A woman, but not really a woman." Now his voice was a sibilant hiss. His mood was clearly making pendulum swings. He'd been the pathetic victim; now he was the psychotic killer. "How do you do it with her, Landers? Do you suck her? How does it feel, having a man's cock in your mouth, getting hard that way? Does she fuck you? No, I don't guess she does, not with this—this..." He moved the razor in a quick downward jerk. I saw the slash of silver, and I knew where it was headed, but my eyes never left his face.

He smiled big enough to show some teeth. "It doesn't work worth a shit, does it? But it turns you on anyway, feeling that cock rubbing against you. You fuckin' pervert."

Galatea groaned and made a slight move as if to shift away, but he pulled her tighter against him and brought the blade quickly back to her neck. I saw her pulse beating fast and hard below the edge of the blade. A rivulet of blood had worked its way down her throat to her chest, scarlet against her pale skin. Tears streamed down her cheeks, and she avoided my eyes. Locke's free hand moved up to her breast. "Nice little titties, though." Still the psychopath. "She told me she grew them herself." He pinched the nipple and I heard Galatea's quick intake of breath and a kind of grunt that came from deep within her.

I said to Galatea," It's okay, baby, you are being too cool." I looked at her. "Too cool. Just hang in there."

She looked at me, briefly, uncomprehending. Then turned her eyes away.

C'mon baby, please figure it out.

Locke said, "You were supposed to stop all of this. I paid you well to stop it." In a very soft voice he said, "I have lots of money."

C'mon baby. "Cool, baby, will you say it so I'll know you're okay? Can you tell me you're staying just too cool?"

She and Locke both stared at me, but underneath the terror, I sensed something. An understanding? C'mon baby, please. "If I tell you I love you, will you tell me that's just. Too. Cool."

She stared at me. I said, "Galatea. I love you."

Suddenly the light of understanding went on. She said, in a clear, strong voice, "Oh Samuel, that is just TOO COOL!"

Through the gaping hole where the door had been flew a blur of chocolate fur. Galatea screamed, "Cool!" Locke screamed something high and inarticulate. In an instant the dog was leaping toward Galatea. She ducked suddenly, screamed again, and rolled into a ball on the floor.

As Cool leapt, I lunged for the gun on the bed, got it and turned it toward Locke. He was skittering in short steps across the floor, almost comical in his half-mast pants.

The razor wasn't funny at all. Still holding on to it, he fell toward the bed, sweeping the razor in a long shiny arc. I brought up a forearm and the blade connected, sliced deep through flesh and muscle. I felt it lodge against bone. I screamed and fired.

The slug caught Locke right in the mouth.

He stood up, as if at attention, with an astonished look in his eyes. His mouth was a ghastly mangled puckered thing, and a great deal of the back of his head blew out and hit the vanity mirror. He stood there a moment, as if contemplating this sudden turn of events. The puckered hole might have moved a little. The eyes stayed open, but they lost the astonished look, and he crumpled to the floor, not a foot from Galatea. The razor was still a glittering thing in his hand.

I got myself up off the bed, threw down the Sig, and staggered over to Galatea. She lay on her side, arms in front of her face. I gently rolled her over on her back.

Her throat was slashed deeply on one side. Pink froth bubbled when she took a breath.

But she was breathing. Oh, baby, hold on.

I got up on the legs of a drunk man and made it to the bathroom. I took a towel and wrapped it tightly around my arm. I took another towel and made it back to Galatea. I folded the towel and pressed it against the wound. I held her cheek. I said, "Hey, listen. Can you hear me?"

She took a couple of breaths, a little steadier than the ones before. Then, ever so slowly, her eyes opened. They took an eternity to focus on me. But then they did, and the slightest of smiles tugged at her lips. She tried to talk but it came out a muttered rasp. A little pink blood ran from the corner of her mouth.

I looked frantically for the cell phone. Then I heard a voice behind me say, "What the fuck is going on, man?"

I turned and stared at the clerk. He stood there, immobile, his face ashen.

"Call 911. Hurry." My voice seemed to echo in the suddenly still room. "Move."

He went. I looked at Galatea, at her nakedness. I reached behind me, grabbed the corner of the bedspread and pulled it to me. Then, keeping the towel compressed on her neck, I used my other hand to carefully cover her with it.

I was sitting beside her, holding her hand, willing her to keep breathing, when the first sirens sounded in the distance.

The first medic did quick triage. Looked at my arm, turned quickly to Galatea and motioned to the others who were coming in. As they set up he went over to Locke. He bent down, studied his face for a moment, said, "Wow," and came back to me. He took a cursory look at the depth of the cut, then wrapped it with gauze. "Need the ER for that," he said. "Let's go down to the ambulance."

I sat still, straining to see what was happening to Galatea. He looked at me and said, "Buddy, it ain't gonna help for you to be up here. Downstairs. Now."

Reluctantly, I got up. When I did, the room tilted, but the paramedic offered a steadying hand, and with his help I made it out of the room and down the stairs to the ambulance. Another attendant got me up on the gurney and he and another white-shirted attendant hefted me inside. No matter which way they turned me I tried to crane my neck to catch a glimpse of the upstairs room.

The driver got the motor started and just as the other attendant was about to shut the rear doors I saw a stretcher being carried down the stairs. On the stretcher was a white sheet. Panic shot through me, and then I saw a shock of dark hair, and a medic carrying an I.V. drip.

I tried to raise up, but the beefy guy who was handling the chores in the rear of my ambulance put a surprisingly gentle hand on me. “Hey, she’s hanging in there. They got it under control.” He smiled at me. “We’re good, man. The best.”

I prayed that they were.

The driver was just getting the ambulance going when I screamed, “Hold it!” so loud that my attendant jerked back and the driver hit the brakes. My attendant said, “Ah, c’mon —”

“No!” I said. “My dog. My dog’s back there. I gotta know if he’s safe.”

The attendant started to argue, but then he said, “Hold it Jake, lemme go see about the man’s dog.”

He swung the doors open and left. A minute later he came back with, no big surprise, Capt. Scanlon in tow. And Scanlon was towing Cool, who was tied to a piece of rope. When Cool saw me he tried desperately to climb into the ambulance, but Scanlon held on to him.

“Sorry,” I said. “He’s kinda strong-willed.”

Scanlon gave me a hard cop look, but then the hound-dog face softened. “You go get yourself taken care of. I’ll take your doggie down to the station, give him a room with a view.”

Chapter 68

I spent two hours in a small, curtained-off area in the emergency room of West Palm Regional waiting to see a doctor. The triage nurse had taken a fifteen-second look at it, said, "You'll live," and assigned me to the waiting list. At least someone came by and put a tight bandage on the wound. No one offered pain pills.

Finally a fresh-faced resident who looked as if he hadn't slept in at least thirty-six hours took a thirty-second look at it and said, "You'll live." He spent the next fifteen minutes cleaning the cut, removing threads from my shirt and the towel, and stitching me up. "Might have some nerve damage," he muttered. "Too early to tell. See an ortho man tomorrow." Then he drifted out of the room humming Ticket to Ride.

No one knew anything about Galatea, or at least no one was talking. She might have been transported to a hospital with different trauma resources.

She might not have been transported to a hospital at all.

At least I had a clue about Cool. Scanlon, of all people, had shown an unexpected soft side. I knew Cool was okay. I'd told him to get hold of Lipscomb. And I gave him MaryAnne's number as well. She'd want to know about Galatea. "I'll let you know where they take her," Scanlon said. I tried to explain that she was a transsexual and that they were often discriminated against in hospitals. He nodded slowly. "I'll make sure that doesn't happen. Go on."

When I'd finally been stitched up, X-rayed, bandaged and had my arm trussed in a sling, I went through the lobby of the emergency room clutching my new bottle of pain pills. I found Scanlon slouched in a chair, looking grim.

He hoisted himself up when he saw me, looking for all the world like an exhausted old basset hound. I went over to him. "Where is she? Is she alive."

He said, "She's alive. She's here. They took her directly to surgery. She's still in there." He stopped and wiped his eyes. "Look, Landers. It's touch and go. The guy, he cut her really deep. What did she do, duck or something?"

I gave him a quick summary. He nodded and said, "He cut into her trachea. He might have even gotten the larynx. She lost a lot of blood. I'm not gonna shit you, man. She's barely hanging on."

I sat down, dizzy.

Scanlon was still talking, ". . .got him back at the station. We even got him some dog biscuits, like really expensive ones. He's eating us out of house and home." He tried a smile. Then he gave me an expectant look. Ever the cop, he wanted to know about Darwin Locke, and how we both came to be in that motel room at the same time. But I wasn't ready to talk. There would be plenty of time for talk later. I told him that.

He nodded again, looking wearier than ever. He said, "We can set up our interview for later, tomorrow. Anything I can do for you now? I could give you a ride back to your car."

I wasn't about to leave. I said, "Could you have someone bring it over to me. I'd be grateful."

"I can do that," he said. I gave him the keys and he went off, his walk a tired shamble.

I found the nurses station for surgery on the third floor. An ice-blonde with a threatening figure was womaning the desk, and she gave me a piercing stare as I shuffled up. The sling didn't cause any sympathy bells to ring.

I told her who I was here for. She snapped, "Wait," and walked back through double doors. A minute later she was back. "He's still in surgery." She glared at me as if I shared some kind of unfathomable perversity with the wounded person. Then she began riffling through charts.

"The milk of human kindness is alive and well," I said pointedly. Then I went over to an uncomfortable-looking bench and sat down. The bench was indeed uncomfortable.

It was uncomfortable for varying lengths of time over the next six hours. I took a trip to the cafeteria for some soup and coffee. I peed twice. I waited a lot. I might have dozed, but it wasn't the kind of sleep that would do me any good at all.

The ice-blonde was replaced on the next shift by a steely eyed redhead. She nodded when I asked about Galatea, went through the double doors and came back. "She's in recovery —" she held up a hand when I started to speak. "She's stable, but in critical condition. As soon as they can, they'll take her to ICU on the fourth floor. You might want to wait up there." She gave me a gentle smile.

"Thank you," I said, "for showing us the courtesy of referring to her by the proper gender."

She gave me an odd look as I shuffled upstairs to Intensive Care.

Chapter 69

They let me see her, briefly, at midnight. MaryAnne, who'd been with me for the past several hours, waited in the sitting area.

Galatea lay on freshly tucked-in white sheets, her left arm hooked up to an I.V. drip, with wires running from various part of her to various machines around the bed. The room, cast in an eerie gloom, was like something out of a Kubrick film, a sound-and-light show of blinking reds and greens, and the muted clicking and whirring of machines.

She was asleep when I came in. I listened thankfully to the steady rise and fall of her chest. I took one of her hands. Her eyes fluttered for a moment, then they opened. She smiled and mouthed the word, "Samuel."

The nurse, who hovered nearby like a mama hummingbird, told me not to let her talk. "Doctor says she can't use her vocal cords at all or she'll have scarring."

I looked back at Galatea. She looked at me for a long time, and then her eyes brimmed with tears. And my heart cracked.

I took a tissue out of the dispenser on the night table and wiped her face. "Hey, it's okay. You're a trooper. You just cut yourself shaving."

We both realized the inappropriateness of the remark. She rolled her eyes and I said, "Whoops. No shaving jokes, okay?"

She rolled her eyes again and smiled a little. I felt the nurse's hand on my arm. "Enough for now. Come back tomorrow. You can call later to see how she's doing. I'll be on 'till 9:00 a.m. Name's Lucy."

I thanked her. As we got out to the hall she said, "I just want you to know that I'm aware she's a transsexual." She looked at me steadily. "She'll get good care. I promise. I won't let anyone harass her."

"Thanks. For understanding. For taking care of her," I said.

Just then MaryAnne nudged my elbow, eyes full of questions. I just nodded. That was enough of an explanation for now. “Seems like everyone I love’s all banged up,” I told her. She smiled, understanding me better than I understood myself.

I left MaryAnne with Nurse Lucy, which doubled my confidence that Galatea would be in good hands.

I wasn’t sure I had enough strength left to get out to the lobby much less to my car, but there was one errand I had to complete if I was to get any semblance of peaceful sleep. I used the phone at the nurses station to call the Emerald City police station. The duty sergeant told me that there was one very lonely dog there, watching the door every time it opened.

I told him to please inform Cool that I’d be there in twenty minutes. I heard him giving the message very reasonably to the dog when I hung up.

Chapter 70

Cool and I had been working on the deck, painting over the bloody graffiti on the back door left by his attacker – by LeGrand (I painted, Cool supervised) — when I'd heard the crunch of tires on gravel and gone around to the front to see who'd come.

What had come was a black Lincoln Town Car stretch limo. The side windows, both front and back, were deeply tinted in direct violation of Florida law.

The face behind the tinted glass of the rear window was almost invisible. Just the merest shadowy movement gave any hint that someone was inside.

Then the rear window drifted down silently, and I found myself face to face with Frederico Corcacan. No surprise there, I thought. The front window was still up, but it didn't take a lot of imagination to figure out what kind of guy was driving.

The dwarf's face barely showed over the window opening. He gave me a smile that might even have been kind and said with the utmost courtesy, "Would you very much mind sitting with me?" He tilted his head slightly to the seat opposite his.

I told Cool to "stay," not expecting him to listen and waited while the driver — the same thug I'd bashed with the trash can during my earlier encounter with Corcacan— got out and came around and opened the door. His fists clinched and his eyes brimmed with hate. I said, "How's your head, big guy?" and dipped into the car to a muttered, "Fuck you." The door closed behind me with a lot more force than necessary.

The interior of the Town Car was deliciously cool; the light that filtered through the darkened windows was soft and enveloping.

Corcacan sat by himself on the rear seat; another wide seat faced rearward, just behind the glass partition to the driver's compartment. Corcacan nodded toward a small fold-down table just to the side of the rear-facing seat. On it were several silver decanters, a bucket of ice and two glasses.

I sat facing the dwarf. I poured a drink, but I didn't pick it up. The partition, which was rolled up, was at my left shoulder. I heard the driver's door open, then shut. Then there was a muted snuffling sound from the front, then a muttered, "Hey, don't."

The dwarf leaned back against the seat, where it connected with the door. His legs stuck straight out, his feet dangled in space just in front of the seat cushion. His tuxedo and shirt were soiled and rumpled, but his hair was combed and styled perfectly, and shone brilliantly in the soft light.

"You've been busy," he said.

I nodded.

He looked out beyond the smoked window, then back at me. "You solved the murder of that girl."

I nodded again.

"Bet you never had a serial killer for a client before."

"Did get a bit confusing," I said neutrally.

"And LeGrand. Pity he had to get caught in some kind of, ah, crossfire just before you showed up. I wonder. You were about to give him some trouble, weren't you?"

"Yeah," I said. "Too bad he had to be the dead hero just when things were getting exciting."

"Coincidences are a very strange thing, are they not?"

I gave him a narrow look. "What brought you to my home, Mr. Corcacan?"

"Why, this Town Car!" He cackled and a little spittle formed at one edge of his mouth. "Forgive me. I've always wanted an opportunity to use that little joke."

I stared at him and said nothing. The smile drifted away and he shrugged. Then he shouted, "Michael, hand me Vladimir!"

The partition came down and a tiny dog — a toy poodle — came out of it as if suspended in space. Then came the hand that held it. The hand dropped the dog on the seat. It immediately spied Corcacan, yelped a couple of times, jumped off the seat — quite a drop for the little fellow — and hopped up into the dwarf's lap. Corcacan held it to his breast, and the damn dog nearly obscured his upper body. The poodle was that extreme white which suggests a dye job, and Corcacan's dark face peered from behind it like a specter. The dwarf's eyes gleamed. Vladimir licked at the dark face. The partition went back up, but stopped a couple of inches from the top.

"As to the answer of what brought me here," the dwarf said. "Coincidences." He paused and stroked the dog's head. "I think it's time to let, no pun intended, sleeping dog's lie." The poodle, as if on command, closed his eyes and sighed.

I saw it coming. The clerk. I had made inquires. I had wondered how the police were doing at solving the shootings of LeGrand and the clerk. And suddenly my suspicions were confirmed. I shook my head, as if to ward off a moment of infinite sadness. Then I looked at Corcacan.

"I don't give a rat's ass about LeGrand. But I have a problem with the dead clerk. He was 22 years old, he was supporting a wife and a kid while he went to the community college. He didn't have to happen.

The dwarf held my gaze and shrugged. "Sometimes it is necessary to sacrifice a few for the greater good."

I felt the anger well, like a suddenly boiling spring. "That clerk," I said, "had nothing to do with any of this. He had a two-year-old daughter. He was enrolled at the community college."

Corcacan shrugged elaborately. One dead kid was well beneath his level of concern. His cocoon, his arena, was here, in this rarefied air of power.

I shook my head. "Not good enough. I don't walk away from this without some assurances."

The dwarf's eyes bore into me. His cackle was dry and without any mirth at all. "You, sir, ask for assurances? You think you have any influence at all here?"

I didn't, really, but I had come too far to back down. Corcacan still looked at me, but he was losing interest. He stroked the dog's head, absently. "So if there is nothing more . . .," he said as much to the little dog as to me.

I said, as evenly as I could, "Fuck you, you spineless little shrimp."

The dark eyes blazed. His mouth dropped open, but no words came.

Finally, in a strained voice, he shrieked, "Michael!"

I yelled, "Fuck you too, Michael!"

There was a flurry of movement behind the smoked glass. Then the partition begin to glide down. "Hurry," I said. I kicked a foot at the dwarf, who cowered against the seat back. The dog whined.

The partition glided downward. I saw the menacing tip of an automatic's barrel extending through the opening. Then the gunman's face came into view. And by that time he was staring into the barrel of my gun, which I'd yanked out of the waistband at the small of my back. The driver stared at the muzzle, his gun pointed in the general direction of Corcacan, who screamed, "Shoot him, not me!"

Maggione, or whatever his name was, looked confused. The dwarf wielded absolute power, or at least he did before he was competing with the dark hole of the Sig's barrel.

"Try it," I said. "Follow the boss's orders. Or drop the gun, it's your choice."

We stayed in a frozen moment of time, then the hand that held the automatic slowly let the gun slide off and fall onto the rear compartment's carpeting.

"Corcacan yelled, "Michael, you're fired!"

I cut a glance at Corcacan. He hadn't gone for a gun, probably left the heavy work to his minions. But the man was seriously dangerous, and it didn't pay to take him for granted. But for now he was simply a tiny, deformed creature cowering in a corner.

The hand that had dropped the gun still hovered in the air. I kept my gun aimed and with my other hand found the little switch that controlled the partition window. I pushed and the window began to rise. The thug started to pull his hand back, but I said, "No!' and it went still again. After a few seconds the top of the glass nudged his forearm, then began to push it up. In another moment the arm was shoved against the upper lip of the partition. I prayed for a strong motor. "Move your arm back a little, asshole. Let your fingers rest on the glass. Pull them back and I got no problem shooting you."

He did as I instructed. I hit the switch again and the glass began to squeeze against his fingers, between the knuckles. Suddenly the fingers twitched and I heard a yowl from the driver's compartment. I kept the pressure on the switch and said, "Turn off the motor. Hand the keys."

The driver muttered, “Fuck you,” but I heard the motor switch off and then the keys materialized next to the trapped hand. I took them and let the fall on the seat.

The interior of the limo immediately began to heat up. I turned to the dwarf. “I realize the house ape in the front seat isn’t much of a concern to you beyond his ability to keep you safe. But I suspect his hand is beginning to hurt him something awful.”

From behind the dog he hissed, “This gets you nothing. You are a dead man.”

“I don’t think so.” I was about to play a hand and I had no idea who held the better cards. With my left hand I carefully pulled out a cloth I’d tucked in my trouser pocket while I was painting. Using the cloth I picked up the thug’s gun. I sniffed the barrel. Nothing. I looked into the black hole. There were some dirty flecks just inside the muzzle. It might have been fired since it had last been cleaned.

I pushed at a button at the top of the grip and the magazine dropped out and landed on the carpet. I glanced at the dwarf; he sat motionless, fascinated. I sat my gun on my leg, took the other gun and, still using the cloth to avoid touching it, ratcheted the slide. A shell flew out and nearly hit the dwarf in the face. He flinched momentarily, then brought his gaze back to me. His eyes were dark and depthless.

I tossed the empty weapon to him. It landed on his lap. This time he didn’t flinch, simply stared at the thing as if it were a serpent. The little dog scuttled out of his lap and huddled against the seat back.

“Pick it up,” I said. “Hold it as if you were going to shoot it. Give it a nice healthy grip.”

“Fuck you,” he hissed.

With my left hand I picked up my gun. I twisted a little and with my right hand took the index finger lodged in the window. The man tried to hold it against the glass but the circulation was about shot and he had very little strength. I straightened the finger and glanced at the dwarf. He gave me nothing but a glare; the gun lay untouched.

I sighed. I do not consider myself a man of violence, though twenty years of police work will teach a person a great deal about the subject, and its appropriate applications. I hesitated only a moment before I slipped the palm of my hand under the outstretched finger and began to apply upward pressure. The finger bent, resisted. The skin stretched and grew pale under the stress. I took a breath, suddenly pushed upward as hard as I could. The finger gave, the sound of the bone snapping was sudden and loud. The man in the front screamed, a high keening wail. I took my hand away and the finger fell and hung at on odd, splayed angle. The wail had quieted to a low, muttering moan. The finger twitched a couple of times.

"Got no problem breaking yours," I said conversationally to Corcacan. "Pick up the fucking gun, you little prick. Don't point it at me. I get a bad reaction to a gun pointing at me, even an unloaded one."

He never let the stare flicker, but he slowly, slowly picked up the gun. He held it in a shooter's grip. He kept the thing pointed well away from me.

I tossed the cloth at him. "Now, wrap the gun up and hand it to me."

He did that.

"Here's what I think," I said. "I think there's blood on this gun. I'd bet some serious money it was used to shoot LeGrand and the kid." I paused and gave him a grin. "Even if I'm wrong, I suspect we could eventually tie it to some kind of crime. And now I've got an excellent set of your prints on it — probably two sets." I kept the smile at a high wattage.

"You are a dead man," he muttered again, but there wasn't a lot of power in it. And then I knew the gun was dirty, because his next words were, "What the fuck do you want?"

"I want the widow and kid taken care of. I want a substantial amount of money set aside in a trust fund, enough that she can live adequately on that alone. I want a separate fund set up for the child, so that she'll get a specific amount each month for her care. I want it set up so that she'll be able to go to college."

We set some amounts. The dwarf worked on keeping his glare up, but there wasn't as much energy at all now. The whole thing was just a business deal, even if it was a deal consummated in the presence of a man whose mangled hand was snagged in a power window. The dwarf and I did a good job of ignoring the low moans of the injured.

The business deal done, I took the keys to the limo in my hand, reached behind me and opened the door. I went out backwards, moved a good ten feet from the vehicle before I tossed the keys back onto the floorboard in front of Corcacan.

“Have a good day,” I said. Then, holding the weapon — all the leverage in the world I had against the malevolent little bastard — I turned and walked back to my house. Cool scampered along in front of me as if he didn’t have a care in the world.

Epilogue

We did have our date — finally.

For the first couple of days that she was in ICU, I stayed at the hospital day and night, except when I had to give my statement to Scanlon, and when I went home to take care of Cool and catch a few hours' sleep.

On the third day she was moved to a private room — courtesy of Emerald City PD — but she still was under orders not to talk and writing on a pad seemed to sap her strength. So mostly I held her hand and rambled. I didn't talk about the night in the motel room, or about Darwin Locke, though I had been able to put together a great deal about the man, and surmise the rest. Wainwright and I had had a couple of lengthy and entertaining telephone calls, if you can call dissecting a serial killer's psyche entertaining.

When Galatea was discharged she went home with MaryAnne. And suddenly she asked that I not come over for a few days. She must have seen the hurt in my eyes. She smiled and patted my hand. I just need a little time to think, she wrote. Just a little time.

I could not bring myself to ask her what she needed time to think about.

Cool needed attention; some of his stitches had been ripped loose during the tussle, and he had perfected quite the forlorn-puppy look when he knew I was leaving the house.

The morning after Galatea had gone to MaryAnne's, I got up before dawn and hauled the flats boat down to the marina. After I'd gotten it in the water and parked the Defender, I walked back along the row of yachts. Locke's boat was still there, still looped with some weathered crime-scene tape. A lonely lady riding the gentle swells.

I took my boat straight out twenty miles, cut the engine and drifted. It wasn't advisable to be out this far with only one outboard. It was unthinkable in a flats boat that drew eight inches of water. But I didn't care, and the day was extremely calm.

I ran a trolling rig and fished blue-water for awhile, but nothing hit, so I dropped a deep line and hoisted a few grouper out of their holes. Not much in the way of fighting, but a tasty treat on the table.

I had had virtually nothing to drink since the night in the motel room. I had felt that spiraling, getting a hold of me I didn't like. Now it seemed pointless to medicate. I wanted to feel everything that had happened.

By late afternoon I'd come back close to shore and trolled for Spanish mackerel, then worked the flats and caught one good-sized redfish. Then I went back to the marina, passed by Locke's yacht once more, and hauled my boat home. I was sunburned, exhausted and too full of caffeine.

Knowing Cool wasn't a fishy kind of dog, I stopped at a meat market on the way home and bought him two pounds of prime rib. Go figure. I grilled three macks and even threw his meat on the flames. We had ourselves a regular feast, sitting on the deck watching the light fade from the big sky over the ocean.

Galatea went home from MaryAnne's the following Friday. She called me and whispered, "Watcha doin', big boy?"

I damn near had to sit down when I heard her voice. I must have been speechless for a beat or two too long.

"Samuel? It's Galatea."

"Hell, with that voice, I couldn't decide if it was Lauren Bacall or Lauren Hutton."

"Very funny. And I worked so hard to make my voice not throaty."

There was another moment when neither of us spoke. Then she said, "As I remember, you asked me out on a date, didn't you? You aren't gonna renege, are you?"

Renege? Like hell I would.

I picked her up and drove her to a cozy seafood place on the ocean in South Palm Beach. The decor was typical — rustic wood, fish nets and plastic crabs and starfish. The fish and shellfish were fresh, and it was rumored the chef had retired from a five-star restaurant in Switzerland and settled down in Florida. The food certainly substantiated the rumor. So did the prices.

Galatea wore a white gauzy thing with a low scooped neckline. A scarf circled her neck to hide the scar from Locke's razor.

She caught me looking at the swell of her breasts and laughed. "Wonder bra," she said, in a still-raspy whisper. "They work wonders, don't you think?"

I smiled. She smiled. I indulged myself in a couple of more glances at her cleavage. It was fine cleavage, especially if you were more into quality than quantity.

I had dressed up for the occasion by exchanging my Wranglers for a pair of Dockers khakis. I'd kept the shirtsleeves rolled down on a freshly pressed Brooks Brothers button-down in a soft Indian Madras. The sleeve covered the bandage; the slice was healing, but I still didn't have any feeling in two of my fingers and the arm was stiff and sore. I'd strapped on my grandfather's Bulova Accutron wristwatch, the very cool kind with the alligator band and the little tuning fork that hummed and kept perfect time. I'd buffed up my Johnston & Murphy saddle oxfords, put on some socks with little clocks on them. I'd worn my Worth & Worth Montecristi Panama that I took out of its box about twice a year. As icing on the cake, I'd slipped a Cuban Romeo y Julieta Churchill into my breast pocket. And I'd even thrown vanity to the winds and brought my reading glasses so I wouldn't have to squint at the menu.

"Don't you look dapper as hell," Galatea had said when I picked her up. "Though that cigar looks a lot like something Cool'd deposit in the yard. How far'd you have to chase the guy for the hat?"

"I know, you can dress a country boy up, but then all you've got is a dressed up country boy," I'd said as I opened the door of the Defender for her.

We got a corner table with a lot of privacy and an exquisite view of the Atlantic. When the waiter came Galatea ordered a glass of white wine. I ordered iced tea. She gave me a funny look but didn't say anything.

She touched her neck and told me that the cut was healing nicely. "I'll have some scarring on my vocal cords, and it could make my voice a little breathier, but I've worked hard on it before. I can do it again."

I told her I liked breathy voices. The bandage on her neck now was just a thin strip of cotton held by a few strips of flesh-colored tape. It looked as if she'd gotten a nasty cut, nothing more.

After she's wolfed down a huge order of fried calamari — the injury hadn't had any long-term effect on her appetite — she said, "Tell me everything."

So I did. I told her that Darwin Locke had been my client, that he in effect had hired me to catch him, before he killed again. "But I never had a clue," I said. "I was completely astonished when I came into the room and saw him."

"So in a sense you were successful at doing what he hired you to do," Galatea said.

"In a sense. But he killed at least two people after he hired me, Shelly and the other hooker."

"Why did he kill Shelly? I thought he loved her." she asked.

I shrugged. "Wainwright and I have some theories. We think Locke was damn near multiple personality. At the very least he was some kind of paranoid psychopath. And of course there was a part of him who wanted to get caught, to stop the insanity."

I took a sip of tea. The sky was absolutely cloudless and thousands of stars had come out.

"Locke's disorganized side was typical of the serial killer spiraling out of control. His was a special case, though. He only went after pre-op transsexuals. Wainwright and I are doing a fair amount of postulating here, but we think Locke killed because he couldn't tolerate the possibility that someone would know about his dark side. As if by possessing that knowledge, they also possessed him. So he killed the ones who knew. Ironic, isn't it? He killed only the ones who satisfied his fantasies."

"That doesn't explain Shelly," she whispered.

"Locke lied to me at the beginning. I think he had known Shelly when she was pre-op. Knew her before he started killing. He may have gone on for God knows how long picking up transsexuals and not killing them.

"I think Locke actually did fall in love with Shelly. I think he probably paid for her operations, made her his complete woman, so to speak."

Galatea nodded. "Gives me the creeps. It's Pygmalion, but with a twist. Once she became the woman he wanted, she ceased to be as attractive to him."

"Maybe. Or maybe she was too perfect. Whatever it was, they had some kind of falling out. She probably suspected he was still picking up pre-ops."

"And she left him." she said.

"Yep. All of a sudden, she was gone. And whatever hold he had on reality started to slip away. His intervals between transsexual encounters were decreasing. He was killing them all by then."

"More than likely Locke began to think of Shelly herself as a liability. She'd done him wrong, plus she knew his dark secret."

"So he found her and killed her?"

"I think he found her by accident. After all, he'd hired me to find her, and I hadn't had any luck. I don't think he was using The Club at all to find his marks. Shelly had gone back to hooking. He may have spotted her. Or he may have been looking. In any event he found her and convinced her to go somewhere with him. And he killed her. I suspect he might have gone back and killed others like that as well, if he hadn't gotten caught."

"Which still leaves some questions," Galatea said. "Such as, 'Who shot Cool?' and 'Who shot LeGrand?'"

"I'm pretty sure LeGrand shot Cool. He's probably the one who killed the egret, too. He wanted to warn me off. Looking back, I think he was keeping an eye on me the whole time I was following him around. Some detective I am."

She smiled. "I think you are a great detective. You saved my life."

"Yeah, well, I have some questions about that," I said.

The waitress came by to clear our plates — we'd managed to have the whole discussion while wolfing down our entrees. She showed us the dessert tray but we both passed and just ordered coffee.

Over the coffee I said, "The question I have for you, Galatea—"

She gave me a grimace. "Oh, oh, here it comes."

"—is, why in the hell did you let Locke into your room?"

She shook her head slowly. "His call came a long time after you left. I thought you'd be back before he got there. I wasn't planning to answer the door at all. He knocked, and I just kept quiet. But then he said something like, “It’s okay, honey. I know Lieutenant Landers. He told me about you.”

God. Suddenly it all came together. “Of course. He must have recognized my cell phone number from the ad. God, talk about skating on the edge of catastrophe.”

She was quiet a little while. Then she asked, “So was all the work you did staking out that house, and looking into that escort agency, was that all wasted effort?”

“As it turns out, no. After Locke’s death they went through his records and found some pretty interesting pieces of information. Locke actually started The Club, and he apparently was the guiding hand in its operation. He was the one who hired LeGrand. Locke’s secretary took the phone calls and passed the information to LeGrand who then set up the hookers with the johns. Several of dead girls had at one time or another all worked out of The Club, but maybe not Shelly. So even if Locke was picking some girls off the street, he could also have continued to use the agency’s files to locate victims.

“Emerald City is in an absolute uproar,” I said. “The police chief resigned before he got fired. The mayor quit — did I mention that I saw him coming out of The Club one night with LeGrand? Capt. Scanlon, the only cop over there who’s been decent to me, is the acting chief, and that’ll be permanent when the city council meets. So I suppose there’s some good that’s come out of this mess.”

Galatea nodded. Then she looked at me with soft eyes and said, “Samuel, how do you feel about killing Locke?”

I looked out at the ocean, collecting my thoughts. “Locke was a monster. God knows what the final death count will be when the FBI gets finished with its investigation. And —” I smiled at her — “I really didn’t stop to think about it when he had that razor on your neck.”

She grimaced, but gave me a steady look and said, “And I thank you so much for that. For saving my life.”

There wasn’t much to say for a little while. We finished our coffee and the waiter brought the check. I grabbed it and Galatea said, “Hey, hey. Wait a minute.”

“Last I checked,” I said, “I asked you out on this date.”

She grinned at me. “And last I checked you shot your own client and didn’t get paid a dime.”

“And let’s not forget the $8000 in computer and surveillance equipment.” I grimaced, but I didn’t let go of the check.

We walked out to the Defender. As we got close to it, she stopped and turned to me. She said, “A lot has gone on. I haven’t been able to ask you about . . . about how you are doing about your daughter.”

I faced her, and she put a hand on my arm. We were very close. “I have those nights,” I said. “I’ll always have those nights.” I paused. “We only had one conversation about her, but that talk gave me some hope that I might get outside my own head on this. I want to talk to you again.”

She smiled. “Of course,” she said. “Of course.”

I deposited my pricey fedora in the driver’s seat of the Defender, made double-sure the doors were locked, and then we walked down to the beach. We took off our shoes and tromped along in the sand for a few hundred yards. I took the cigar out of my pocket. Galatea said, “Don’t even think about it.” I slipped the cigar back.

We walked a little ways farther, our feet making imprints in the soft sand. Then Galatea said, “Do you think I’m repulsive?”

I looked at her. “My god, Galatea! I think you’re gorgeous.”

“Do you think —” she paused for a long moment — “do you think of me as — a woman?”

“I think of you as a really beautiful woman.”

She kept walking, looking straight ahead. She said, “In the motel room, you saw me.” I glanced over at her. She said, “You saw me in a way that I never wanted you to see me.”

I stopped and turned to her and put my hands on her shoulders. “When I look at you, I see a brave, wonderful woman.” I smiled.

Her smile was tinged with sadness. “I’m kinda stubborn —” she poked a finger at my heart — “just like you, Samuel Landers. Remember what I told you the first day we met? That you have a stubborn heart. Well, you do, but I’ve watched it open up. I know sometimes you hate it, but your walls are breaking down.”

And she said, “You know, Samuel, we both have stubborn hearts. I’ve held everything inside my whole life.” She smiled at me, a little wistfully. “It’s been different with you. I talk to you. I want to talk to you.

“I want to do this whole thing —” she brought her hand up to her breasts and swept her hand down her body — “I want to do it right. I’m going to finish counseling and save up my money. By then, I'll be ready."

We walked a little ways down the beach, hand in hand. Something tilted inside me, those colliding forces that I'd struggled with my whole life seemed to suddenly become consonant.

I stopped so suddenly that she kept going until her hold on my hand stopped her. She turned around. I put my hands on her shoulders again.

"You know, my stubborn heart is feeling a little less stubborn all of a sudden. After knowing you, Galatea, there're a lot of things that I can be okay with now. Like this."

I brought her to me, and tilted her face up to mine, and I kissed her, and I let my lips linger on hers and then we got into it a little more.

After awhile we broke apart, gasping for air. "Wow," I said. "Oh, man," she said.

And then, to my utter astonishment, I said, "Do you want to come over to my place?"

About the author

Larry Patrick Shriner was raised, and lived for many years, on Florida's West Coast. He began his writing career as a journalist covering the crime beat for a major daily newspaper, and has taught writing extensively. He now resides in Durham, North Carolina with his wife Elaine.

Books by Larry Patrick Shriner

Epilogue for Murder
Angel, Falling
Shadowstalker

www.ingramcontent.com/pod-product-compliance
Lightning Source LLC
Chambersburg PA
CBHW060517180626
46817CB00002B/393

* 9 7 8 0 6 1 5 7 6 0 4 7 6 *